SEA OF GREEN

Also by Thomas Adcock:

Precinct 19

SEA OF GREEN

Thomas Adcock

THE MYSTERIOUS PRESS

New York • London

Tokyo • Sweden • Milan

The Mysterious Press, 129 West 56th Street, New York, N.Y. 10019

Printed in the United States of America
First Printing: October 1989
10 9 8 7 6 5 4 3 2 1

Library of Congress Cataloging-in-Publication Data

Adcock, Thomas Larry, 1947–
    Sea of green / Thomas Adcock.
      p.   cm.
    ISBN 0-89296-384-0
    I. Title.
PS3551.A397S4   1989
813'.54—dc20   89-42602
                                                    CIP

For Kim

Stolen waters are sweet, and bread
eaten in secret is pleasant.

Proverbs 9:17

PROLOGUE

The house was square and small and wedged between an empty warehouse and a taxi garage on West Fifty-second Street near the Hudson River. Most of the white paint was gone from neglect and harsh winters. A pair of tiny upstairs windows were blackened from a long-ago fire. Pigeons roosted there by day in the rotted wood and glass shards. Rats fed on the moss by night.

It was set in about eight feet from the crumbled sidewalk. A wire fence with a padlocked gate, taller than a man, enclosed the little yard. Three dressmaker's dummies occupied the yard, held up like scarecrows by poles run through them and sunk into the ground. One wore a dress with lace around a scooped collar and puffed sleeves that fluttered, armless, in the damp breeze off the piers; another, a man's shirt and tie; the third was pinned full of ribbons and dime-store jewelry, so it looked.

Beyond the dummies were two wooden steps, then a narrow door. Windows on either side of the door were covered over with scrap boards. The chinks around the boards were filled by tinfoil and wads of yellowed newspaper.

Midnight was minutes away. I stood in the heavy darkness, listening.

1

The wind gusted. A coffee can blew along the sidewalk. Cars and trucks raced downtown over rain-soaked pavement on Eleventh Avenue. Foghorns sounded softly on the water.

I stamped chill from my toes. And waited for what I had come to hear.

Beneath my feet was a long crack in the concrete. I imagined this as a tightrope that stretched between all I had seen in my life and those next few minutes into the blind future.

Across town in the better blocks of Fifty-second, the signposts identified it as Swing Street in honor of the jazz clubs, where my mother used to wait tables. One night when she could not find a sitter, I went to work with her, and the boss was a good guy and said it would be okay so long as I did not get in anybody's way. Billie Holiday sang "God Bless the Child" that night and told the crowd it was just for me.

That is how I like to think of New York. . . .

From inside the house, a ragged voice: "Up from your defilement!"

And then, the sound I had come to hear. . . .

ONE

And so, I was back.

There was I, with a new lease on the old life; freshly settled into three drafty rooms of a shabby old walk-up in the tired-out part of town, where I grew up seeing how regular meals were achievements and getting drunk was total victory. There was I, who used to believe that none of this would ever again be a part of my off-duty life.

Outside my new battered door, the hallways and the stairwells smell permanently of fish and earnestly boiled beef and simmering tomatoes and fried chicken. Babies cry in this house, and couples fight, and women in hairnets lean out pillowed windows to monitor passersby down in the street.

In Manhattan, an apartment like mine may still actually be afforded by a regular person who is lucky enough to stumble across it or, in my case, lucky enough to know somebody to help him stumble.

Before I got lucky, I was staying in a small room with large pests down on the Lower East Side. This was only temporarily for two long years while I waited for my wife, Judy, to come to

3

her senses about us, which she ultimately did not do upon the advice and counsel of her lawyer.

We had been married nearly fourteen years, Judy and I. Our life together was sweet and sick, like the life of the city itself. We owned a pretty house out in Ridgewood, Queens, with a fence in front and a flower garden in back; where we never had any children, or time; where gradually and inevitably we became a departmental statistic.

And where one day a judge of the Queens County Civil Court decided that in all due fairness and equity I should get lost out of my pretty house in Ridgewood, officially as well as in fact.

Which is why I am now living in the neighborhood where I was born and raised, because it's cheap and divorce is expensive.

Once, it was a respectable slum. Everybody called it Hell's Kitchen.

The tenements were populated by and large by dockworkers and printers and peddlers and saloon-keeps and small-time hoods and hard guys. And jazz musicians, lots of them. And also lots of working women with kids, like my own mother and me, with their husbands and fathers off fighting the war against Hitler and Tojo. I remember wearing knickers and a necktie to the Holy Cross parish school, with its separate arched entrances for boys and girls. Television was not around yet, and very few people had telephones in their apartments; nobody had air conditioners, of course, and not too many had the kind of cash it took then to own a Frigidaire. We played Annie-over and cally-up and stoop-ball and ballie-callie in streets we shared with drunks, whores, thieves, grifters, and gangsters with pistols and big cars. The Irish priests prayed for our souls, one and all.

Now it is changed and changing.

It is called Clinton. Only the socially incapacitated call it Hell's Kitchen anymore, as I do. I have read that the new name represents social progress, and that all the newcomers who use it have pronounced a blessing on the place.

The newcomers—myself excluded, as I am only going home again—are young and unfailingly attractive. They work at jobs where they can keep their fingernails clean all day, and they will pay big rents for renovated apartments with "character." And they seem to know everything about excellent food, save how to cook it for themselves in their own renovated kitchens.

But they know nothing of how it used to be here, nothing of the unresolved sorrows of Hell's Kitchen; nor do they care to know. They are too busy building the ghetto of their dreams.

And then there are the others. The suckers. They hang on for dear life to cramped apartments and cramping jobs, in a city that seems hell-bent on evicting anybody who hasn't the decency to be a bond trader or a real estate prince or a media tycoon. They are the people slipping and falling around us, or else they are pushed to failure; either way, more of them wind up each year at home in the streets.

Suckers claim that there once was a time, by God, when certain things were always for sure: Franklin D. Roosevelt was always the president, Joe Louis was always the champ, Paul Muni played everybody in the pictures, and the general idea was that we were all in it together.

I generally like hearing these sentiments because it is soothing to me these savage days, and because I notice that I have always gravitated to life's suckers. This is my nature and so I cannot help it and maybe I'm a sucker myself.

Which is to say, the day I found myself back in Hell's Kitchen thanks to the help of a guy called Buddy-O, I had no more useful understanding of the neighborhood than one of the attractive young newcomers or one of the old-line suckers. For instance, I did not know about the past and how it is never past no matter how people will try to bulldoze memory.

But I would learn this in spite of myself.

I would learn, too, that in Hell's Kitchen there is a nightmare on every corner.

Neil Hockaday is my name, but almost everybody calls me Hock save for my only living relation. Which would be my uncle Liam Hockaday over on the other side, which would be Dún Laoghaire, Eire.

I carry a detective's gold shield for the New York Police Department, which for the past fourteen years has seen fit to assign me to a plainclothes detail officially known as Street Crimes Unit—Manhattan. But which everybody on the force and all the snitches and perps and assistant DA's and bailbondsmen and wiseguys call the SCUM Patrol. This is a good shorthand way of describing the general character of my clientele.

When I say the SCUM Patrol is plainclothes, I mean very plain clothes. So plain I mostly look like any of the customers in a diner called Munson's, which is very near where I now live on West Forty-third Street and Tenth Avenue, as in *Slaughter on* . . .

Inside Munson's, time froze in about February of 1955. Guys in there dress in khaki or green twill work shirts and matching pants, with their names embroidered in red over the breast pockets. And white socks inside black steel-toed construction boots, jackets and quilted fatigue vests, and olive-drab watch caps that came government-issue from when they visited Korea for a while.

On the job, I try to look like a Munson's regular who hit the skids. I shave maybe twice a week, and I am the type who needs it twice a day. I will walk around the streets like I'm not aimed anywhere in particular, and it might look like I'm drinking out of a paper bag with maybe a pint of rye inside of it and that I have got troubles you do not want to hear about. You might imagine that a guy who looks like this spends a fair part of his day talking to himself or listening to voices that nobody else hears and that probably he smells bad. So when you see him coming at you, you naturally hold your breath and look way past him because you do not want to make eye contact and run the risk of being panhandled and you only hope to God he hasn't got lice jumping off of him.

That is no pint of rye in the paper bag, by the way. It's my point-to-point shortwave radio. And besides the usual .38 police special in my belt snap holster, I carry a .32 automatic Beretta Puma strapped to my left ankle and a nice big ugly heavy piece in my shoulder holster—a .44 Charter Arms Bulldog. My gold shield is usually on a chain around my neck, tucked into my shirt or sweater.

The purpose of my looking like a strip of Munson's wallpaper makes sense when you understand that in addition to media, entertainment, publishing, the rag trade, the Mafia, your various political graft, espionage among the UN crowd, and the usual genteel swindles and property theft committed in boardrooms with mahogany desks, there is also the lower element of the New York criminal industry: boosters, dippers, clips, yokers, smash-and-grabbers, runaways from apple pie America, your complete line of killers, your regular two sexes of pross and your cross-dressers, pigeon droppers and assorted other bunco artists, purveyors of all manner of dubious gift items, and entrepreneurs of the informal branches of the pharmaceutical business.

My job is to be ignored, or to be at least inconspicuous, so that I might once in a while get the drop on at least some of these perps in order to prevent their scoring against at least some of their natural prey: out-of-towners, matinee ladies with blue hair, big-ticket shoppers of Fifth Avenue, women with lines in their foreheads like men and suits like men and Reeboks on their feet in the morning, blue-eyed guys with imitation leather attachés, and matrons lined up outside Radio City Music Hall with their big snatchable handbags full of credit cards good for a twenty-four-hour shopping spree before anybody catches on.

I like to think I am good at what I do, even though there is not exactly an abundance of what I would call public gratitude for my services. I know this from too many times I am looked at by people who need me around more than they actually want me around.

Despite the aggravation and the way I have to dress, I look on SCUM Patrol duty as one of the department's most prestigious assignments. This is mainly because I am able to work pretty much unsupervised. Which means I am trusted to be at least a half-honest cop by a city that is about three-quarters on the take.

Also I am able to say that my job is *interesting*, which you cannot truly say about most jobs anymore, and that includes most cops' jobs. The way it plays on my beat, I am out in the streets alone on an hour-by-hour proposition: fifty-eight minutes of walking around with my pores open, then two minutes of surprise.

No matter what, I have to be ready. This is because surprise ranges from delightful to deadly, and comes from absolutely anywhere.

Take, for instance, this last time I heard from Buddy-O.

TWO

It was a quarter past four on a Friday afternoon on the ninth of November, one of those smudgy gray days when the city looks like it's all 1940s-style snapshots, the square kind with curly edges. I'd been back at work about ten days since settling into my new place. And I was working on a big stack of arrest reports in a claustrophobic second-floor office of the Midtown-North station house where I had been posted until New Year's.

The men's room was on one side of me and the lounge was on the other side, where about two dozen uniformed cops were eating sandwiches out of delicatessen bags and watching a movie on WOR-TV, *Gorilla at Large*, with Lee J. Cobb, Cameron Mitchell, Raymond Burr, and Lee Marvin. This was all about a mutant circus gorilla who liked biting and pummeling human beings and the love triangle among the beautiful female trapeze artist, the shady ringmaster, and an earnest young leading man who was apparently the only person in the world who believed the gorilla was a gentle creature at heart.

I could hear through the wall to know all this about the movie. My office was done up in government green, including even the glass in the one window that otherwise would have provided a

fine view of the central air shaft. There were two little beige steel
desks in the office, and I used the one with the telephone on it.

I'd been eating a Blimpie hero and thinking about breast of
turkey and Thanksgiving Day and Christmas trees and how the
season of peace and goodwill and rather serious depression
would be my ex-wife's first one with her new flame, a guy whose
named sounded like a respiratory disease—Pflam. She and
Pflam, who was not even a cop, were planning to spend the
holidays out west in some rectangular state where all the other
Pflams grow turnips or something. Also, I was trying to type a
report on the entertaining details of a collar I had made the night
before involving one of the oldest cons in New York City, the
talking dog number. Typing was difficult, since the letters *k*, *m*,
and *d* were missing from the Remington manual standard
keyboard and I was unable to make use of the words *sucker*, *mark*,
or *dip*.

The bust was made inside a dive near the Port Authority Bus
Terminal at the edge of Times Square. The terminal itself is
situated at the southwest corner of West Forty-second Street and
Eighth Avenue, an intersection known by its professional habi-
tués as the Deuce and the Stroll. The bar is back behind the
terminal building and caters to a slightly higher life form than
some of the other nearby establishments.

As these places go, the bar is semihonest most of the time and
does not suppose itself as much more than what it is—a
hiya-sailor dump. A guy in a three-piece wanders in, somebody
quickly tries to sit him down at a table near the stage; but maybe
if the guy has been there a few times and is wise to the formula,
he insists on a bar stool and makes it there all by himself. And he
sits with a glass of six-dollar booze and unwinds after one-
of-those-days before he has to ride home to the wife and tykes
and he enjoys the show across a crowded room. A half-dozen
wigged and perfumed females largely beyond the age of forty
earn ten dollars hourly plus tips to wiggle to rock and roll on a
runway. They are experts at covering up stretch marks on bellies
and hips with Maybelline basic pancake and a few daubs of
talcum. Then maybe somebody on her break from dancing
comes up behind the guy at the bar and her breath is candied and

her voice is all baby-doll and she nuzzles him for a drinky and the tab on her bottle of phony champagne runs twenty dollars; which if he does not buy her one means she is gone quick—house rules, nothing personal—and which if he does means she is then tremendously interested in his life story for about five minutes before she invites him to join her back in one of the nice cozy booths, where the larger jug of champagne runs to a cool hundred bucks. The guy does what he has to do.

But this three-piece was having nothing to do with this champagne business, not even for twenty bucks. That's how wise he was to the hustle. One tough customer, this one with the wing tips and the college ring.

So that is how it happened that the dog talked. Which is a grift that very few New Yorkers have witnessed in the past half century, and which most have never even heard of.

I was sitting at this bar myself since I needed to speak with Buddy-O, who had suggested the place since it was convenient to us both now that I had taken the apartment he had found for me across the way from his own place—and also convenient since nobody that either one of us knew was dumb enough to be doing his drinking here. Anyway, Buddy-O had called me up at the station house to see if I was interested in hearing some loose talk in certain Hell's Kitchen circles about a big black guy nobody knew who was recently asking lots of the right questions in some of the right places as to the most favorable contract rates on wounds that do not heal. I said I might be interested.

So I was waiting for Buddy-O to show when a slow-moving guy with a limp walked in. He was wearing an overcoat and a black turtleneck sweater and dark glasses and was holding on to one of those kindly-faced golden retriever dogs with a harness for leading around blind people. He walked up to the tough customer in the three-piece at the bar and said, "Would you mind very much if I sat next to you on this empty stool?"

Something told me the guy with the dog had just dropped a hook in his gull, who was saying yes to the poor unfortunate crippled-up blind man and even helping him get up onto the stool where the B-girl had struck out. But generally speaking, I do not pay much attention to what goes on in dumps like this. I figure everybody there is all grown up and should know where they are most of the time without my help and they should know that Times Square is not Kansas. However, there are certain things I am not supposed to ignore as a cop. So I felt professionally obligated to watch over this particular sucker.

"Buy you a drink?" the sucker said to the blind man.

"Okay, that'll be fine, young man. I'll get the one for my dog."

"Your dog drinks?"

"Terrible, ain't it? And he's on duty, too. But he's a good old dog just the same, and so that's how come I overlook his drinking."

The bartender poured out a dish of water and spiked it with Duggan's Dew Scotch, then put it down in front of the blind man, who thanked the bartender and then asked the sucker if would kindly set it down on the floor for the dog. Which the sucker did. And then the dog lapped away at it.

The sucker shrugged and looked like he was happy to have a great story for the water cooler set the next day, and then he sat back on his stool, watching the dog drink and the dancers dance. And then he got curious.

"Mind if I ask something personal?" he said to the blind man.

"Not at all. Ask away."

"Well, I don't mean to be rude or insensitive, but why would you want to come here when . . . well, when you can't see what's going on up there on the stage? I mean, why else would anybody come here and pay what they charge for bad drinks if he couldn't see some tit?"

"Hell's bells, son, I wasn't always blind! Used to come in here all the time. I was the emcee of this here joint. Retired now. I drop in once in a while with Rex here, my wonder dog, and I visit the girls."

And then sure enough, the B-girls and the dancers who were on break crowded around the blind man, cooing and all kissy. And he pinched their bottoms and they squealed and all the other suckers at the bar moved in closer. Two guys even I had not noticed before moved in tight around the suckers, thin little nondescript guys with long quick fingers.

Then the dog talked.

"I'll have another," Rex said.

The blind man and all the B-girls looked down at Rex looking up at them. The dog's tongue was hanging out. Odd that the blind man should look down at the dog, I thought.

Then the sucker next to the blind man looked down at Rex, and all the other suckers did, too.

Rex lowered his head and said, "I said I'll have another, please."

Nobody but the suckers were surprised to hear Rex talk. One of the girls bent over and picked up the bowl from the floor and handed it back to the bartender, who fixed up another drink.

"What the hell?" said the sucker next to the blind man.

And several of the other gulls said approximately the same thing and crowded around the talking dog and the general excitement.

"Oh, they're surprised about Rex," the blind guy said to one of the girls. Then, to the suckers, "Gentlemen, this here's a talking dog. One of the only ones in the entire world."

Like maybe there were a few more, I thought. I noticed how the girls began giving more room to the thin little guys bumping around in the crowd of suckers.

"Say, you're a ventriloquist!" the tough customer crowed.

The blind guy smiled and extended his hand and said, "Well, son, I guess I can't fool you. You're a sharp one, that's for sure. Waldo's my name. Used to work carnivals all over the country until I had a terrible accident and lost my peepers. Now I just do bar tricks, for the hell of it. Like throwing my voice so it looks like Rex here's talking. Anyhow, let me buy you a drink now, okay?"

So the sucker who was wise to the phony champagne scam was played out on the talking dog routine. The dippers who had cleaned out the sucker's pockets and those of the small knot of fellow suckers were beating it quick to a side exit. Waldo the phony blind man would keep his sucker occupied with a drink so that he wouldn't have to notice things were missing from his pockets right away. And the house was no doubt taking a cut of all this action, which I decided as I took in the picture that I could not in the best conscience tolerate occurring right in front of my face.

Even so, I might not have done anything if Buddy-O had been on time, which he wasn't. I checked my watch and noticed he was almost thirty minutes past due. So I figured I would make the necessary collars to have a bust on an officer's complaint. I busted one of the dippers first, who turned out to be holding the original sucker's wallet with about a hundred fifty in cash and the better class of credit cards and Kodaks of an overweight wife and two freckle-faced kids and a couple of different colors of Trojan rubbers. I next busted Waldo and the bartender.

The sucker whose wallet I retrieved started giving me a hard time about how he didn't want to get involved. So I said I would have to keep his wallet for evidence, which I could for about a day until the property division had time to tag and photograph the contents. Ordinarily, I will return to the victim the cash, or at least part of it so he can be on his way without major inconvenience. But I feel like going strictly according to the book when somebody starts giving me a hard time; so in this case, and at my own personal expense, I telephoned his wife over in Jersey and told her to come get him because he had just been robbed inside a girlie bar.

I then called the station house for some uniform backup to take over my bookings since I still had to wait for Buddy-O the snitch to arrive.

Which he never did.

So I was trying to get all this down on paper, without benefit of the three significant letters, when my telephone rang.

"Hock, it's Neglio here," my boss said.

"What's on your mind?"

"Same things that'll be on your mind some year soon when you're thinking what to do while you're on pension. Open up a bait-and-tackle shop out on the Sound? Write up your memoirs for some publisher? Like that. Also, I want to see you tomorrow."

"About what?"

"About a delicate," Neglio said. "Just be in my office in the morning, nine sharp."

One of the nice things about working out of Midtown-North nowadays is that I can walk to work. And the nicest thing about walking back and forth from home is that I am able to stop off at Angelo's Ebb Tide on Ninth Avenue at the end of a day.

This is a place that has seen better days and worse and is currently in between.

Less than a year ago, nobody ate anything at the Ebb Tide unless they had to. Then, it was something meaty and soggy that came floating in gravy from a steam table, or stale peanuts in cellophane bags to go along with beer that sold for forty cents a draft.

Some decades back, the curb outside was lousy with Packards and Lincolns and Frazer Manhattans, and the owners would check their sidearms at the door and then step inside to a place lit in dark pink, with plenty of shadowy alcoves. The customers drank French wine and twelve-year-old Scotch and ate well-aged porterhouse steaks and smoked dark brown prerevolutionary Cuban Macanudos afterward. Joey Adonis, the big West Side gangster, was a regular when I was a kid.

Now the place is going through its third incarnation.

A great many white wine spritzers are served to a great many pretty people flocked around the far end of the bar, and they pay with plastic. The back dining room is crowded with a lot of customers who order a lot of things that their favorite magazine has declared fashionable; when they are not looking about to see who else might be there, their conversation runs to health clubs or personal therapy or other restaurants. The younger females, I have noticed, almost all smoke cigarettes and sometimes right along with their food. This is because they have come a long way, baby.

Despite the new riffraff, I do considerable business at Angelo's Ebb Tide to this day. This is because of the Ebb Tide's constant namesake, Angelo Cifelli, the bartender. Since the 1950s he has been faithfully on duty in his stiff white shirt and black bow tie, black vest and red apron. And since then he has played his jazz recordings for the customers and has held forth with his unfailingly astonished view of a world generally run by men's darker angels. Angelo is partial to the front end of the bar these days, which is where I sit with the other old loyalists and drink Johnnie Walker red and Molson chasers and maybe have a boiled egg.

When I dropped by after shift that early November Friday, Angelo was playing cuts of Lester Young, Mabel Mercer, Jack Teagarden, George Shearing, and John Coltrane, all run together on one glorious reel-to-reel. He brought me a red and a Molson without my having to say anything, and he also set down a copy of the late edition of the *New York Post*.

"I see by the paper that we have had ourselves another fine old day in the U.S. of A.," he said. "It's been some year for news, hey?"

"The best," I agreed. "Mencken would have loved all of it."

"You're telling me. Every other day we had Wall Street suits on a daisy chain of manacles being hauled off to the federal jug for using coke the way the rest of us use cash. An old Miss America embarrassed herself right out of a job with the city. I think everybody in the Bronx by the name of Stanley is under indictment. And also we come to find out that one of these TV preachers finally found some babe in his flock worth a punch in the pants and how he's praying to God to help him keep his fly zipped up since the bribe he put out to the bimbo to keep her mouth shut doesn't look like it's working out so efficiently."

"We are living in a truly wonderful age," I said.

Angelo poured himself a red and put back about half of it. He said, "So, I ask you—how come anybody votes?"

"I never vote," I said. "I don't see any reason to go out of my way to support redundancy."

Because I made Angelo laugh, I got another red and Molson on the house.

Somebody down at the far end of the bar in a cable-knit sweater and a cashmere jacket started snapping his fingers. Angelo turned at the sound, then looked back at me and rolled his eyes.

"I got to go now. The guy down there? Eight to five he is going to want a pitcher of margaritas for him and his friends and here it's November. What can I tell you? They all voted for the foozle, twice—and they don't know enough to be embarrassed about it. And even worse than that, they do not know how to drink right. I tell you, we're doomed."

Angelo went away, and I sat there listening to the jazz and I put away the second Scotch and sipped at the Molson and turned the newspaper pages. I was not reading anything, though. I just let the block letters of the headlines and the cheesecake photos and the advertising messages drift into view. . . .

Friday?

When you live alone like I do, days are long and empty enough so that weekends are not the stuff of great expectations. But this particular Friday, Inspector Neglio had called about a meeting first thing the next morning, which of course would be Saturday. Which according to my tour assignment was a day off; that and Sunday, too. Neglio had some delicate case all right, to call me in on a day that would cost the city double overtime.

I could use the extra money. My ex, Judy, had not yet said "I do" to her Pflam, so the court still had teeth marks on my bank account.

I finished going through the paper and I finished the rest of my ale and I felt smooth. I wanted to go home for a nap before I sat down with the usual takeout Chinese in front of my black-and-white Philco to watch Dan Rather and his sweater. And then intuition kicked in, and I started thinking hard about Buddy-O and how he had not shown up last night, which can happen; but he had not telephoned later on, either, to explain himself. Which is something that never happens when a snitch has something for sale as good as what Buddy-O was claiming.

Thought you ought to know, Hock— there's this nigger runnin' around askin' about contracts for permanent violence, like in the old days, you know?

And I mean, he's right in the neighborhood. People I talk to, they don't know the coon. But he sure as hell knows where to do the right kind of askin'.

Just for you, Hock, and in light of my duty as a public-spirited citizen of New York, which don't laugh but I mean it this once anyhow, I done a little investigatin' on my own.

What I got to tell you, I think is goin' to be very profitable for everybody concerned—exceptin' for certain ones very high up. And I ain't sayin' no more on this telephone, okay?

So, you want more you have to meet me. Bring along your very most generous expense account, Hock, and I will consider it as a down payment. I got confidence you're goin' to see your way to payin' more than you ever paid me for anything before.

No kiddin' now, Hock, this is choice stuff. . . .

If I could get the information I need to do my job from the League of Women Voters, then that is where I would go get it. This would save the city plenty of money, and I would not feel so cruddy like I do so much of the time when I talk to my snitches. I do not especially like snitches, and I would not like living next door to any of them, which naturally causes me to especially dislike Buddy-O, being that we are, in fact, neighbors.

Nevertheless, there I sat thinking about a snitch like he was a person. Maybe this was because he had for once done me a favor by putting me on to a cheap apartment; maybe it was because we were a couple of kids together in Hell's Kitchen a long time back.

Sometimes Buddy-O would be at the Ebb Tide when I was there. But we would never speak to each other on these occasions. This was Buddy-O's choice since he did not want to be seen too much in public chatting with a known cop. Besides, when he was at the Ebb Tide he was almost always in a booth trying to keep his hands from sweating while he was being cool about telling some out-of-towner he had dragged along how he could currently afford the time to assist in certain fiduciary matters since he was temporarily between a couple of very big deals.

I would have broken this compact and talked to him if he had walked in that Friday afternoon. Instead, I asked Angelo if he had happened to see Buddy-O lately.

"I saw him maybe two days back," Angelo said. "Yeah, Wednesday it was. He came in for a veal sandwich and a

Moosehead, along with some black guy who had the same thing. Which I thought was funny. . . .

"I don't mean it was funny about the veal and the ale. I mean it was funny about the black guy. Buddy-O was not exactly in the habit of having too many friends outside his own gene pool, and he wasn't exactly a paid-up member of the N-double-A-C-P."

"I know what you mean," I said.

Angelo turned around and changed the tape on the stereo. A few bars into "Bloos for Louise" by Zoot Sims, he thought of something else he could tell me about Buddy-O.

"Say, I just remembered," he said. "Somebody told me the cops were all over his place. That was just about an hour ago."

THREE

This being the planet we are obliged to occupy and these being the sorry times they are, it no longer surprises me when somebody dies with a big smile on his face. But poor Buddy-O was not among that happy number; from all appearances, his plans to stick around with the rest of us for a while had been rudely interrupted.

Down on the street from his place, I had had to shove my way past the usual mob of droolers, gawkers, and lawyers in shiny suits drawn to a murder scene like rednecks to white socks. And then I had had to clear my way past the uniforms loitering around the doorway of the building on Tenth Avenue and Forty-third where Buddy-O kept a couple of dumpy rooms over Runyon's wholesale pinball shop. For the first time in our many years of association, I was in Buddy-O's parlor, along one edge of a continuous white line on the black linoleum floor that a detective of my acquaintance from Sex Crimes by the name of Aiello had chalked around his sprawled and naked body.

In death's repose, Buddy-O bore a certain resemblance from the neck up to a carnival freak I had often seen as a kid in the summertime out at Coney Island. He was called Popeyed Pete, the freak, because he was able to push his eyeballs most of the way out from their sockets.

Only Buddy-O did not look like Popeyed Pete on purpose.

"Here, have yourself a cigar," Aiello said, holding out an open pack of Te-Amos. "The stiff's going a little gamy on us now."

I said thanks and he lit me with a Zippo that leaked and I joined every other cop in the little apartment and the police photographer and a couple of guys from the medical examiner's with stethoscopes dangling around their necks besides in puffing up gray cloud covers from the odor of day-old blood, urine, and feces. Through an archway to the other room, I saw a sweaty middle-aged guy sitting in a wicker chair. He was the only one who was not smoking, and the abstinence was making him woozy. He wore one of those cheap suits like you see on life insurance guys. There was a briefcase in his lap and he wore a pinky ring and his shirt collar was tight and his skin looked like butter. Altogether, he looked so damn guilty of *something* that it was only natural how an apartment full of cops figured he was no doubt innocent of at least whatever in hell had happened to the late tenant. A couple of Aiello's men were asking him questions and writing down his answers in notebooks, but they were not too excited about what they were doing. Corpses make rooms calm like that.

"Who's the civvy?" I asked Aiello.

"Says he's from the landlord's, says he came up here to try and collect on the rent. Or throw the guy out, one or the other. Says he found him this way."

I nodded. The photographer finished up a roll of film, then stepped across the corpse while reloading his camera to get the other side recorded for forensic posterity. The medics packed up their instruments and rolled out a green plastic body bag and gurney.

"Hell of a rotten thing, hey?" Aiello said, shaking his head. "A guy gets checked out like this and the first person noticed anything is the landlord he's owing big."

"Well, it doesn't matter anymore about the rent," I said. Buddy-O's body was wrapped and removed, leaving only the three different colors of his body stains inside the chalk lines. "What's your angle in this?"

"Nothing specific, just your routine look-see and I cover for the precinct detective unit. Nowadays, the station house gets something on a naked dead man and they right away call us up at Sex Crimes because it might be a case of fag bashing, which is very popular lately on account of all the scary business about AIDS. I can't figure the bashers, though. Maybe they think if they don't do what they do, then everybody'll think they got lace on their own drawers. I don't know. Anyhow, we have to come out to pretty little scenes like this, which is nowheres near the worst thing I ever seen nor you neither, Hock. It's at least a change of pace from our nunrapers and kiddy diddlers and guys who like waxing their otters on the Lexington Avenue local when all the young babes are going to work in the morning."

Aiello finished his cigar. He walked over to the Pullman kitchen against a wall near the apartment door and doused the butt in a sink full of greasy water with small brown dead things floating on top.

"I don't think we got ourselves a gay blade here, though," he said. "Nothing that shows it anyhow, not even a stack of weenie magazines. What he was doing naked, who knows? There was a towel still sort of damp hanging in the can where he's got a shower-bath, so maybe that's all there is to this drama. As far as that goes. Every American's got the constitutional right to prance around bare-assed, I say. But anyhow, I had the medics check out his pecker and his bum and the plumbing looked good to them."

"Some bedside manner."

"Aw, hell, you know how it is, Hock. You don't try getting a laugh off all this god-awful stuff when you can, then all you can do is cry or drink. You want I should cry?"

"Drinking's more subtle."

"Ain't it the truth."

One of Aiello's men in the other room gave him the sign that they were through with the sweaty rent collector. "By the way," Aiello asked, "what's your angle on the dearly departed?"

"He's a snitch of mine. *Was* a snitch. And it happens he tipped me to a good deal on the apartment where I live, right around the corner."

"Jesus, Hock, you *live* in this neighborhood?"

"Well, it's where I grew up."

"Nobody ever taught you about moving up in the world?"

"I'm not much of a striver. What can I say?"

Aiello shook his head and opened his notebook and looked at it and got off the subject of where I make my home, choice or no.

"So anyway," Aiello said, "we got here one DOA by the name of Aloysius Patrick Xavier Devlin. Would this be your boyo?"

I nodded and said, "Everybody called him Buddy-O since I don't remember when." I was one of maybe three or four people in his life who remembered him all the way back to his real name. And so after all that time, hearing Patty Devlin's true birth name sounded as final as falling soil on a lowered casket.

"And did everybody know also how he used to be hooked up pretty tight with the Westies?" Aiello asked. "That's his rap when I sent for the once-over-lightly from the computer downtown."

I knew that, but in no great detail. I explained to Aiello how the neighborhood had declined over the years and how it was therefore not too surprising that a high-ranking Westy might slip down the social scale as well. How he had slipped from his position with the preeminent criminal gang of Hell's Kitchen all the way down to the lowly status of Buddy-O at his passing— that I did know. In addition to snitching for me, he worked just about every con and small-time grift he ever heard about from his pals around the neighborhood and in Times Square.

For many years, for instance, Buddy-O kept a postal box to collect responses to his standing advertisement in one of those tabloids crammed full of edifying stories about two-headed babies, cannibalism, UFOs, amazing diets where you drink all the beer and eat all the chocolate you please and lose flab in your sleep, ghosts of Elvis Presley, and wild wolf-boys prowling the countryside. Buddy-O's ad was smaller than most in the paper, almost lost in all the offers for loans by mail with no collateral required, elevator shoes, flying saucer radar detection kits, vinyl repair franchises, and Rosicrucian secrets of the universe. But he

was very proud of being in the business and he had shown me
the ad many times:

> *U.S. citizen? Thousands of government-backed jobs at top wages
> are yours for the asking! Exercise your God-given rights to
> America's vast bounty! Hurry! Send $10 for value-packed list!*

For their tenners, Buddy-O's suckers received a photocopy of
the latest U.S. civil service hiring sheet, which he obtained from
the post office free of charge.

That and a hundred other scams over the years.

As for the Westies, there probably wasn't anybody around
Buddy-O's age or mine who came out of Hell's Kitchen without
some involvement in the gang. I myself had a job sweeping up on
Saturdays at the Leprechaun Bar, which was the front business
for the Westies and which was where my mother worked behind
the stick for a few years during the war until she could land
waitress jobs in legitimate places where they would have had
waiters in white gloves if not for the draft. The Leprechaun is
gone now, ever since one evening in 1971 when Mickey Featherstone had a few and wound up pulling a .25-caliber sleeve
pistol on the late Linwood Willis, whose final moments were
spent informing other patrons at the bar that Featherstone did
not look so goddamn tough to him even if he was the number-one
cannon of the neighborhood outfit that ran the docks and the
unions and won subcontracts every time the mafiosi down in
Mulberry Street wanted somebody missing up on the West Side.

All that is left where the Leprechaun once stood is a vacant lot
full of broken bricks and glass and rodents surrounded by a fence
topped out in razor wire. That and Linwood Willis's widow, who
left a time bomb in the ladies' room that just about blew the bar
across the river to Jersey. Mickey Featherstone was acquitted of
the murder charge on his plea of innocent by reason of temporary insanity. The last I heard, he was living out of town under
the federal witness protection program in exchange for once in a
while ratting out diehard Westies. But the Westies do not matter
much in the scheme of things now since Hell's Kitchen doesn't
have ten percent of the dock action it used to have and since the

neighborhood is nowhere near three-quarters Irish like it used to
be, let alone English-speaking.

"What's your pleasure on this?" I asked Aiello.

"Well, I'll tell you, this here's one of your everyday cheap
murders. Nothing happened that anybody's going to be complaining about, and nobody's gone over who is going to be
missed by anybody else."

"So what about the guy you're sweating in the other room?"

"Him? He don't know nothing but what he found here. He
came for the rent like he said, and then he seen what he seen and
called up 911 right away, just like a good little citizen. Devlin'd
been stiff from the day before. Sure as hell looks to me like we
got a whole lot of nothing.

"Anyhow, it don't matter to me," Aiello said. "This is nothing
for Sex Crimes. So I'm kicking it back to the station house PDU
and somebody's going to have to keep it around in some manila
folder until it gets all yellow and cruddy from dust and one day
it slips off the edge of somebody's desk by some accident and
then it maybe falls into the wastepaper basket and then it's off to
open-file heaven."

Aiello had his mind made up, so I did not mention to him how
Buddy-O had set a meeting for us the other night, which I
calculated would have occurred pretty much on schedule if not
for some person or persons unknown having dropped by his
place without an invitation.

I kept to myself. Not out of any professional disrespect for
Aiello, but in consideration of how the scene played: while I
might argue that Buddy-O's murder was not cheap in the classic
sense by which cops rate these events, I could not get around the
bigger picture and how it looked to be what cops will call a
public interest murder. Sometimes in the criminal justice system, we public servants will decide to forget about something in
the public interest, even a homicide from time to time. Take for
instance mob icings. In New York, there has not been a single
successful prosecution on a mob hit since the electrocution of
Louis "Lepke" Buchalter of Brooklyn's Murder Incorporated,
which was about a month before the Japanese attacked Pearl
Harbor.

So somewhere along the twisting line and under certain circumstances—like the grisly end of a down-at-the-heels Westy like Buddy-O—a cop might keep a little back for himself, as a practical matter in the longer-range interest of the general public. Maybe something might compute later on.

Aiello and I understand all this without having to waste words about it. This is because we have reached a point in our careers as New York cops where we possess no more illusions of riding about on white chargers. We know we are simply in the business of emptying out the ocean with teacups.

So I asked Aiello, "Do me a favor and let me ask your little man in the other room a couple of my own questions?"

"Oh, sure, why the hell not. Just don't take all freakin' night with him, that's all. We'll be sealing up the scene and then I got to get home. It's Friday and my wife and me always go to the parish fish fry."

"Think of the lovely table talk you'll have."

He muttered something and went about the job of securing the late Aloysius Patrick Xavier Devlin's premises for the full forensic team to sweep through, and I went to the other room. From one of Aiello's men, I got the fact that there had been no forced entry to the place, that it was a pure hit, that nothing had been stolen, and that the clammy little rent collector had a house key on him.

"Hey, but I didn't use no key!" he said when he heard us talking about this aspect of the case. "I just knocked on the door and walked in, and Devlin, he was croaked out on the floor there."

He pointed in the direction of the parlor and asked one of the detectives, "Is he gone, is the body gone?"

"Relax, pal," I told him. Then I asked his name.

"What the hell is it to you?"

I showed him my badge and he looked me up and down.

"Well, these other guys, they seem to know you, so I guess you're okay even if you don't much look like any detective I ever seen."

"What's your name?" I asked again.

"Howie Griffiths, and I already told that to these other guys, along with my address and all."

"How are you feeling, Howie?"

"Like something you pick out of the bathtub drain when the water won't go down, that's what. How the hell would you feel?"

"About the same, I expect. I don't blame you."

I took a look around the room where Buddy-O slept, and it personally depressed me since it closely resembled my own bedroom. There was a steel-spring bed with a twin mattress on it and a radio on the windowsill, with a wire hanger for an antenna. A couple of dozen empty beer cans in a plastic bag in the corner were ready to take back to the deli; there were old copies of the racing form in piles mixed in with the occasional *Daily News* or *Post*; clothes were heaped on a chair and mostly on the floor; and there was a basin in one corner with a dripping hot water tap.

"Howie, was there any particular reason you picked today to come collecting on the rent?"

"I come 'cause he owed, that's why."

"You don't personally collect from all your tenants, do you, Howie?"

"When they owe like Devlin, yeah, I do."

"How much was he back?"

"Six months."

"Now how about an answer to my original question?"

"What was that?"

"I'm asking you, did you have any special reason to come by Devlin's apartment today?"

"Well, maybe I heard he was going to be good for settling some of his markers. Devlin was a guy always owing everybody. Bar tabs, accounts at the deli, where he bought his clothes. All over town. So, as I'm one his many creditors, it's my job to pay attention to whatever I might happen to hear about the guy."

"Where was the money coming from?"

"How the hell do I know? I don't pay attention that close. I just heard he scored, that's all. And that's all I need to hear."

"And where did you hear all this?"

"One day I'm in this deli over in Times Square buying a

provolone sandwich and some cream soda for my lunch, and I hear this bum who hangs out in there talking with the counter-man about Devlin. Actually, he was called 'Buddy-O' in case you didn't know."

"I'd heard that."

"Well anyways, these two guys were just generally talking as to how Buddy-O was about to come into some serious money, that's all."

"What day was it when you were minding your own business and overheard this little chat in the deli?"

"Couple of days ago. I was on the horn to Buddy-O right away, day and night. But no answer. I don't think the guy ever answered his telephone."

"Who was the guy in the deli with the news about Buddy-O's finances?"

"Don't know him by name," Griffiths said. "But he's this old loon you see around the neighborhood all the time. Always going around with a priest's collar even though he ain't no priest I ever knew. This guy, he goes through the trash baskets for deposit bottles just like all the regular skels."

The loon in question would be an old fellow named Lionel, who had forgotten his last name many years ago. He wore a clerical collar he had found lying on the street because he had the bright idea it would make things go more smoothly when he redeemed cans and bottles. Which naturally earned him a street name: the Holy Redeemer. And he happens to be a man I talk to on a regular basis about what a harmless loon comes to know by keeping his eyes and ears open. So the Holy Redeemer is one day chinning about a fellow snitch and how his colleague's boat is due to come in, and it just so happens that a character like Howie overhears this item. By this and certain other occurrences, I have learned that New York is an awfully small big city.

"Who do you work for?" I asked Griffiths.

"A little property management company right here in the area." He took a pack of True mentholated cigarettes from the pocket of his polyester coat. "Look, I told all the other cops already."

"So tell me, too. Who exactly do you work for?"

"Christ almighty! I work for Empire Properties up on Forty-eighth Street, okay? That a crime?"

"Some people might say so."

Griffiths stood up and buttoned his overcoat, and his jowls shook. "Would you mind too freaking much if I leave now?" he said. "I done my damn duty. I called you cops when I come in here and nearly tossed my cookies by what I seen and then I answer a bunch of questions I don't have anything to do with anyway and right about now I'm sick and tired of you guys, okay?"

"Okay, Howie. Maybe we'll have a nice visit again someday."

"Not if I can help it."

"Oh, you never know with murder and Manhattan real estate."

Griffiths' jowls shook some more and he left the room without saying anything more, but I heard him complaining to Aiello out in the other room. And I heard Aiello tell him, "Get the hell out of my face."

I was about ready to leave myself when I happened to spot the first thing in Buddy-O's place that told me anything besides how he lived alone, how he was pathetic, how he never committed anything to paper, how he did not have anything worth stealing, and how his apartment was nothing but a place to keep dry. What I saw was an orange card, about three inches by two. Business card size. It was on the floor with the rest of the mess under Buddy-O's bed, mostly a thicket of socks and shoes and underwear and beer cans and dust balls.

At the top of the card was thick black lettering:

MANNA FROM HEAVEN?
FAT CHANCE!

Then below this, there was a fine scripted message:

Get your personal pile, right here and right now! I'm the man to tell you how!

I looked some more under Buddy-O's bed, but I did not come across anything additionally revealing, save for the last three consecutive and well-thumbed issues of *Big Bazooms* magazine. Otherwise, it was more socks and dust and some old matchbook covers and lots of unsuccessful OTB slips.

The orange card had a telephone number on it with an uptown exchange. I slipped it into my pocket and said my good-byes to Aiello and his crew and left for home.

FOUR

Dinner was the Hunan flower steak, a side of fried dumplings, a dish of noodles in sesame sauce, and a couple of Mon-Lei lagers. My ex, Judy, used to say this was one of most disgusting traits, my ability to eat right after seeing something splattered all over the place that used to be a person.

Well, so be it. Buddy-O had been killed next door and there was nothing I could do about that. The food and the beer helped.

I sat in a green silk brocade chair from the Goodwill, balancing the food in my lap. The chair was fringed at the bottom and stuffed with goose feathers. I had picked it out from all the other chairs nobody wanted anymore because it looked like something that might have graced the parlor of some genteel bordello down in Chelsea or Greenwich Village back during New York's gilded age. This helped me face the fact that it was November and that I lived in a drafty tenement again in Hell's Kitchen, alone.

I thought about how I should look up the Holy Redeemer to see what he might know about any events leading up to the untimely demise of Buddy-O. And I was watching my favorite Ronald Reagan picture on the tube, *King's Row*, where he gets cut in half.

The apartment was dark except for the blue glow of the Philco screen and a white pool of light from a reading lamp over my shoulder. This suited me. I knew where all my belongings were, and I owned little besides books and clothes and enough of a kitchen to make chili and coffee and a sideboard to hold the Philco and my Johnnie Walker red. So there was no pressing need to see any of it.

My home life would be brighter if there were women around from time to time, but women are not abundant in my life. This is not altogether by choice. I would like to be able to believe in a certain legend about single male cops in New York and how women are all over them all the time. I have heard this legend propagated many hundreds of times by lonesome single male cops putting back shots and beers in lonesome cop bars, which are the foulest rag-and-bone shops of the heart you're ever likely to encounter.

The only woman I had had up to my place, in fact, was Judy herself. I invited her for dinner and promised that it would not be chili, so she came over. I should have stuck to the chili.

We rutted around some on a couch under the window that overlooks Tenth Avenue, but this was not satisfying for either one of us, though it undoubtedly entertained the old lady who lives downstairs. And then since she had me in a generally incapable frame of mind, she chose that moment to tell me all about her wonderful Pflam.

After which we argued and insulted one another. As usual, the theme of this discourse was money.

"So this is the roach hole you picked out for your first really truly bachelor pad?" Judy walked around the place sniffing and turning up her nose. I watched the way her body moved. "It figures you'd go right back here. I suppose now you're hanging out in all sorts of dives again with your bummy friends? How come you never could pal around with somebody who'd do you a little good?"

"Somebody like who, exactly?" But I knew who she meant.

"Like Eakin. You went to academy with the guy, and the two of you were friendly enough then."

"What do you like so much about Eakin?" As if I didn't know.

"What's not to like? He's made lieutenant, he's off the damn street, he lives up in Rye, in a house with a swimming pool. He's got three cars—"

"He's dirty."

Judy raised her hands and let them fall back down. They slapped against her bare thighs. Then she quickly pulled her clothes back on again, as if I should not be seeing her naked all of a sudden. Flustered, she said, "So he's dirty a little, so what?"

"So someday the guy who holds the pad on him will want to be collecting. That's what happens to dirty cops. You're forgetting already about Knapp?"

"Oh, to hell with those old Knapp Commission hearings. There were lots of dirty cops before those days, then a few of them became guests of the state. So what? I notice that New York's finest still has plenty of room for goons and crooks and thieves. So don't always be such a goddamn choirboy, Hock."

"You've got it way too simple. Before Knapp, you had no say about what kind of cop you were going to be. It all depended on who you fell in with. Now you have a choice: you can be dirty or you can go straight. No matter which way you choose, you're always sure of having one-half the department behind you."

She clapped her hands. "A pretty speech, Hock. But I still say, so what?"

"So there are shadows now. Something I always knew, even before Knapp. You want to be a good cop, you watch out which way the shadows move."

"Oh, to hell with your shadows! And to hell with you."

And then she cried, right there on my crummy couch under the window. I thought if maybe I could bend her way some, there was a good chance she could change her mind about leaving town for the holidays with Pflam. Maybe.

But it had gone on this way between us for too many years, during the marriage and after. We had been right to split up, and we both knew that corrosive words cannot be taken back, how time does not heal everything; how we had wound up with nothing but aches and pains, not even any kids of our own.

The more she cried, the more I hoped she was doing the right thing with Pflam.

And I wished I had had sense enough a long time ago to get a regular job, maybe selling refrigerators at a Sears Roebuck, something like that; something so that when I woke up in the middle of the night in bed it would not be because of a cop nightmare.

Now the holidays were coming.

Soon they would light up the giant fir tree behind the statue of a golden Prometheus overlooking the ice-skating rink at Rockefeller Center and Christmas in New York would have us all by the throat. About five hundred street corner Santas, temporarily sober and no happier about their condition than I would be myself under the circumstances, were ringing their bells uptown and down. The support pillars at Macy's main selling floor had been dolled up like candy canes since the last week of October. And before too long, the tipping season would arrive all over the city with a vengeance. And total strangers would be insisting that I have a nice day, and my Con Ed bill would read HAPPY HOLIDAYS at the top of the page in a festive red-and-green dot matrix.

And I didn't have anyplace to go on Christmas Eve, the year's big payoff when everybody out there with kids and wives and roast turkeys and plenty of money for presents are anxious to let the rest of us know how deliriously happy they are.

Every Christmas since our divorce, which had been two now excluding the one upcoming, I had gone by the house out in Ridgewood and Judy would be waiting and we had not planned anything. I would manage to look pretty good for the occasion. Vincenzo down at my barber's would cut my hair and give me an extra-close shave, and I would wear something from Paul Stuart, on the order of flannel trousers and a suede vest and a tweed jacket and shoes with tassels. I would bring along Perrier-Jouët in the flowered bottle, Judy's favorite, and oysters and an expensive gift. And high hopes of spending the night, hopes that had thus far been fulfilled.

But now it was all over.

Which meant that this Christmas Eve, I would more than likely be right where I was now. In my green chair, probably with takeout Chinese stuff in my lap if I did not feel like making

some yuletide chili. I would drink, of course. Alone or maybe
with Angelo at the Ebb Tide. And I would probably end up
watching my Philco: *Christmas in Connecticut*, followed by *Miracle
on 34th Street*, followed by *A Christmas Carol*, followed by *March
of the Wooden Soldiers*, followed by midnight mass from St.
Patrick's Cathedral, where I had once in my life sung—when I
was a boy soprano in the choir at Holy Cross, just like Judy said.

I got up from my chair and turned off the movie right after
Reagan said, "Where's the rest of me?"

Then I went to the window.

My view was the neighborhood spoon, a day labor hiring hall,
a perfectly habitable tenement house with tinned-up windows
and boards covering the doors and squatters inside and a store
with a red neon sign that flashes LIQUOR-LIQUOR-LIQUOR
all through the black night and two spires of a Croatian church
that mostly does funerals now and bingo on Wednesdays and
rents out its ballroom for Puerto Rican weddings.

And, of course, I could see a corner of the building where
somebody killed Buddy-O the scammer and snitch who once had
been a somebody. And somebody else would get away with his
murder now in the ashes of a neighborhood where he didn't
matter anymore, where Aloysius Patrick Xavier Devlin had
become a zero.

I went to the sideboard and poured myself a nice big tumbler
of Johnnie. And then I stood over at the window again and stared
at the night.

Patty Devlin and me, I thought; we had wound up the same in
two different styles. But alone is alone. And loneliness comes up
so slowly on a man, it can leave him helpless. And often with the
extra regret that in the end, nobody much even notices or
remembers he was there.

I went and poured myself another drink, put it back, decided
I was drunk, poured another, and went to the window to sip it
until I could not stand up anymore.

Down on the street below me, a couple of hookers were
sauntering up to cars in the thinning uptown traffic that had
come to a stop at the light over Tenth Avenue and West
Forty-second. Both were skinny and around eighteen. They

moved lazily in their drug hazes from one car to another, on tall spiked heels that kept their feet wet and cold in the night mist and blasts of Hudson River wind.

A fat guy in a red car with Jersey plates and two gawping pals in the backseat hired them both.

Under a canopy outside the red neon light of the liquor store, a tall black man stood smoking a cigarette, his face uptilted. He stepped back into darkness and flicked away his cigarette when I noticed him.

I decided to sleep on this.

FIVE

Saturday morning was damp and dark gray. I awoke on my couch, still dressed in yesterday's clothes. The first thing I thought about was how I had to see Neglio at nine o'clock. The second thing I thought about was my hangover and how there was a chance that eggs and bacon might ease it some.

Outside, it looked as if we would have our first snow. So after I showered and brewed some coffee and ate a few aspirin and gauged the weather by the feel of the drafts inside the apartment, I decided on Levi's, a Ragg sweater, wool socks, Weejuns, a peacoat, and a tweed cap. Relatively speaking, I would be natty for the boss. Since it was officially my day off, I decided to pack only my department-issue .38 special.

My head started clearing up on the third cup of coffee, so I left the rest of the pot on the stove and started down the stairs. Old Mary Rooney, the lady who lives in the flat right under mine, stuck her head out into the hallway and asked, "How come it is you're up so early and on a Saturday besides? Sure, it's usually the crack of noon for you, ain't it, Hock?" From behind her, I could hear *Adam Smith's Money World* on the television.

I explained to her about being called downtown, and then she

37

asked, "Well now, as it is you'll be out and about, would it be so much trouble to be picking up a few little things needed by a poor woman?"

Always, she needed the same things: Lipton tea bags and L&M cigarettes. Otherwise, she survived on cans of lunch and dinner when it struck her that she required solid food. The Korean superette down the street delivered everything for her once a week, including a supply of Meow Mix and 9-Lives for her companions, the exact number of which I did not want to know.

I said I would be happy to run an errand for her, even though this was not so.

"Let me go get you the money you'll be needing for my things, then," she said.

I listened to some televised chatter about debentures and futures and pork bellies, and Mary Rooney shuffled back to her door.

"I'm giving you four bits and you can keep the change of it for your small troubles," she said, extending the money to me. "Don't be forgetting now, if you please. It's two packets of the L&M brand and the red-and-yellow box of Lipton's, sixteen bags to the count."

I would not forget. But I did wonder which year it was that remained as the present in Mary Rooney's mind. Which year was it when two packs of cigarettes and a box of tea bags cost less than a half-dollar? Had tea bags been invented yet?

Mary Rooney closed her door and locked it. I heard the police bar slip into place. Then I went downstairs to the street.

The wind was sharp and I turned up the collar of my peacoat and stuck my hands into the slitted side pockets and headed for the only sign of warmth and light in the morning gloom. Which was the bright window of the spoon across the way, Pete Pitsikoulis's All-Night Eats & World's Best Coffee.

I pushed open the door to Pete's, and a swirl of warm steamy air was sucked outside into the cold. I looked for someplace to sit down, which was not going to be easy. The restaurant was full of taxicab drivers who had spent the tiny hours booking all the extra fares they could before Christmas, off-duty bartenders from the late joints in Times Square, doormen in their brown-and-maroon livery on their way to day shifts at the apartment houses uptown with names to them, amiable drunks here and there, and an old-fashioned kind of Broadway dancer of my acquaintance by the name of Mona.

Mona was minding her own business with a cup of cocoa and a glazed cruller and a copy of the tabloid *Post* spread out on the counter in front of her; the headlines contained the words *horror* and *granny* and *maniac* whenever possible. On the stool next to Mona was some character in a Burberry trench knock-off who looked like he did not belong on the scene but who was nevertheless trying his best to make a hit.

The air smelled of sausages and eggs and hamburgers and fried onions and coffee, which in actual fact was not the world's best. I saw Pete's head and shoulders on the other side of the pass-through shelf, where at the age of seventy-five he still worked fourteen hours a day as his own chef.

Mona had had it with her admirer. She looked up from her newspaper and told him, "Drop dead, why don't you, creep?" And she arched her eyebrows toward me, and the guy in the suit looked me over and then took off. So I sat down on his empty stool.

"That there is one of the biggest problems with this city today," Mona said after she'd said hello. "There is very damn little sense of civility anymore."

"You're right."

"Damn straight I'm right."

A waitress with a wet rag stopped in front of me and cleared crumbs off the counter and set down a mug of coffee. There was a tag shaped like a Santa clipped to the apron strap along the curve of her right breast and it said "Wanda." I told Wanda I wanted the number two and that my friend Mona would have another cocoa. Wanda snapped her gum.

"How've you been?" I asked Mona.

"Oh, I don't know, kind of lousy since you ask."

"What's the matter?"

She sighed. "This is going to sound nutso, but I'm getting the feeling lately like I'm one of those old lovely buildings around town that's right in the way of a wrecking ball. You know, like old Pennsylvania Station that was torn to hell and thrown away or the Morosco and the Helen Hayes Theatres that were knocked over to make room for the Marriott Marquis that I suppose might look swell in Omaha, maybe."

I told her I knew exactly what she meant.

Wanda brought what I had ordered and set it down. I ate and Mona watched me for a while. And when I looked up, I saw she was wearing a devastating smile.

And she said, "In your mental file cabinet, how do you have me pegged, Hock? Maybe under 'Broadway Babe'?"

I could not say anything, what with the unchewed eggs and toast in my mouth.

Mona nodded a yes for me and then said, "But—do you have any idea where Mona Morgan comes from? Do you have any real idea what I'm about?"

Only by label, I admitted to myself. My loss. Mona knew what I was thinking and laughed lightly at me. But it was a tolerant and friendly laugh. She made me like it.

I swallowed and said, "I would like it if you told me."

"And maybe I will someday. You'll have to remind me."

"It sounds like that could take some time."

"Oh, I think you'd find it time well spent," she said. "When I entertain a gentleman outside the club, I do it the old way, you know? Refined-like. A gentleman sees my show, he sends back flowers with a note, he takes me out to supper someplace nice, I listen to him, I make him laugh maybe. . . .

"I even laugh some myself. Later, maybe we end up at my place. Naturally, I accept gratuities. Which I earn. If the gentleman doesn't leave in the morning feeling like about a million dollars, then the guy's dead."

One or two scenarios of an evening at Mona's place reeled around in my mind.

"You see, Hock, I'm a classic. I should be respected, like old Penn Station. I have a life with background to it . . . and details, subtle details. But respect is rare nowadays, and they went and killed subtlety. So since you went and asked me, that's how come I'm feeling a little lousy."

I took out my wallet and laid down money for the number two, for Mona's cocoa, and for Wanda's tip. And I said, "I think you ought to do most of the talking when your gentlemen come calling. I'll bet you're lots more interesting and complicated than they could ever pretend to be."

"Maybe you want to find that out yourself, Hock? You could stop by the club one night. Send back some flowers, take me to supper. That sort of thing. And, you know—etcetera."

"I don't know—"

And Mona laughed at me again, and I liked the sound of that again. "That's not just me," she said. "There's also maybe a half million more women out there willing to give. Or haven't you noticed?"

"I notice. The trouble with me is, I'm not up to taking just now."

"Well, I love you anyhow, Detective Hockaday." Then Mona slid off her stool and folded her newspaper and yawned. "So long now. I've got to be running along home to bed. Alone, unless you feel otherwise."

I kissed her on the cheek and she left and then so did I.

Only when I left, I picked up company. Maybe this should have surprised me, but it did not.

He was slender, tall, and black. And dressed in a dark raincoat and a brown felt hat with a wide brim. I could not see enough of his face to guess an age. Besides which, he was standing way over on the other side of the street when I spotted him. In a doorway, smoking.

I decided to let him follow me for a while.

SIX

Inspector Tomassino Neglio is a man of the bureau, as compared with a man of the streets. Which is to say, he is a man of files and memoranda and City Hall luncheons and smart cocktail parties and moonlight dinners on yachts hosted by the people who own New York and attended by some other people who are under the impression that they run the city due merely to the fact that they were elected to do so.

Once, Neglio was a street cop himself and a good and tenacious one. He knew the world was then close and dark and crowded with strangers who could hurt him at will or help him if they happened to be listening to their better angels. But now his days and nights are mostly filled with the best people, if not always the best of intentions.

Neglio's office occupies a southeast corner of a high floor at One Police Plaza in lower Manhattan. He has two secretaries, one of whom is competent, and four telephone lines, at least one of which he assumes is tapped by the U.S. District Attorney's Office out of long-standing federal tradition. The outer office is full of cops pulling bow-and-arrow time, meaning the department has reason to be temporarily nervous about their carrying weapons on the job. He has a departmental lawyer on call, two uniforms to run around with him wherever he goes as a means of discouraging somebody with a small brain and a big idea, and a personal driver.

At my disposal was the subway shuttle from Times Square to Grand Central, where I changed trains for the IRT local down to its terminus at City Hall, which is a short walk from Police Plaza. At nine sharp, the ham-faced sergeant in charge of Neglio's outer office let me in to see the boss.

He had been standing at a window looking down over the gray harbor. When I stepped in, he waved me over to an alcove where he keeps a couple of leather club chairs and a table with a tea service and a view of the Brooklyn Bridge hanging pretty over the East River.

"I'll make this as short as possible," Neglio said when we settled ourselves. "That's for two reasons: one, there isn't much detail I can give you; two, I'm on my way out to JFK and a plane to Bimini for some sun. You ever been to Bimini, Hock?"

"I get my sun out in Far Rockaway," I said blankly.

Neglio shrugged.

I said, "What's this all about, then?"

"What's it always about?"

And this is pretty much like it is in every delicate I have ever worked. I am always up against the same thing. Nearly half the trick of solving the case is figuring out what murky information is being hidden from me by whoever it is happens to want the case solved—in this instance my own Inspector Neglio, which meant the case must be extremely delicate.

I said, "Supposing my first wild guess involves a big pile of cash in small denominations and nonsequential serial numbers that wound up in the damp paws of somebody on the city payroll? Could I call myself a detective headed part way in the right direction?"

"You're good, Hock. You're very good." And then he pulled an envelope from the breast pocket of his suit coat. Before he gave it to me, he said, "But I don't know if we're talking about just money this time around, which is generally uncomplicated.

What we're talking about is death threats from some kind of bedbug out there, somebody badly off his nut."

So far as I know, nobody had ever taken a scientific measure of the frequency of death threats in New York. On a nice tree-lined street in Staten Island or Queens on a quiet night of a pleasant month, maybe it would occur twelve or thirteen times an hour. That would represent the low end of the scale. Here and there around the city, there are some more vengeful precincts. I have worked many station houses, and no matter the local atmosphere, an idle homicidal threat is nearly always treated as a low priority. People who are not cops think this is callous and shocking until it is pointed out to them that very few murders are premeditated, that very few murders even begin with threats no matter what the mystery novels say; and that anybody who pops off about killing somebody has just gone and got rid of about ninety-four percent of the pent-up rage required to actually carry it off.

Of course, all that wisdom can be beside the point if the threat happens to be against somebody with the ear of a guy like Inspector Neglio or one of his fine friends.

"You want me to have that?" I asked, indicating the envelope. Neglio gave it to me.

"Ever hear of a guy with a sweet little tax-exempt dodge up in Harlem by the name of Father Love?"

"The Jesus jumper on the radio?"

"That's the man. The Most Reverend Father Love of the Healing Stream Deliverance Temple."

I tore open the envelope and found four orange cards inside— all the same as the one I had found under Buddy-O's bed the day before:

MANNA FROM HEAVEN?
FAT CHANCE!

Get your personal pile right here and right now! I'm the man to tell you how!

But the cards Neglio gave me were not blank on the reverse sides like the one in Buddy-O's room. Each of them had a biblical quotation written on the back, neatly in pencil. And below each quotation, in angry gashes of black from a wide felt-tip pen, there was the threat, "DIE FATHER LOVE."

When I looked up, Neglio said, "We're after somebody who's likely to be running around on your turf. We're talking bedbug here, and you're the best man I have for the job of getting inside a bedbug's head."

And then he said lots of other things, none of which mattered too much at the moment. Which was just as well since I could not focus on anything besides the picture I had of Buddy-O with his eyes popped out from being strangled.

"Where did these come from?" I finally asked.

"Four weeks in a row, they showed up inside of envelopes in the collection plate at the church. Father Love and his crowd, they put these cards out all over town to drum up some business. So there's a malcontent, maybe he got run over pretty good by Father Love. Maybe he wound up hurting himself real bad after he tossed up his crutches when the padre was rolling holy one Sunday. Maybe he got bilked down to nothing and his old lady left him. Who knows? Anyway, now the bedbug's out to kill."

"How did you come by these cards?" I asked.

"They came to me through a friend."

"A friend you have in common with Father Love?"

"That's right."

"And you're not going to tell me who this friend is?"

"That's right."

"But it's a friend in a high place?"

"I'm not going to play twenty questions with you, Hock. Like I told you, I want to get to Bimini. And like I said, the case is delicate."

"Just find the bedbug, right?"

"Right. From now on, you got this case exclusive. You work your snitches, we'll put extra money on the street for you if you want, you check the flops and the pervo joints and whatever else you can think of. You report to me exclusive. I want this creep and I want him bad."

Naturally, I decided for the moment to hold back from Neglio the business about Buddy-O's murder and how I was naturally thinking it connected somehow to Father Love. Since the boss was not at liberty to tell me all that he knew, he was in no mood to entertain what I might know or come to know. Full disclosure emerges slowly in delicate cases, if ever at all. We both knew the drill.

Neglio saw from my face that I thought he was being even less helpful than usual. "Look," he said, "I really don't know a lot, except that it's probably going to get real damn complicated."

"I've heard about complexity. You think I recently arrived in the city with a round haircut?"

"No—"

"You have to give me something to go on," I said. "Like for instance, a real name would be nice to know."

"Samuel Waterman. That's the padre's name. Mean anything to you?"

"Offhand, no. Should it?"

"No."

"Tell me something else. Is this politics here?"

And when Neglio answered this one, there was a lot of breathy sound in his talk, as if words that meant something could be covered up with air that meant nothing. "Well, politics . . . you're talking a very big subject. Strange bedfellows, money, power. It's a lot like religion, wouldn't you say? The fear of the many and the shrewdness of the few?"

I suppose he was trying to tell me something, but it did not register then. So I did not bother asking Neglio anything more. I sat looking at the cards he had given me. And Neglio sat looking at his watch, which I took to mean that our meeting was over. Which was correct.

"When's the last time you were in church?" Neglio asked.

"My wedding day. They told me that marriages are made in heaven."

"All of us get bad information, Hock. You go along in this life, you have to forgive and forget that sort of bum steer."

I told him that was better advice than the priest had dispensed.

"Anyhow," Neglio said, "tomorrow's the Lord's day and I'd like it very much if I knew you were on the job up at the Healing Stream Deliverance Temple."

* * *

So I had my marching orders.

As I traveled back down the elevator on my way out of the bureau and into the streets where I belong—as I thought about poor old Buddy-O, some Harlem radio preacher who some bedbug wanted dead, Mona Morgan, about Howie Griffiths the landlord's shill and how his hands sweated, about how somebody was shopping my neighborhood for a contract killer, about how Christmas was coming and my ex was leaving town—it occurred to me that everything going on around me for the past few days was all jumbled up in a blur and moving along like some very fast train.

Sometimes all I have to do is wake up in the morning and I feel like I'm already on the far side. That's the place where quite a number of occupational hazards come crashing down on my head like a pile of wet snow off a time-weakened roof.

This was one of those times. So I was not in the best frame of mind to have to deal with the first person I saw once I left the lobby of One Police Plaza.

That would be my tail.

He was so familiar by then that I recognized him from the back. He wore a dark olive raincoat and a brown Borsalino with the brim snapped down in front, which I thought made him look like a stock character in a spy movie; he held a cigarette in one hand and a furled umbrella in the other, and he stood in front of a vacant shop window, watching me by reflection.

I felt like taking a couple of swings at the guy right then and there since I do not take well to being followed and since I was sore about having to get up out of bed with a hangover. But I figured that I had to make absolutely certain this was the same guy who was so interested in my apartment window from the night before. And besides, I also figured it would not be in the best interests of public relations for a white cop to be mugging a black civilian in the immediate vicinity of police headquarters. So I walked over to Broadway and headed uptown.

At Chambers Street, there was a skel with a big sign around his neck trying to cadge quarters off motorists entering Manhattan from the Brooklyn Bridge. When I got near enough to read his sign, I liked the enterprise I saw: "TRYING TO RAISE $1,000,000 FOR WINE RESEARCH." So I donated a buck. The skel put a hand on my shoulder and said, "God bless you, boy." And I turned my head to avoid the muscatel fumes and got a good sidelong glance at the guy in the olive trench coat.

I then cut into the south tip of the park out in front of City Hall and walked diagonally toward the center, as if I were on my way to the IRT subway station. The only others in the park that morning lay on their backs on strips of cardboard they had set atop benches for insulation from the cold, with newspapers for cover and pint bottles of Thunderbird wine for warmth. When I heard dry leaves crunching underfoot behind me, I walked toward a stand of trees where I would not be seen by passing cars on Broadway.

When I stopped, so did he.

And then when I turned and dropped to one knee and drew out my .38 special and made a tripod out of my arms and one cocked leg and directed the business end of the revolver at my shadow's face, his umbrella and cigarette flew out of hands and then the hands went up high in the air and he puffed up quite a lot of frost in the air between us before he was able to get out the words: "Hey, man, you don't have to do that. . . . You got it wrong. . . . Hey, man, I'm not armed. . . . Put that thing away. . . . Oh, please, man. . . . "

For a couple more seconds, I said nothing. Silence and a pointed gun command rigid attention.

"Hit the ground and spread out on your belly!" I yelled at him. "Now!"

He did what he was told, and I walked over to him, slowly. I kept my gun trained on him. You never really know.

Standing over him, just outside his reach, I let him worry about what I might be thinking of doing with the revolver I had fixed on his head. And I sized him up.

The hat he wore was a good one, maybe worth a couple of hundred dollars. Now it would need a good cleaning and blocking since when he fell it had rolled off his head into a patch of mud and dead leaves. The raincoat was genuine Burberry. He

wore charcoal-gray corduroy trousers with maroon flecks and a
pair of pebble-grain English walking boots. The guy had obvi-
ously been to school.

I stepped around behind him, out of his sight, and let him hear
the sound of the revolver hammer clacking back.

"Oh, please, man," he said.

"Shut up."

I sat down on his rear end and jammed the barrel of the .38
against the back of his uncovered head. He made noises in his
throat like some forest animal caught in a trap. I used my left
hand to hold the gun against him while I patted him down with
my right. No weapons.

So I slipped off him and told him to put his hands behind his
back, which he did. Then I locked him up with the cuffs and told
him, "Roll over so I can get a look at you, chump."

He was a couple of inches over six feet and slim, and he looked
as if he had just walked out of an old sepia photograph. His hair
was short, with a part cut in the middle. His face was light
brown and smooth, and his eyes were hazel.

I showed him my gold shield, then put away my .38 since I
did not figure I would need it anymore. Then I informed him
that he was under arrest.

"You have the right to remain silent," I said, starting in with
the Miranda. "Any statement you make may be used against you
in a court of law. You have the right to an attorney. Before
answering any questions, you have the right to have an attorney
present at any time. If you cannot afford—"

"Save it. I know all that," he said. Since I had put the gun
away, he had suddenly become cool even though there he was
lying on his back on the dank ground with cuffs on his wrists.
"What's the charge?"

"I don't know yet. Maybe I'll decide on something by the time
we get to Central Booking and we put some ink on your fingers
and take your picture front and profile with a little necklace full
of numbers."

"Take my advice, tell me the charge now."

"Suspicion of interfering with a police officer. That gets you
twenty-four hours in a holding pen until you manage to get in

front of a judge who can hear for himself what a smart mouth you've got. You can call up your lawyer and he can come down and rant and rave and hold your hand and tell you how I can't get away with it—which I can't, not entirely. But the lawyer will charge you by the hour, and I can make sure it's all going to take him many, many hours to see to it that your constitutional rights are all preserved."

"You do what you have to do, Detective Hockaday." Then he grinned at me. "And I'll do what I think is right. From what you've just said, I imagine I'll start by filing a brief of particulars with the Manhattan Criminal Court on a complaint of abuse of police authority. Chances are, you'll take a walk on that charge. But along with it comes an automatic IAD investigation, and maybe that's something you wouldn't want to tempt."

Oh yes, this guy had been to school all right. Like maybe Harvard Law.

So I said, "Okay, let's save each other a little time and trouble. Where were you last night about half-past eleven?"

"Outside a liquor store on Tenth Avenue. If you want to know any more, you're going to have to let me get up off the ground and you're going to have to take the cuffs off."

Instead, I reached inside the breast pocket of his coat, where I guessed I might find a wallet with instructive things inside it. I was right. He carried about a hundred dollars in cash, the various gold credit cards, an alumni charge plate to the Harvard Coop, and a New York State driver's license that told me he was born on the twenty-second of March 1952, that he lived in a pricey block of the West Village, and that he had a very interesting name: Samuel Waterman, Jr.

SEVEN

So after I let him up and freed his hands and he had picked his Borsalino out from the mud, I asked him, "How about squaring a little with me now? What's the idea of tailing me?"

"Am I still under arrest?"

"That I am thinking over, Counselor."

Waterman rubbed his wrists and gave me another one of his lawyerly fish grins, which reminded me how I am not fond of talking to members of the bar of justice. With maybe a couple of exceptions at certain points in our history, lawyers are the sort who come down from the mountains after a war in order to shoot the dead.

"You haven't got anything on me that's going to turn out anywhere near the way you'd want it, Hockaday. True enough, you could irritate the hell out of me for several hours today on some nuisance rap. But you want to know what you'd be buying for that kind of two-bit cop intimidation? About ten grand worth of hell in the courts."

"Are you threatening me, Counselor?"

"I am advising you. Be smart and you won't find my bill in your mailbox."

51

All I needed in my life besides my hangover was one more unpleasant conversation with a lawyer. The idea was creeping into my mind without too much trouble that Waterman, Jr., here was the guy behind my drawing watch duty on Father Love. I made a mental note to check out Junior and his law firm for their respective statuses at City Hall and police headquarters and among the fraternity of the assorted multitudes of open-palmed VIPs in the city of New York. I also decided to back down from him since he was now all puffed up and ready to fight with me, which is an old-school method used by a tired detective to get what he wants the soft way.

"You've got to be really upset, Mr. Waterman. I can understand that, really I can. All these threats against your old man, the Most Reverend Father Love."

Junior nodded. Then he looked away for a second like maybe he had the habit of wincing whenever somebody said his father's trade name out loud. I congratulated myself for striking a nerve in record speed.

"So under the circumstances," I said, "how about we just forget what happened here today? You're a free man again, okay? That make you feel better?"

Waterman shook his head, but I could not be sure he meant yes or no by this. I don't think he knew either.

"You're hard to figure," he said, "and I haven't got all that much time to wonder anymore. So like you say, I ought to try squaring with you. It might be easiest and fastest."

"It's also possible we're both trying to get to the same place."

"Yeah, I thought of that. I thought about a lot of things since yesterday."

"Like what things? And forgive me, but let's cut the crap as much as we can from now on. It's cold and my head feels like it's something dead and full of stale water."

"One straight answer for starters—"

"Which would be more than I've got so far from you."

Waterman ignored that. "The guy they found murdered the other day in the building near yours. The guy named Devlin who they called Buddy-O. What's he mean to you?"

"He was my snitch, a stool pigeon. Also, he very recently did me the good turn of flagging me on an apartment that I needed."

"Why do you think he'd do that for you? I mean spot you the apartment like he did?"

"I don't know. Snitches like to be ingratiating, I guess." But the whole truth was, Waterman had asked me a very good question, which I had not stopped to consider in my greedy rush to sign up for something as rare in Manhattan as a place to live where you pay regular rent instead of monthly ransoms.

"I answered you straight," I said. "So now it's your turn. You're playing detective on me. Not a good idea. How come?"

"Because all of a sudden I haven't got better ideas, all of a sudden I can't make any sense out of what I'm hearing from anybody. First, I heard about some psycho up at my father's church who's been dropping little threats into the collection plate on Sundays. Then, since I have a couple of friends with the city, I'm told the police department is going to put its very best man for the job on the case. That would be you, Hockaday. I hear you're a Boy Scout, but that it hasn't made you stupid."

Waterman lit a cigarette for himself and continued. "Then things start moving fast and too furious. Like I suddenly hear there's a contract out on my father and that some guy called Buddy-O is the broker for the hit. Then Buddy-O turns out to be a guy named Devlin, who turns out to be not only Detective Hockaday's neighbor, but Detective Hockaday's informer besides, which you confirmed yourself a minute ago. And then Devlin gets knocked off.

"I naturally start asking myself questions. But all I can see to do is follow you around, Hockaday, to see if there are any answers in the places you go."

"What have you found out so far?" I asked.

"Only that you spend your nights alone and drink too much."

That sounded like an epitaph, I thought. "All this stuff you tell me that you've been hearing, where exactly did you pick it up?"

"Let's consider that information on the order of what you told me I have the right to keep quiet about."

"That was if you were busted, Counselor. Which is what I

have generously decided to forget, you'll recall. You're now very close to jerking me around, which I might resent."

Waterman grinned, and for a second or two I thought about decking him. But I could see that would be a waste of time; he was not going to be any help to me except maybe later when I might have something to bounce off him. Now he was holding back, like Neglio was. So I threw him something straight out of the blue again to knock him off balance.

"By the way, how do you and your old man get along?"

He looked quickly down at the ground so that I could not get the immediate reaction on his face. He dropped his cigarette and stamped it out vigorously. I liked it that I had riled him.

"Not so good," he said. "And not so bad that you'd logically consider me a suspect in the threats, so in the interest of efficiency, I'd stay off that trail if that's what you're thinking."

He expected me to say something in response. But I did not.

"We've had battles," he said, "just like every other father and his son, I expect. But I never wanted to kill the man—or have him killed. I didn't have to. The guy was already dead to me."

Naturally, I asked for some elaboration on that pregnant thought. Waterman tossed out something far too quick and glib by my lights.

"My mother died before I was old enough to have any memories of her," he said. "My father sent me off to all the best schools from day one. So I can't honestly say that I knew him any better than I knew her. Get the picture, Hockaday? My father was right there all the time, and yet he wasn't. Can you imagine?"

Yes, I could, I answered.

"Well, if you come up that way, then you would hardly want your old man dead. Quite the opposite. You'd want him to someday come to life for you, don't you think?"

That time, I didn't answer. Waterman brushed his hat with his coat sleeve and muttered, "That old stuff doesn't matter anyway."

I shrugged. "I'm not so sure about that, pal. Maybe the old stuff matters a lot, whatever it really is. You think that over, why don't you. Between now and the time I want to talk to you again since I know where you live. And think about how you can help me, all right? I'm warning you, though, playing shamus isn't the kind of help I need. I have to go now and see about keeping your father alive."

So I left him standing there in the park with his muddy hat and his open mouth. Maybe he would talk plenty later on. I walked over to the subway station and caught the number 6 uptown to Forty-second Street.

There was a number of good reasons I wanted to walk back to my place from Grand Central instead of taking the nice warm shuttle train to Times Square, chief among them being that I might run into the Holy Redeemer somewhere along his Forty-second Street hangouts. If I did not see him, though, there were plenty of spots where I could put out word that I wanted to buy some of his conversational time, and then sooner or later he would make it his business to find me. Also, I might want to stop somewhere for a few jars to help my head. Angelo would not be on at the Ebb Tide until five, so it would have to be the Landmark pub on Eleventh Avenue or Mike's American Bar & Grill on Tenth, or maybe Robert's farther up the avenue. And of course I still had to pick up the L&Ms and the Lipton tea. Besides all that, a walk on a cold day helps me think, and I needed help.

When I got to the corner of Fifth Avenue, I slowed down as I passed by the public library where my mother used to take me even before I started school; where later on I would go myself after a day's work shining shoes; where I first was taught that New York means, among so many things fair and otherwise, that anybody in the city is welcome at that great house of education and learning, even an ignoramus shoe-shine kid from Hell's Kitchen.

It was the library where I headed when my arms and back ached too much to slap another speck of polish on leather. I would walk up the limestone stairs past the stone lions named Patience and Fortitude, then inside to the call desk on the first floor, where I was obliged to check my wooden box of wax brushes and stained cheesecloths. An elderly man with a neat white mustache and a green linen jacket would take it from me with the greatest dignity every time, as if I had handed over a fine Brigg umbrella and an Englishman's proper bowler. And then, after this elegant kindness in the middle of a rude and inelegant city, I could go upstairs to read. I chose books and magazines about County Carlow and County Dublin and the Wicklow Mountains on the other side, where I had roots in another world. And I would also read about the war. The war that meant I could never know my father because he did not return from it.

And if I had known him, my father, what of the two of us then? Would we have battled? If this man had been in my life, if he had held me and kissed me or beat me and cursed me or helped me build things or told me how much there was to do in this world, or all of this—how would I have described the man to others? What would I say, especially, of the two of us were someone to ask me how we fared as son and father, as I had asked Waterman that day of his father and himself?

And if it had gone mostly bad between us, as can be the case between a man and his boy—then might even regret provide me now more comfort than the emptiness of knowing nothing at all of him?

I picked up my pace and moved on, and the sky darkened and its clouds shifted and rumbled.

Five blocks I had walked without laying eyes on the Holy Redeemer. I did, however, develop a question that would inevitably have an answer: How did Waterman know my apartment so well that he was able to stand on the street knowing which window to watch for me?

At Seventh Avenue, I stopped in at the deli next door to Hotaling News and bought the things for Mary Rooney. I told a counterman that I was looking for the Holy Redeemer for some information and that I was willing to pay by the word and that if the counterman could deliver the Holy Redeemer within the next forty-eight hours, I would see that there would be something in it for him, too.

It began to snow.

Light and very wet at first, it felt more like the heavy rains that come at the graying end of a New York autumn. But then there was sleet, which by the time I had made it to Eighth Avenue had become sheets of undeniable snow. Winter had made an early debut.

I turned up the collar of my peacoat to keep my neck dry, and I was glad I had had the sense to wear a cap. Everybody else had covered their heads with whatever was at hand—newspapers or handbills or cardboard signs ripped off walls or sandwich wrappers, anything that might offer even the flimsiest shelter from the storm.

Every year for some time, I know a singular moment that marks the bitterest change of seasons; one moment at the outset of another New York winter when I am struck by the only pure thing that distinguishes the comfortable of the city from the miserable. Which is luck.

I came on this theory when I was eight years old and the youngest choirboy at Holy Cross Church and fortunate enough to be allowed to tag along with the older fellows whose voices were starting to change when they ran off to the cloakroom behind the side altars to play dice in between the Sunday masses. In this sport, they were ably and discreetly assisted by an aged parish priest with a nose full of broken red veins who was known as Father Cash-Box Kelly. This was for two basic reasons— Father Kelly's proficiency at any game of chance you chose and the delight he took in handling all the special money-raising projects assigned to him. None of us boys ever knew him to have celebrated a mass, heard a confession, visited the sick, or given last rites. Old Cash-Box Kelly was not that sort of priest; he was the sort who turned up at the bingo games, who did not mind sitting at a card table outside the church on warm Sundays hawking raffle tickets, who especially did not mind making the rounds of the neighborhood bars on Sunday nights when a priest's money is known to be no good, and Cash-Box in his Roman collar was prepared to accommodate any Catholic invitation of a drink. Also he would collect a little cash from his hosts, for this worthy project or that. And from this latter endeavor, my own mother was often assisted with her monthly obligations, making Cash-Box Kelly a most favored priest in the Hockaday household and never mind the rumors about his habit of wagering with choirboys.

"There now, lads, is as good and sound a lesson as so many others you'll be hearing from the sisters in the classrooms." He always began this way, bones rattling in his hand as he knelt in his black cassock on the cloakroom floor, his right arm cocked for the sidewinder toss of the dice and his accompanying *"Hail Mary, Mother full of grace!"* for the encouragement of holy odds, so often in his favor.

An early snowfall over an afflicted part of the city, and a fugitive memory of old Father Kelly. These were the elements of the singular moment that marked the winter's onrush. These and the sight of a bag lady of my acquaintance who calls herself Heidi.

She lives on handouts of coffee and some of the finest Italian cuisine to be had in Manhattan, by way of the scrap bin outside Giordano's restaurant on West Thirty-ninth Street. She picks through the bin every night, and what she does not eat on the spot, she will carry off in her bags for later consumption.

Now I saw her sitting on a standpipe on West Forty-third Street, against a sheltered brick entrance to the Times Square IND subway station. Her red and bloated legs stuck out in front of her, and people had to step over them as they went down the stairway to the train platforms. Snow piled up on her ankles and her bare, blackened feet.

Heidi's legs were full of ulcers because she has to sit up all the time, even in the drift of cautious naps. A woman on the street, even the foulest-smelling crone, is vulnerable to rape if she dares to lie down. And so she sits up, the result of which is ulcers from constricting the flow of cleansing blood. Gradually the skin rips open and sores are exposed to soot; and soon the leg goes bad as rotten meat, which it in fact has become.

I do not know Heidi well. She distrusts all men because she knows they are stronger; her face looks as if it has been punched by quite a number of men. From the times we have talked, I know she has some education, as many bag ladies do. Heidi owns a balding fur coat she wears year-round, and she is always reading. She scavenges only for the more serious newspapers; I have seen her throw away the tabloids in disgust while rooting through a wire trash can.

Now she sat on the standpipe reading the *Times* in the snow, her bent nose running. The front page carried the story of how the president saw a communist threat in Nicaragua, but apparently no threat of winter to homeless women in America.

I went into a deli for a cup of coffee with cream and sugar for Heidi. Next door at the liquor shop, I picked up a fifth of Johnnie Walker red for myself; I would have bought the same for Heidi, but she's a teetotaler.

Then I crossed Forty-third Street. I stopped where Heidi was, extended the coffee container, and waited several seconds before she took it. Many people have the idea that the homeless and the helpless are supposed to slobber with gratitude when you offer them a handout, as if this is their obligation for petty charity. In her own due course, Heidi would look up from her paper and take what I had for her, and this was our understanding.

She looked at me with a kindly expression, which was unusual. Every other time I had met her and tried talking to her, she was impassive, like a tattered queen. And then she did something remarkable. She had a friendly word for me.

"It's snowing," she said. "Isn't that lovely?"

"Yes." I opened up the coffee for her, and the steam rushed out. She took the cup but did not drink it right away. She stared at me instead and smiled slightly. "Drink up before it gets cold."

"I will. Oh, I will. But tell me, did you hesitate getting this coffee for me?"

"I always get you a cup when I see you. Regular coffee, cream and sugar."

"Yes, that's right, isn't it? That's good. One should never indulge in hesitant mercies."

I told her I agreed with that and that I could help her more if she would trust me.

She thought this over, then shook her head. "Never you mind. I'm going to be all right. It's snowing. Isn't it lovely?"

Then she drank about half the coffee, looked up at me again, and smiled like she was once a lady accustomed to many ordinary pleasures. And then she said in a voice from her past, "Merry Christmas."

EIGHT

Mary Rooney was waiting for me, listening outside her door for the sound of my footsteps. I saw her poke her head over the rail up on the second-floor landing as I went through my mailbox in the vestibule. Her gray hair was done up in pink and yellow rollers, as if she had plans for a big night on the town. But so far as I knew, Mary Rooney went nowhere besides church and the OTB parlor up on Ninth Avenue, and then only by day.

She was highly agitated about something. When she saw it was me on the way upstairs with her cigarettes and tea and my Scotch, she started hopping up and down and screeching, "Come in here and please God be quick about it!"

I took the stairs two at a time. "What is it?" I said when I'd reached her. "Are you hurt?"

"No, 'tis nothin' like that. Just come in my place, quick now, and I'll be tellin' you."

I followed her through the door, and she slammed it behind us.

"Did you manage to find what I was askin' after?" she said. She threw all four dead bolts into place on the door and slid the police into position besides. "Did you now?"

I handed over the bag of L&Ms and Lipton tea.

"Good, I'll make us a nice pot now. I'm already at the business of cookin' a bit of lunch, so this will fit in fine."

She turned from me to the Pullman kitchen between the heavily secured door to the corridor and the door to the bathroom with the big clawfoot tub. The configuration of my flat one floor above was identical—the same kitchen and bathroom, the same parlor with the bricked-up fireplace and two windows, the same tiny adjoining room barely big enough to keep a bed and bureau.

Mary opened a pack of her cigarettes, put an L&M between her lips, and lighted it the way people do when they have lived alone for a long time, when accouterments do not matter and no longer occur. She lowered her face toward the teakettle on one of the stove burners, then dipped the cigarette tip into a flame jet.

"You're still standin' there with your hat and coat on," she said. She wore a housedress herself, light green with pink cabbage roses all over it. "You'll now take them off and sit yourself down in my house like a right gentleman, if you please."

So I pulled off my hat and my peacoat and set them down on top of the radiator to dry off.

"Would you be wantin' to share a bit of the beef stew in the oven?" Mary Rooney asked.

"I don't think so. Just tell me what's happened here that has you upset."

"Well, you will sit down and have some tea, isn't that right?" She pronounced it "tay."

"Mrs. Rooney, please. What is it?"

"Oh, that. I'll be comin' to that soon enough."

She pulled open the oven door an inch or two, peered inside, and then shut it.

"Go on now, sit you down. You'll have to content yourself with a nice relaxin' wait for your tea. White or black will it be?"

"White and sugar."

And so I sat, at the card table in the center of the parlor where she spent most of her days writing letters to dead relatives in Ireland. It was the only place to sit. The couch by the windows was full of snoring cats. I faced the mantelpiece over the idled fireplace. There was a portable television set on the mantel and crowds of photographs in plastic Woolworth frames on top of that and along each side pictures of many generations of Rooneys. Fair-haired, light-eyed, solid-legged, and all wearing the same dour expression. They looked precisely like Mary herself, every one of them.

"If you've a mind to, you may tune in the afternoon movie on the telly," she said over her shoulder. She was busy pouring boiling water into a brown pot full of Lipton bags. "I know you fancy the Reagan pictures. There's the one this afternoon where he's playactin' with the chimpanzee."

"That's all right, I've seen it many times in reruns on the evening news."

Mary laughed like a young girl and then brought the brown pot and the saucers and spoons and cups and a bowl and plate for herself to hold the stew when that was ready. Along with an ashtray and matches, all this was set atop the mess of her correspondence.

She poured us each a cup, and I drank patiently and then said, "You have my fullest attention, Mrs. Rooney. What is it you hauled me in to hear?"

"Oh, crikey, I nearly forgot that now, didn't I?"

She rummaged through the papers on her table until she found something she was looking for, stuck under an ashtray. She slipped a letter out of an envelope already slit open and handed it to me.

"This here is the latest from the landlord," she said. "It came slitherin' under me door today, right when you left the house this mornin'. You'll be findin' the same nasty thing upstairs. But I wanted to see your reaction right off. So tell me what you think now."

Mary lit up an L&M while I read:

Dear Tenant:
As mananging agents of your building, we would like to take this opportunity to extend to you the offer of $2,500.00 in exchange for the surrender of your apartment lease.
This tender offer is good only during the next sixty (60)

days. Should you accept, we will in addition be most happy to assist you in securing suitable resident-guest lodgings in a nearby property likewise under our management, the Flanders Hotel, on a strictly first-come, first-served basis.

Should you be interested in this generous, limited-time offer, kindly telephone the office at your soonest convenience.

For Empire Properties, Inc.,

A. Griffiths.

H. Griffiths.

I looked up, and when I did Mary Rooney said, "All this mornin' since the evil thing came, I don't know whether I'm supposed to be frightened or furious."

"Furious gets my vote." I thought about Howie Griffiths and his clammy skin and how he was the innocent rent collector who happened to find Buddy-O, the dead tenant, so he said. And now it turned out that this fat weasel was my landlord's agent.

"Ay, and it's where I was leanin', too." Mary Rooney sucked hard on her cigarette and her eyes blazed.

"You know the Flanders Hotel?"

"Oh, Jesus!" she cried, pronouncing it "Jaysus." "Jesus, Mary, and Joseph, don't I know the place. There it is right in my path on the way to Holy Cross, that bawdy house the landlord wants me livin' in now. Well, I ain't goin' to a house full of harlots from Hades!"

The Rooneys up on the mantelpiece looked every bit as shocked and outraged as Mary sitting across the card table from me. I put my hand on hers and said, "I promise, you won't be having to move there."

But I had no solid reason for saying that. Only the first brightening premonition that events whirling even as fast and loose as those around me during the past two days could eventually connect; and that when they did, a slime like Howie Griffiths might get tripped up on his own trail of gummy footprints, which very well might lead to some interesting places.

Griffiths had made the mistake of getting personal with me. First, he was there where my snitch was murdered. Then he turns out to be my own landlord's shill. Then I am only just nicely settled into a flat thanks to Buddy-O and now the weasel who tried collecting rent from a corpse wanted to cash out my neighbors and me for a lousy two and a half grand apiece and rooms at a hot-sheet dump of a hotel.

"I don't know that I should hold you to such a promise, Hock. We got us a landlord who's wantin' to empty the building like they're doin' all over town, and it's a landlords' town, that's sure." Then she spat, "They ain't lords of the land, neither! They're the scum of the earth!"

"The landlord can maybe empty the building," I said, "but only in time. He can't do it anywhere near as fast or as cheap as he thinks. Not if we stick together. Then when we leave, it will be more or less when we feel like it—and when the price is right."

Mary Rooney jumped up from her chair. "Oh, 'tis grand! We can soak the rich like the Little Flower used to say!"

I had the idea that Mary Rooney would be the perfect candidate for keeping the tenants of our building whipped to a fine and productive fury on the issue, and I told her so.

"Sure, I'll do it, Hock! Oh, and I'll make it a lovely donny-brook for us all."

Then came a muffled rumbling sound from somewhere near the door, followed by a wet-sounding explosion.

I dived out of my chair and grabbed Mary Rooney by her slender shoulders and took her down to the floor, covering her body with mine for protection.

Then quiet.

I looked toward the kitchen, where I figured the explosion had occurred. And sure enough, brown liquid blotches covered the walls and cupboards and the refrigerator next to the range. The oven door had blown off its hinges.

Mary Rooney got herself up from the floor and walked over to the kitchen to inspect the mess.

"Crikey," she said, slapping her forehead. "It's me Dinty Moore can that I'm always forgettin' to cut open before heatin' up the insides."

I successfully begged off helping old Mary Rooney clean the slop off her kitchen walls and the rest of it. Then I went upstairs to my own place, where I could take a good stiff drink and a long nap, both of which I badly needed.

At half-past one o'clock on a Saturday afternoon, my day thus far had brought me an assignment from the boss to drop everything I was doing in favor of a delicate investigation of homicidal threats against some politically connected, soul-saving Harlem holy man; a disquieting run-in with the padre's own son down in City Hall Park, who had been tailing me in a trench coat; and the detonation of a can of Dinty Moore, which did not have a calming effect on me.

This was not to forget my breakfast chat with Mona Morgan, during which she laid out her grievances with the Philistine vagaries of Manhattan real estate. Which I myself was about to face with my own dear landlord.

Speaking of which, there did not seem to be a letter from Howie Griffiths under my door. So when I got inside, I looked up the number for Empire Properties in the telephone book, dialed, and wasn't too surprised to get an answering machine that sounded just like Howie. I hung up.

I flipped on the radio and tuned in WBGO-FM, the jazz station from Newark. I listened to Charlie Parker and then Ella and then the Duke, and outside it kept on snowing.

Then I sat down in my green whorehouse chair and set out the four MANNA FROM HEAVEN? calling cards from Father Love's church on the side table. I picked one up to read the Bible quotation scrawled on the blank side along with the death threat, and then my telephone rang.

"Aiello out of Sex Crimes," the caller said. "Where you been today? I only called up about a hundred times, you Irish hump, you."

"I been in and out. What's up?"

"Nothing official, but since you got a personal angle in that public service homicide yesterday that we're kissing off, you'll be interested maybe in a couple of things that come to me on it."

"Like what couple of things?"

"Like a pair of telephone tips that come in to me since I'm the one who's still officially catching on the Devlin hit yesterday, even though I'm about to bump it down to the PDU. So just because I'm a sweet guy, I remember this morning how you were so interested. So I figure maybe if Detective Hockaday wants the glory here, then he can have it so far as I care. And I also figure you'll be wanting to hear what I was told before the PDU, which is how come I'm trying to reach you. Am I right?"

"You're maybe right. Maybe I'll wind up owing you a steak."

"That sounds right." I could hear Aiello light a cigar. Then he continued. "So first, the guy downstairs from your snitch Devlin's place, the guy who owns Runyon's pinball shop, he calls and says he's been thinking about this Buddy-O, or whatever his name was, and the murder and all. He says he doesn't know if it means anything, but all day long on Friday there's this character who don't belong hanging around the block.

"Like a mope the guy was, Hock. Runyon, he don't know any connection, of course, even if there is a connection. But he wants to get it off his chest, so he calls the cops. Can you believe it? A public-spirited citizen in this town? Jesus H. Christ, and I was thinking this town was nothing but Beirut West, especially your neighborhood."

"Never mind about that," I said. "What did Runyon say about the mope?"

"Said he was a slow-moving kid and he pegged him at seventeen, eighteen. A geek who drags himself around with his mouth hanging open. Not your kind of the senior prom type of a guy.

"Anyway, Runyon got some real good close looks at him since the kid was moping on the street outside his shop half the day Friday and since a lot of that time he had his face mashed up against the windows checking out the pinball machines. Especially the ones with the naked ladies that light up when you get the steel pellets to land right on the tips of the old melons."

"How about something a little more in the way of a basic description now?" I asked.

"Well, Runyon says he's black, very light-skinned, and he's got blue eyes. So you'd remember him pretty good if you seen him yourself. Tall kid, six two or better, and like I already said, he's clumsy as a three-legged camel. He was wearing some kind of old man's suit and overcoat and hat, like he got everything from the Goodwill back when Ike was warning the Chinese commies to lay off Quemoy and Matsu.

"What did you do, Hock, lend him some of your threads?"

Aiello had himself a good laugh at this, and I waited it out and then asked, "What about the other call?"

"That one came first thing this A.M. I'm in at my desk at Sex Crimes on the weekend on account of I have to get my October monthlies written up, and who should I get on the blower but that creep rent collector, Howie Griffiths, a character you will of course remember from yesterday when your neighbor and your snitch was canceled out. Anyways, he remembers you.

"So this morning, he's calling to ask me to verify that Neil Hockaday is a cop, which I naturally do. Why not? Then he asks me to verify that Neil Hockaday the cop is the same Neil Hockaday who is a tenant at West Forty-third and Tenth Avenue. So I ask him who the hell needs to know that.

"Howie, he says it's on account of the late Mr. Patrick 'Buddy-O' Devlin had a certain message for this particular cop. So I confirmed. Why not?

"Then Howie says he's going to try to get ahold of you as soon as he can."

I thought how it would probably be a better idea for *me* to get hold of Howie Griffiths as soon as *I* could, and I thought again how it seemed that everything was going at high speed on me all of a sudden.

I thanked Aiello for the information and told him that I would let him know how things turned out. He told me that he likes the porterhouses over at The Palm restaurant on the East Side, medium rare.

And then for more than one reason, I had to use the loo. Which is finally where I came across my formal Empire Properties offer of twenty-five hundred bucks to vacate the premises I had only just begun to occupy. That and the official messenger, too.

Howie Griffiths lay on his back in his birthday suit in my clawfoot bathtub, which had been white and clean until things started spilling and dribbling out of Howie. My "Dear Tenant" letter was pinned to his hairless pink chest with an ice pick.

NINE

Two naked dead guys in two days in Hell's Kitchen, and both hits relate to me.

Quite a welcome back to a fellow's old stomping grounds, that; that and Judy's touching holiday engagement notice a few nights back right while we're groping around together on my couch like a couple of moony teenagers in the backseat of a Chevy coupe. *What in hell does it mean when a man finds a fat corpse in his bathtub and one of the first things that runs through his mind is his dead marriage?*

And now I could not even do what I needed to do in my own bathroom. Or else I would maybe contaminate the crime scene.

So I took a couple of short steps backward from the toilet, careful not to touch the doorknob or the light switch or the towel rack. I still had a fairly complete view of Howie Griffiths' carcass from the door. He was sprawled in the tub with one pudgy leg up along one side and one arm slung over the other side and turning blue. From the expression on his pale, ashy face, I guessed that Griffiths felt sadly unsurprised the last time he was able to feel anything.

Blood oozed slowly from three tiny punctures I counted down

at the bottom of his deflating belly, then I stopped counting; maybe there were more holes, but I could not see them from where I stood, and it really didn't matter. What mattered was the meaning of the Empire Properties letter spiked to his chest, not to mention the fact that all his clothes were missing. Any moron could see there was a statement here. *Would I be turning up another of Father Love's calling cards?*

Somebody got to Howie Griffiths the same way they had done in Buddy-O, which was quick and quiet and under the benefit of familiarity. *The big geeky kid in the old clothes?* Otherwise, old Mary Rooney downstairs would have heard the ruckus up in my place, and she would have told me all about it when I was sitting with her at the card table in her parlor.

That much for starters.

Griffiths must have come by the house in order to slip his cruddy little form letters under the tenants' doorways, timing his rounds just late enough in the morning so that anybody who had to work would already be gone and early enough so that everybody else would still be sleeping in on a Saturday in November. That way, he would not have to encounter anybody who might want to pester the management about rubbish in the air shaft that needed cleaning up, or cracks in the walls that needed plastering, or the boiler room down in the cellar that needed repairing—or any of those other contractual niceties that are theoretically part of a New York City standard apartment lease.

I had learned moments ago, of course, that the late Mr. Griffiths in my bathroom had begun his day with a telephone inquiry to Detective Aiello and that in the course of that conversation mentioned something about a message he had for me from the late Mr. Devlin down in the morgue. Presumably, Griffiths felt he should deliver such a message from beyond the grave in person, along with the cheap regards from the landlord.

So I suppose he knocked on my door, learned I was gone, and stood out in the corridor debating whether his business was urgent enough for him to use his agent's passkey to enter my place and wait there until I got home. Maybe that is approximately what happened yesterday at Buddy-O's place, too;

maybe Griffiths thought murder was like lightning and could not strike twice in the same neighborhood.

But it turned out Griffiths was dead wrong. Maybe somebody followed him into my apartment from the hallway. Or maybe somebody was already inside my place waiting for him—or, more likely, waiting for me. *Like Sam Waterman, Jr., who knew the layout of my apartment so well?*

Nothing made sense. Everything made sense.

I went and poured myself a sensible Scotch.

Then I telephoned Aiello to tell him how things had turned out.

A couple of uniforms were dispatched to secure the scene at my place for the homicide and forensic teams that would be coming. And Mary Rooney became agitated all over again when I told her about the murder upstairs. She hopped up and down in the hallway and then fetched a couple of pots from her kitchen and banged them and rousted everybody out of their apartments with the news.

For the first time since I had moved in, I met all my neighbors. Nobody had seen or heard anything suspicious that morning. And nobody seemed sorry to hear that Howie Griffiths had become a memory.

Babies screamed; dogs barked; cops clumped up and down the stairway, their hip radios crackling with static; an ambulance sounded from somewhere down in the street; somebody was yelling about how this was a good time for a rent strike; the television set in Mary Rooney's flat was running, and I heard a promo announcement for next Monday's *Donahue* talk show— "Rock star marries gay porno star. . . . Can this wedding last?"

And now, since I had to use the loo more than ever, I put on my hat and coat and went off into the snow. I thought of the one place where I had a shot at getting all three things I needed just then—bladder relief, maybe a little insight, and possibly a chat with a coot named Lionel.

So I turned the corner at Forty-second Street and headed east, for the bar at the Flanders Hotel.

The bar—a one-story establishment with a plywood door and no windows—is appended to the twenty-eight-story Flanders

Hotel, which is one block down and one over from my own dear tenement house. And which I have been informed is managed by the same Empire Properties Company that used to employ the stiff in my bathtub.

The prices at this bar are not to be believed: a draft of Coors goes for a dollar (half a dollar for senior citizens), and for a nickel more you get your choice of a frankfurter, a small dish of chili (not as good as mine), or a tuna sandwich; three frozen White Castle hamburgers from the South Bronx radiated for a couple of minutes in the microwave are a dollar and a quarter.

The scene at the hotel has never been confused with the bright urban pleasantries presented on the *Sesame Street* television show that youngsters watch on a beat-up Sylvania in a dingy alcove in the rear of the lobby, back where off-duty hotel clerks with pistols under their shirts sell dope to whoever wishes to smoke, snort, or inject his way to someplace between paradise and suicide.

Half the rooms at the Flanders are under a semipermanent contract to the city, as so-called temporary quarters for families with no homes and nowhere to turn. These are families headed mostly by poor, uneducated, unskilled, unmarried women with young children who were evicted from their three-hundred- and four-hundred-dollar apartments with kitchens because they were no longer able to hack it on welfare allotments or from pushing brooms and scrubbing floors off the books at minimum wage, or mostly both. And so the city of New York, in its wisdom and mercy and in concert with the prevailing winds from Washington, houses such families of hopeless women and suffering children in roach-infested ten-by-twelve-foot rooms without kitchens at the Flanders—which bills the government for daily hotel rents that pro-rate to an average two thousand five hundred dollars monthly. The other rooms are filled with the paying transients—low-echelon pimps and hookers, drunks, drag queens, drug pushers dumb enough to use their own merchandise, and aging Times Square hustlers whose hands shake too much to make a living anymore.

A few months ago in one of the newspapers, there was a story about how the Flanders Hotel that reaps a fortune from the city and from the feds had slightly more than one thousand open and unresolved violations of municipal, housing, health, and building codes. And how none of the politicians in town or up in Albany were inspired to rush forward with a reform bill that addressed something that for once actually needed reforming. Thus is the state of desperate shelter in New York: at the Flanders Hotel, there are seldom vacancies.

The bar next door has a history as hazy as the stale cigarette smoke that hovers in blue clouds up against the tin ceiling. One of the older regulars says the joint opened in 1939 and was an immediate hit with merchant seamen and German spies who eavesdropped on loose chat about traffic along the Hudson River piers even though America was not in the war yet. Somebody else says that's all wrong, that the place did not go up until after the war, in 1946, and then it was an after-hours spot where jazzmen got together and drank wine and smoked "tea," as they called marijuana in those days. And still others say the place first started about 1950 when has-been athletes on the new professional wrestling circuit stayed at the hotel and needed a convenient place to drink and brawl.

I do not go to the Flanders too often because I cannot relax there the way I can at the Ebb Tide, where few of the customers look at me and right away say to themselves "cop." Which is exactly what seemed to be happening as I walked through the plywood door of the Flanders and headed for the urinal in the men's room. After that mission, I used the phone booth in back and rang Information for a number to Sam Waterman Jr.'s place in the Village. I dialed the number the operator gave me and was not surprised when I was answered by machine. At the sound of the beep I hung up.

Not too many of the customers can afford music on top of the cost of drinks, cheap as they are. Which is a shame because over the years the Flanders Bar juke has become a fine and varied collection of tunes. I fed a couple of quarters into the box and punched up some numbers I favor and which I thought would go over well with the crowd.

The Mills Brothers' 1943 hit, "Paper Doll," started up as I took my stool at the bar. I ordered a draft and three hot White Castle sliders. Somebody named Mario, who was celebrating his release from prison by nursing *cervezas*, thanked me for the first tune. "Nice pick, pal."

Then came Hank Williams and "Your Cheatin' Heart," and I watched a guy up front tip back a bottle of codeine cough syrup. And somebody else wearing a Hawaiian shirt and a raincoat was telling the sleepy-eyed bartender that he was a tourist, that it was his third day in town, and that he had not bargained on the rotten weather. And then right when Ray Charles started singing "Born to Lose," I saw a familiar old man with a thirsty look on his stubbled face shuffle through the door.

He spotted me, smiled, and headed down my way. About medium height, he was rail thin and time-ravaged, with lots of white hair, thick and brown cast, like his complexion. Around his watery blue eyes and his pinched lips and hollow cheeks were dark gray creases and darker shadows. He was a man whose appearance was marked by a long life of discomforts, a life that alternated among jail cells, cold rooms in cheesy hotels, the Bellevue psychiatric ward, and the larger asylum of the streets.

He carried a big wet canvas bag over his shoulder, as if he were St. Nicholas. But the bag only had empty beer and soda bottles in it. And he wore a tattered Roman collar around his neck. Lionel the Holy Redeemer, my snitch.

I ordered him a draft, and he drank it down with one swallow before he took the bag off his shoulder. And then I ordered another for us both. "Bless you, son," he said. He waved his hand at me in a priestly way and then used his sleeve to wipe his lips.

"You need something to eat?" I asked him.

He took a stool and sniffed the air and said, "Sure, I could stand it. What'd you just have, some of them thawed-out gut bombs?"

"Yes."

"Sounds swell to me."

So I set him up with the burgers, and he settled his bag down on the floor. When the food came, he ate it slowly.

"You heard about Buddy-O?" I asked Lionel.

"I heard he's gone west. Too bad about that, I liked the guy mainly." Lionel turned to look at me. "How'd he get it, any-ways?"

"Somebody laid for him up at his place over Runyon's, and it looks like—"

"Yeah, I know that place of his."

"It looks like a piano wire job to me. What do you hear about it?"

The Holy Redeemer shook his head and crossed himself like some priest in a movie would do. "Hock, I can only tell you the man was not playing too smart lately. He was spreading it all over the place how he wasn't going to be no cheap grifter like the rest of us cheap grifters, right? He's telling this to us, which is insulting, and he's telling it to God knows who else. Saying he's going to get 'back on top,' as he puts it.

"You don't go stepping out of your place and expect there ain't a price to pay, know what I'm saying? I mean, you leave well enough alone. Otherwise, you complicate things. You asked me, I could of told you Buddy-O was either going to get like he did or else he was going to kill himself to get the jump on being killed."

Lionel went back to chewing a White Castle. I asked him if he wanted another draft, which he did.

"There's a lot of blank spots in a job I'm working," I said. "You could maybe fill some of them."

"What's it worth to you?"

"Double the usual."

Lionel smiled sadly. "It ain't worth double to *me*, friend, and that's even if I was able to tell you something worth your knowing, which I ain't, really."

"A few days ago there was a man who heard you talking about Buddy-O. This was at the deli next to Hotaling's, and Buddy-O was still very much alive. You were talking about how he was coming into some serious money."

"What man?"

"It doesn't matter now. He's dead, too."

Lionel smiled again and looked even sadder, like all the air had been let out of him.

"Well, it's only the dead who'll tell you the truth," he said.

* * *

I spent two more hours in the bar with Lionel, and nothing he had to say meant anything more than his ideas about truth and death. And I did not have the heart to press him further. Besides, I was dog tired.

When I left it was dark outside and raining, and anybody out walking was covered up by a black umbrella. And so I almost missed Mona.

"So, here you are out on the town," she said, raising the umbrella so I could see her face. "Why don't you drop by and catch the show?"

This she said to me without the preface of hello. Her voice was low and gorgeous, like one of those lady disc jockeys on midnight radio for all the bachelors who can't sleep.

"You're on your way now?"

"I am, and on foot, too," Mona said. "The first lousy day of winter when you really need a taxi and they all disappear."

A Midtown-North squad car moved slowly down the avenue toward me. I stepped off the curb into the street and flagged it to a stop, identified myself with the shield, and asked the professional courtesy of delivering Mona Morgan to her theatre.

"You're a doll," she said as she got into the backseat of the blue-and-white. "Any time, you know. Just say so."

"Maybe tomorrow night," I said.

"Don't say it unless you mean it."

The squad car took off, and I watched it turn on Forty-second. And I thought about Mona Morgan sitting in her parlor, and I pictured me sitting there with her. And I meant it about seeing her.

Until then, there was the little matter of Howie Griffiths' dead and naked body reposing in my apartment.

I stopped at a supermarket before heading home. I needed stewing beef and peeled tomatoes and a couple of onions to make a batch of chili. I had all the spices already and lots of mushrooms and a can of black olives. If there was anything that might get the smell of a fresh murder out of the place, it would be chili.

When I got back home, a uniform posted there to wait for me

passed along the fact that Aiello had been and gone. "Detective Aiello would like you to know," the uniform said, "that he's going to kick this case to the regular precinct detective unit. He says, quote, 'Nobody's after Howie's fat bum,' unquote, so it's not his job."

The officer also told me that everybody in the house had been questioned, that my apartment was dusted for prints for whatever good that would do, that Howie was checked into the morgue for an autopsy on Monday that would confirm what was plain to see happened to him, and that somebody, presumably, had notified Howie Griffiths' loved ones.

The officer left. My place was mine again.

I took down my cast-iron chili pot and rubbed it with salt and olive oil. Then I set up my chopping block and got out the meat and the vegetables, and I opened up the tomato can and dumped the contents into the pot to start boiling this down to liquid.

Outside, it was raining. I stirred the tomatoes with a wooden spoon and then poured myself a nice big glass of Scotch and went to the window. I heard the occasional swish of a car going through a pothole puddle of gray snow. Plumes of steam hissed from grates in the streets, like geysers from the subterranean. The top of the Empire State Building, which I could just make out by standing at the far end of my window and stretching for the look, was a gauzy red and green for the holidays. Down below, a few game hookers worked the johns in the cars. And I thought I saw Heidi walking along on her decaying legs.

I drank the first of many drinks that night and remembered the Holy Redeemer's curious remark about the truthfulness of the dead. It was not the usual thing I heard about the truth.

Many people in the world, maybe most, have an unnatural respect for the truth. Many would have us believe that the almighty Truth represents the only way to unravel complexity, the light and the way toward keeping a story straight. Newspaper editors, lawyers, holy men, newly elected politicians, and certain other ignoramuses of my acquaintance dearly love hearing such a homely notion. They would rank truth right up there with morality, though it is entirely possible that a fair number of these characters would fail to recognize a moral issue were they to wake up in bed with one.

One of the most valuable things I have learned since becoming a cop is that there is nothing more revealing about why somebody does something to somebody else than a great fat pack of lies. Lies are strategic markers in every life-and-death struggle; they are like the red thumbtacks on a war map we kept on the parlor wall when I was a kid and everybody in the whole world fought for good or evil and both sides lied through their teeth every day in the name of their brand of the Truth.

And once, my father wrote from wherever in the war he was, *"The world's gone cockeyed and a moral truth doesn't have a tinker's chance against the Devil without vast armies; and God's very own sweet army doesn't have a chance without spies and betrayals and secret codes and treacheries and propaganda and the very thickest plots and all manner of deception and cruelty required to preserve a man's civilization. . . ."*

That, I suppose, is when I first learned that to study lies was to know something practical, something useful, about the human condition. That is when I learned that lies have important motivations.

Truth, on the other hand, is something that simply happened. Like the piano wire around Buddy-O's neck, like the ice pick plunged into Howie Griffiths' belly and chest. I had an accurate view of these two truths, yet I knew nothing beyond the events themselves. The simple truth is simple indeed, and nowhere near enough. Something happened. So what, and so what now?

If truth stalked the world, as so many liars so prayerfully and so publicly desire, there would be no place for the artful precision of nuance, no need of faith or optimism, no measure for beauty or clarity, no balm of extenuating circumstance, no perspective on dignity, no room for justice.

If truth prevailed, I would be unemployed.

So many times when I am considering life's restless contradictions, which is often when I am working a case and often when I have had one or two jars, I wonder if my thoughts are mine from the beginning. I wonder if the ghost of my father who never came home from his war is maybe telling me things.

*   *   *

I took my glass and my bottle and sat down in my green chair next to the telephone. I dialed Sam Waterman Jr.'s number and reached his machine again.

Tonight I would eat chili and watch the movie on television, *The Petrified Forest*, directed by Archie Mayo and starring Leslie Howard, Bette Davis, and Humphrey Bogart.

Tomorrow was the Lord's day.

TEN

"**F**olks out there before me—"

He stopped himself for a moment, and scattered voices responded, "That's right . . . all right, now."

"All you dear folks in the shining pews that God in heaven has sent to us right down here in little old Harlem for our holy use and for our earthly comfort . . . *hallelujah!*"

His voice was deep and creamy, his diction elaborate and precise. He paused to wipe his glistening brow. White linen against clear, light brown skin the color of fine caramel.

An acolyte stepped quickly and purposefully to the preacher's side. He was a boy of ten or so. He extended a small round silver tray that held a silver goblet encrusted with sterling vines and ruby and garnet grapes. The preacher drank, and his hazel eyes danced. He wiped his brow again and then returned the handkerchief casually to the breast pocket of his well-shaped black mohair suit coat. Shafts of white light from the chandelier flashed off the big square-cut diamond ring he wore on his right hand.

Congregants began swaying in their seats, right to left. Maybe a thousand people, most of them black, moving in a gentle rhythm as they sat in the red plush chairs of a church that was once a marble-and-limestone movie palace.

Scattered voices began forming a throaty chorus. *"Amen . . . amen . . . amen, Father Love."* And then the preacher leaned forward, lips nearly pressed against the microphone attached to the burled oak pulpit in front of him:

"And you folks out there someplace in the dark void beyond my sight . . ."

His voice now grew more intimate with the waft of extra breath amplified by the microphone.

"Somewhere out there in this great and frightful and tempting city that swarms upon the rock that splits the water into the great rivers—"

He paused for accompaniment.

A small straight-backed man in a choir robe with the pan-African nationalist colors of red, black, and green sat at an enormous organ, a mighty instrument enameled in black and white. He riffed two decks of the organ keys, and the tremolos floated through the congregation, soothed and stirred them all at once, made a thousand people feel a single tone.

And then the men and women of the choir surrounding the organ, clad in the tricolored robes and seated in rows in four tiers, slapped their knees in unison.

Then Father Love resumed his greetings to the radio worshipers:

"Oh yes, Jesus, all my people! Wherever they are! All of you!

"We're all of us going to have one *shoutin'* good time this Sabbath, hear?"

"That's right!" answered row upon row of voices, the words tumbling and rolling through the church. "Amen, Father Love!"

And up in the pulpit, Father Love twirled on his heels, and then the congregation shouted and clapped their hands over their heads. Many wept helplessly. A woman in back, not far from me, ran out into the aisle with a tambourine and began spinning and banging the bells. A smiling usher in a neat gray suit put a calming hand on her shoulder and guided her, firmly, back to her seat. And from many places all through the crowd, open-palmed hands shot up as gestures of spiritual surrender.

Then Father Love raised his own arms, exposing crisp ivory French cuffs and buffed nails and the handsome diamond ring and the silver band of a bejeweled Rolex. The small man at the organ bent over his keys and pumped up the volume; the pitch grew and swelled, the notes carried such power that I felt vibrations through the heavily carpeted floor.

The crowd took several minutes to quiet, and through the tumult Father Love smiled broadly and waved at those privileged to have seats in the front few rows. He turned to his choir and blew kisses to its members. And then finally, when he could again be heard, Father Love leaned to whisper dramatically into the microphone:

"Oh yes, my beautiful brothers and sisters and my children one and all—and you doubters, too, whom I love as well. It's Jesus who gives us the power and the reason to shout for joy!"

The organ riffed lightly. Father Love spoke quickly again, his voice rising:

"All of you—you better believe we have Jesus with us this glorious Sabbath! Right here in the Healing Stream Deliverance Temple. Right here in Harlem, U.S.A.!

"Oh yes. Jesus is here!

"My Jesus, your Jesus, is here—and you all better know, Jesus is no pie in the sky today or any other day!

"Jesus is here—*right here, and right now!*"

All the congregation rose to stand, save for the unfortunates down front and left of the long stage covered with potted roses and lilies and the pulpit and the choir. They sat in wheelchairs, with canes and crutches held in their laps, yet even from here, withered arms reached high and faces brightened.

And everywhere, there was the chant: *"Amen . . . amen, Father Love. . . . Bless you real good, Father Love . . . and God bless us all."*

The tambourine lady near me was back out in the aisle, whirling and shouting and banging in full abandon. And she had plenty of company, so many so overcome with spiritual fervor that the gray-suited ushers could do no more than stand aside to let them worship free and raw and at the top of their lungs.

Men whose faces were uptilted to the shining dome overhead

cried openly, allowing all their pent-up anguish and disappoint-
ments and fears to give way to the hope that had brought them
to this moment; young boys, some of them clutching their
fathers' big hands, saw the men in tears and then cried themselves in terrible excitement.

"Hallelujah!"

Father Love shouted from the pulpit. *"Hallelujah!"*

And his shouts of encouragement for the chanting and the
dancing and the weeping spread out below him, from the altar
down through the aisles and the red plush seats and the
wheelchairs and clear through the whole church right to the door
out to St. Nicholas Avenue and the wintry wind, came over and
over again: *"Hallelujah! . . . Hallelujah! . . . Hallelujah! . . .
Hallelujah!"*

Then again, up went his arms. And again after several
minutes, the crowd dropped to near silence to hear their
preacher whisper into the microphone:

"And now all of you within the sound of my voice and the
voices of all of those who have made it here to sit before me along
with the Lord. . . . If you haven't guessed it by now—"

And the organist riffed the keys.

"This here is Father Love talking to you. I'm going to tell you
the truth, the whole truth, and absolutely nothing besides Jesus'
own sweet truth—*so help me God and help me plenty!*"

And the choir jumped to its feet. So did the little straight-
backed man at the organ. They began singing the song the
congregation knew from Sunday after Sunday came next in the
theatrical order:

> *Something real good's*
> *Going to happen to you . . .*
> *Happen to you,*
> *Happen to you!*
> *Something real good's*
> *Going to happen to you . . .*
> *Jesus of Nazareth*
> *Is passing your way . . .*

Four times on such a day as this, in the very same jubilant church where Father Love talked and where his followers responded to him with such full-throated joy, had come the threats of death. And I stood now with all the singing around me, assuming that somewhere in the church right at that moment there was someone ready to drop the fifth threat into the collection plate.

I slipped my hand into my coat pocket and pulled out the four cards that were there, four deadly little two-by-three-inch orange cards. I stared at them like I had been staring at them since breakfast. . . .

That morning, by habit, I opened up the closet where I keep my regular work clothes, the things I buy from the Goodwill or at the Salvation Army or that I find in the streets. But since it was Sunday and all, I went to my other closet and picked out a blazer and trousers. I also wore a tie and shaved close and used bay rum.

And for the Sabbath artillery, I loaded up my .32 Baretta Puma and strapped it to my left ankle; then I clipped my .38 special to my belt; and then in the event I would maybe need to make a big impression on somebody, I put on my shoulder holster and filled up the .44 Charter Arms Bulldog.

I put away the calling card threats in my blazer pocket, along with my gold shield. Then I slipped into a gray hat and a dark blue overcoat and maroon muffler, and I stuffed gloves in one coat pocket and NYPD bracelets in the other. And then I headed to Pete's.

Wanda the waitress brought me sausages and scrambled eggs that were too runny, so I knew that Pete himself was off. When I finished, there was an hour to kill before I would have to take the number 3 IRT subway train uptown from Times Square to Harlem. So I set out the calling cards on the counter in front of me and read the Bible quotations:

There is none righteous, no, not one.

Rom. 3:10

*The heart is deceitful above all things, and desperately wicked;
who can know?*

Jer. 17:9

*The fathers have eaten a sour grape, and the children's teeth are
set on edge.*

Jer. 31:29

As a dog returneth to his vomit, so a fool returneth to his folly.
Prov. 17:21

The verses were all written in pencil, neatly and carefully and
in a clear hand. Below each was the identical threat, "DIE
FATHER LOVE," written in a crude slash with a broad-stroke
felt-tip pen. I stared at the cards as if just by looking at them long
enough they would begin speaking to me, as if they could tell me
right out loud who killed Buddy-O and who killed Howie
Griffiths and who wanted to kill Father Love.

I switched the cards around, arranged them horizontally and
then vertically and then in an end-to-end square. I read them and
reread them. Yet all I knew were the simple facts: Father Love,
Samuel Waterman, had a strained relationship with his son;
Father Love was a longtime widower; he was somehow connected in a major way with the big rich of New York, which also
naturally meant he was connected in a big way with the mayor
and assorted pols.

Father Love had been around just about forever in the religion
dodge, during which time he had scored significant bundles of
loot by charming his fans and his detractors with an unabashed
pride in material acquisition and with his boundless and infec-
tious self-confidence.

And that was about all I knew.

Nothing nearly specific enough for me to begin making any
sense from the fact that there was a bedbug out there somewhere
after Father Love. My only chance of sense could only begin
from meeting Samuel Waterman—Father Love. . . .

*   *   *

One of the deacons was finishing up a list of churchly announcements.

"And Friday, we'll be having Brother Tyrone's Miracle Fish Fry. . . . Now, you can pick up tickets for the whole family right out in the lobby after services. . . .

"And don't you forget, if you don't have your very own copy of *Father Love's True Guide to Self-Esteem* or your very own copy of *Father Love's Ten Steps to Fiscal Blessings*, then you just stick up that hand of yours and make sure there's five dollars on the end of it and an usher will gladly sell you any one of these most valuable new and exciting tracts. . . ."

Hands shot up and ushers went about their business, and Father Love, meanwhile, sat up behind his temporarily occupied pulpit in his purple wing-back throne. Surrounding him were vases of lilies and red roses and potted ferns. And back behind the throne were black velvet draperies across a doorway, over which hung a sign with gilt letters:

Since the people began to bring the offerings into the House of the Lord, we have enough to eat and plenty left over, for the Lord has blessed His people.

II Chronicles 31:10

When the deacon was through, he turned and saluted Father Love, who then stepped up from his purple throne and beamed at his congregation as he resumed his place at the pulpit. And then he raised his arms and face upward, and the congregation joined him in silence; then the Praise-Sayers rose and their robes rustled and they sang:

There's a garden where Jesus is waiting
And He bids us to come to Him there,
Just to walk and to talk with the Saviour
In the beautiful garden of prayer.

Oh, the garden of prayer is within you,
In your heart and your soul and your mind.

When you turn to the presence within you,
All you need you will surely find!

Oh, the beautiful garden, the garden of prayer,
Where my Saviour awaits, and opens the gates . . .

And when the choir was finished singing, Father Love, with his face still uplifted, declared, "Be what you want to be!"

The congregation shouted back, "Hallelujah!"

"Do what you want to do!"

"Hallelujah!"

"Have what you want to have!"

"Hallulujah!"

"Health, happiness, love, success—and *money!*"

"Hallelujah!"

"Right here, and right now!"

"Hallelujah!"

And then Father Love leaned into his microphone and said with breathy intimacy:

"And never, never forget—money is the *root*—"

The crowd began rumbling its approval.

"I say, money is the *root*—"

The organist riffed the keys.

"Money is the root of all—*good!*"

And the congregation broke into wild cheering and whistling and foot stomping. I would have given a lot if old Father Cash-Box Kelly could have been sitting next to me to witness this service.

"The positive pocket makes for the positive mood!" Father Love declared.

"Hallelujah!"

"Oh, it's so important to be positive on all matters of finance, my brothers and sisters—"

"Hallelujah!"

"Why, just the other day, one of our brothers came to me and he said, 'Father Love, you talk fine and all about thinking positive about money, but I got real money problems, don't you see. I owe the IRS ten thousand dollars—and I ain't got ten thousand dollars! Father Love, I got trouble!"

The congregation murmured, and Father Love continued with his story.

"I said to our brother, 'Friend, you never truly listened to the message. Else you'd know, *you* ain't got trouble—the IRS has got the trouble!'"

The organist riffed, and the congregation laughed and shouted, "Hallelujah!"

And when the people had settled and were wiping their eyes, Father Love said, "Now then, nobody here's got the money problems today, ain't that right?"

"That's right!"

"Then this would be the good time to take up the collection to keep our good works and our good words going. . . . All right now, all right," Father Love said, raising his arms. "We are now about to pass the plate."

He dropped his arms to his sides then, and he dropped his head and closed his eyes in prayer. And the congregation did the same. All through the auditorium, among a thousand people, eyes were clenched and hopes were concentrated on what Father Love had preached for years was the only means of freedom—money.

Father Love said softly, "All right now, brothers and sisters. The ushers will pass amongst you with their collection plates. . . . Listen close to me now!

"I want you to put your hands into your pockets, every one of you beautiful brothers and you beautiful sisters.

"I want you to keep your eyes fiercely closed . . . and dig deep into every corner of those pockets. I say *deep*!

"And I want you to feel around for the paper inside. I don't want to be hearing no clinking and clanking in those plates now!" He laughed, and the congregation, heads bowed and eyes closed, laughed in response.

"You just touch paper. Touch that currency. It don't matter now whether you touch a one or a five or a ten or a twenty! Don't matter a'tall!"

And the congregation roared back, "Don't matter!"

"Some of you got *fifties*!"

"Hallelujah!"

"Some got hundreds!"

"Hallelujah!"

"Some so poor they only got one little bitty old George Washington!"

"Hallelujah!"

"But we love them all!"

"Hallelujah!"

"Amen . . . that's right, *hallelujah!*"

The congregation laughed.

"But what I'm saying to you . . . and what I am saying to God here in this church with us . . . and what I'm saying to all you fine folks out there hearing my voice on your radios . . . I'm saying, it don't matter what you got to give so much as that you give to somebody else so they got some, too. Then you're blessed, and you're bound to prosper!"

"Hallelujah!"

"You give to me, and I help you!"

"Hallelujah!"

"I help you keep that money going round and round. And you know what goes round comes round!"

"Amen!"

"All right, then. You just grab hold of whatever it is you're fingering down deep in your pockets. Don't matter what you got, just bring it out. And you hold it up straight in the air toward God's heaven with your eyes tight shut!"

"Amen!"

"And you beautiful brothers and sisters who tithe to the Healing Stream Deliverance Temple, you hold up your green envelopes with your checks and money inside and whatever else you want to give extra from your pockets this morning, too. . . . You all are doubly blessed to be pointing your offering up to God's heaven."

"Hallelujah!"

"Hold those bills and envelopes high now! Wave the money at God now!"

"Hallelujah!"

"The ushers are commencing to pass amongst you now.

They'll just pick those bills off your hands, like they was cotton off the stalk. Hold your arms high now, wave to God now!"

"Hallelujah!"

"And I'm going to commence my prayer to God for you all and for your generosity. And so I can see it for myself to tell God all about it, I'm going to open my eyes and look out amongst you fine and beautiful folks with your eyes locked shut."

"Hallelujah!"

"Keep them eyes shut now!"

"Amen!"

"And wave that green to God!"

"Hallelujah!"

"And when I look out over you, what I want to see . . . is a sea of green!"

ELEVEN

"**I** have the feeling, Detective Hockaday, that I am not quite the man you expected to meet today."

We sat across from each other in leather club chairs flanking a marble fireplace that burned sweet-smelling apple tree branches and birch logs. Between us was a mahogany gaming table with brass legs.

An usher whose name turned out to be Roy had shown me to this room when I asked to see Father Love after the service. So I had waited about a half hour in his private study while he showered after all his contortions and exhortations, then changed his clothes. I had not seen a room like it since back in my uniform days and the three years I spent posted to the Nineteenth Precinct on the Upper East Side where I answered my share of Park Avenue and Sutton Place burglary calls.

There might have been five thousand books on the shelves that ran floor to molded ceiling against three walls. Two big Oriental rugs covered the floor, and there were a couple of hand-carved tables with lamps and flowers and stacks of even more books. And a big mission oak desk in one corner with a pair of Tiffany chandeliers overhead.

Samuel Waterman, Sr., was trim and handsome and looked more like his son's older brother than his father. He must have kept two closets like I did. One for his flash—the black mohair suit and the shirts with French cuffs and the gaudy Rolex and the diamond ring—and the other for the sort of wardrobe somebody with money would have, along with sense enough to keep quiet about it. Now he wore a white cashmere sweater and gray corduroy trousers with tweed socks and slip-ons and a plain tank watch.

"Who do you think I should expect?" I asked.

"Somebody who doesn't know much besides playing the dusky for the folks on Sunday?"

"I know about taking a pose on the job."

Waterman laughed, and I felt it might be possible for me to like the guy, at least a little.

Then he opened a humidor on the table, took out a cigar for himself, and offered me one. I lit up with a lighter that was gold and heavy and that felt good in my hand, and I heard my darker angel telling me something about slipping it into my pocket. But I set it back on the table next to the humidor.

Roy poured coffee with anisette and put down two cups for us, then left us alone to talk.

"Nice," I said, exhaling the soft smoke and taking another sweeping look at a place where I would not have minded living for the rest of my days. "Very nice, especially the cigar."

"Well, Father Love is obligated to smoke the finest. Macanudos from seed grown in and harvested from the blackest Cuban soil you ever saw and hand-rolled by Havana tobacconists. All according to God's plan for the cigar."

He puffed, then added, "You're a policeman and I'm a preacher. Would you like to know what I consider both a crime and a sin?"

I told him I would like to know that.

"Banning Cuban cigars from this country," he said.

I said, "But I suppose it gives the politicians something to do. They can say they're fighting godless communism without actually killing anybody for once."

"Of course you're not here to talk with me about cigars, are you, Detective Hockaday?"

"You can call me Hock like everybody else. And no, I'm not here to talk about cigars."

He nodded and said, "Hock, as you like it."

"I've met your son—"

"My son?" Waterman said this like Sam Junior was some kind of news flash. Then he recovered his normal tone. "Yes, yes . . . my son has been in communication with my office here. It seems he's concerned with these threats, so-called, against my life. We were told to expect a police investigation. And now here you are."

I reached inside my coat pocket and removed the calling cards with the Bible passages. I dropped them on the table for Waterman to see. But he wouldn't look at them.

"They're not *so-called* threats, they're threats," I said.

"Detective Hockaday . . . Hock, I have to tell you that I personally believe this is all a very large waste of your time and the city's money. You would expect that a man in my circumstances would be frightened by these threats. I am not. When you've been in the religious service as long as I have, you learn to live with certain extreme elements that come with the calling. Now surely you can understand that, being a policeman?"

The man was either very smooth or believed he was right, or he was hiding something from me like everybody else was. For the time being, I had to suspect him on all three counts.

"Do you know a man named Aloysius Patrick Xavier Devlin? He's called Buddy-O on the street."

Waterman's answer came fast. "No."

"Howie Griffiths?"

"No."

Then I told him how they'd both been murdered. Waterman puffed his cigar and looked about as interested in what I was saying as if I were trying to sell him some life insurance. I told him how Griffiths had supposedly discovered Buddy-O's body, how I'd come across Father Love's calling card in Buddy-O's apartment, how Griffiths was then killed in my own apartment. And before all that how Buddy-O had wanted to tell me about a murder contract. And how Waterman's own son believed the contract was meant for his father.

I left out lots of curious details, of course. But I gave Waterman enough pieces of the picture so far that he couldn't fail to see the weird and dangerous symmetry of it.

But he sat there across from me and puffed his cigar impassively.

"I wonder about people who don't tell me things they should to keep themselves safe and sound," I said. "It's been my experience that they're either worried about my finding something unpleasant, or that they have a death wish. So here you are in this palace of yours, and somebody's out there closing in on you fast, and you're trying to sugar me off the case. So I naturally ask myself, what kind of trouble do you have here in paradise?"

"I'm not at all sure I appreciate the sound of your voice anymore, Detective Hockaday."

"So I don't get to sing in your choir. I'm still going to be here in your church."

Waterman shrugged.

There was a knock at the door of the study.

Waterman opened the door and Roy stood there, then followed Waterman back to where we were sitting.

"Give it to him, Roy," Waterman said.

He sat down and Roy dropped the fifth death threat on the gaming table, along with the other four. There was the same "DIE FATHER LOVE" gashed in pencil, along with a neatly penned Bible passage:

> *If a son shall ask bread of any of you that is a father, will ye give him a stone?*
>
> *Luke 11:11*

"Did this one come the usual way?" I asked Roy. He looked at Waterman, who nodded to him, then Roy answered me.

"Like usual, yes. This came in one of the green tither's envelopes, stuck in the collection plate like the other ones we gave to young Mr. Waterman." He said to Father Love, "You know, Pastor, since we were all worried and everything."

Waterman said to me, "You can see now there's nothing sinister here, only some of my nervous subordinates acting against my wishes."

To Roy he said, "You can leave us now."

"Today there's something besides," Roy said.

I asked what that was.

Roy addressed Father Love. "Downstairs in the community room, behind where we count the money. You know the piano that's down there?"

"Yes," Waterman said.

"Well, it's not there anymore."

"The piano was stolen?" I asked.

"At last," Waterman said, "we have a legitimate crime on the premises."

"Let's go take a look, then," I said.

An alleyway runs along the north outside wall of the Healing Stream Deliverance Temple as a service drive for heavy deliveries and trash collections. There is a doorway leading to the main floor and another leading to a wide steel stairway that empties into a big open room used for socials and rummage sales and child care. The missing piano could easily be taken up the stairway by two men maneuvering the load on a skid. Once at the top of the stairs, they would be out the door and into the secluded alleyway, and the church would be minus one piano.

Which from the looks of things was exactly how it happened. With a bit of help from someone on the inside.

"I'm sorry it's gone," Waterman said. The two of us stood at the bottom of the steel stairway. "It wasn't worth anything, monetarily, that is. Just an old upright that needed tuning. It was the first one I ever had in my ministry. I used to play it myself before I was able to hire a real pianist."

"You don't have any alarm system on those outside doors?" I asked him.

"None. There aren't any alarms anywhere in the building."

"Who has keys?"

"Oh, lots of us. We have a board of directors, and most of them have keys, I believe. Then we have our various organizations, and the officers and the custodians, of course. All of them have keys."

"And the ushers?"

"Yes, most of the regulars."

Waterman looked up the stairs to the big steel door at the top with bars covering it. "Most of us don't carry keys to that particular door," he said. "No need to. It only has locks on the inside, as you can see. From the outside, there's no way anybody can get through. No handles, no keyholes. Nothing. Somebody inside has to open the lock and pull the door in when we have scheduled deliveries for down here, which isn't all that often."

"What went on down here this morning, in this community room?"

"I don't believe anything was scheduled down here, actually. Just the accounting in the adjacent smaller room, but that doesn't get under way until after the first service."

"Show me the lock on that door up there, will you?"

I followed behind him up the stairway. The door had two heavy steel flanges that overlapped to the inside cinder-block wall. These were fitted out with keyed dead-bolt locks, securing the door to stone from the inside. In addition, there was a steel sliding bar over the door that fitted into brackets on either side.

The locks were open, the sliding bar upended.

I pushed the door open to the alleyway and stepped outside. It was a narrow alley, barely big enough for a city garbage truck. St. Nicholas Avenue access was down at one end of the alley; at the other end was a high fence covered in leafless vines, with thin trees and weeds on the other side, where there was a vacant lot and a crumbled building. Beyond that, I could not see.

I turned to Waterman, who stood behind me just inside the doorway. "I want to check around here for a minute. Wait there for me, will you?"

I walked the short distance in the alley toward St. Nicholas Avenue in search of anything that might have been left behind by whoever it was who ripped off the piano. More commonly than anyone might believe, thieves are sloppy. I once found a wallet at the scene of a cat burglary. There was nothing in it but a strip of penny arcade photographs, but it was enough. The burglar was smiling in six consecutive frames with his girlfriend. I scored an identification of the girlfriend at a pinball and novelty parlor on Mott Street down in Chinatown, where you find a lot of those photo strip machines. Inside an hour I made my collar with the help of an ident from the obliging girlfriend when I told her I was from the City Health Department checking up on venereal disease traffic and did she happen to know the name and address of the young man in the pictures with her.

But this time, no such luck. I could tell that a vehicle of some kind had been in the alley that morning from the fresh tracks in the slush. But that was all.

I looked around the corner of the church wall. The last of the worshipers were straggling out from the main door of the temple just up the avenue, which was starting to get crowded with pedestrians.

I turned to walk back to the delivery door. Waterman stepped out into the alley to wait for me.

I started to tell him how I did not think it was a good idea to stand out there in the alley. But I heard heavy steps behind me and turned, and I only saw an arm collide with my head. I lost my footing and went down, and I slid into the brick wall of the adjoining building and cut open my forehead. Then the footsteps loped past me.

I stood up and slipped again and banged my knee on the ground. I saw the back of a man in a long overcoat running clumsily toward Waterman, who only stood there, unmoving and vulnerable.

Then two shots fired. The gunman in the overcoat hit Waterman at point-blank range, in the face or neck. Then he ran, slowly, to the fence.

Waterman fell and he twisted and went down on his chest and held his neck with his hands and the blood poured out between his fingers. And when the warm blood fell to the snow, it steamed.

I could have dropped the gunman if I had fired at him, but I could not spare even the few seconds it would take to draw one of my weapons. If I was going to save Waterman, there was no time for sharpshooting.

I turned him onto his side and steadied him, so that the blood would run to the ground rather than collect in his wounded neck and drown him. I pried his hands away and groped with my own in the hole in his neck until I found the jugular vein.

"Roy . . . Roy!" I screamed. "Help, Roy!"

My voice echoed dully in the alley. I heard my words bounce from one brick wall to the other.

I pressed Waterman's jugular vein delicately, between a thumb and my first two fingers, stanching the flow of his blood maybe by half. I used my free hand to part his lips, and blood and mucus poured from his mouth. I used my fingers to bail his mouth of fluids, to keep his windpipe free.

Waterman's eyes filled with red. I knew he was hemorrhaging badly. At best, I had him for ten minutes before he would go into comatose shock. Then it would be up to the doctors, then to forces beyond medicine.

The quiet and the slowness was overwhelming. The gray peacefulness of Samuel Waterman slipping away. Second by suspended second.

Then I heard Roy shouting from somewhere inside the church. I heard him clattering up the steel stairs.

"Father!" he shouted. "Father Love!"

And the big slow guy in the overcoat started up the fence. I could only see the back of him. He was thickset, like a middle-aged man, but even in his slowness I had the sense that he was younger than he looked.

Awkwardly, he made his way up the fence. He reached the top as Roy emerged from the steel door.

"Father Love!"

The big guy on the fence turned once and looked my way. But I could not see any of the detail in his face. The blood of the man I held had splattered everywhere, including over my forehead and into my eyes.

The gunman dropped to the other side of the fence, crashing

in the dry, winter-brittle leaves. Roy turned with the sound of it. Then we watched him run through the vacant lot.

"Call an ambulance, Roy! And get it here fast!" And then I thought about where I was. "Tell them it's for a cop."

Waterman's eyes dropped shut.

TWELVE

There were now all the grim and familiar clean-up events that follow a shooting, so grim and familiar to me over the years that they have become abstractions. Neither the stunned victim nor the fleeing assailant nor even I seem to have any true involvement in what has occurred, as if we have all become the audience to our own dream of a crime movie, all of us seated in the dark, numbly watching our respective scenes.

How many times now had I seen a man gunned down, in the movies and in real life? How many times had my hands raced routinely over a shocked, still body in hopes of finding some tiny pulse beat? How many times had I looked at my hands and seen them red and glistening and gummy with another man's congealing blood?

At that timeless moment as I knelt over Samuel Waterman's wounded body, as it seemed I was watching myself as a player in that same old movie—as dozens of Father Love's congregants surged into the narrow, snow-slicked alley from the avenue, some of the men storming past me and up over the fence in vain pursuit of the gunman, the others encircling me and screaming prayers into the wind—I knew finally the natural miracle and the value of abstracting all the murderous violence I have witnessed in my career as a New York cop. The abstraction has been my own necessary self-defense against the sight of so much depravity, it has kept me from toppling over the edge and into the puzzle house; now it would be Waterman's only chance to survive the bullet that had ripped through his neck, now his future was in my hands.

I heard Roy's voice cut through the howl of the frightened crowd pressing around me.

"Clear the way! Clear the way!"

Then there was Roy, kneeling opposite me. He put a big hand on Waterman's unmoving shoulder. I scooped more blood and mucus from Waterman's mouth, held my fingers clamped against his jugular.

"On the way," Roy said. And in some foggy distance I could hear the piercing siren of an ambulance, followed by the low blasts of its air horn.

I saw there was no more heaving motion to Waterman's chest, a bad sign. He had stopped breathing.

"What now?" Roy asked. "What do we need now?" His voice had fear in it, fear for Waterman's life. But he was struggling to speak evenly; he did not shout.

Roy leaned closer to me to hear clearly. "Waterman may be going into seizure soon," I said. "That's going to scare the crowd, but it looks worse than what it is—and besides, I know how to handle that. What I need is for you to keep the people away, and out of the alley altogether if it's possible."

Roy nodded.

"Okay," I said. "First, keep in mind the crowd here doesn't mean any harm. They're only frightened. So get some of the taller men and women—tall so everybody can see them—and appoint them to help you. By involving people, the crowd is less resistant. Understand?"

Roy nodded.

"We've got to have room for the ambulance to back in here so the paramedics can take over. Every second counts, understand? Get a man out into the street to wave any traffic off to the side, and to guide the ambulance in here. Understand?"

And then I had done all the talking I had time for. The rest was up to Roy.

I bent over Waterman and covered his bloodied mouth with my own, pinched his nose shut, and blew several quick pops of air down his throat. Then I sat up and slapped his chest with my flattened hand, striking him square in the sternum. I repeated the mouth-to-mouth, then the slapping, then the mouth-to-mouth . . .

The siren grew louder, quickening my pace. I heard Roy's commanding voice above all the rest. And I hoped desperately that he could manage the crowd.

I felt people stepping back from me, then feet moving quickly past me and out toward the avenue. I sensed the hysteria coming under control, thank God for Roy.

But still, Waterman's chest was stone still.

I ran my hands down over his arms again, down to the wrists. His pulses were still. I felt below his armpits. No pulses there, either.

I raised my head, turned from the blood and the sickening gray and the stink of Waterman. I sucked in the cold air, turned back, and blew into his mouth. And I started praying. I prayed, I blew air into Waterman's mouth, I slapped his chest, I prayed.

And still he didn't respond. I then cursed him, Waterman's own blood spraying from my lips, "Breathe, you son of a bitch, breathe!"

I blew into his mouth again, and finally Waterman's back arched and his upper body jolted and thrashed.

And then someone in a white medical coat pulled me off Waterman's fallen body, pulled my stiffened fingers away from his wound. Two more in white coats with oxygen masks dropped to their knees in my place, in the snow and the blood. I got to my feet, none too steady, and I heard one of the paramedics saying, "We've got him, he's making it—I don't believe it, the guy's making it!"

Then Roy strapped my arm around his shoulders and walked me back toward the door to the church cellar. And as he walked down the steel stairway, I could feel the blood and the muck

falling off my shoes. I tried opening my left hand, the one I had
used to stanch Waterman's neck, but I could not.

For thirty minutes, maybe more, I sat alone in a wicker chair
in the enormous bath and dressing room off Waterman's study.
My hand soaked in a basin of hot water and Epsom salts, and I
felt the muscles in my wrist and fingers start to relax. I had now
made the acquaintance of my own death grip.

Meanwhile, the ambulance crew had taken Waterman to the
emergency room at Harlem Hospital. A two-man detective unit
from the Twenty-eighth Precinct was interviewing church members and passersby willing to talk, and a forensics squad was
combing through the side alley, the fence, and the vacant lot
beyond. Uniformed cops kept the traffic flowing along St.
Nicholas Avenue, kept the curious and the ghoulish and the
variously outraged pedestrians from trampling through the crime
scene before anybody had the chance to make something out of
any nascent clues that could be lurking about in the wet alley
slush. Which to me seemed about as likely as a ten-term
congressman volunteering for a fact-finding tour of Detroit in
January.

Roy and one of the janitors had taken my clothes and my slimy
shoes off someplace to get them cleaned good and fast, so that I
could then get the hell out of their church before anything else
happened. That is not exactly the way they put it, not in so
many words, but the sentiment was there. Somehow, Father
Love would be his same old self, waiting around for the
accountants to add up the day's receipts, if not for my poking
around the temple. Public gratitude, like personal welfare,
cannot be considered a perquisite in the police trade.

Now I was left in the eerie comfort of Waterman's private
quarters. Here I had been only about an hour ago, chatting with
a supremely confident Samuel Waterman, flush from his Father
Love stage show, splendid in his carefree white cashmere sweater
and gray flannel slacks and Guccis and not quite understanding
how some detective wanted to be trifling with some lunatic's
pathetic threats against his ministry.

I have found it useful in my business to think of a crime as something quite more than an illegal act or two, something beyond the simple collision of a couple or more opposing forces. I try to imagine how the commission of a crime lodges in the perpetrator's heart and mind, how it marks him—how it marks the victim, too. Whenever I am assigned a case, I try paying the closest attention to the atmosphere of the thing. And I let this atmosphere lodge into me, as if I had been the criminal myself, or at least the victim. I try to let this atmosphere affect the way I see all things, including the telltale logic behind the crime.

Most every crime has a certain logic, though it might be peculiar or weird or off-key to everybody else; sometimes a killer, say, is the kind who listens to personal demons the rest of us do not wish to hear. Homicides especially have logic to them, and that logic translates into leads for even the most modestly alert detective, and it is often a more concrete clue than even fingerprints. Besides which, killers mostly fall into time-stained categories: loose cannons, who leave bloody trails; average Joes provoked by simple and sorry combinations of passion and convenient weaponry, who leave bloody trails; dim bulbs and brutes, whose entire lives are bloody trails; and the contrite, who run straight to the nearest precinct station house to confess the whole bloody thing.

So now that I had a break in the mere act of a crime, I began to consider the atmosphere of Samuel Waterman, AKA the Most Reverend Father Love of the Healing Stream Deliverance Temple. And the first picture that formed in my mind was Waterman in his cashmere sweater and Guccis, looking nothing like Father Love in the shiny black suit and the French cuffs and the Rolex . . .

. . . Standing there for that suspended second in the pale alley light, about thirty feet behind me. And then the shot and Waterman stumbling and reeling and his hand clamped against his reddening neck. Then he fell down, chest to the ground covered in snow and ice. The wounded body sliding a few inches on the frozen alley floor, arms flapping and blood oozing underneath. Waterman looked like he was riding a surfboard on a wave of blood, and I noticed how the index finger of his free hand pointed to something. I don't know, maybe the

future. . . . And there was the look in his eyes when I turned
his body over on a side, the look I saw in the eyes of all who
crowded around me, which was the unasked question on everybody's lips—why?

And there were the earlier atmospheres surrounding the more
successful attacks on Buddy-O across the way from my own
apartment and Howie Griffiths in my own damn bathtub. There
could be little doubt about the connection between Buddy-O and
Howie. Among other revealing curiosities, both their corpses
were naked as jaybirds. And I naturally had little doubt that
somehow or other these murders had some link to the attempt on
Waterman's life.

But what logic could I find as common ground to all three? It
was not going to come easily this time.

And I also thought about a couple of telephone calls that
weren't going to be easy either. One to Sam Waterman, Jr., and
the other to Inspector Tommy Neglio on a beach somewhere in
Bimini.

So until my clothes came back and until I could be in some
more proper sort of place to make the tough calls, I believed it
only helpful to the cause of detection that I sit where Waterman
had surely so often sat—and sat at length—and that I spend this
time soaking in the luxury of the place. I had had my long hot
shower, my knees had stopped knocking, my forehead was
bandaged, and I was bundled in a big terry-cloth guest robe and
the brine had greatly soothed my left hand. Nearby was the
invitation to further balm, a heavy glass decanter that Roy had
generously set out for me before leaving for the cleaner's.

I pulled my hand from the basin, dried it, and shook away
some of the painful tightness. Then I helped myself to the
refreshment of eight-year-old Macallan single-malt Scotch whiskey, which greatly warmed me as I studied my surroundings.

The wicker chair I sat in was alongside a wide marble-and-teak
double vanity, set off by a bronze statue of a nude Egyptian
serving girl whose modesty was for the moment protected by
Turkish towels draped across her extended arms. There was a
brass reading lamp posted behind the chair and a low wicker
table in front, full of lacquered foreign magazines and the

decanter of Macallan and a few of Waterman's precious cigars in an open humidor and a half dozen or so of the current best-selling novels. In a far corner, set below a vertical stained-glass window that apparently looked out to nothing more than an air shaft, there was a vaulted black-and-green-veined marble bathtub with elaborately curved and filigreed gold fixtures and an adjacent shelf neatly filled with sea sponges, colored salts and soaps, brushes, and bathing rags. Near this was an oak-topped commode under a brightly tiled water closet with a gold pull chain, next to which was a bidet. And so I made a mental note to check on Waterman's circle of lady friends.

In the opposite corner was an antique nickel-and-glass pharmacy counter that housed every conceivable sort of men's and ladies' toilet and grooming compound, open to selection. The counter was handy to the immense hexagonal whirlpool shower stall I had already used. Inside the shower, six stone lion's heads spat out streams of water. And the shower steam nourished a small forest of date palms just outside the dimpled glass-and-silver door.

I thought about the bathroom in my own flat down in Hell's Kitchen, with the holes in the floor and the ceiling that was caving in and Howie's dead pink body that had so recently been reclining in the clawfoot tub. A bathroom very familiar to most of Father Love's poor flock, except for the pink corpse of a rent collector, though such might well have been a favored dream.

Across from where I sat was a pair of French doors, tall with big gold handles that led into Waterman's dressing area—a huge square of trisected space. In the middle was a Queen Anne leather chair, a book rack and an Oriental rug. On either side of this were polished mahogany cabinets and open shelving for accessories and full-figure oak-framed mirrors for complete front-and-back viewing.

And beyond the dressing area, of course, was the impressive expanse of books and more leather furniture and Tiffany lamps and the fireplace and paintings and library green trim and all the rest of the select atmospherics and privately enjoyed accoutrements of this wealthy, wounded religious impresario whose life mocked those of all his trusting followers—those without faces, left outside to survive as they might in an unmerciful world apart from the burnished comforts of the walls that surrounded me now, walls so easily penetrated by threats of death, walls that had ruptured and now bled.

Samuel Waterman lay in a hospital not far from where I sat among these comforts and my uncomfortable thoughts. And there in that same hospital, too, I imagined a Harlem baby uttering his first cries; like all newborns, he was aware of sounds and warmth, of soothing voices and the proximity of love. But what this ghetto baby could not know is that, unlike most other American newborns, the prospects of his greeting tomorrow are quoted at odds that ought to be unacceptable to a country with such a high opinion of itself. But if indeed that baby survived his birthday, he would grow to know the score—and to rightly hate it. And then we may be sure of many more bleeding walls to come.

I poured myself some more of the Macallan.

And then I stood up and drew the belt tightly around my robe and walked through the French doors and through the dressing room and on out to the softly lit library.

By now my left hand was strong enough to support the heavy drinking glass. I used my right to touch the spines of Waterman's vast book collection, or at least some of them . . .

. . . the way my mother told me to pick up books and touch them whenever I had the chance, even books a boy might only barely comprehend, even books I might never grow up to read. *"Love the way a book smells under your nose, Neil, and love the way its binding feels to your hands, and, aye, go on and dirty your fingers in the dust that will settle onto a book."* There was little money for books, so she told me what she could of them, if only she knew a book from touching it. . . .

And so I touched many of the treasures that lay on the shelves around me now. I walked the length of one whole wall, running my fingers across the books and wondering if Father Love truly cared as much for the souls of his believers as my mother had cared for mine. Had he ever invited the children of his church to come here to this big silent magical room to take down the books and learn about loving them?

I pulled down Boswell's *London Journal* from a shelf, and Leslie Marchand's biography of Byron, and Frank Budgen's memoir of James Joyce. And I found a nearly mint copy of Ford Madox Ford's *Great Trade Route*. And a collection of English tributes to Proust, brought out in 1923 by Thomas Seltzer, according to the fly page. These I found wedged between a pair of jade bookends in the shape of Chinese palace dogs. And I found a signed copy of Wyndam Lewis's *Apes of God*. And on one proud shelf, all of James Baldwin.

Then my eyes drifted along the lower shelves, the ones so accessible to the chair where I sat. And there was Anaïs Nin's *Delta of Venus* and Henry Miller's *Sexus* and some other tony erotic works, along with lesser titles of the genre.

A voice from behind me interrupted my assessment of Father Love's literary tastes.

"You're a reading man, Detective Hockaday?"

It was Roy, and he seemed as surprised at seeing a cop with a book in his lap as I had been seeing the works of Anonymous and the others on Father Love's shelf. Roy had entered the library soundlessly, or maybe I had not heard him, absorbed as I was in the range of Waterman's literary tastes. Now he stood beside me with a paper shopping bag. He handed me the bag and expected I would stand up, get dressed, and disappear. But I sat where I was.

"A detective, a good detective, has to be a reading man," I said. "The best writing is about discovery, and you can see how one thing improves another."

Roy said nothing. He was not unpleasant with the silence, but he was impatient with me, so it seemed. So naturally I felt I should take my time.

"Besides," I continued, "I always find it revealing to take a look at the sorts of books a man chooses to keep around him, if any. It's as revealing as learning what he likes to eat for dinner, or what he likes drinking, or what he likes in his women."

Ignoring everything I had said, Roy pointed to the unopened bag in my lap and explained in a monotone, "There's your clothes, sponged and spotted clean. Best we could do in a hurry."

When he saw I was in no hurry, Roy added, "I want you to

know that we're deeply grateful for your saving the life of our dear pastor." But the way he spoke and the now unmistakable impatience in his expression made me feel as welcome in the Holy Stream Deliverance Temple as a condom in one of the collection plates.

"Sit down, Roy." I motioned to the chair across from me. He sat down and I looked him over.

Roy was about my size, six feet. But he was heavier. Not fat, but more bulky in the chest and shoulders and legs than me. He had dark brown skin, clear black eyes, and a self-assured look. The kind of man who could put on a uniform and lead anybody's army anywhere. His hands were large and well kept, a gentleman's unscarred hands. He held them laced in his lap, and he sat straight in his chair. I guessed him to be thirty years old, give or take two.

"Tell me about yourself," I asked him. "For starters, what's your full name?"

"Roy S. Dumaine. The S is for Saunders, which is my mother's maiden name." He returned to the monotone.

"How long have you been with Father Love, and what is it, exactly, that you do for him?"

"Oh, I've been part of the church here since I was a kid. I come from right around here in the neighborhood, and, you know, we grew up with Father Love on the radio every Sunday night."

"And you thought you'd like to be like Father Love, is that right?"

"Well, I remember being seventeen and thinking how I might want to be a preacher. I was good at dealing with people, and I always cared about seeing them get ahead and beating the odds against them."

"So, do you preach now?"

"The only real and true preacher around here is Father Love. That's it. You might hear me on the radio sometimes, but just to announce things. It's Father Love's show all the way."

"Where do you fit in, then?"

"If I had a job title, I guess it'd be executive assistant. I generally do what needs doing, ever since I was seventeen.

About four, five years ago I started getting paid for it, and now I give Father Love all my time."

"And do you buy the whole show, Roy?"

Dumaine smiled, coldly now. Like he had heard this snide sort of questions before, especially from white folks. He asked, "You're what, Hockaday, a Catholic?"

I said I was.

"Well, then since you're used to the biggest and gaudiest production we have in town, I guess you maybe look at us here in Harlem and you think we're nothing but some little-bitty tent show by comparison." And then he unclasped his hands and leaned forward and jabbed a finger at me and said, "But if you please, don't be coming uptown to tell me that Father Love is any more—or any less—then your man downtown with all the rings and the funny hat, hear?"

There was an unlovely challenge to his tone and an even unlovelier glint in Dumaine's black eyes. But even so, I might have given in to his point—if not for the dread thought of having to confess for it later. So instead I provoked him some more, out of what I have come to value and respect over the years as my perverse instinct for taking a man's measure.

"I look around here and I ask myself, can this guy Waterman— sorry, Father Love . . . , can this guy pass through the eye of a needle?"

Roy shook his head. "Let me tell you something about the people of this church. We know all about poverty here, and so we're sure as hell not about to be wishing it on Father Love or anybody else."

Again he had a point, and I knew it. I was enjoying this conversation as much as Roy was hating it.

"Well, let me say this," I said. "You and I are sitting in a room here that's like the other side of a mountain to the folks who come here Sundays. You know it and I know it—and Father Love knows it. What's true about the folks out there in the pews is a lie in this room, what's true here is a lie out there."

"With all due respect," Dumaine said, "and I'm keeping in mind what you've been through for us, your bravery and all, and seeing how you're a reading man like Father Love himself—well,

I'm surprised you don't have respect for the great difference between facts and truth."

I thought, Here we go again with an outsize regard for the truth and all of that. But I said, "And please, the fine difference here would be what?"

"The fact of our members here is that they're poor, as you say. But that's not the truth of them. The truth of them is as rich as this room we're in."

"Father Love tells them this sort of thing in exchange for their pennies?"

"It's the truth as he sees it, and there's people here every Sunday who know it's the truth—no matter what the poor facts of their lives happen to be. I believe this is the truth.

"Now, can you understand that? And if you can, would you say it's any damn different than what you've been taught in your Catholic church?"

I smiled and said, "Roy, how about having a drink with me?"

"I'm not a drinking man, no thanks."

Then Roy asked, "What do you know about people like us, anyhow? What do you know about being sick in your stomach in the morning from being hungry the night before? What do you know about hopelessness? And people looking at you with cold eyes because all they can see is your hopeless damn black face and your hunger?"

"I can tell you I know enough not to be making assumptions about any man," I said. "And I can tell you that in Hell's Kitchen where I come from, I learned a long time ago that you don't have to have the same mama and poppa to be brothers. How about where you come from, Roy?"

Dumaine did not answer.

I tipped back the last of my Scotch and said, "So, being a reading man from Hell's Kitchen and a drinking man besides, I know about hunger and hopelessness from my very own times."

Then I stood up and opened the paper bag and looked into it. Everything was there, shoes included. I had kept my .38, of course, and I had left my hat and overcoat in the library from the first visit.

So I went over to Waterman's dressing room to slip out of the robe and back into my own things, which had never been cleaner, truth to tell.

Back outside the church, I found a lieutenant in uniform sitting in an unmarked squad car from the Twenty-eighth that was idling on Lenox Avenue and blocking the entrance to the alley where Waterman had been shot. A couple of the forensics stragglers in raincoats were tramping about the edges of things.

There were still some patches of snow that were visibly, brightly red. Somebody who didn't know what had happened earlier might have thought a wagon full of cherry-flavored Italian ices had taken a spill. That is because ordinarily you do not right away think some preacher was gunned down right alongside his very own church, not even in New York, not even in Harlem; certainly not when the preacher could be presumed to have God and the SCUM Patrol on his side.

I remembered then about the telephone calls I would soon be making and the hell to pay for them. And my head started aching; not a whole lot, not like there were ten-penny nails breaking through the bone, but enough of an ache to nag me about the error of my ways in failing to opt for the peaceable little career at the Sears Roebuck out in some peaceable little place like Nutley maybe, over in Jersey. Who needed this?

The lieutenant rolled down a window when I tapped on it with my gold shield. Heat and blue cigarette haze curled out into the cold and mixed with gray plumes of auto exhaust.

"So, Looey," I said to him after I had read the title in front of his name on a silver tag that rode his lumpy chest, "any word from the hospital yet on Father Love's condition?"

"You'd be Hock, is that it?"

I told him that would be it.

The man I was talking to was one Lieutenant G. L. Keene, and he was looking at me through unfraternal slits below the shiny black brim of his commander's hat. So I couldn't be sure about the top of his head because of the hat, but I pegged him for bald. He had a bald guy's face, anyhow. He was maybe fifty-five and pillow-shaped, and he seemed about as sweet on life as a fat man with a neck full of boils.

"Okay, let's see here, Hock. You just so happen to be up in my precinct, on a Sunday morning, which I understand is usually your day off. And you're hanging round with a pack of these holy-rollin' niggers here. And then you just so happen to be havin' a walk-about in this here alleyway and you wind up savin' the padre's grapes."

He paused, sucked his teeth, and said, "That about the size of it?"

My saying nothing by way of response gave Keene no pause.

"Jesus H. Christ," he went on, "I wish't they'd tell me when they got some VIP deal going down, I really freakin' do! Look, tell me this, at least—is the captain here in on all this?"

"I don't know," I said. "Probably not."

This seemed to be of some relief to Keene, a naturally paranoid sort due to the sour circumstances of a certain stripe of bigot-cop I am pained to acknowledge is something of a cliché in a system as substantially imperfect as the New York Police Department. But sometimes an imperfect system finds the perfect means of dealing with this type of cliché, by way of promotion to purgatory; in Keene's case, he had one day realized how he had been made the butt of a joke somewhere up the line when somebody posted him to central Harlem, where he was certain to spend the rest of his career surrounded by those well outside his own ancestry.

"Christ a'mighty, Hock, you ought to see all the offers I get to become chief of police for little dinky-ass outfits in dinky-ass little places like Coconuts, Florida. Oh, every day in the mail I get the offers. I swear to God, they keep tunnelin' under me like they been doin' and one of these days I'm going to say yes to Coconuts."

And of course, this was the other method found by an imperfect system of dealing with its Keenes: circulate their résumés to out-of-town police departments. My own boss, Inspector Neglio, did this routinely when confronted by undesirables. When it brought about the desired result, Neglio would be the first one to slap a Keene on the back and tell him how New York's loss was going to be Coconuts' gain.

"Well, we'd sure miss you around here," I said to Keene.

Keene took off his hat and rubbed his hairless scalp, and suddenly all desires of the good life at Sears Roebuck evaporated as I envisioned a Nutley full of Keenes.

Then I asked him, "Until you've moved on to someplace, could you give me the late word on Father Love like I asked?"

"Oh, yeah. They told me about two minutes ago the padre's in critical. It don't look the best they ever seen, but it don't look the worst neither. They got a transfusion on him, though, so they're hoping to perk him up some that way."

"What do you know about his scam up here? I mean, he can't be just living off the take from services."

Keene shrugged. "I don't know much, I don't care much, you know? Father Love's like all the rest of your bright-faced niggers up here doin' it the worst to their own people—playin' the mitt game, you know? Open up their mitts and hold them out for the regular suckers to fill up with cash.

"I tell you, Hock, these people up here—they love bein' suckered out of money almost as much as they love bein' suckered out of a night's sleep when somebody says they been hexed. Harlem's a different planet, I'm tellin' you."

The forensics cops walked past us, finished with their job. Keene returned their salutes.

"You can't tell me anything else about a guy in your precinct who leads a church as big as this one?"

"Well . . ." Keene tried to think of something helpful. "Well, I always wondered one thing, and that's how come in this day and age he didn't do his thing on TV? I mean, how come just the radio all these years?"

"Interesting," I said, which was the truth. I would have to ask Waterman that question myself.

"Would I be correct in assuming you've got yourself a delicate assignment up here, Hock?"

"That's right."

"So you'll be seein' us again?"

"I expect."

Keene rolled up his window and shifted the squad car into forward gear and drove off, leaving me standing there on Lenox Avenue in search of a public telephone that might be working. I walked a couple of blocks downtown toward 125th Street, where I could catch the A train back to Times Square.

I stopped at the Baby Grand club a couple of doors past the Apollo Theatre. Somewhere in the back of the place, I heard a young singer rehearsing an old song. *"You're fat and forty and over the hill/But baby, you're my meat and I love you still . . ."* And I felt like having a few and staying there for the rest of my life, but instead I made my phone calls from the booth at the front end of the bar.

First, I rang up Neglio's office and spoke to one of the inspector's bow-and-arrow boys, who told me how the boss was vacationing in Bimini, which I knew, and how he was sorry but there did not happen to be any telephone contact between New York and whatever kind of grass shack Neglio had rented for the duration. Which maybe I should have figured.

Then I telephoned Sam Waterman, Jr. I was not surprised to get his answering machine again, so I left a message for him to reach me at the Ebb Tide bar. I said it was urgent.

Then I walked out of the Baby Grand and headed for the subway.

And I felt like a cop feels so much of the time, as effective as a man chasing a spider with a bowling ball.

When I got home, the first thing I did was check the place for somebody who might have recently died there. But I was alone and that was good since I do not know if I could have put up with another stiff.

I telephoned Harlem Hospital. Father Love was still in critical. I telephoned the Twenty-eighth Precinct station house and was assured that a couple of uniforms would be posted through the night outside and inside of Waterman's room. And then I telephoned Waterman's kid again.

And again I reached his answering machine. And again I left an urgent message for him to call me, at home.

Then I flopped on my back on the couch beneath the windows and sank into a deep blue sleep. I dreamed of the Christmas Day coming and how I would not be spending it with Judy. And I dreamed of my father, whom I had never met, who was dead to me; I dreamed of him as I always did, as the man in the picture frame.

And in my dream, the frame had two legs and a soldier's boots, and the picture of my father was marching through a battlefield.

THIRTEEN

I stood in the doorway down behind the crumbling limestone stoop of the Paris Nights Transient Hotel, a half step below the dark and the grit of Fifty-fifth Street at the northwest corner of Eighth Avenue, where Times Square porn and tourist shops and the Broadway theaters and cinemas start giving way to Hell's Kitchen tenements and Irish saloons and OTB parlors. I was waiting for my eyes to adjust to the murk of the place when a girl sidled up from the bar. The girl had a big grin on her face, which was not actually the first thing that happened to catch my eye.

"Girls" is what they prefer being called at La Club Pigalle, which is the last mastodon of a certain ancient race of New York burlesque house that has mercifully survived the various winds of the day. It has survived all the usual low and squalid forms of righteousness; it has survived the holy wrath of Fiorello La Guardia, an otherwise brave and sober mayor with the unfortunate tendency toward axe-swinging whenever his nose turned blue from thoughts of garter belts and G-strings and tassels twirling around pasties to the pungent beat of a brassy tune; it has survived the endless extortion plots of cops, crooks, and capitalists—the civic trinity that has made urban America what it is today; it has survived the decades of backstage jealousies, betrayals, squabbles, phobias, and all else in the vast range of emotion-soaked female caprices. La Club Pigalle has survived even the recent plague of mindless raunch that has trampled so much of the dear, decent wickedness of Times Square, the plague that has probably killed the imaginations of an entire generation of sailors.

When I was a kid, the priests at Holy Cross Church railed from the pulpit against La Club Pigalle right there in the neighborhood, as if it were an evil greater than poverty itself; then with sweeter voices, the priests would follow with homilies about the humble glories of regular Bible reading as the antidote to erotic temptations so rampant among the men of our parish. And then when I was at long last tall enough to pass by the Pigalle's indulgent and drunken doorman, I had the very good fortune to see these opposing persuasions in the very same place at the very same time—in the magnificent person of a baggy-pants comic called Scurvy, whose crowd-pleasing act consisted of his buxom second-banana wife and himself burlesquing their way through a prurient selection of biblical passages that he would first solemnly read aloud to the audience, right out of a regular leather-bound King James, with his missus there by his side to punctuate each introduction with a lewd shake of her hips and a suggestive high note blown on a slide whistle.

On that first wonderful night of mine at La Club Pigalle, I noticed the presence of quite a lot of the parish men. Practically a delegation they were, stamping their big feet and hooting merrily at the scenes enacted from Judges and Deuteronomy and Ruth by Mr. and Mrs. Scurvy; and it seemed obvious to me that these were more valorous men who defied the lightning to strike than men who presumed God unable to cope with bawdy satire. Right then and there I wished to be a priest myself and able to grant all of them their immediate absolutions, the poor sods from their rock-stolid Irish New York homes where dinners were sternly boiled and taken in the kitchen at six sharp and noiseless sex was taken in a room without lights, provided first that all the young and innocent were safely off to sleep.

Years ago the Pigalle and the Paris Nights were as elegant as they were forbidden places, so it seemed to us. There was an out-of-town sporting crowd that stayed in the hotel and played cards in the lobby; some still wore spats over their shoes, everybody wore hats. And there was a jaunty neon sign in the shape of a lady's slippered foot that pointed the way down to the club door. But the whole place is tattered now and as gray and shabby as an old lady with a snootful of booze. Even so, I am grateful for her. She is still here, and she has not yet lost her soul. The Pigalle is a genuine fleshpot in a sexless desert of glass and chrome that is creeping all over Manhattan.

Maybe the only reason the Pigalle now survives is because its unlikely owner of the past thirty years or thereabouts, a sultry old transvestite cabaret singer named Labeija, had the very good sense to have bought the entire premises for a figurative song— the club space in the cellar, with its liquor license and its helpfully sinful repute; the Paris Nights Transient Hotel, which she filled over the years with her aged and exotic friends; and the top floor with the terrace and garden she built, where Labeija still lives in splendor, in surely the only penthouse in all Hell's Kitchen.

And maybe it would all die one day with Labeija. In the meantime, it was Mona Morgan's kind of place. And mine. And I was not in the mood for a funeral just yet, certainly not with the reception I was getting in the doorway. . . .

The girl clutched at my hand, pulling me into the warm darkness and the warming sounds of La Club Pigalle. A muted trumpet and a raggy piano, glasses and ice, brush strokes on drums and a muzzy trombone, and the stamping feet of parish men, what was left of them.

She was tall and her hair was long and light brown, hips slim and round. She had a big stagy bust that was getting almost no shelter whatever from the red-sequined dress she wore. She was beautiful in her way; but then all the club girls were beautiful in this way, in the kind softness of colored lights and the haze of drink; even old Labeija, in his own tormented way, would be beautiful when she sang.

I stared at the girl, wondering if she might be also beautiful in

the natural light of day. Probably not. She said to me, "Hello,
baby . . . long time no see."

And then I handed her a dozen white and yellow roses
wrapped in foil, which I had picked up along the way from a
Korean greengrocer. She squealed pleasantly and really did
sound like a girl, like a young girl on her prom night. So I felt
lousy when I had to tell her, "They're for Mona . . . could you
get them backstage to her?" She looked at me like she was maybe
thinking about how many men she had hugged in her time, how
many mouths she had had to kiss.

So we stood there for an awkward couple of seconds until I
said brightly, "I remember this place had a sign outside."

"A couple of blocks from here, they got all the signs you'd ever
want to see, mister," she said. "The result of which is those joints
are full of the type who come to the city in cars, to bring us
everything they're opposed to back home.

"This here club, baby, is for the rest of us. It's a good old spot
that's still real as a dream. So we don't bother about advertising
anymore."

I smiled and told her, "Then I'm happy to be in the right
place."

"You're cute," she said. "I like you, even though you got
another girl in mind. At least it's one of us girls."

Then she showed me to a little table with a candle in a glass on
the top of it and said she would be happy to take the flowers back
to Mona, right away. I sat down and flagged a waiter for a drink.
And I took inventory of a place I had been away from for far too
long.

La Club Pigalle is a long, narrow, low-ceilinged barn of a joint,
with a stage in the back that is surrounded by beer drinkers
smoking cigarettes like their lives depended on it. They're guys
who look like everybody's shy bachelor uncle, men who inhabit
an unornamented world. Along the walls, in the patched vinyl
banquettes or in the shadows, the old girls in their fishnet hose
and their spangly gowns pressed themselves against the livelier
customers.

The last of a set of strippers had finished, and now she bowed demurely from the stage. Bits of her feathered boa danced in the spotlight that faded gradually to dark.

Then, after some silence, an alto voice sang from somewhere on that darkened stage a song I have heard Sinatra sing a dozen times on Jonathan Schwartz's Sunday morning show on WNEW-AM, "A Man Alone." Only this voice was more sinuous than Sinatra's, lower and huskier.

And then a strong light filled the stage, light that sliced through the hands of smoke hanging in the room. And Labeija was there in the light, both hands clasped around a microphone, singing with her eyes closed, her voice so textured and sad and alternately bright and happy. She moved to "How Little We Know," then "Fools Rush In," then "Harlem Butterfly" and "Skylark" and "Arthur Murray Taught Me Dancing in a Hurry."

And a tap on my shoulder, light and feathery as the stripper's boa. A feminine voice:

"You're listening so nice and close, I see. That's good for the singer, shows you're a real friend of the house, Hock. Beside being a friend of mine for coming up here to see me finally."

Then Mona leaned over and kissed me on the cheek and sent my blood pressure on a wild goose chase. Which was a pleasant surprise for me.

"You could ask a girl to sit down for a drink since you just went and bought her flowers," she said.

I stood up and caught my foot on a table leg and felt about as smooth as a bag full of fingernails. Then I pulled out a chair and said, "Oh, sure, sure, sit down, won't you?"

And then we sat. I picked up a book of La Club Pigalle matches from the ashtray and lit the candle between us. And the yellow light caught in her black hair. And I saw her dark liquid eyes like I had never seen them before, and her fair skin and her red lips and her perfect white teeth.

She laughed at me. And I liked it.

And I blew out the match and remembered the other day at the spoon how we had started talking, how it had been important talk. And now I began wondering where Mona Morgan had come from and what had brought her here. I imagined her in some little town upstate, walking along Main Street in the wintertime, bundled up in a fur coat and her arms full of parcels and snow in her black hair. And she would be smiling with her perfect teeth, like now.

"Those teeth," I said to her. "I'd love to see you bite into an apple."

She laughed again. Then she leaned forward and touched my hands. Our faces were close, and I saw the tiny creases around her eyes and mouth, but it was all right by me; I had so many more creases of my own, and I hoped that was all right by her. We listened to Labeija sing "Old Devil Moon."

The waiter came by. I wanted another red and rocks, Mona asked for a club soda with a lime twist.

She sat back with her drink and said, "Beija's a good singer, don't you think?"

I said yes, I thought so, too.

And Mona said, "I was a singer once. Well, a singer and a dancer. I'd have rather just been a singer, but you know how it is. Do you know how it is, Hock?"

There was a general rippling of applause, then a general shuffling forward as the crowd of shy bachelor uncles made its way to the favored ringside seats around the stage—for the resumption of the meat-and-potatoes entertainment, another round of strippers.

We watched Labeija take elaborate bows in the foggy blue light. Some of the older, drunker customers had tears streaming down their noses and they clapped their hands like sentimental seals, and it hardly mattered what they knew about the husky-voiced singer or what they did not. What mattered was a moment's bittersweet oblivion.

We clapped, too, Mona and I. Labeija blew kisses to the old blubber boys.

When the applause died, I said to Mona, "You were saying?"

"Was I?"

"About singing and dancing."

She pulled a strand of her black hair and looped it over an ear, and then something melancholy came to her voice. "One time or another," she said, "I guess I did about every place there is up and down the East Coast. But the Pigalle . . . I guess it's best for me now."

"I saw you at the Melody once," I said.

"Oh God, Hock, that was so long ago! Where've you been?"

I told her about living in a house in Queens and how that tends to take you out of the know, about my room on the Lower East Side until I got it through my head I was divorced, about how I was back home in Hell's Kitchen. About marriage, and regret. Funny how it didn't take so long to tell, I thought.

"You sound like you're mostly sad from being married," she said. "I guess sad's better than being mostly angry."

"Oh, I got angry some of the time."

"Like how angry?"

"Let's just say I went to confession an awful lot when I was married."

Again she laughed. Those teeth! I sipped my drink and felt my head and the skin on my face going fuzzy from booze.

"I got one good piece of advice from a priest one of those times I had to go and confess," I said. "The priest told me, 'My son, you know what they say about women—you can't live with them, and you're not allowed to shoot them.'"

"A rare priest. He was wise to the fact that God's an ironist." Mona did not laugh after she said this.

"Is He?"

She looked away blankly, toward the stage where some skinny blond number was wriggling to "Let Me Entertain You," which was not doing a whole lot for the uncles watching her closest and even less for me. I thought about how I had neglected to call up Sam Waterman's machine again to tell him to try me at the Pigalle.

"Me, I think I probably would have liked marriage," Mona said, her voice very far away. But then she looked back at me. "But you know how it is—I'm a dancer, not a singer. You know?"

I did not actually know, and Mona did not actually expect me to. She stood up and said, "Well, let's see what you think about the costume."

She opened up the front of a long green dressing gown, closed almost to her neck and loosely draped down well past her knees.

She did a couple of neat turns, and I saw flashes of a body-hugging gold lamé sarong with slits high up the thigh. The rise she got out of me lifted her oddly shifting spirits.

"Anyhow, I'm at least the featured dancer here," she said. "So tell me, what do you think?"

"I think I'm going to love your act, and so will everybody else if they know what's good for them."

"My hero."

Before she sat down again, she slipped off her shoes and had me get a load of her toes. She'd painted them ten different colors.

"You like?"

"Yeah, I like, but . . ."

"Part of the act. You'll see." She put her shoes back on and sat down. Then she looked a little blue again and said, "I'd give a whole lot if you'd have come along when I was an ordinary girl."

"What's an ordinary girl?"

"A pretty girl from Nowheresville, that's your ordinary type. Like Mona Morgan from Rhinecliff. . . ."

So she was from a little town upstate, I thought to myself.

"I was pretty as all the rest, and I sang as badly as all the rest; I had better legs than most, though. Lucky me."

She looked away again to some blank spot. I almost did not hear her say, "I wish I could make all the ordinary girls stay put. I should have stayed put. I might have been sensationally beautiful up in Rhinecliff."

"You're beautiful here and now," I said weakly. But the words tasted like lint. Mona smiled patiently at me, a woman accustomed to limp words from men.

"Beautiful enough," she said, "but not so bright enough. If I were bright, I would have known to stick around my hometown and help beautify the place. But even if I'm not so bright, I try to learn.

"So far, I've learned that a pretty girl like me is needed in a place like Rhinecliff. Down here in the city, nobody needs me but the boys with the eyes for business, you know? They can use me all right. That I learned real quick.

"Also, I learned that if I don't like it, I can go right on back to Rhinecliff and let the pretty girl from Schenectady or Bridgeport

or Worcester have a go at it, and the boys with the eyes for
business—they'd never know the difference.

"You know how it is, Hock? Do you?"

I was looking at my hands and thinking of someplace in the
world where I could maybe take Mona Morgan so she could
forever be a pretty girl bundled in a fur coat, with parcels in her
arms and snow in her hair. And I was thinking of some way to
say this to her so it would not sound hollow.

And then, as if I were sitting in some revival movie house
down in the Village on a rainy afternoon half listening to familiar
lines from Lorre or Garfield or Greenstreet or Ladd up on the
screen, there was Labeija's raspy voice. . . .

"Hiya there, Hock. You come by to haunt my place again?"

"No, Labeija," I said. "You've got the face for that."

Labeija gave me a manful slap on the shoulder. Mona stood
up, kissed her boss on the cheek, and said to me, "Good—now
you'll have company. I got to go and get ready for my act."

I told Mona I'd look for her after the show, and she said, "You
better, Hock. I want a supper out of you, then we'll have a time
later on."

My face was hot. It was not flushed; I do not blush anymore.
I'd like to, but I can't.

Labeija planted her big camouflaged man's body into the chair
Mona had vacated. I wondered how she might look with a cigar
and a beer bottle and her face washed.

She was wearing a big curly auburn wig, one of a large
collection of wigs. Her face and throat and décolletage were deep
orange from all the Max Factor body pancake plastered on with
water and alcohol and buffed to a shoe shine to prevent streaking.
Her eyes were done up in extra-length showbiz lashes and so
much cocoa-colored mascara that it looked like she might have
mashed a couple of Hostess cupcakes somewhere between her
nose and where she plucked her brows.

"This visit for old times' sake, Hock?" Labeija asked. "Or you
on some business? Or you just after a little peach off of Mona?"

"Old times, mostly," I said. "I don't have any specific business
here, but sometimes business isn't so neat, you know. And I
don't know much about peach anymore."

"'Course not, you being a married man and all." Labeija poked my shoulder again and said, "Oh, all you good ones are taken."

"Judy and me, we're split," I told him. "It's been a while. I guess you didn't know."

"Well, it ain't easy, is it?"

No, I said, it was not easy anymore.

Labeija shrugged. "So what's up with you and Mona now?"

"The other day, I bumped into her. After a lot of years . . ."

I did not bother telling Labeija how I had first bumped into Mona along about 1975, when she was working the lobby of a hotel full of evangelists whooping it up in the banquet room for some actor making a big speech about how he wanted to play the White House someday. I was still in uniform in those days, and it was starting to chafe. So I did lots of favors for certain ones I planned to make useful to the cause once I got my promotion—favors like not pinching them for reasons that were not particularly hurting anybody at the moment.

"She turned up in my coffee shop," I said. "Or I guess maybe I turned up in hers. I just moved back to the old neighborhood, Beija.

"Anyway, Mona and I got talking. And I guess that's about all, except she wanted me to come see her work some night. And tonight I need the diversion."

"Besides which," Labeija said, snapping her fingers at a waiter, "she looks damn good, don't she?"

"Well, that, too."

When the vodka came, Labeija said, "So many good-looking girls come here, so very many of them over the years. This ain't a pretty business, but it's a business full of pretty girls. Go figure. Some of the girls turn out lucky, some don't; practically all of them wind up with nobody who honestly cares one way or the other."

"Which way has it been for Mona?"

"Well, Mona, she's lucky, I guess you'd have to say. Her legs are good, and nothing ever happened to her face—and you should see to it nothing ever does. Know what I mean?"

I finished my drink and thought vaguely about how many drinks I had had that day. And from the slushy sound of

Labeija's voice, I thought she might have matched my own tally. She ordered another vodka.

And I was aware of a lot of different sounds around me and how it confused me. The schmaltzy music from the house band, camping it up for the last bump-and-grinder before Mona's featured act, the feet stamping around the runway, waiters thumping by with trays full of beer. Or maybe all my thoughts were loudly caving in on me late in the night of an awful day.

I was aware, too, that Labeija sat waiting for me to say something.

I managed, "No, what do you mean?"

"I mean, when you're in show business, you shouldn't let your face get rearranged too much. If you ever get mad enough to swing on somebody in the business same as you, you're obliged to keep your blows as low as possible. The lower the better.

"It's only the decent thing to do. People who don't understand the reasoning that's back of this rule, they call it dirty fighting. But you can really see how it ain't.

"I mean, Hock—you can see, can't you?"

How many of us ever do?

The emcee's voice boomed through the smoky dark of the room, and the crowd hushed.

"Ladies and gentlemen . . . which should cover some of you out there—"

The drummer banged out a rim shot, and there was a deep rumble of laughter.

"—La Club Pigalle, where the finest in good old-fashioned burlesque lives on and might set you back, oh, maybe half a week's paycheck—"

Another rim shot.

"—is proud to present for your enjoyment our star attraction . . . the lovely, the curvaceous, the charming, the captivating, the bewitching, the enchanting . . . the one and only, Mona Morgan!"

The band went into an overture. Spotlights played leapfrog in shades of coral and yellow and green, and the crowd whistled and stamped and called out Mona's name.

She floated in from the offstage wings, free and light and smiling with her perfect teeth. She wore long white beaded gloves that came up past her elbows, and a matching cloche over her head, and soft white fur pieces wrapped around her shoulders and hanging down around her body in front and back like Spanish moss on southern pines.

I stood up and started walking toward the stage; I was unaware how many steps I had taken, until I was right up close enough to feel the burning of the lights and the heat of the tight-packed audience. Mona spotted me in the dark, below her. She waved, pointed at me, winked. Some of the uncles turned around to have a look at lucky me.

Mona started moving around in circles on the stage, establishing eye contact with every one of us, pointing and winking. She tossed a glove to the crowd. She dropped a fur from one shoulder and paused for us to see that first exposure of her creamy skin. I knew desire again, and I knew how it was the human race carries on. And the uncles around me shouted and stamped, like a herd of hogs that had finally discovered the meaning of mud.

She dropped more furs, until all eyes were transfixed on the gold lamé sarong and the slits in the sides that framed her legs. And then she pulled the cloche from her head and shook out her long black hair. All of us gasped.

She bowed. Then she took a microphone from the bandleader, moving toward a stool that sat by itself in a shaft of pink light at the edge of the runway.

She leaned on the stool at first, then raised one leg and glided up atop it. And then she asked her uncles, "Would you like a little song?" Her lips touched the microphone.

Her uncles very much desired a little song.

And so the band segued from the vamp to the melody now, and Mona pouted up her lips and closed her eyes and crossed her devastating legs. Then crossed them again.

She let her shoes fall off her feet, as if they were overripe grapes. And she wriggled her ten painted toes and sang an old double-entendre song like maybe Betty Boop would have sung it—a wonderfully arousing song about a lady sorry for not having a proper birthday gift for her beau, and how she proposed to make this up to him by offering her "Popsicle Toes." And at that moment in the tenderloin of Times Square, where imagination has mostly been killed, Mona's old song and the soft slow way she moved were lovely and thrilling.

Mona would tip her head as she sang, as she worked her way delicately out of her gold lamé; with the faintest smile, more than anything else she showed of herself, she made us reach back into the depths of our instinct to desire her. For she was beautiful and a star and an enigma.

FOURTEEN

While Mona changed after her show—while she got herself dressed suitably for supper, actually—I made three telephone calls.

The first one was to Harlem Hospital, where I spoke with the head nurse on the overnight shift.

Father Love had responded satisfactorily to the blood transfusion, it seemed, but he had also entered into a semicomatose state, which the doctors said was sometimes a natural stabilizing influence under the circumstances, but sometimes not. In any case, they wouldn't know anything for forty-eight hours.

"And then what?" I asked.

She took her time before answering this one. I heard sputtering on the line, which could have been spandex having a time of it beneath her white starched uniform—or else the sound of her exasperation. I have dealt with hundreds of nurses in my time, and I have never known one of them to be happy about having to say anything that was not a direct quote from a doctor. This one said, "Well, I suppose in forty-eight hours he'll either still be with the rest of us . . . or, being a reverend, he'll be in heaven."

131

I told her it probably made little sense to hold out blanket confidence in choice reservations for holy men hanging by a thread. She told me how she did not think it was a good idea for somebody in a dangerous profession like mine to be cracking wise about religion. She probably had the finer point, I thought.

"Anyhow," the nurse told me, "all we know tonight is that he's in critical condition."

"I guess about as critical as you can get."

"Yeah, I guess."

There was some more sputtering, and that call was over.

I next telephoned young Waterman. I got the usual results.

Then I telephoned for reservations at a place I know uptown where Wiener schnitzel is called *scallops vienesse*. I thought Mona would appreciate it.

She did.

When we stepped out from the taxicab and made our way to the door under a long red canopy, Mona squeezed my arm and nuzzled my ear with her soft lips and whispered, "Mr. Hockaday, what can all this mean? How did you know I love roses and supper at places that come with canopies out front?"

"I am sensitive, yet flashy. What can I say?"

"Don't make me laugh."

"I don't make people laugh much. Ask anybody in town. They'll laugh."

Which is what Mona then did. I felt her cool laughing breath on my neck and knew if I was not careful that I could fall, but hard.

Inside the restaurant, I liked the way she let her lynx coat slip off her shoulders into the fluttery hands of the maître d'hôtel. I liked what she wore underneath, too—something black and shiny that caught light in all the right places.

We followed the maître d' and his clicking patent-leather shoes through the dining room, a sunken square of tables and candelabra and champagne buckets. Our setup was in a good corner, and the table was full of purple flowers and crystal and heavy silver and enough linen to make a parachute. We might have been seated dead in the center of the room from the way people stared at us, mostly at Mona. She enjoyed the attention, and I had the feeling she was looking back at a couple of guys here and there who might have been instrumental in her career; also a couple of wives she had heard so much about.

And I was considering my answer to Inspector Neglio when he complained about the tab from this place showing up on my expense report. I decided to remind him about his taking off on a vacation where they do not have telephones, and how this is technically speaking a direct breach of the rules covering time off for brass hats.

I heard the maître d' click his heels. It sounded like he was wearing castanets instead of shoes. "Very *goot*, sir," he said to me, even though I do not remember saying anything to him.

Then the sommelier dropped by, and his feet clicked, too. Mona said she would stick to her club soda, thanks just the same; I sent him away after something red and pricey anyhow, and he said, "Very *goot*."

I asked Mona, "You like?"

"Yeah, I do. But I don't picture this place and you going together, Hock. You come here often?"

It was Judy's favorite place, but I did not tell her this. My wife liked to get dolled up at night, and her taste in restaurants was what you might call royalist.

"Often enough so I'm getting to suspect that Hans and Fritz and their tap shoes all had something to do with the Third Reich."

"I told you not to make me laugh," Mona said. Then she leaned forward and touched my arm, and I heard a waiter sigh. "I'm happy to see you in these surroundings, Hock. I'm so used to seeing you dressed like you're some slug who lives in the park.

"But you look at you now! You either have a good lady dressing you right for once in your life, or you're bucking for a promotion."

"I wouldn't mind some extra pay."

"Good for you," she said. "Then you can afford to see the ladies more often. We're very big eaters and drinkers, you know."

Her remark made me instinctively slip a hand down into my coat pocket to see if I still owned a wallet, which is something you do several times a day in New York unless you are destitute or think your life is charmed. I still had the wallet. And next to that the five death threats on the cards dropped into collection plates at the Healing Stream Deliverance Temple.

When my hand came up out of my pocket, the five cards came along with it. And then my elbow was bumped by the sommelier, who was suddenly clicking all around the table and fussing with his corkscrew. So without thinking about it, I set the five cards next to my bread plate.

I tasted the Givry and smelled the cork and decided it was burgundy all right. I said I would go ahead with the proposition. And then we ordered supper.

I do not remember what we ate or whether it was any good. I do remember watching Mona lifting bites of food from her plate and placing them gently into her mouth; and how I had not seen anything so naturally elegant since I watched her daub her lips with a paper napkin the other day at our spoon on Forty-second Street.

And I remember wondering for maybe the thousandth time how it is so few women have any clear idea of the power their ordinary beauty holds over so many of us men.

The coffee came.

"Pumpkin pie," Mona said. "I can't get it out of my mind. I suppose it's the time of the year. What are you doing for Thanksgiving, Hock?"

"Waiting for it to pass."

After I said this, I realized how sour it sounded. So I asked Mona to pay no attention to me under the circumstances of this being my first holiday season on the stag line.

"You just went and killed my appetite for the dessert," Mona said. "Sitting across the table from a guy still hung up on his ex-wife does that to a girl, in case you didn't know."

I told her I was sorry about that.

"So you're sorry, so what? Better you should learn what obsession is, Hock, and how it's not healthy for you."

"What's obsession to your way of thinking?"

"It's what's left when a love affair has lost its respect."

I started to pour myself another glass of burgundy. Mona made me put the bottle down.

"Save something for me," she said. "And I don't mean I want a drink."

"All right," I said. I sipped coffee. "And there there won't be any more talk about any woman besides yourself."

"Now you're talking."

Mona pointed to the five cards I'd put down on the table. "By the way, what in the world are those?"

"Clues."

"Oh, I like it."

Until then, it had not occurred to me that I might talk to Mona Morgan about clues in the case I was working, such as they were. Mona had been a regular contact of mine for years, usually good for confirming useful items I would pick up from my snitches since she heard lots of things she was not necessarily involved in herself. But if I talked about clues with her now, of course, I would not have the least trouble about putting in the bill for expenses, would I?

"By any chance are you familiar with the Bible?" I asked Mona.

"Not hardly."

"Well, look at this stuff anyway."

Mona picked up each of the cards, looked at both sides, and read the Scripture passages:

There is none righteous, no, not one.

Rom. 3:10

The heart is deceitful above all things, and desperately wicked; who can know?

Jer. 17:9

The fathers have eaten a sour grape, and the children's teeth are set on edge.

Jer. 31:29

As a dog returneth to his vomit, so a fool returneth to his folly.
Prov. 17:21

If a son shall ask bread of any of you that is a father, will ye give
him a stone?

Luke 11:11

"As far as the verses go," Mona said, "I can only tell you that
they're from both Old and New Testaments."

She ran a finger over one of the "DIE FATHER LOVE"
scrawls at the end of a verse. "This is the part that's scarier than
the verses, although the verses are scary enough themselves."

Mona handed the cards back to me, looking at the printed side
with Father Love's slogan and telephone number. She said, "I
guess I'm supposed to figure that somebody wants to kill this
guy? Who is he, anyway?"

"Father Love is a radio preacher, he has a church up in
Harlem," I said.

"Since when are the cops interested in a Harlem radio
preacher?"

"Since he's more than he pretends to be. Father Love is a stage
name, you might say. It's a beard for a very well connected guy
called Samuel Waterman."

"Where's he well connected?"

"The usual circle," I said.

"Oh yes, the circle. The one that starts with the well-dressed
gentleman who takes out his well-padded wallet and makes a
loan to the types who find a way of getting the rest of us to pay
off this loan." Mona sighed. "And so in a very little while, this
money goes around and around and it winds up back in
somebody's wallet as a very fat wad—somebody's wallet we
never heard of, like this Waterman fellow."

"Yeah, that circle," I said.

"So what's Detective Neil Hockaday's involvement in this
unlovely enterprise?"

"I come into it by way of my well-connected boss downtown,
who assigns me to hold Father Love's hand—only before I really

get the chance, funny things start happening on the way to the church."

"Funny like how?"

I told her about Buddy-O's murder. I told her about Howie Griffiths dead in my own bathtub. I told her about the apparent connection between the two. I told her about bumping into Sam Waterman, Jr., then how Junior dropped out of sight.

And then I told her about Father Love being shot that very morning and how he was lying uptown in Harlem Hospital, in critical condition. "Not that I'm saying I always need an excuse," I said, "but you can now maybe see why I'm drinking so eagerly."

I poured some more wine into my glass, and this time Mona did not do anything to stop me. And from the stricken expression that played across her face, which began several minutes ago when I told her about lying in the snow with Waterman in the alleyway and stanching the flow of blood from his bullet-ripped neck, it looked like Mona might want something stiff in the way of a drink herself.

So I held the bottle poised and arched my eyes, and Mona found an empty water glass and pushed it near the wine. She took a drink, touching her throat with her free hand as the wine went down.

"Well," she said, "you're telling me all this now and I'm supposed to do what—sing for my supper?"

"I don't know, I just thought you might be able to help me think."

"What am I supposed to give you, the woman's point of view, so-called?"

"Don't knock it. Women have built-in antennae that pick up supersonic nuances. It's what makes you all so scary, to tell the truth."

She laughed and I was relieved.

Then she shivered, like a snake had just run up her leg. She said, "Hock, you have to be careful here—I mean really *careful*, like you've never been careful before about anything. I'm only sitting here listening to what you've been through in the last few days, and I'm scared out of my mind for you. I think you're right up against the steam on this one, sooner or later. And you might get burned . . . and I don't want you burned, not for this."

My response wasn't the best, but I was facing Mona's wet eyes. "Well, it's what the department calls a 'delicate,' so there are higher-ups who are aware . . ."

But I trailed off, thinking how I'd never told Neglio about Buddy-O or Griffiths and about how he was down in Bimini now—maybe in violation of departmental rules, but in possession of plausible deniability. Which given the circumstances myself were I in Neglio's shoes, I might have chosen for myself.

Mona took another sip of her wine and said, "So they call it 'delicate,' do they? That's a goddamn cheap way to put it."

I put my hand over hers. "I've been run over a couple of times, I got a better-than-average way of looking out for big long cars coming at me from alleys without headlights."

"Yeah, and I know about the big talk from you men, too. I know where your big talk's got us. Oh yeah, your big talk and your big circles."

Mona finished what was in her glass, draining it away angrily. Then she took the bottle from me and poured all that was left, all for herself, something just shy of another glassful.

"I'm scared for you, that's what I'm saying here," she said. "From all the times you've been run over like you say, can't you see that possibility?"

"Sure," I said.

"You talk about how it's women who pick up nuances better than men, right? Well, I think the nuance here is all pretty much money, Hock, which is what scares me. But if you're going to go after this, which I suppose you are no matter what, then just take it easy—but follow the money trail. That's how they cracked Watergate, too. Remember? Remember how Deep Throat kept telling Woodward and Bernstein to 'follow the money trail'?"

"I remember it was good advice," I said.

"Yes, but that was only Washington, and it was only newspaper reporters and politicians," Mona said. "This is New York, this is for real. And when a serious cop in New York starts following the money trail of a serious crime—"

"Sooner or later, he's going to find steam," I said, interrupting her. "Like you said."

"And so I'm scared, like I also said. And I'm drinking, and I'm maybe going off the deep end a little because I'm scared you might laugh me off."

"I'm not laughing."

"Good. So I'm telling you again, *be careful.*"

"You're telling, I'm listening. I promise."

Mona looked at her empty glass again. She seemed sleepy. "Now if you don't mind too bloody much," she said, "could we please get on to my place?"

Not even the time I spent in Waterman's baronial quarters could have prepared me for Mona's place. Inside, that is.

Outside, it was an ordinary red-brick-and-stone tenement house, six stories high, the legal maximum for residential buildings with no elevator. There was the usual bank of broken mailboxes in the lobby, which was the usual cramped common space of dirty tiled floors and graffiti-smeared walls and a single circular fluorescent light hanging from the ceiling. In Hell's Kitchen, we call this the landlord's halo; it gives off the kind of light that makes everything look cheap and ghastly.

Across from Mona's apartment house was a row of loft buildings in various stages of destruction. A crane with a wrecking ball strung up on it sat in the middle of the rubble. Tomorrow, maybe, the crane would finish off the job. Tonight it was a vandal at rest.

I followed Mona up the steep central staircase. The stairs creaked and smelled of ammonia, and there were deep grooves along the way, where other men had been in my shoes exactly. We walked to the top.

Mona's apartment was the big one in front. She opened the door and touched a foyer light switch and walked into the parlor ahead of me, looking back over her shoulder to catch my reaction.

I stood in the foyer with my mouth open and looked in at the several chairs and tables, all brocaded and covered with good books and flowers that looked as if they'd just come in from the

garden. And a big Chinese lacquered screen in back of a
damask-covered divan. Cherrywood tables at the sides, with
lamps and candles in brass holders. Mona lit these.

Then she came over and pulled me into the parlor, and we
stood on a Chinese rug of red and blue underneath a chandelier.
I looked up at a couple of hundred crystals and a dozen or so soft
lights; it was a chandelier meant for a drawing room in a mansion
out in the country someplace and yet here it was in the parlor of
a Hell's Kitchen walk-up.

"It's a Baccarat, from my hometown . . . you know, Rhinecliff. It's a gift from a great lady in Rhinecliff called Miss Jessie.
Did I ever tell you about Miss Jessie and the house on the hill
that my daddy built for her?"

"No."

"Most of my things here come from Miss Jessie." Mona looked
around her apartment. And so did I, my fullest attention coming
to rest on a corner alcove with a window over the street and a
cabinet full of books and what I might have called a desk but
didn't since "desk" seemed too shabby a word for it. I walked
over and ran my hand along the smooth wood of the desk. Mona
followed behind me and said, "That's my favorite piece, actually.
My papa Sam made it. Did I ever tell you about Sam?"

I said, "No."

"Well, he was a carpenter and a cabinet maker." She put her
hand on the wood, next to my hand. "This is something he
copied from a picture in a lady's magazine, a picture of a
Fifteenth Louis *secrétaire*. Sam could reproduce it, but he
couldn't pronounce it."

I looked out the window over the *secrétaire*, at the rubble down
below in the construction site, bathed in a dim white light from
bare bulbs strung along a fence topped in razor wire. West of the
fence was a low cement wall that ran along a stretch of sidewalk
where there were no buildings. Below this part of the sidewalk
was a deep ravine, the old New York Central railroad tracks
running down along the bottom. When I was a kid, hobos
sometimes made camps down there, even when some of the
trains still ran.

"There used to be some fine buildings down there," Mona

said, looking over my shoulder and out the window. "They were beautiful big hulks, brick and limestone with terra-cotta cornices and gargoyles and iron railings under some of the windows. There were offices and loft shops on the upper floors, and shops at the street level. And of course the trains once upon a time. Now they're taking all of it down, everything from here to the river."

"What's going to replace it?"

"Who knows?" Mona said. "I went over and asked just that one day. I spoke to the foreman of the wrecking crew down there. He said to me, 'What the hell do I care, lady? I only knock 'em down.' Which he does, all together—brick and mortar and framework and all the carved lions and griffins and eagles. All of it's rubbish to this guy, all of it's the same. There's no shame in that man, or men like him."

I shook my head.

And Mona said, "Growing up the way I did and having the people I had around me, I can only look at life these days like it's some kind of lunacy. I mean, I had my papa—my mama died when I was a baby—and he was a man who was always fiercely proud of his work. And there was Miss Jessie—"

Mona stepped away and turned her head. And then she went on. "Papa was a carpenter back when one man built one house, all by himself starting with digging a hole for the foundation. And he built his very last house when he was just about ready to retire. He built it for the town rich lady, this wonderful lady we called Miss Jessie. She never had a husband, and no family. But she had plenty of style and money and friends. The town loved her and would have loved her without her money. I especially loved her.

"She owned a great piece of land in the village, about a half acre with a hill on it that gave her a fine view of everything in Rhinecliff. You could have made postcards out of those views from the hill. She wanted a house up there, and she wanted it to be a masterpiece, and so that's what she got.

"Miss Jessie interviewed the best architects and carpenters and contractors she could find. Lots of them came up from New York. But she wound up hiring Sam, my papa, because she liked how excited he got about her idea of the house and how he'd suggested it should have a verandah all the way around the outside and how he thought a central library with rounded walls would be perfect for her collection of books and clocks.

"I think I know how Miss Jessie must have thought when she talked to Papa, and watched him come alive when he spoke of building things and how his hands moved when he talked of his work, like he'd much rather be hammering and sawing and pegging than just talking.

"So Papa built her house. It took him better than three years. Oh, it was something, Hock! I wish I'd known you then. I'd have had you come with me when I walked up the hill to Miss Jessie's and went inside the round library to wind up all her clocks. That was my first paying job—twenty-five cents a day, a cup of tea, and Miss Jessie would teach me how to act like a lady.

"She was so happy with her house that she gave away a little bit of her land to Papa when he was all done building. It was a nice lot with fir trees, down from the hill. She had him build a retirement cottage there, with a front porch that faced the grand entrance to the last thing he built—which was his masterpiece.

"Papa sat out on that porch of his every evening almost, and he'd look up at what he'd done with his hands. And that's how I was raised, Hock, believe it or not."

Mona ran some fingers through her hair and cleared her throat. "So guess what happened to Miss Jessie's house, my papa's masterpiece? Guess where it went?"

"You say 'went,' so I suppose it was torn down?"

"Torn down wasn't all," Mona said. "They even leveled the hill. And now the whole place is an A and P with a great flat parking lot around it."

"My God," I said.

"I'm only thankful that neither one of them lived long enough to even suspect that Rhinecliff could do such a lousy thing."

She turned and looked at me again. And I could see she'd been remembering how life looked, through a prism of tears. She said, "Now you know quite a lot about me."

I told her I was proud to know about Mona Morgan from Rhinecliff, and Sam and Miss Jessie. And there was a very young and fluttery tone in her voice as she said, "Well . . . why don't you look around if you like, and I'll go make us some tea?"

I said that was all right by me.

There was a reading lamp on the lower writing surface of the *secrétaire*. Its base was a one-foot brass likeness of Mars, the Roman god of war. I reached up under a gray cloth shade and switched it on and noticed a telephone.

Toward the general direction of the kitchen, I said, "Would you mind if I made a quick phone call?"

"Sure, okay, just so long as it's not to some other woman." The sound of Mona's voice was mixed with the sounds of clinking china and running water.

I rang Waterman Junior and hung up when I heard the familiar sound of his answering machine. Then I walked to the divan in the center of the parlor and sank into it, grateful for its softness. And grateful for the candle that burned next to me so fragrantly; for the sudden sight of Mona flitting barefoot from the kitchen, down a little hallway and into the bedroom.

In a few minutes, she was back in the parlor and standing in front of me under the soft light of the chandelier. She wore a loose-fitting blue dress, and it make her black hair blacker. I looked at her bare feet, the colored toes.

"So you liked them?" she asked.

"I liked them."

She took a half step backward, reached behind her, and unclasped the blue dress and let it fall down around her ankles in a silky pile. And there she stood, now in white lace.

I had watched her strip before. That night, in fact. And other nights, too. And I knew all that to be illusion. But this moment in Mona Morgan's parlor, there was illusion's mirror opposite; there was possibility.

"Please you?" she asked.

And all the other things I had to think about—all the awful things, all the things that didn't yet add up—were things I decided to consider some other day.

"Yes, I'm pleased all right." And I felt like I was in that revival movie house in the Village again, and there was Bogart. "You got a figure like a shot of brandy on a winter's night."

She laughed.

I said, "Just tell me hello and I'll know all I have to do is send up a flare and relax."

"Hello."

The tea we had later.

When I woke up, there were pleats over me—cream-colored silk pleats that formed the inside top of the canopied bed we had moved into following our get-acquainted session in the parlor. I remembered Mona telling me how much she loved going to places that come with canopies. Now I did, too.

I sat up and my hip brushed against hers. She made a low sound and her body shifted a bit.

The headache I had been expecting—the one that made me feel like an out-of-town visitor—did not materialize. To make sure of this, I pitched forward at the waist and then from side to side. No pain. I was amazed at the happy side effect of sex after a long day's drinking.

There was a struggling early morning light in the bedroom window, which faced south. I could see that the walls were deep red and glazed. And I could see myself in an antique oval mirror on the wall beyond the end of the bed.

I swung my legs over the side of the bed. It was high off the floor, in the old-fashioned style, and my feet did not touch the rug. I wondered if the bed had once been Miss Jessie's, if the bearskin roll snugged at the foot of the bed had belonged to Sam . . .

And I wished—how desperately I wished—that I had something of my own father's, some small thing even. Anything I knew he might have held in his hand, or worn. But it was all gone. Even the letters from the war that I remembered my mother reading to the other soldiers' wives; and me in the kitchen listening, straining to memorize my father's words as they were spoken from paper. And why had I known that would be necessary? Where had the letters gone?

. . . and if, by possessing these things that had belonged to those she loved, Mona could feel that no matter what else in her life, she was not so oppressively alone.

I found my way to the bathroom and swished water through

my mouth and showered and combed my hair. Then I picked up my clothing from the floor around the divan and dressed, and stacked Mona's things neatly in a chair.

And I found the kitchen and the kitchen things in the usual places. So I made a pot of coffee while Mona slept on to some more sensible hour.

I took a cup of coffee with me to Sam's *secrétaire*, where I stood looking out the window over it to the bleak Monday morning below. Early workers walked the streets, presumably to their bus and subway stops. Maids, deli countermen, janitors, mechanics, busboys, drivers, mailroom stiffs. Taxis from the neighborhood garages headed crosstown to where business was best, on the East Side. Cardboard boxes hugged doorways, and inside them was where the homeless had sought shelter from the night winds.

I thought I might read something from the book-crammed cabinet until Mona awoke. Then we could walk down to Pete's together for breakfast—and wouldn't Pete be surprised by that, and wouldn't Wanda's tongue start wagging?

I turned to look at my choices on the shelves. But something distracted me, something below.

What I saw was desperate and pitiful; that much I knew, even though I could not get a completely clear view in the morning half-light from my perch six stories up. But still I could sense the uneasiness of it.

Eyes now.

Only eyes below the snap brim of an old hat. Wary eyes that watched the waking street, from a V-shaped crack in the low cement wall that bridged the railroad ravine beneath the street; eyes that belonged to someone who needed to wait for the secret moment to vault the wall, from the ravine side.

A head rose.

I saw flashes of a face. A young man's face, dull and brownish like the cement. Something about it—the tilt of the head, maybe, the shapeless jaw, the fleshy brow; I did not exactly know—put him in the category of the big quiet kid who clumps around the house for ten years until one morning he gets up, washes and dresses, gives the blade a couple of licks on the whetstone, and dices the family and half the neighborhood.

I had seen it before.

I had seen it recently.

I grabbed my .38 and my coat and ran downstairs to the street.

FIFTEEN

From the number of times I almost went sprawling on the narrow creaking stairs, and crashed about trying to keep my footing in that ghastly staircase light of landlord's halos, it's possible that the big quiet clumsy kid in the ravine actually heard me coming after him long before he spotted me. The street had grown that still.

And maybe that was why when I reached the doorway, when I looked through a filmy pane of glass in the window on the upper half of the door before I pushed it open, the kid in the old snap brim hat was looking right back at me. In that frozen moment, across all that divided us, we silently introduced ourselves—hunter to quarry.

This was, of course, the kid who had tried gunning down Father Love only yesterday morning up in Harlem—and right in front of my face. The kid I could not draw on because there was no time what with Father Love crumpled in the snow and his neck torn open from bullets; the kid who clambered over the fence at the end of the alleyway outside the church and disappeared into the leafless thicket; and the kid who left me there with my hands full of Samuel Waterman's gushing blood.

And he was the kid who matched the description given to
Aiello from Sex Crimes—of the mope hanging around where
Buddy-O was murdered, in his apartment over Runyon's pinball
shop right across the way from my own place. . . .

Runyon got some real good close looks at him since the kid was moping
around on the street outside his shop half the day Friday and since a lot
of that time he had his face mashed up against the windows checking out
the pinball machines. Especially the ones with the naked ladies that light
up when you get the steel pellets to land right on the tips of the old melons.

Runyon says he's black, very light-skinned, and he's got blue eyes. So
you'd remember him pretty good if you seen him yourself. Tall kid, six
two or better, and like I already said, he's clumsy. . . . He was
wearing some kind of old man's suit and overcoat and hat, like he got
everything from the Goodwill. . . . What did you do, Hock, lend him
some of your threads? . . .

No mistake about it.

And as soon as I pushed open the door, the kid sank back
behind the wall. Like a big rat, he skittered down out of sight.

I unsnapped the safety hitch of my belt holster and started
sprinting across the street, dodging taxicabs and ankle-breaking
potholes. I pulled out my .38 when I reached the sidewalk on the
other side, skidded over a patch of thin ice along the concrete
barrier over the ravine. And there I stopped, to look down;
carefully, in the event a gun barrel was waiting to greet me.

When my frosted breath cleared away, I saw tall clumps of
weeds and saplings and sumac, stiff from the onset of winter.
They lined the steep, litter-clogged banks of the ravine that
sloped down deep—maybe a hundred yards—to a straight line of
rusted iron railroad tracks. The wood ties between the tracks
were split and charred, burned long ago by camps of hobos
huddled over the fires for heat. About half the stretch of track I
saw was standing beneath black oily water, an open sewer.

I turned my head at what I thought were the sounds of big
slow feet running through the brush, somewhere out of my
vision, back below the lip of the wall I hung over to look into the
ravine.

I heard branches snapping, the sound of stones and rubbish
and broken bits of withering brush *ping*ing and splashing in the

standing water on the tracks down below and under the sidewalk where I stood. The kid was running down there someplace, completely gone from my sight—running away from me, again.

And then I saw the handholds and toeholds along the west ravine bank he had climbed, to my right and beyond the cement wall. The barely perceptible holds he had used to climb from below, up to the surface of the city, to the wall where he had waited, hiding; waited for his chance to jump up to the streets, and the upper world.

I reholstered my revolver and opened my coat so that my legs could move freely. I stepped carefully over the wall and made my way down slowly, hand over hand and my feet wedged into earthen slots—down and down, into the dank and the rubbish and the dark and the smoke and urine stench of the ravine.

Rock and soil gave way beneath my feet as I scaled downward, and these bits of the ravine bank fell to the black stagnant water. And the farther down I went, the stronger the smell of trash and paper fires, the pungent wreath of marijuana, the stink of the sewer; I began seeing bodies dozing and dazed, bodies against bodies sleeping through the night like litters of dogs tightly butted together for the shared body heat; and sometimes faces, awake and watching me—a man in a warm topcoat and good trousers and the luxury of a clean shirt and sturdy shoes that kept out water; a man who had known a hot shower that morning and a cup of good coffee; a fool in some arrogant pursuit on behalf of some meaningless gold badge, down where he could not possibly belong, in a river Styx unspeakable to those floating just above on the island of Manhattan; a fool cop down here hunting for one of their untouchable own; a good cop gone very seriously beyond the upper pale, to where outlaw is the law.

I saw faces half-hidden by cement pillars that supported the great thumping humming street and sidewalks—where trucks and taxis streamed endlessly across town, where bulldozers and cranes toppled buildings so that flesh and blood could be replaced by glass and chrome, where tired working people in shabby old neighborhoods like Hell's Kitchen hurried back and forth to their wage-paying jobs in the homely belief that money could buy back the time of their lives. I saw faces in parted weeds—as soldiers in Korea had seen them, as soldiers in the villages of the Mekong Delta had seen them in their Vietnam nightmares: faces on prone bodies, lying inside low shacks of wood and sheet metal debris and long strips of cardboard; the collective dead-eyed gaze of eyes burning into me from all sides now, the silent contempt of people cheated by birth.

And I knew where I was, though never had I actually been here before in this America. Now I knew this ravine for the truth of what it was: the deep and dirty green sea where one side of a city had tried to bury its shame. And I was deathly aware that down here *I* was the wrong side of my city; that no matter what good I had ever done or spoken or thought above, down here below I was a fool who knew nothing.

Behind me, a scavenging dog made a tubercular rasping sound as it limped across the frozen mud and the broken, blackened glass shards of the ravine flats along either edge of abandoned tracks. I looked at ribs standing out harshly from thin, mangy sides. The dog had come stupidly in search of food, unable to know or to even imagine how quickly and easily it could be snared and strangled, how its hide could be boiled away for the meat.

Then I looked north, through the arched tunnel formed by the overhead streets of the other side of the city. And somewhere dimly on the dark horizon was my meaningless prey, galloping off and away through a world in which I was a trespasser.

I walked slowly—I did not run—back toward the bottom of the ravine bank and ended my dogged, stupid search. I pulled myself up and up. And when I reached the street again, my hands were torn and bleeding and I was soaked in sweat and a fear I had not known in more than twenty years and would not care to know in a hundred and twenty more; and I was most grateful as hell to be alive and able to breathe and bleed and sweat—grateful to the point of pledging myself to a visit later in the day to Holy Cross Church, where I would take a kneel at the stations of the cross as I did when I was a boy, where I would today tell somebody up in heaven that I had once more learned how humbling it is to know when you have been a lucky man.

And although the first shift for one side of the city had only just nicely begun, and the sun was still a cold orange blot hanging low in the eastern gray of a November day, I very, very badly wanted a drink.

At Munson's diner, where I had had to go for my drink since I was of course locked out of Mona's place and did not want to ring her doorbell from the lobby and wake her up, I ordered steak and eggs and coffee so that the beer I actually wanted all for itself would not look so unseemly so early in the morning. I drank and I ate, and I also looked over Monday's first edition of the *New York Post*.

Under the newspaper's logo and the silhouette of *Post* founder Alexander Hamilton and the dubious claim that the *Post* is the fastest-growing daily newspaper in all of America, there was a big grainy photograph of Father Love on the tabloid cover. He was standing dramatically in front of his usual bank of microphones attached to his preacher's podium and his mouth was wide and I could remember his sound . . .

I want you to put your hands in your pockets, every one of you beautiful brothers and sisters.

I want you to keep your eyes fiercely closed . . . and dig deep into every corner of those pockets. I say deep!

And I want you to feel around for the paper inside. I don't want to be hearing no clinking and clanking in those plates now! You just touch that paper. Touch that currency. It don't matter now whether you touch a one or a five or a ten or a twenty!

Hold those bills and envelopes high now! Wave the money to God now!

The ushers are commencing to pass amongst you now. They'll just pick those bills off your hands, like they was cotton off the stalk. Hold your arms high now, wave to God now!

Keep them eyes shut now!

And when I look out over you, what I want to see . . . is a sea of green!

. . . and there looked to be lots of gold in his back teeth in that big oval mouth, and plenty more gold in the stiff French cuffs at the wrists of his upraised arms.

And below the photo:

HARLEM RADIO REV
IN BLOODY SABBATH SHOOTING
[Details, pg. 5]

Inside, there were three more photographs of Father Love, none very recent. One pictured him with a baton leading his church choir, the Praise-Sayers, along with the small straight-backed organist I had seen pounding the mighty Wurlitzer; another pictured him wearing a Santa Claus hat, dispensing toys to Harlem youngsters and turkeys with twenty-dollar bills stuffed in their beaks to their parents, with a beaming Roy Dumaine at his side; and the latest picture was of Father Love shaking hands with a befuddled politician in a South Bronx disaster zone that everybody knows from presidential photo opportunities.

With the additional photos, there was this story:

FLAMBOYANT PREACHER IN COMA
TOP COPS CLAM UP ON SHOOTING
—By Ned Blunden

The self-styled faith healer and Holy Roller preacher— "Father Love" of upper Manhattan's Healing Stream Deliverance Temple—lies in comatose condition today in Harlem Hospital following an assassination attempt Sunday morning on the grounds of his church. The armed assault was brazenly carried out in the presence of at least one plain-clothes undercover police officer, apparently on top-secret protective assignment in the wake of earlier death threats.

"Father Love," whose true name has never been revealed, is a pioneer in the field of raising vast amounts of money over the airwaves, purportedly for the good works of his church. Unlike newcomers to the broadcast churches, Father Love has shunned television, however.

The Harlem minister's radio programs are immensely popular with his faithful followers, especially in New York's

black community where his message is particularly tar-
geted. The programs are a blend of gospel music, an appeal
to old-fashioned morals and self-sufficiency that comes as
the result of generous donations to Father Love personally,
and to his Harlem-based church.

Neither money nor any other obvious motive has been
suggested as the reason for the mysterious death threats
against the somewhat mysterious radio minister. The *Post*,
at this report, could not determine the exact nature of the
threats, nor the number.

Roy S. Dumaine, executive assistant to Father Love,
would say only, "The police have been informed, in detail,
of the several threats against our leader's life. The New York
Police Department has responded by assigning an elite-force
officer to investigate, and this officer was in attendance for
the first time during our services today [Sunday], after
which this officer witnessed the shooting on the grounds of
our church."

Dumaine declined to elaborate. He would not name the
police officer involved, he would not tell the *Post* the true
name of Father Love, and he would not describe the
would-be assassin.

"The shooter got away," Dumaine said. "And right under
the nose of the police, so let the police explain."

Spokesmen at the Central Harlem Precinct station house
and police headquarters would confirm only that a complaint of "recent vintage" was under review by "the appropriate command." Asked about the identity of a so-called
elite-force officer on scene at the time of the church
shooting, a spokesman at police headquarters said, "There's
only one inspector who would know anything about that
and he's on vacation somewhere."

As to exactly how Father Love was shot, neither the
police nor Dumaine would give the *Post* or any other media
details. No reason was given for this unusual news blackout.

Followers of the wounded minister expressed varying
degrees of shock and outrage—and numerous theories as to
the motive of the escaped gunman, as well as the news

blackout by police—as word of the violence spread through
Harlem and the larger black community of New York City
and elsewhere in the metropolitan area.

Meanwhile, clergymen throughout the city contacted by
the *Post* reacted with sorrow . . .

I did not think it would enlighten me to read of the merciful
sentiments of a random sampling of the cloth. So I ordered
another beer. Then I tore out the article from the *Post* and
thought about the implications of a news blackout, Father Love's
double life as Samuel Waterman the pol, and Roy Dumaine's
shrewdness in dealing with the press and his thankfully dealing
me out of the story.

And I also thought about Mona sleeping back up in her
apartment.

I borrowed a pencil from a waitress and wrote a message to
Mona along the top margin of the clipping, by way of explaining
myself and how I was not there beside her in bed when she woke
up: "Sorry for ducking out, kid; but as you can see, something
came up—steam, I think."

Then I left Munson's and started walking down to my place on
Forty-third. Along the way, I stuffed the *Post* article into Mona's
mailbox in the vestibule of her building. In a manner of
speaking, it was too early to ring her bell.

SIXTEEN

No doubt it was because I fully appreciated how I had been drafted into the very puzzling struggle against a web of insidiously linked and noxious things—a "delicate" situation, so-called; steam, I should say now—that I chose to walk down the sunny side of Tenth Avenue toward home. There would be strong light under which to think of the shadows I had to battle.

And on the avenue in the warming Monday morning was a bit of scenery I could no more easily ignore than I could the talking dog routine or any of another thousand daily scenes that, taken together over time and through our civic history, make New York City the hands-down capital of the ace-up-the-sleeve.

There at the center of a knotted crowd of clerks and secretaries in tennis shoes and the occasional suit-and-tie, all of them waiting for the uptown M-11 Broadway bus, was a con gone careless by half. He knew enough to steer clear of Times Square, now depleted of the seasonal horde of tourist marks but still full enough with officers of the SCUM Patrol, but here he was right where it so happens I live.

The trouble with cons at the time of year when it is still possible to loiter in the out-of-doors is that they can become too eager for the flash of any available sucker's cash, as the plucking season draws to a close with the first frosts. And the difference between grabbing a sucker's money from his hands and coaxing him into laying down his own bet on a game of skill and chance is the crucial difference between felonious larceny and the misdemeanor of promoting gambling. A larceny collar pads out a tour of duty rather nicely since the arresting officer is generally obligated to do his own booking and shipping work, and since it happens I myself am a slow typist; and maybe in the hopeful recesses of my soul, I was looking for a way to avoid the real work at hand.

Anyway, there he was—working a top-of-the-ball con on the crowd.

Ordinarily, this is a team effort shell game consisting of a "springer," two "sticks," and three "wall men." The sticks and the springer work a salt-and-pepper routine. The springer is always a black guy with talented hands for the basic crossover shuffle in three-card monte, only for top-of-the-ball he uses three bottle caps—one of which covers a little red ball. The sticks are always white and wide-eyed, maybe one of them a guy in wing tips and a suit and the other one a woman who looks like she spends most days driving kids around in a station wagon somewhere over in Jersey. The sticks seem to be winning regularly off the fast-talking springer, and the marks are reassured and start lining up for the fleece. The wall men are lookouts and give high signs in the event they spot a plainclothes cop like me, in which case the springer kicks over the cardboard box he is using for his table, the game is struck, and the team moves on. At the end of an average day at the shank of summer, a modestly accomplished team will split five grand six ways, and nobody bothers about filing with the IRS.

But this time, just one lonesome springer was braving the odds. A solo act, and sort of pathetic he was, the poor sod. He wore a bulky sweater and a T-shirt underneath, and he was pounding his feet for warmth. He looked like he needed the money a lot more than his marks, and I felt sorry about what I was going to do to him.

He shuffled his bottle caps and chanted at the small bus stop crowd, "Don't be a jerk and go to work—make it here quick, and call in sick! Spend your dough on a New York show—come one, come all, lay your money on the ball!"

A couple of secretaries in down jackets and finger-waved hair stopped chewing gum and watched closely.

"See it crawl, like a little red fly on the wall—top-of-the-ball!" And then the springer did his crossover shuffle, and anybody would swear the ball was under the middle cap.

"You see where the ball went?" the springer asked.

One of the secretaries laughed and pointed to the middle cap.

"Show me your forty dollars to go 'gainst mine and I be pressing dead presidents into your pretty pink hand," the springer said. He pulled a twenty and two tens from his pocket and thrust them at her.

The secretary rummaged around inside her pocketbook for money, pulled out two twenties, and said, "Well, I don't know—"

At this point, a stick would have jumped into the situation and allayed all doubt by taking the bet. And the springer would reshuffle and smile and make the ball come natural for the wing tips and the suit, who would then be loudly delighted to take forty bucks off the black guy so nice and easy. And then the secretary would no longer be reluctant and the springer would reshuffle and cross over. Only there were no sticks now. And the springer was desperate and cold and careless.

"Gimme that bet!" he snarled. And he grabbed the secretary's forty, and I moved up behind him and tapped his shoulder.

"How you doing this morning, Friendly?" I said.

"Oh, sheeeeet!" the springer said. "You the damn Murphy?"

I said I was and showed him the gold shield in the case in my coat pocket. And I also pulled open my coat a bit to let him see the .38 in the holster. "I'm going to read you now, Friendly. We've got felony larceny here, so listen up."

"Sheeeet!"

The secretary started screaming something about a broken nail and being late for work, and the springer lurched, like he might try running off someplace—*maybe the ravine?*—and so I caught him at the neck with the crook of my arm, squeezed, and

sted it was the better part of valor for him to come along
me peaceably. He saw things my way, largely in the
interest of breathing, so I let up on his neck and locked one end
of a pair of NYPD bracelets to my left wrist and the other
end to his right, and together we strolled down Tenth Avenue
and took a right at the corner of West Forty-second Street, then
west to booking and shipping out of the precinct station house
across the way from the NYPD Mounted Division livery stable
and part of the block I could see from my parlor windows.

I had given the station house telephone number to the
secretary and told her, "Go on to work and call me up when you
get there, ask for Hock." And she had said, "Okay, yeah," and I
knew she would never call, which she did not. I would write up
paper for what it was worth, and the springer would get jugged
maybe at Riker's Island for a few days; he would ultimately not
be convicted of larceny in the absence of a material witness
besides the arresting officer; and so it goes in the criminal justice
system of New York City.

Thoughtful men with weight on their minds do their thinking
in many active ways—by taking long walks along country lanes,
or sailing pretty ships in the Long Island Sound on weekends
with attractive women, maybe, or batting about tiny balls with
little racquets on squash courts at their lunch hours, or chasing
tinier balls yet with skinny wood-and-steel clubs along fairways
of green grass cut through forests and hills and bogs. But I, Neil
Hockaday, when deep in detective thought, affect absentminded
busts of tiny little men.

And so now as I slowly typed—and listened to frequent
expletives of *"sheeeeet!"* from the poor sod of a shell game springer
I had cuffed to a chair joined to the floor with four bolts—some
few of the gossamer threads of the web that held Father Love,
the same web that had killed Howie Griffiths the sweaty rent
collector and an obsolete Westy hood called Buddy-O, began
actually appearing to me. No more than shimmers in my mind's
eye, but there was something like a vision all the same; and I saw,
too, the thick steam clouding through and through that delicate
web and the vaporous wisps that escaped—to float off high and
fine, above it all.

Then it was that I knew.
Wisps was what I was after.

When I had finished booking junk counts on the springer, I
left him with the khakis for holding and shipping, and then I left
the station house and headed for the newsstand outside Pitsikoulis's coffee shop. I bought the *Times* and the *Daily News* and
Newsday, too, none of which did anything to amplify what I had
read in the *Post*, except that *Newsday* ran a blurry color photo of
the church up in Harlem with the American and African
nationalist flags crossed over each other on poles above the main
entrance, and Roy Dumaine in a black suit standing around with
his big arms folded against his chest, not so much like a man
whose mentor lay comatose in a hospital as the self-satisfied new
owner of some tax-free Harlem real estate.

None of the newspaper reporters had apparently troubled
themselves to wonder why it was that Father Love, an hour after
he had finished preaching and dressed in his decidedly unpreach-
erly clothes, was prowling around in the alleyway at the side of
the church with the likes of me in tow. And so there was no
mention anywhere of the piano theft.

I walked across the street to my building and climbed upstairs.

When I got to my apartment, I tossed the papers on the couch
for a later read. Then I carefully pushed open the door to the
bathroom and snapped on a light. No dead body in the tub this
time. I wondered how many years it would be before I would do
something as simple as opening my bathroom door without
thinking anything of it.

I had time enough to get some coffee going before the
telephone rang. It was not so hard to guess who might be finally
returning a call.

"Hello," I said.

"Well, so you're finally someplace I can reach you."

"That's a funny thing for you to say."

"How's that?"

"Oh, I don't know—just offhand, I guess if it was my father
who'd been shot, then I might be thinking about something a

little more significant than my own convenience in calling somebody back on the phone."

"Look, I know all about the shooting, and—"

"Hard to miss the news."

"And we didn't get along, like I said, okay? I told you all about that. But it doesn't mean I don't care about my old man being shot, all right? In fact, I'm up at the hospital with him now. I'm calling from the hospital, okay?"

"What's the outlook?"

"He's . . . well, still in coma. There isn't much to say. The vital signs are good. Really, they won't know anything for sure until he comes around—or until he doesn't."

I thought about that one for a minute and shook my head. "Sam," I asked him, "where the hell were you all the times I called?"

"What are you trying to suggest, Hockaday? I think the real question ought to be, where the hell were *you* and the cops when my father was shot down?"

"Actually, my hands were full. Full of your dad's blood, to be exact, which I managed to keep from pouring out of him too fast, which is how come he's now alive."

Waterman was rattled. Like I had hoped.

"Look, I have a little summer place," he said by way of answering my question, "out on Gardiners Island. So that's where I was the whole weekend."

"It's not summer, Junior."

"I go out there one last weekend every year, to work. You know, to shut everything down for the winter. Stack away furniture, seal up the windows and doors, cut the power, turn off the water . . . you know."

"No, I wouldn't know. I want a beach, Counselor, I take the D train out to Coney Island."

"Be that as it may, Hockaday, I was out of town all weekend."

"Really cut you off from the world, I guess."

"I guess."

"I got to ask this, Junior—can you prove it?"

There was now a lot of irritation in Waterman's voice. And

noises that sounded dangerous, like if I had my fingers near his mouth, he might snap them off.

"If I had to, Detective Hockaday, I could prove my whereabouts."

"So . . . what, somebody out there with you?"

"I have neighbors."

"I see. You say you cut off the power?"

"Had it cut off, about ten Sunday morning I think was the effective time."

"Let me ask you about that answering machine of yours I kept getting."

"What about it?"

"Is it one of those models where you can call up the machine and have your messages played back?"

"It so happens it is."

"So how come you didn't call your machine?"

"I had the telephone shut off out in the country. That was effective Saturday morning."

He said that quickly, which I did not like. Most things about this guy, I decided at that moment, were far less than what I usually like in people.

I was silent for a second or two, and there was light static on the line. Waterman got flustered into adding, even more quickly, "I drove back to the city this morning, and that's when I played back all the messages . . . and got your numbers all over town, including even your girlfriend's house."

"Well, I guess you've got all the bases covered then, Junior."

"I'm not trying to 'cover the bases,' and I resent the implication . . . and please don't be calling me 'Junior' anymore."

"Sorry." He expected me to say more, but I wouldn't.

And now Waterman sounded like he was trying to recover some advantage, in a manner that did not seem at all like what he probably used to hear in classroom lectures at Harvard Law on methods of disarming one's conversational adversaries.

"Let's just cut the crap now, Hockaday."

"Okay, let's."

"What I want to know is—what in hell happened? You were

supposed to be protecting my father, and he winds up getting it right at church!"

"I'm sorry. We try, but cops don't guarantee anybody a charmed life."

"What have you got for leads? Anything?"

"There are some leads," I said, though I would not have said so if I was talking to another cop. "How about if I get a squad car to run me up to the hospital right now? We could go over the leads together."

Junior hesitated. "Not now. I've got somebody waiting . . . I have to make a living, you know."

"Oh."

And then quickly, "I'll be calling you, Hockaday. To see how you're progressing."

"Stay around town, Junior."

When he hung up, I telephoned Harlem Hospital and asked to speak to the nursing station near Father Love's private room. I asked then to speak to one of the police guards assigned to protect the preacher.

"Who's callin'?" the cop asked.

I identified myself and said, "Anybody in there with the reverend right now?"

"Naw, Hock, it's just him and the intravenous bacon-and-eggs."

"Visitors is what I mean."

"My orders is, no visitors allowed."

"What about his son?" I described Sam Waterman, Jr., to the officer: tall, black, slender, dapper.

"Nobody like that, and nobody else, neither," the officer said. "There's just a doctor I got clearance on, and a technician and a couple of different nurses to monitor the gizmos. Nobody else. So it's nobody here but us cops and quacks."

"Anybody show up to ask for a patient named Samuel Waterman?"

"Who?"

I told him again.

"The name don't mean nothing to me."

"No, I didn't think it would. Thanks."

So Junior was lying.

I called his number at home. And reached the answering machine.

Over on the sideboard, I found the notebook I had started on the case and jotted down this interesting lie, next to where I had already written down the name of Junior's law firm over on the East Side. Which was near where I had written down the late Howie Griffiths' home address and telephone over in Jersey.

I dialed Griffiths' number and reached his widow and offered my condolences, and I also asked when it might be convenient for me to come over the river for a talk; and how I thought that should be absolutely as soon as possible in the interest of keeping the investigative trail warm. There were sounds of children and television commercials in the background, and a parrot making hollow clucking noises.

"Well, lookit, I already talked to some New York detectives all about this," the widow said. She was annoyed, like Howie himself had been when I walked into the late Buddy-O's scabid little bedroom to talk to him about Aiello and his Sex Crimes crew had already sweated him on how it was he had happened to find Buddy-O dead and naked. "So how come I gotta talk to you on top of that?"

I said, "It was my apartment where your husband died, and—"

"So you're that cop, the one who found him in the bathtub stabbed." The widow Griffiths sounded as moved by the circumstances of her husband's murder the other day as if someone had told her that her pet parrot had died during the night. "What's your name again?"

I repeated my name.

"Hockaday, yeah. Now I remember; the other cops, they called you Hock. I got some things I could maybe tell you, Hock—stuff them other cops didn't seem too much interested in hearing."

"I'll be happy to listen, Mrs. Griffiths."

"So why don't you come by tonight. After *Wheel of Fortune*, though, okay? That's my favorite show, and I don't like missing it for nothing."

I told her I could see her about eight o'clock.

* * *

I rang up the desk sergeant at Midtown-North and asked him to reserve me a plain car for around seven or so that night.

And then I unhooked the phone and lay flat out on my back on the couch under the window, and I fell asleep in about five seconds flat.

I dreamed I was watching a springer working a shell game down on the street. Bottle caps moving left and right, left and right. The ball under only one of the three caps. And the springer's thin quick fingers and his quick talk.

See it crawl, like a little red fly on the wall—top-of-the-ball!

And the springer looked just like Samuel Waterman, Jr.—in his lawyer's three-piece custom-tailored suit and custom English shoes and a shirt with a collar pin and a patterned tie from Hermès.

I was the guy who knew all about the trick shuffles and all about the wall men and the sticks. For all the good it was doing me.

Wasn't I a stick myself . . . a shill? A plainclothes SCUM Patrol cop in a greasy coat and a watch cap and a radio in a paper bag most of the time? A strip of Munson's wallpaper, somebody who was not what he seemed to be?

But no matter all that I knew, I couldn't pick the right bottle cap. . . .

There was somebody knocking at my door.

A couple of hours' sleep dropped out of my life, like threads brushed off a raveled sleeve.

"Hock, you in there?"

It was Mary Rooney's croaking voice.

More knocking.

"Hock!"

I got up off the couch and started toward the door, and when she heard my step she stopped knocking.

When I opened up the door, there was Mary Rooney in a housedress and a sweater and rollers in her hair. And the

Dominican janitor who lives in the basement was standing next to her out in the corridor, with his chin curled into his chest like he was obliging a hangman and his noose.

"This here's Ricky," Mary Rooney said. "I told him he should talk to you since he's all on about how he done something to the rent collector what was disemboweled up here at your place."

Ricky looked at me, and beyond me into my apartment, and crossed himself in the name of the Father and the Son and the Holy Ghost.

SEVENTEEN

When we had settled in my place—Mary at one end of the couch, sitting ramrod straight and looking at my books suspiciously, me at the other end, and Ricky in the green whorehouse chair, his hands spread nervously over the arms like he was expecting an executioner to throw the switch at any moment—Mary explained:

"Like I was telling you I'd do, Hock, I been round to this one and that one in the house—you know, about this business of our bloody landlord and his little note asking us to kindly leave the premises. You know, the note?"

It would have been exceedingly difficult to forget about a note that had come spiked to the chest of a naked dead man I'd found in my own bathtub. I said to Mary, "Yes, I remember."

"And then it turns out," Mary said, "that the very man who signed the nasty thing—"

"Oh!" Ricky cried. He crossed himself again.

"Griffiths was the name," Mary said. She adjusted an errant hair roller. "Our very own rent collector, murdered he was. Right over there, beyond that door to your loo."

She pointed to the bathroom door. Ricky followed her finger

with his eyes and shuddered. Then he turned to me and said, "I doan never mean nothin' to happen to dis man Greefeth. I doan believe in dis *santería* too very much, I tell you that honest, sir."

"*Santería?*"

Ricky put his hands together and looked up and whispered something to God, and then he said to me, "The black magic, sir. Very bad foking black magic!"

I looked at Mary, and she rolled her eyes and said, "He thinks he might have killed Griffiths with black magic and he should hire a lawyer."

I shook my head, but it didn't help anything. "Why would you want a lawyer?" I asked Ricky.

Mary spoke before Ricky could. "I tell him all lawyers are crooks and molesters and liars. I tell him the devil makes his Christmas pie from lawyers' tongues, but still he wants to hire one. So I talked him into seeing you first."

"Ricky?" I asked.

"Dis man Greefeth, he come to me one day and he say to me, 'Ricky, you job ess no needed no more,' and I say to dis man, 'What do buildin' do now without janitor?' And Greefeth, he laugh and he laugh!"

I shook my head again.

Mary said, "Oh, the evil bunch! You see? They're planning on reducing the services, such as they are. Meanin' to force us out and meanin' to be ugly brutes about it, too."

I asked Ricky, "What did you do when Griffiths laughed at you?"

"I ask Greefeth, 'When I got no job, no more here?' He say, 'Ricky, you better get out now.' So, I am so mad with dis man I think of old *santería*—I think about what curse I want on dis man's head."

"Exactly what do you do?" I asked.

And of course Mary was quick with her own two cents: "If he done what we know happened, it wasn't cruel enough."

"Ricky?" I asked.

"I got drunk, sir. And I remember the *santeros*, the priests. Here, I doan believe in the power of dis *santeros*, but I got drunk. . . .

"One time in my country, I see dis *santero* put the blood on the coins, then he throw dis coins on a man and curse him. When Greefeth tell me I no more have job, I am fear to go back to my country. I no want that!

"So, I am drunk, sir. And I find chicken in my house, I squeeze blood from dis chicken and I put dis blood all over pennies. And I go lookin' for Greefeth, and when I find him, I throw dis bloody pennies on him, and"—Ricky made a chopping motion with his hand—"dis bad man Greefeths, he dead two days later!"

Mary jabbed a fist in the air and hooted, "Good for you, Ricky!"

Ricky crossed himself. I shook my head.

"You don't need a lawyer, Ricky, you're in no trouble," I told him.

"No trouble?"

"No."

"But when I see Greefeth and I throw dis bloody pennies . . . Oh! . . . He is with the priest!"

"What priest?"

"I don't know name," Ricky said. "Just a priest, just a old priest."

"A priest from over at Holy Cross parish?" I asked him.

"I never see dis priest nowhere in church."

"What did he look like?"

"He old, his hair white. He thin. I don't know, just a old priest."

"Where did you see Griffiths and the old priest together?" I asked.

"I find them in the street talkin', outside dis buildin'. I lookin' for Greefeths, and I find him talkin' to dis priest."

"Did the priest have a bag with him? A large bag?"

"I don't know. . . . Oh, I think maybe yes." Ricky's face brightened.

"Anyway, you threw the pennies at Griffiths?"

"Yes, I very foking drunk."

"What happened?"

"Greefeths laugh and he laugh and he say, 'I take care of you spic, I get you later, spic!'"

"What did the priest do?"

Ricky rubbed his head. "I think he run away. I doan remember dis too very much, I very foking drunk."

"Don't worry about the curse you put on Griffiths," I told him. "You didn't kill him, did you?"

"I only threw dis bloody pennies!"

Ricky seemed relieved, like a man on death row whose sentence had just been commuted by the governor. He had confessed to me what he thought was his sin, and I had absolved him. This made me uncomfortable.

Mary lit up an L&M, and she was beaming, self-satisfied. She said to Ricky, "See, and did I not tell you all the same myself?"

"Okay," Ricky said.

He stood up and so did I. And I hoped they would both leave. I wanted to sleep some more. And then I would have to hit the street in search of Lionel the Holy Redeemer, who had some answers due.

"Oh, I only wish't it was me what done in that snivelin' little bastard from the landlord's," Mary said. "Speakin' of which, will you be comin' to our demonstration, Hock?"

"What demonstration?"

"Crikey, I forgot to tell you?"

"I guess."

"Hock, in my organizin' efforts amongst the tenants here, I come to find out we're not the only house in Hell's Kitchen that's been asked to turn itself inside out. There's good people all up and down the neighborhood's been gettin' nasty notes like the ones we got! All of them in buildings owned by Empire Properties."

"You've been very busy," I said.

"Indeed I have, Hock. Organizin' is what I've been doin' with myself, like you told me I should. . . . And oh my, Hock, I feel I'm a girl again—and I feel like it's springtime over on the other side! You know, when the milk all tastes like onions because the farmers are puttin' the cows to pasture and the cows

are eatin' the onion grass, which is what grows after the pussy
willows come, but just before the forsythia?"

Mary stopped for breath, and then, "It's just the best thing I
done in years, Hock, that's all. I'm stickin' us together so's we
can stick it to the landlord!

"And so, we'll be demonstratin' up the street, in the park.
Tomorrow night. Can you make it?"

"I'll try," I said.

"I promise you this, it'll be a donnybrook."

Mary patted her hair rollers and Ricky smiled at me and they
left.

I had not found the Holy Redeemer anywhere, and I'd left
word at all the usual places up and down West Forty-second
Street. In about two and a half hours, I would have to go over to
Midtown-North and pick up my car and drive over to Jersey to
see the widow Griffiths.

So to fortify myself for the upcoming evening excursion out of
town, and because I was hungry besides being thirsty, too, I
gave up the search for Lionel the "priest" for the while. I headed
over to Ninth Avenue and the Ebb Tide.

The sun was on its way down, making the very unseasonably
warm day grow suddenly quite seasonable. And the river winds
were picking up. I had visions of a nice jar of Johnnie Walker red
and feeling it burn inside me on its way down.

Angelo was on the job. And it was too early by an hour or so
for the wine spritzer set of a weekday afternoon. The bar was full
up with the old sorts from the neighborhood, the ones with time
and money to spend—not a lot of either, but some. Plaid shirts
and corduroy pants held up with suspenders, and caps with
union buttons, and a lot of talk among the old fellows about some
supervisor down at the meat packer firing somebody for stealing
a steak while the big shots in the suits were stealing the company
dry; complaints about everybody they used to know who moved
out to the suburbs and forgot about when they were kids in the
neighborhood all eating salami sandwiches together.

The music was cuts of Lester Young and Roy Eldridge—"This
Year's Kisses" and "I Didn't Know What Time It Was."

There were many crumpled wet tabloids strewn across the bar, evidence that the old boys had spent a fine productive day soaking up noteworthy news events and beer, culminating in red-faced debates. They were not talking about the Father Love shooting when I happened in, thankfully; this was an Irish crowd and thus far more interested in the bloodier criminal sport of politics—especially with a presidential election on the docket.

Gnarly fists slammed against the bar as agreeable punctuation to the various notions put forth by Angelo Cifelli, an Italian through and through who nonetheless served up the hyperbole that draws Irish to a pub like peat to bogs. They could take their pleasure either in favor or in opposition to whatever he had to say, so long as it outraged.

Angelo thumped a newspaper photograph of George Bush and told somebody down at the end of the bar named Flaherty, "You think this guy's scary? Wait until you see the delegates to his nominating convention—retired Nazis, crazed hemorrhoid sufferers, TV evangelist perverts, pyramid sales grifters, young stockbrokers. Flaherty, I'm telling you true—we're doomed."

Angelo stepped over to set me up with a red and a Molson. I told him I would appreciate fish and chips besides, and he passed this order along to a waiter. And then he said to me, loud enough for everybody's ears and by way of inviting me to jump into the fraternal dialogue, "Ethel Merman, she knew all about politics—there's no business like show business. And baby, is this showtime or what?"

I tipped my glass to the bar and offered, "Here's to politics in the U.S. of A.—to the gentle art of getting votes from the poor and campaign funds from the rich, by promising to protect each from the other."

Every fist in the place slammed the bar on this one, and I enjoyed the prospects of several free rounds. And I silently congratulated myself for once having read the essays of Oscar Ameringer.

Somebody wanted to watch the early evening television news, speaking of show business. So Angelo switched on the TV set over the back of the bar, which was mostly used for watching wrestling and boxing and baseball. Instead of turning up the TV

audio, Angelo left the jazz playing. The video kept switching
back and forth between a reporter with thick hair and dazzling
teeth and a herd of smiling men with equally dazzling teeth that
the reporter seemed to be taking seriously as presidential possibilities. And nobody in the Ebb Tide bar on Ninth Avenue in
New York City that day thought there was anything particularly
unusual about watching all those moving lips on a soundless
screen.

Somebody called Mogaill said, "I been able to read those lips
for years now. See that one guy, he's saying he's for better
jobs and better pay; the other guy's saying he's for good jobs at
better pay, or maybe this year he's for better jobs at good
pay . . . that I don't know. And sooner or later, one of them
bozos is going to say, 'I'm just plain for jobs, jobs, jobs!'"

To which Angelo added, "There's not a man of them there
bright enough to stop and ask what a 'good job' *is*, or why
anybody would necessarily want one."

And Mogaill muttered his bleak vision of an ever less gentle
and less kindlier nation. "Oh, today they're yelling about 'good
jobs for good pay'—a couple of years maybe what with all the
bodies we'll still be stepping across in the streets everywhere,
they'll start yelling about 'good food for good people' and they'll
be asking questions they'll say is only good logic, questions like,
Why feed a dead man even if he is still walking?"

I said quietly, "It's already the idea."

Branches snapping, stones and rubbish and broken bits of
withering brush *ping*ing and splashing in the standing water on
the tracks . . . and the smell of trash and paper fires, the
pungent wreath of marijuana smoke, the stink of the sewer;
bodies dozing and dazed, butted together like litters of dogs for
shared body heat . . . faces, and the collective dead-eyed gaze
of eyes burning into me from all sides, the silent contempt of
people cheated by birth . . . *"Why feed a dead man, even if he is
still walking. . . . Good food for good people. . . ."*

It had been quite a day. And the day before had been quite a
day. And the day before that. . . .

* * *

I telephoned Mona from the booth up near the front door.

"Hello, lover, you miss me crazy?" she asked.

"I do, I guess I do."

"Didn't I tell you I was a cure?"

"I'm on the path to recovery, I'll give you that," I said. "A cure's going to take a longer time."

I listened to her breathy laugh and thought about what she looked like then—sitting in the window at her papa's hand-built *secrétaire*, the telephone cradled between her shoulder and her chin. And I thought about the sight of her biting into an apple; and how much I would like to have known her way back when; how much, as the years passed, I had come to realize that time is a vandal.

"You got my note, on the newspaper clip?"

"I did, yeah. Are you being careful?"

"I guess."

"Am I going to see you tonight?"

"Maybe. What's your schedule?"

"I'm working at the club, two sets of 'Popsicle Toes,' you know."

"Me, I have to drive over to Jersey," I said.

"Oh, Hock, poor thing. Something about the case?"

"Well, it relates."

"God, how long are you going to be on this?"

"That's up in the air."

"Be careful!"

"You told me that. I won't get hurt, honest."

Mona laughed, but not because she was amused. I thought I maybe heard ice clinking in a glass on her end. She said, "Nobody gets hurt honest, it's the other way I worry about."

"How about I pick you up at the Pigalle after the show? I ought to be back in the city by then."

"That'd be swell, Hock. You know what I'm thinking I'd like to do tonight?"

"I'm tired, baby. Real tired."

"Good. Because tonight, I'd love to come see your place."

"My place is a dump."

"You have any food in your dump?"

"I make chili, that's about it. Most people, they don't like it."

"I'm a lot of things, honey, but 'most people' isn't one of them."

And so it was settled about later that night when I got back from seeing the widow Griffiths in Jersey.

When I stepped out from the phone booth, I sadly noticed it was that time of day when the old Irish boyos in the plaid shirts and suspenders and bald heads and gnarly hands start giving way to the newer neighborhood crowd in gray flannel and paisley ties and expensive haircuts and camel topcoats.

I had about twenty minutes before it was time to get going over to Midtown-North for the car. So I took a stool at the bar. The television set was still playing the news, still minus the sound and still making perfect TV sense. The reporter on screen now was a lady with rosy cheeks, and she was interviewing a vaguely blond-headed man about something.

He was hatless even though he was being interviewed outdoors in the cold, he was forty some years old and wore a good dark double-breasted suit and violet foulard and a topcoat that hung back over his shoulders. His brown-yellow hair was ragged and choppy, as if he had recently bought the three-dollar trim at the barber shop down in the Times Square IND subway station. The face was bland and a little puffy and white as a Maine potato. He had tiny feminine lips that protruded when he spoke up there on the soundless screen. And he had muskrat teeth.

I heard somebody at the bar whose name I did not care about say, "Hey, I read that guy's book! That's Daniel Prescott—he's awesome!"

Prescott was saying something with his tiny puckered lips and muskrat teeth. I turned to Angelo, who was wiping glasses nearby and sneering at Prescott's face, and I asked him, "Who is this guy anyhow?"

"You been living on Venus the last couple years or what?" Angelo said.

"Or what, I guess. I've been going through my divorce."

Angelo shrugged. "Oh that, yeah." Then he asked if I would

have another drink. To which I painfully declined since I had to drive over to Jersey yet that night.

He shrugged again and said, "Well anyhow, Daniel Prescott's a real estate developer, so-called. He went and hired a press agent a while back. You ever hear of a landlord who needs a press agent?"

I said I had not.

Angelo said, "The guy's a braying turd, so naturally he's got the story of his dumb life out there on the market and naturally it's a best-seller. Also—and I am not making this up, Hock—this *landlord* is about to announce he's going to run for president."

I had a little time before I would have to get the car, so I dropped around to the Flanders Bar in hopes of catching up with Lionel the Holy Redeemer. But he was not there. I left word I was looking for him and that there was a twenty in it for whoever could connect us together first.

Then, I left for Jersey.

EIGHTEEN

"**W**ell, I don't know, you don't look like any detective I ever seen."

She poked her hand out from the door and ran her fingers over the gold shield I held outstretched for her inspection. I also unzipped my bomber jacket so she could catch a glimpse of the .44 Charter Arms Bulldog snugged under my armpit in a shoulder holster.

"I'm telling you, lady, it's me. Hockaday, the cop you talked to on the telephone the other night. And what's a detective supposed to look like anyhow?"

"Well, when I was a kid they mostly wore brown suits that looked like cloth boxes and ties that were brown, too, with big fat Windsor knots in them. And those kind of black shoes with the zigzag crepe soles like you can buy over at Bamberger's basement. And hats—they always wore hats, like in the old movies on the TV. . . ."

To me, Lynette Griffiths looked even less like a widow than I did a detective. And she looked very out of place in a suburb like Englewood Cliffs. Her hair was dyed a jet black and there were dark blond roots showing at the forehead and crown, and she wore it in a ruthless permanent wave. Her face was oddly orange, the result of a lot of pancake, I thought; and dried bits of pale red lipstick had worked into the spaces of her teeth.

She did not sound sorry like I think a recent widow should probably sound. And I wondered if I would ever be able to stop her from talking at me on the front porch of her fake-Tudor house. An airplane droned overhead somewhere in the Jersey night, and a car siren across the street on a Mercedes-Benz made blooping noises.

"Then there's your detectives today, the ones that think they got to look like they're cops on the TV shows you got now. They're wearing those suits with the no-vent jackets, and pleated pants and pastel shirts like from Saks. And those Italian loafers with less honest shoe leather on them than my house slippers, and—"

"Mrs. Griffiths, it's getting cold out here. Would you mind— couldn't we just step inside and talk? Remember you said you had certain things to tell me—things the other cops didn't have any interest in hearing from you?"

"Oh yeah," she said. "Well, come on in, then."

We settled in the living room, the heart of the late Howie Griffiths' home. I had walked into it the way I usually enter an unknown room—a little warily, my eyes working over the place to catalogue the contents in case it might be important later. This is an occupational hazard of cops, this way of walking into people's houses.

Mrs. Griffiths sat down on an early American–style couch covered in a brown-and-yellow-plaid fabric. Above the couch was a velvet painting of Christ, flanked by wood-grain vinyl sconces filled with wax grapes. I sat in a maple rocking chair with a plaid cushion that matched the couch. Between us was a honey-maple coffee table holding a Revised Standard Holy Bible bound in white leatherette, a big glass ashtray with some burned-out butts in it, a half-consumed jar of Gerber apple- and-plum-flavored baby food, and the current issue of *People* magazine opened to something about Oprah Winfrey.

A little kid in diapers was standing inside a playpen cage over on the other side of the room, with its back to us. I could not tell whether it was a boy or girl. The kid was mesmerized by *The Newlywed Game* on the nearby color television console. In another cage, not far from the playpen, a red-and-blue parrot cracked seeds in its beak and stared at me like I was still wearing stripes after breaking out of Sing Sing.

Lynette Griffiths fingered a silver necklace pressed close to her throat, and she stared at me, too; watched me catalogue everything in her place, seeming to worry about my opinion of the decor. Then she said, "Howie, my husband . . . my late husband . . . he bought me this necklace. I got married wearing it, in fact. . . . We were crazy happy then. Sure as hell didn't last too long, though."

And though I had stood outside listening to her talk, it was not until now that I was inside in the light and looking at her that I heard the Appalachia in her voice and how some of her words came out as if she had a catfish stuck sideways in her mouth. She lit up a Vantage.

"Yes, ma'am," I said. And then, "Mrs. Griffiths—now, please don't think I'm accusing you of anything, but . . . your husband died a violent death, he was murdered—and just a couple of days ago, in my apartment!—and here we are, and, well . . . you just don't seem upset about it."

She shrugged. "Bingo. I'm not upset, okay?"

"Okay. How long were you and Howie married?"

"We were coming up on a fourth anniversary."

"And what—it didn't look so good for a fifth?"

"That didn't look likely according to the case pending in the Bergen County Divorce Court. I guess now it's going to save me some lawyers' fees." She took a long draft of the cigarette and said, "I know that sounds cold as hell, Detective Hockaday—"

"Hock you can call me if you want."

"Okay then. It's cold, but I guess money's the only thing that mattered to Howie anyhow. See, I threw him out because of money, I guess. Howie, he hasn't been here with me and the baby for the past year thereabouts."

"What happened?"

"Little things first. . . . I tried saying this to the other cops, but they kept telling me it wasn't relevant, you know? . . .

You sure *you* want to hear this, Hock? I mean, I can't promise you that I got something that'll guarantee you can go back to New York and right away crack open the case of my Howie's getting himself murdered. I guess what I got to say is more like . . . like a woman's intuition."

I told Lynette Griffiths how I was a very big believer in that sort of thing.

"Well, okay then. . . . You see, I just figure that my Howie—"

She turned abruptly when the baby made a sound like a farm horse blowing off air. The baby seemed much relieved. Lynette turned back to me and said, "You want maybe a drink or something?"

I told her no, and she looked disappointed.

"Anyhow, back to Howie. You ever meet my Howie?"

"Once I talked to him," I said. But I did not tell her this was on the occasion of Howie being the person who discovered Buddy-O's naked dead body.

"A real jerk, wasn't he?"

"Ma'am, I don't like speaking ill of the dead."

"Oh, yeah. Well, he *was* a jerk, though. He lived like a jerk and he died like a jerk. For a while there, he was my jerk. At least there was that."

"How did you meet him?"

"Well, back four, five years, he was a salesman out on the road, and his territory was right around my hometown of Henderson. That's in Kentucky. Those days, he was calling on hospitals and clinics and such, selling all kinds of medical equipment and pharmaceuticals and such out of the head office in New York, which is Howie's hometown.

"Oh, I'd never met anybody from New York before, and I was kind of thrilled. I was working as a cocktail hostess at the Holiday Inn in Henderson, where he stayed, see. I didn't look so bad in those days, and neither did Howie since I hadn't fattened him up yet. . . .

"I suppose I had this feeling about him right off, right at first. But I didn't pay attention to myself. I just let the heat take over. Know what I mean?"

"Yes, ma'am, I think so."

"He was one of these guys who thinks it's important to find some way of having all the answers. You know? Today I can tell you that listening to some guy with all the answers is no answer. And I guess I knew that in my gut, but like I said, I didn't pay no attention to myself.

"Well, one thing leads to another between men and women, you know, and Howie and me are married and he says we'll be on top of the world if he can just get back to New York and somehow make a killing. . . .

"Oh, jeez, now ain't that an unfortunate way of putting it? A *killing*. But that's the way Howie always talked.

"Anyhow, I started having the feeling how Howie was going to end up just the way he did practically the first day we're back in New York, which was two years ago. I think once I told him so, but he brushed me off."

I asked her, "What made you feel like that?"

"'Cause Howie was all the time wanting to get into places where he didn't fit. . . . Probably you got no idea what I'm talking about."

"Suppose you tell me and I'll just listen to you and maybe I'll come to understand."

"Jeez, you're even better'n Donahue, Hock. I mean, I really got the feeling like you want to hear me talk. Them other cops—"

"Other cops have their way of investigating a crime, I got mine."

"Yeah, I guess I can see that. . . . Well, anyhow, my Howie was always thinking he was a guy on the make type, some really slick number who was someday going to be the real big shot on Easy Street and all. Well, hell, you seen him—he don't even know how to dress like the striped-pants boys, let alone talk like them."

I nodded.

"Howie, he figured all it took was for him to somehow get his carcass in the right place and he'd have it made, and that's all there was to it. That's what I mean when I say he was sort of a jerk—may the poor dumb jerk rest in peace.

"Like, he goes and buys this house we're in, and he can only just barely afford it from what he's saved up being a fairly successful salesman, you know? Howie the big shot with a house in this fancy Englewood Cliffs here. You know? Hell, the neighbors around here made us know every day in a couple of thousand ways how we didn't belong, and how we never would. Probably, Howie didn't mind so much getting thrown out of this house."

Lynette tamped out her cigarette and lit another. "See, we're just your average workaday middle-class suckers, Hock. You know what it's like to be middle class these days?"

"I got some ideas," I said. "What's your idea?"

"Well, I think it's like living somewheres between success that you know damn well down in your secret place inside yourself where you don't lie even to yourself is just always going to be out of reach, and flat-out failure that's so sickening and horrible you don't want to mention it."

I said, "That's more or less along the lines of the way I look at it, too."

"So, that's Howie and me. Only Howie, a classic sucker, don't know that about himself. He don't know it because he's all the time signing up for them idiot classes and seminars and whatnot at the hotel. You know, them Dare to Succeed scams? Oh, my Howie fell for every damn one of them. Somewheres around the house here, there's all kinds of three-ring binders with all the phony crap he got over the years from these scam classes.

"Well, that wasn't the worst of it! A couple years back he picks up this book all his fellow suckers are buying up even though they ain't read a book since they were in school. The book's the life story of this New York guy called Prescott. Prescott writes this book called *Me First*, and I guess it's how to be polite and respectable even if you're actually just a dumb hog who thinks it's all about money and shiny objects. Anyways, it's the hottest thing between covers for guys like my Howie, of which there are millions."

I told Lynette I had just recently heard of Daniel Prescott and his book and how it did not sound like anything I would care to have on my shelf at home. Not any more than I would like to be wearing underwear with holes on a day some car ran over me for fear of what the doctors would think about my character when I showed up at the hospital on a stretcher.

"This book, it changed Howie's life. And that's actually even what he told me one day: 'Lynette honey, Daniel Prescott has changed my life.' Like he'd actually met up with this guy who wasn't even decent enough to be embarrassed about writing a book called *Me First*, and like his fool book was the Holy Bible itself and he was God."

She put a hand on her white leatherette Bible on the coffee table. I noticed how her name was stamped in gold leaf on the binding of the good book.

Solemnly, she said, "Hock, you can see plain I'm a sinner. I smoke, and I drink, too. But even so, I'm still a God-fearing woman. That's the way I was raised up in Henderson, and I ain't ashamed—and I ain't some sophisticated blasphemer like these folks here in this snobby-nosed town where I don't belong, okay?"

"Okay."

"So, my Howie starts talking like he's putting this man Prescott way ahead of the Lord—and I can't stand it. And the even more disgusting thing is, I pick up that book of his and read it for myself . . . and I'll be damned if Prescott himself just about puts his own money-grubbing life ahead of Jesus, too!

"Now, that's what I mean when I say I figure my Howie's headed for real trouble."

"Did anything specific happen?" I asked her. "I mean, anything to confirm your suspicions here?"

"Well, Howie being Howie, he right away goes out to see how close he can get himself to this Daniel Prescott character. He finds out all about the couple of hundred companies or whatnot that Prescott and his bunch control, and Howie winds up getting a job with one of them.

"You know what Howie tells me then?"

I asked her to tell me.

"Howie says, 'Lynette honey, I'm going to be a disciple.' Like he's found a guy with all the answers, see what I mean? And the blasphemy!

"Well, so Howie signs up with this company called Empire Properties—"

"Which is owned by Prescott," I said.

"Yeah, his master. Anyways, he gets himself a really nothing kind of a job where he's got to collect rents from people in some slum over in Manhattan . . . and he's also running some lousy hotel over there, too—"

"The Flanders," I said.

"Yeah, that's it. I seen the Flanders Hotel on the TV news lots of times. What a dump!"

"And you sensed trouble, somewhere down the road?" I asked.

"Sure I did. Ain't money a caution, though?"

"I guess."

"You guess right," she said. "Besides which, Howie started telling me how he was really catching the big boy's eye—that'd be Prescott himself—since he was personally responsible for getting a whole lot of folks kicked out of their crummy little apartments so the landlords could start really hauling in the loot from what they call redevelopment.

"And Howie, of course, being a sucker, he thinks just because he's on hand there doing the dirty work it means he's going to be sharing in the big score. Like anybody pays attention to guys like Howie doing the dirty work."

Lynette sat shaking her head for a second.

I said to her, "And so you say you threw him out of the house?"

"Well, it wasn't so dramatic. He wasn't here half the nights in the week anyways, he was always prowling around over there in New York with who knows what. I just told him one time he ought to get the hell out for good since he wasn't around for me much. If that's throwing a guy out, that's what I did.

"I ain't ashamed of throwing him out. I am sorry he got killed, though; but I'm not surprised, like I said. Oh, I try being ashamed, but it don't work. I guess I can't help it, you know. I was raised the way I was raised, and that means I was raised by the Bible and the Scriptures; you know what they say about men like my Howie?"

"No, ma'am, I'm afraid I don't know. Not right offhand anyway."

"'Whosoever shall worship money before the Lord brings hellfire and damnation into his heart and home.'"

She put out her second cigarette. Then softly she added, "So for the sake of the baby and me, Hock, you can naturally see how I couldn't hardly afford to love my Howie anymore."

And then I asked her, without first thinking how she might answer me, "Mrs. Griffiths, do you happen to know a lot of Bible quotations by heart?"

"Well," she said, blood rising in her neck and face, "I should say I know my Holy Bible!"

She stared at me suspiciously, and so did her parrot.

And so for the time being, I decided not to ask whether Lynette Griffiths also happened to know the Most Reverend Father Love—perhaps from his business cards. In the business of being a detective, I sometimes find it practical to hold off asking questions until I know the answers.

And just now, I was a long, long way off from knowing the answers I needed. So far off that I could not yet see all the questions to come in need of all the difficult answers, all of it waiting for me across the river in Hell's Kitchen.

"You'd be Hock, that right?"

It was one of the bartenders at the Pigalle talking. He'd poured me a Johnnie Walker red, and I was sitting there listening to Labeija singing in the blue light up on stage, a song called "Paradise Cafe" that was pretty good. The bartender was a guy about fifty wearing a jet-black toupee that didn't much go with fair skin that had not seen the earlier end of twilight in decades.

I said I was Hock all right.

And then from top to bottom and from side to side, his moon face was covered with a leer.

"Mona Morgan, she come in here a little early tonight and asks me to be on the lookout for you. She says you should go right on up to her dressing room when you get here." And as I got up from the bar to go, the guy said, "Don't do nothing I wouldn't do, Hock!"

I walked along the front of the ringside seats, mostly unoccupied since it was only singing up on the stage and not stripping. I looked up at Labeija as she sang and noticed the scribble of fear in her mascara-clogged eyes—fear or maybe its next of kin.

Then I took an open stairway to an upper corridor outside a short row of dressing rooms for the girls. Anybody outside the burlesque business would call these rooms closets. I came to a red-lacquered door with a silver star hung over the name Mona Morgan, and I tapped. I did not hear anything, so I tapped again. Then came the clink of glass against glass, and Mona's strangely coagulated voice, "If that's you, Hock honey, then waltz your little ol' self right on in here . . . door's off the latch."

Mona was, to put it kindly, a mess.

She sat splay-legged in a high-back wicker chair that might have been a throne in some movie about a Polynesian princess. But Mona did not much look the part of a movie star, or even the star of La Club Pigalle of West Fifty-fifth Street off Eighth Avenue. And surely not the girl in the fur coat with bundles in her arms and snow in her dark hair. In fact, some falls of that dark hair of hers were perched carefully on a Styrofoam wig stand.

One of Mona's knees was bruised. She wore a cheap plaid robe and a sloppy smile, and she'd been painting her toenails for the show, but the colors had sloshed clear up to her ankles in some places. On her dressing table were all the different vials of nail polish and a tray full of stage makeup and some spangly gewgaws and also a nearly dead pint of Jack Daniel's and a small water pitcher that had not seen much action and a single lowball glass.

She had recently screwed open a tall bottle of Wild Irish Rose muscatel, perhaps to clear the palate, and she drank this now from a green-and-yellow-striped juice tumbler. A goodly bit of the wine dribbled down over the lapels of her robe, and Mona now brushed at the red blotches, but it was not doing much good.

"What's going on here, Mona?"

She laughed at me as I stood in the doorway. There was no

charm in her voice as she said, "I'm trying to put the vineyards out of business . . . care to join my crusade?"

Mona took her lowball glass and held the sticky thing out toward me. I shook my head no, as much in bewilderment as anything else. I pulled the door closed behind me and said quietly, "You're drunk." And I felt stupid even before I finished saying it.

"Well, pardon me all over the West Side, but I got complexities like anybody else," Mona said.

"So how do you expect you'll dance your big number out there tonight, bombed like you are?"

She tossed back her head, frizzes of black hair shot with some gray snugged down with a cloth wig cap and bobby pins. There was a glint of dignity in her motion, which I had to regard as both amazing and beautiful under the circumstances.

"Miss Mona Morgan," she said regally, "never ever fails to please a man—alone or a whole damn room full of them, hear? The customer's going to be getting his damn money's worth tonight, like any other night. So who wants to care about anything else besides? You, Hock? *You* want to care?"

I put my hands in my pockets because otherwise I might have picked up a firehose out in the hall to wash down Mona. I asked her, "The bartender told me to come up here—you got some problem?"

"Sure I got a problem. Same problem any woman's got almost all the time. A man."

"I hear that kind of problem's good and bad."

"There's a lot of people would say this man, he's purely good."

I said, "Even so, you leave good silk out in the rain, it shrinks."

"Hock, you got insight. . . .   Oh, baby, I got something I just got to tell. . . . "

And the way she sounded now, the way a tear crept into the corner of one eye, I could not be angry with her for slipping off into the balm of a sad and lonesome drunk. She put a hand to her chin in hesitation, even though it seemed she wanted to pour out news like a rotary press. What news, I couldn't guess. Her eyes were not the clearest I had ever seen them, but I could see how they played the same dread expression I'd seen in Labeija only a few minutes ago.

"I don't know, I can't . . . oh, I can't tell you. . . ."

And then, of course, she started crying. Big long whoops and sobs and her funny-looking capped head down in her arms folded atop the dressing table, her shoulders heaving miserably. The Wild Irish Rose crashed to the floor, and there was a river of wine stink and glass crumbs, and it startled a tiny speckled mouse making its way home to a crack along the baseboard, and Mona shrieked at the sight of it—shrieked until its rubbery tail disappeared into the wall.

"A rat in here!" Mona bawled. "A rat!"

"Oh, come off it," I said. "He was only a mouse."

"He was a damn rat rodent, right around my ankles in this here ratty dressing room!"

This, the classic grievance of the burlesque queen. Everywhere on the circuit, so I was once informed by a dancer I once pinched on a charge of dipping a wallet out of her Uncle Sugar's blazer while he was walking her home one fine evening, dressing rooms in strip joints are teeming with mice. The girls have a theory about this. They reckon that mice are the only creatures besides the male human stupid enough to want to hang out in places where perfectly good money is forked over to see slight variations on one of Mother Nature's more minor designs.

The regular girls in a strip joint accept their mice the same as they accept their audiences; and quite often notice certain striking resemblances in appearance and personality.

Usually, the stripper's shrieks and her outraged threats to cancel out of the advertised star production number—whipsaw responses to the unhealthful, menacing emergence of said dressing room vermin—have to do with the prosaic wishes for higher pay and maybe some plusher fringe benefits. But Mona was already paid plenty, and her accommodations were as good as there were at the Pigalle. In Mona's case, the mouse took her mind off some bona fide terror, for which I was momentarily thankful; at least she had stopped her shrieking.

"Labeija's going to hear about this!" Mona said. "I'm not going to put up with this kind of trash and filth. I'll cancel first, and you can tell her for me!"

"How about if I just bring her right up here and you can tell her yourself?" I asked. I thought maybe Labeija could talk her into just going home for the night and sleeping it off. And I thought, too, that Labeija might be able to help me make some sense of whatever foul thing was afoot at the Pigalle.

"Say, why not!" Mona said. "The cow ought to be done bellowing by now. Send up the old drag queen, why don't you, and let's just see what the hell's what?"

And I stepped back out into the narrow, dark, and comparatively sweet-smelling corridor and headed toward the stairway leading down to the main floor and the runway stage.

As I came to the head of the stairs, I heard the band strike up its schmaltzy rendition of "One for My Baby and One More for the Road," heavy on the percussion . . . and then it somehow felt like my own head was the snare drum I heard, and it felt like somebody was beating on my head with the world's biggest and hardest pair of drumsticks, and I felt suddenly like some waterlogged dead thing floating along in the cold Hudson River, and it was blacker than I had ever thought possible. . . .

NINETEEN

I came to, alone. And in my own bed. I knew it was my place from the chorus of sharp whistles the wind makes as it blows through all the cracks along the bedroom window casing and from the ratcheting engines and hydraulic scoop lifts of the garbage trucks that run up Tenth Avenue around dawn when it's so nice to be rousted awake.

. Also, I could hear bottles and glasses clinking out in the other room. Somebody was rummaging around with his thieving hands in the sideboard where I keep my supply of Johnnie Walker. And the intruder was clumsy about it.

I tried sitting up, but I took this a little too fast. My head felt like a lot of fat people had been sitting on it lately. So my back only made it an inch or two off the bed. Besides which, Mona had a restraining hand on my stomach and she said softly, "Whoa now, boy, just lie there and take it easy."

And then hearing her speak, Mona's companion in the other room stepped in. He held a glass of my Scotch and he asked, "How's the patient?"

I could not answer him right away. For one thing, I did not truly know how I was, and for another, there was Mona Morgan

189

on a chair next to my bed and I was astonished and comforted all at once by this confusing presence. Her dark hair was all back in place, and she had fixed up her face and was wearing a nice dress like a regular lady. She must have drunk plenty of coffee sometime between the last moment I saw her, hollering about a mouse in her dressing room, and now here in my place. She had bathed herself, too, and was back to smelling like I enjoy smelling her.

To the guy standing there with the Scotch, who I presumed was some kind of a doctor since he also wore a stethoscope around his neck, I said, "I got one hell of a head."

But I was looking at Mona and remembering how it was outside of her dressing room at the Pigalle where somebody had suckered me.

Mona said only, "That was a mistake."

"Yeah?" I said. "That's what they told Marie Antoinette, and next thing she knew, her head was forty feet down the block."

And then the rummy doctor moved over near the bed and felt the pulse points around my neck and adjusted a bandage he had plastered around the back of my skull. He said, "Best as I can tell, son, you ain't got a concussion." To the best of my recollection, that would be the first time I heard a physician say *ain't* in the course of stating his diagnosis.

"That's swell," I said to the doctor. I moved slowly now and was able to prop myself up on my elbows. "So you want to tell me the lesser damages?"

"Well, we only know that somebody sapped you pretty good, son. Dropped you like a piece of hardworking lint, they did." He put back the Scotch and licked his lips clean. "But aw hell, you'll be okay, it appears."

He noticed how his glass was empty and said, "You don't mind if I take another jar." And he didn't wait for an answer from me. He went back to the sideboard in the other room.

I looked at Mona. "Who is this geezer?"

"Doc Allingham," she said. Carefully, she touched the bandage at the back of my head and frowned. "I don't know his first name. He used to be legit, a regular surgeon. But you know what booze can do to the surest grip. Anyhow, today he's a kind of an M.D. that certain people need to know."

"What people?"

"Certain people without any Blue Cross or Blue Shield, or any other colors of paper where they make you put down your actual name and address in order to get what you're being gouged for. . . . And people who maybe need a doctor after they get banged up in a club in Hell's Kitchen late."

I touched my head myself and imagined how it looked under the cloth bandage and the gauze and decided I did not want to see it for a few days. I said, "You say this was all just a mistake?"

"Look, Hock, I'll lay it out plain for you sometime soon, okay? For now, just take it easy and mark me off for a very bad night, why don't you. Who needs answers now, anyway? I'm going to stick by you, and we can find better things to think about, okay?"

"I don't know that that's okay, Mona. You have to consider what I've been through ever since moving back to the neighborhood. I have one of my best snitches find me this dump of mine, then the snitch gets it; then the guy who finds the snitch dead turns out to be connected to the dump I'm living in—so connected that he writes me a letter on behalf of the landlord offering me a couple of grand or thereabouts to give up the lease I just got and go take a room at the damn Flanders Hotel; then *this* guy—whose name is Griffiths and who fancies himself a *disciple* of his boss, my landlord, who is maybe running for president!—winds up getting canceled out right here in my own dump, if you please, and it's bloody as all hell. . . ."

I took a breath. Mona put a hand on my chest, which felt pretty good. "And then meanwhile, just for the record here, let's not be forgetting that I'm supposed to find some kind of Bible-slamming psycho who's out gunning for some Jesus-jumping radio preacher up in Harlem who is actually somebody else entirely—and who is now, for the record, lying comatose in the hospital since I didn't manage to do my job too well and wound up with him just about dead in my arms. . . .

"And that brings us right to now. Now I'm lying here after being clouted to the stars in a strip joint, and I wind up with a

bump on my nut that feels like maybe it's a Buick. So honey, let
me tell you: answers are as good as aspirins for me. So maybe
you could just give me two little answers: who the hell suckered
me last night, and how the hell come I found you sitting around
your dressing room like some slobbering dipso?"

Of course, I did not expect answers. But I felt I had cleared up
my sinuses. And of course, Mona's head fell forward and she
started crying a little. And that left me with all the starch of
water in a trick dribble glass.

Mona said, not looking at me, "You know how it is, Hock. You
do know, don't you?"

I mumbled how I did not think I knew much of anything
under the circumstances.

"You got a life like mine," she said, "and one of the thousands
of things you do wrong just all the time is you look for love in
most of the wrong places. . . . I guess maybe that's what I had
to tell you last night, partly. . . .

"After a while, things start catching up with you, and maybe
even if you always figured they would, you still don't see it
coming. Something old and nasty, it can come on you even on a
day that seems so new and clean. . . . Life's complicated, you
know.

"Look, Hock, the guy who put you down—"

"It was a guy?"

She didn't bother with an answer to that. "The guy who put
you down, he's a nothing—a zero, a guy who who never was and
never will be."

"So this guy," I said, "he's prowling around outside your
dressing room last—?"

"Yeah, and in the dark he must have thought . . . oh, I don't
know what he thought. Maybe he figured you were going to hurt
me, I don't know. But what the hell does it matter what he
thought, anyway? The important thing is, he didn't do any real
damage, okay? Labeija called up Doc Allingham, and then Doc
and I brought you home. . . . We did the best we could, the
best we knew how—and why don't we just leave it at that?"

And I decided there was time, some other day, to check into
all that Mona said. So I decided she was right, at least for now,

and that we could leave it lay. And I was just about to tell her this when Allingham walked in with his bony head and his red nose.

"Now that you been sort of up-and-at-'em," he said, "what's it feel like, son?"

"I feel like it's a dog-eat-dog world and I'm wearing Milk-Bone underwear."

And then Mona laughed and made me feel about as right as I could.

Allingham laughed, too, and wiped his mouth with the back of his hand like drunks do and said, "Well then, I'll be clearing out since you don't need me any longer." He hung around, though, and watched Mona while she went through her pocketbook for money.

She said to him, "This will be one of your . . . one of your quiet calls, Doc?"

"Madam, I assure you—medically speaking, I am wallowing in the depths of discretion."

I told him, "That's what I sort of thought."

And Mona handed him a few bills.

He went into the other room and I watched him pick up a hat and coat from the couch under the parlor window, along with a black doctor's bag, like the bags I saw when I was a boy and doctors still came around calling to your house and they didn't go poking around in your liquor cabinet while they were there. Then Allingham left. We listened as he clumped down the stairs.

And then Mona smiled at me and put her hands on my chest again and said nothing. She just traced circles on my skin with her fingers, and then her hands moved lower and lower. And after a while, she said, "You were out there for a good long time, but I don't imagine it was very restful. Now I'm going to make it restful for you, Hock, okay? You think you'd like that?"

I felt her warm breath as she stood over me. Then she put a knee up on the bed and her dress rode up her leg, and a shoe slipped off her foot. And her hands moved lower.

And I closed my eyes and remembered, from the other night.

Just tell me hello and I'll know all I have to do is send up a flare and relax.

Mona had been watching me think. I knew this when I opened my eyes and looked at her. And she knew. And she said, "Hello."

At about noon, there was the strong sweet smell of coffee and chicory in the house. And pecan butter melting over toasted molasses muffins. And I was awake, thinking fondly of what had happened after Mona told me "Hello."

In some ways, I felt good. In other ways, like my head, I felt a little more beat-up than usual.

I turned and looked out the bedroom door, and there was Mona, standing at the window that looked out over West Forty-second Street, the back of my building. She stood there in her regular lady's dress, running a hand through her dark hair and sipping coffee and looking out at the gray day, and she was beautiful—

But how ugly she had been, too. The memory was a fugitive one, but it had not disappeared; would not disappear yet. Mona sitting in her dressing room with a tumbler of wine, and the stains and the misery and her still secret troubles . . . *"I got complexities like anybody else!"*

—and then she turned when she heard me stirring. She said, "Morning, Detective Hockaday. I've been over to Ninth Avenue to get us something to eat. Something besides chili, which I'm not in the mood for now if that's all right with you."

Which it was, I told her.

I got up out of bed, slowly on account of my head. Mona took me by the elbow and steered me into the bathroom, where I took a nice long hot shower and managed, with some considerable effort, to keep my head from getting wet.

When I got out, she had my terry-cloth robe and a cup of coffee ready for me. Then she got me over to the green chair, and I sat down feeling a lot more complete about myself than usual.

She sat on an arm of the chair and draped a hand back around my neck and let a leg swing free and said, "Hock, you should think about you and me for a minute. No kidding, think about us."

I said, "Well, I do, and I also think about how we're all grown up and that we've both been run over more than once, and that we know how words can hurt more than broken bones even."

"So we'd better watch what we say here?"

"Something along those lines," I said. "Talk doesn't get freer and easier as you go along, does it?"

"No, I guess not. After a while, it gets you dug in pretty deep."

"Yeah, I think so. God, I hate being careful."

"So what if you didn't have to be careful, Hock? What would you say then?"

I might say that maybe just for the sheer hell of it we ought to go round up all the cash we could lay our hands on, both of us; and how then we should get over to Grand Central Station and buy a pair of one-ways up to Rhinecliff or someplace easy like that. And we would find ourselves a good hotel room there, maybe a suite; and maybe with a view of the river and the Catskills, which would be gray and snowy this time of the year. We could have ourselves a fine dinner with all the proper wines, and we could talk of the times that got away from us and of our sweeter sorrows, too. And then on the next day we could hunt for a house to live in, to hide in. With furniture and maybe a dog, and new life at our age; and some way of turning our tragedies into memory's jests.

But here I was a man all alone, and divorced, and of the tenderest middle age. A man with little in the bank, yet somehow rooted and established all the same; and every day I spent a lot of time thinking about how it was back when I was a kid living with my mother, and how much I would give to be able to talk to the ghost of my father. And I knew what all of this meant; I knew I was beginning to see that if I wanted to survive the years I had left to me that it was time to become a serious character in the story of my life.

Which required some solitude and some great and certain care, for all concerned. And so, of course, I told Mona none of this. . . .

Instead, I said something I do not remember. Except that whatever it was, it was neither disappointing nor promising—

certainly nothing that resolved anything between us. They were only words that left my lips as if they had heavy weights on them, words that sank into the emptiness of my parlor and then rolled away.

And instead of anything else that might have been said during a moment that might have changed everything for us both, forever, the telephone rang.

It was a bartender from the Flanders with a wheezing voice, and he asked:

"Hock, you still lookin' for the Holy Redeemer?"

I said that I was indeed.

"Well, he's settin' right here."

And, it appeared, he was not anxious about leaving for any place soon.

Lionel the Holy Redeemer had the *Post* spread out on the bar in front of him, an elbow holding down each corner, and a glass of beer with a thin head of foam on it. He was wearing his dark overcoat because it was drafty in the Flanders with only the plywood door for protection against the wind. I could see a bit of the soiled white clerical collar at Lionel's neck. His big bag, the one he used for collecting deposit cans and bottles, lay on a bar stool next to him, flat and empty.

On the juke, Leon Redbone was singing "Mama's Got a Baby Named Ti-Na-Na," and a young man with a ponytail held in place with a rubber band, his head down on the bar in his arms, kept tempo with his foot. There was a slender hooker with a pockmarked face up front at the bar, drinking something out of what I suspect might be the only champagne glass in the place. She gave me a look, I signaled a no, and she shrugged; nothing personal. The only other customers were three old gents, two black and one white, who were probably roomers at the adjoining Flanders Hotel. They played dominoes at a small table in back.

I walked up to the bartender and palmed him twenty. Lionel turned just in time to see this transaction. He smiled slyly and ran a blue-veined hand through his yellowish-white mane of hair, turned back, and looked at his beer.

I took the stool next to him and laid out two crisp dollar bills. Lionel's lips parted and his eyes flickered sideways for a look at the money, but he didn't face me.

"Maybe you heard I've been looking for you," I said.

"So I just seen."

I motioned for the bartender to come over our way.

"What'll it be for you?" I asked Lionel.

"I already got here a while ago," he said, "and I already put out for this-here beer."

I gave Lionel a tenner. "Here's to cover for that, and from now on the city's going to sport you to what you're drinking today, okay? Besides which, I got plenty more for you so long as we keep this little time of ours sociable, and useful. What do you say?"

Lionel took the ten and put it away someplace in the murky interior of his overcoat and said, "Well, I always figure one beer's a refreshment, two's a meal, and three's a party."

I pushed the singles down on the bar forward, enough for a party of beer. Then I added a ten and told the bartender to keep us in drafts and shots besides. And then before I pressed him any further, I waited for Lionel to enjoy his first hit of whiskey.

"What do you like to hear in the way of music for this little party we're having?" I asked him. I fished coins from my pocket as the juke died.

"Your choice entirely, Hock."

I went over and punched up another Redbone tune, "My Blue Heaven," and also "Scratch My Back" with Coleman Hawkins on the sax and a Fred Astaire rendition of "Miss Otis Regrets."

And when I got back to the bar, Lionel was putting back a second shot of whiskey. Which has a fine way of melting most of the natural resistance between a cop and a guy like the Holy Redeemer, who is best off keeping quiet, even despite the fact that he sometimes snitches for me.

"Okay, so maybe I'll go along with you and get a little drunk this afternoon, Hock," he said, "and then anybody's going to say whatever come out of my mouth I couldn't help, right? So what is it you're after me for, anyways?"

"Three things—" I began.

And I laid down three more tenners for Lionel to pick up and stuff away, which he did, quickly and with an eye peeled to make sure nobody saw him with that kind of money. It's a chancy thing for somebody living in the street to be carrying any more cash than is absolutely necessary to scrape through a day on the bum, and now here he was with forty dollars. And which, he and I both knew, made it wise for him to be hanging out with somebody like me, authorized to carry all three of the loaded guns I happened to be carrying.

"One, we already know that you're maybe the last guy I personally know who happened to see a snitch of mine called Buddy-O alive before they wired up his neck and croaked him out . . . and Buddy-O was a guy you mainly liked, I seem to remember your saying.

"Then second, it comes to me that you were also a guy I know who happened to see one certain other poor slob alive before *he* was checked out, too. And that would be one Howie Griffiths, who is—was—a fat little rent collector around here and a guy who also somehow was supposed to be in charge of the Flanders Hotel here, as you probably know, along with many other interesting things I should be knowing, too—"

Lionel looked at me like I had just dropped an ice cube on his fly. And then when the surprise of this line of questions died down, his eyes went dull and compliant again and his shoulders stooped low, as if gravity pulled them down especially hard. I smelled decay on his breath when he spoke.

"Maybe other guys seen Buddy-O alive before he went west, maybe lots of other guys," he said. "Nothing remarkable about me seeing him. Same thing for Griffiths. It's a big city, y'know."

"Yeah, Lionel, but so far as I know, you're the *only* guy who saw *both* these characters alive before both of them got themselves killed."

He turned away from me and stared at the glass of beer he had now mostly emptied. And he said, "Christ Jesus, Hock, this's evil business you're gettin' into whether you think so or not. I'm tellin' you that straight out, with no interest in nothin' by it for me."

"I appreciate that."

"Oh, do you?" Lionel snorted, looked up. "You think you can go away from this neighborhood like you done, and go off and live with working folks and money and all, and then just come back on here and pick up where you left off and everything's going t'be lovely and nostalgic for you?"

"No, I don't think so."

"Oh no—not you, Hock." He snorted again.

I said, "Why can't you cut the cute crap now and just square with me about what I'm paying to hear? I want to know what you think connects two dead guys of your recent acquaintance—Griffiths and Devlin, or Buddy-O to you."

Lionel waved at the bartender, who brought us back the whiskey bottle. I told him to set it down and leave it, and for this consideration I dropped him another twenty.

"And what if I did tell you?" Lionel asked, blinking and pouring out a third shot for himself. He filled up a short glass for me, too. "What's supposed to be in it for me—money?"

"Sure, money."

He tipped back the whiskey and then tightened his hand around the beer glass with foam drying on the inside.

"Money ain't what I need a lot of, Hock." He spoke quietly. "Money's real nice, but they always make sure there's enough laying around easy to lead the bummy life."

"What do you want besides money?"

"I don't even know that no more," he said. "Now ain't that strange? Maybe I'm not so much different than anybody else in not knowing there's something aside of money that's worthwhile. 'Course, I forgot most of my name, too. So what's anybody expect out of an old bum?"

I put back my own whiskey and told Lionel, "What I expect out of an old bum like you, pal, is that since you already went and took the big fall in your own life, you have this one certain advantage over an old choirboy like me."

"Oh yeah?" he said, sneering. "And what's the big advantage I got?"

"Did I say big advantage?"

He snorted.

And I said, "What you have, pal, is what I need right now

with two murders they pay me to worry about—and that's the ability of seeing the rest of us in this fair city of ours for what we really are, and not for what we're too busy thinking we are."

"Oh Jesus, you're asking somebody like *me* to tell *you* what I think about most people in this-here New York City?"

"I'm asking."

Lionel stepped off his stool. "I don't know if this's cause and effect, Hock, but I suddenly now got to go use the crapper pretty bad. I'll be thinking up my answer on the throne, okay?"

While he was gone, I leafed through Lionel's *Post*. Ned Blunden, the police reporter, had another piece about the Father Love shooting and what it all meant, which if all you had was the *Post* to go by seemed to have something to do with disgruntled life insurance policyholders since the Healing Stream Deliverance Temple was very heavy into the whole life racket. Which is a way of providing folks with precious little to invest in savings and security since all they have is pretty much tied up in survival with a whopping three, maybe three and a half percent interest on their accounts. And which is a racket that is technically within the law.

There was also an item in the page-six gossip and cheesecake section about Daniel Prescott and how his backers—who know no shame and have thus profited immensely in the business of American politics, which is also technically within the law— were tossing him a big party in order to help him with a certain hat-tossing decision. That, or else ring him in for a healthy percentage of the really big loot it now takes to find the one American out of about two hundred and fifty million of us with enough ignorant fortitude to suffer fools from coast to coast in order to wind up in a job that inspires the nation's stand-up comedians more than any other single constituency.

Then Lionel returned to the bar, sat down, put on a pair of dusty glasses with thick lenses that magnified his eyes and made them look more watery blue than usual, and he said, "You know me, Hock. I'm a guy who's been checking in and out of Bellevue since about '57, and I been in and out of traps for borrowing lots of stuff that don't belong to me and forgetting about returning the stuff . . . you know."

"I know."

"And you want to listen to me?"

"Yeah."

"Well, ain't that something new, now. All these years they put me in little rooms by myself, which forces me to think more than most folks will ever think, and now suddenly for the first time in my life one of you's actually asking me to express a view. Society says I'm a nutjob and a criminal, just because I steal, and now here you are, a cop, asking me to somehow help you out by telling you the results of all the time you forced me to spend deep in thought.

"I like it! I think this is what I need more than money, y'know? So, I decided to tell you what I first started formulating in my mind one night I'm strapped in a bed at Bellevue.

"So here's what I think of your society, you people with your jobs and your homes and your voter registration cards: You're all like passengers on a train, which you only naturally believe is going to take you to someplace safe and sound. Someplace like what they call the American dream.

"Only, none of you want to pay attention to the fact that your train's just about running clear off the tracks—and you got yourselves an engineer up front who'll tell you, if you bother asking, that you never ever had a ride so good."

Lionel took another whiskey and so did I.

And I said, "Speaking of trains, that's the third thing I want to ask you about."

I told Lionel about my chasing down the ravine where the old railroad tracks were, where hobos made their camps years ago when I was a kid; about how I had been after the gunman I had seen take down Father Love—which was something Lionel knew about, he said, from reading the *Post*. And I told him how I had only been down there a few minutes maybe since I was not quite dressed the right way for any extended sight-seeing; and how I had not seen anything so appallingly desperate since those nightly television pictures of Vietnam in the 1960s and early '70s with all the defoliated villages standing as unholy testament to the great American crusade against godless communism.

"Haw!" Lionel said, nearly shouting this. "I think you just might even mean that."

I said, "Mean what?"

"Christ Jesus, Hock, I think you might really truly be one regular sucker out of a million who might want to see the way things really truly are."

"Isn't that what I've been saying?"

"Okay then, choirboy . . . you want to come along with me to see where the king of the jungle lives?"

TWENTY

At a quarter past two o'clock on what was turning out to be a surprisingly sunny and unquestionably clear Tuesday afternoon of November, there I was walking up Tenth Avenue with the Holy Redeemer—past my own apartment house where Howie Griffiths had been murdered, past Runyon's pinball shop catty-corner where Buddy-O had been murdered in his rooms upstairs; onward to "the jungle," which Lionel informed me "is your fastest-growing neighborhood in Manhattan, only you ain't likely to be seeing *New York* magazine doing a photo layout of the place with little tips on where to buy some snappy Sunday brunch."

And then at West Forty-sixth Street, we turned west into a largely empty block that nonetheless had the power to take me back some thirty years in time . . .

. . . to when I *was* a choirboy at Holy Cross, and a hardworking shoe-shine boy outside the library, and an otherwise perfectly irritating little angel in a place called Hell's Kitchen for excellent reasons; and back to when my mother and all the other upstanding churchgoing Irish ladies of the neighborhood tried valiantly to keep us boyos from knowing what, exactly, went on inside a certain house on West Forty-sixth Street that was run by a scrawny-faced English lady with bad eyes whom everybody called Blind Mary. Blind Mary was famous for two things: she had six toes on her right foot and was happy to show herself off as a freak of nature to curiosity seekers; and she would admit a fellow into her parlor if she felt there was an outside chance he was eighteen years old and therefore, by her lights, man enough to enjoy certain congress with one of the girls in the upstairs rooms.

And back of Blind Mary's house, there used to be a wood-and-tin shed that became the official hangout of a loosely organized gang that came to be called the Buddy-O's because if a cop ever asked how come we were usually together, we had the wise answer, "Oh, he's just a buddy o' mine is all, and so's he and so's he . . ." And none other than Aloysius Patrick Xavier Devlin was our leader, and even then he struggled to make his way in New York with a gang to back him up; and since Devlin was the one who took the gang most seriously, he came to be known as Buddy-O himself.

By the standards of the day and place, the Buddy-O's were small stuff. Contract murders were the bread-and-butter of a certain couple of families out in Brooklyn, extortion belonged to members of the Mulberry Street social clubs, numbers were for the smartly dressed guys up in Harlem, safecracking was anybody's business since this was and still is a skilled trade, kickbacks were the province of City Hall and the true believers of our free enterprise system, and Wall Street had the monopoly on gentlemanly bank jobs and smooth swindles—which goes to show how some things never change. Left to the likes of the Buddy-O's of Hell's Kitchen were the relatively innocent pursuits of tipping over Puerto Rican bodegas up in the West Sixties before there was Lincoln Center, mugging rubes in Times Square—and generally thieving off guys they knew for a fact did not belong to rival gangs, or guys who eventually drifted away because they were too busy being choirboys.

But the Buddy-O's did not spend all their time honing skills in the sociopathic arts and sciences. They did the same things all the rest of the neighborhood youth did—which was mostly street games, since nobody owned a television set or had money for the movies. It was a far piece from the all-American boyish idylls on the covers of the *Saturday Evening Post*, but there were worse things we could have been doing, and the hardworking folks hanging out the tenement windows with their elbows cushioned on pillows seemed to breathe easier when they could watch us playing Annie-over or ballie-callie or stoopball or colly-up. Or Devlin's favorite—all-ee all-ee in free.

And how after I had drifted away from the gang, the Buddy-O toughs, including Buddy-O himself, would knock me down regularly on Forty-second Street for the coins in my shoe-shine box. Could anyone back in those days, watching me and Buddy-O himself from some tenement window as we both chased around the same obstacles in our street games, have known it would turn out that *I* was the one who would today be walking confidently down the streets that Buddy-O and his gang once owned—and with Buddy-O himself now on his way to a grave on Hart Island where a number would indicate his burial spot and inmates from Ellis Island would come periodically by boat to tend the Potter's Field of New York City?

"All-ee all-ee in free." I did not say this loudly, I did not even realize I had said it audibly.

"Say what—?"

"Oh, just something we used to play around here," I said to Lionel. "When we were just punk kids running in the streets."

"Oh Christ, yeah," Lionel said. "I remember them days." And he snorted.

Then he pointed toward a wire fence at the back end of a black-topped parking lot full of cars, mostly station wagons. The lot covered over what used to be Blind Mary's house, and the shed was gone, too. And I began to wonder if parking lots had taken over everything that everybody I knew ever remembered—Mona Morgan's old grandfather's cottage and his masterwork house up on the hill in Rhinecliff, and right where I was walking over what used to be Blind Mary's very own parlor, probably—where she would sit in her big pink chair by the staircase and show off her six toes while young fellows stood around with their hats in their hands, talking in extra deep voices and waiting for their turns upstairs.

The wire fence sloped and dipped along the rear edge of the parking lot and abutted a windowless elevator wall of a sooty red-brick loft building. A dead-looking tree curled up from the slope of the ravine beyond the fence.

Lionel pointed to the tree and said, "That there's the main entrance to where we live."

And as we walked through the last few rows of parked cars, I became aware of the interesting fact that quite a few station wagons and family-type sedans had become very much the same things as the upstairs rooms of Blind Mary's house, only with tires and bumper stickers and tags from the New Jersey Department of Motor Vehicles.

A car door would open, then out would step some guy who was pretty much nondescript except for the satisfied expression on his face. And then up would bob some hooker's frowsy head, and she would just stay right there in the car; maybe she would light something that could be smoked as she waited for the parking lot jockey with all the car keys on a big ring to bring over the next john to the station wagon with the Sea World sticker on the back fender, whatever. And meanwhile, the commuter who had brought the rolling bordello into the city in the first place was off working in some Manhattan office silo, completely unawares.

"How long's this pretty enterprise been going on here?" I asked Lionel.

"You been gone a *very* good long time from around here, ain't you, choirboy?"

Well, I had, I said.

Then very matter-of-factly, Lionel filled me in on this continuum of trade along West Forty-sixth Street. "See now, for close to twenty years, I guess, girls have been making a little daytime money doing . . . well, you know, backseat jobs. They toss a couple of dollars to the jockey supposed to be watching that nobody gets into the hicks' cars, and so everybody cashes in and nobody pays no landlord."

"And the hicks never catch on?" This was a dumb question and I knew it.

"Shoot, Hock—what does the white-shoe trade ever know about anything? I mean, ain't that about half the reason there's such a thing as a SCUM Patrol and you got a job with it?

"These hicks, they come walking through this parking lot full of old rubbers and douches all over the ground every Monday through Friday, and they don't never catch on; they walk through all the other damn miseries here, and they don't catch on to any of that neither, since all they're interested in doing is getting in their cars and honking their way home to where they pretend they have nothing to do with nobody's miseries in the city. Besides which, the girls is smart enough to know they should be careful with the cars and not be leaving too much wear and tear behind."

He pointed over a few rows, to a lineup of cars farther on down the fence on the other side of the center driving aisle, and he said, "Over there's a specialty department—where the johns go if it happens they prefer some nice pretty little chicken-boy."

I wanted a drink.

Lionel said, "Most of 'em—the girls, anyhow, not so much of the chickens—they're living down somewheres in the jungle at least part of the year. Some of them are getting to be old girls, too. . . . But look here, Hock, this little garden-variety vice, it ain't what you're wanting to find out about today, right?"

"Not today," I said. "Today I want to meet your king of the jungle, who can maybe give me a little help with the shooter who ran down here the other day. You think he can help me?"

Lionel said, "Well now, we'll just have to see about that by and by, won't we? Follow me, pal."

Then Lionel bent down and pulled back a flap of the wire fence, crawled through to the other side, and secured his feet in the large, snaky roots of the dead tree. I followed his lead. From the tree roots, we then made our way down along what was practically a stairway built into ravine wall, with handholds and steps chiseled into the steep bank of schist rock.

And once again, I descended into the river Styx of Hell's Kitchen, though now we were several blocks south of where I had been Monday morning in pursuit of the young mope who had shot down Father Love. Again, there were the smells of trash fires and the incense of burning marijuana; now and again, the sounds of skittering rats in the brown weeds, and plopping water.

But it was somehow more peaceful, quieter, in this section of the ravine—the jungle. Here there were no contemptuous eyes boring in on me as they had the other day; here was, so to speak, the better neighborhood of the jungle—where the residents were better fixed somehow, and somehow secure enough in their surroundings to take a visitor like me in stride.

Of course, it helped that I was not wearing a suit and tie and topcoat this time. Instead, I was dressed in some of my working clothes—an old parka, a knit watch cap, faded jeans with paint spots on them, an army sweater, gloves with the fingertips cut out, and a pair of felony sneakers, which is what all the well-dressed New York subway muggers call their Pro-Keds. *And* there was the considerable help of having a sponsor for this walkabout, in the person of Lionel the Holy Redeemer. So now there was no large need of fearing this valley of the shadow of death; besides which, there was the comfort of my full comple-ment of rod and staff—the Bulldog in my shoulder holster, the .32 strapped around my left ankle, and the standard .38 police special in my belt clip.

I looked at about a dozen men squatting around a couple of little fires down along one section of the rails, taking swigs from a bottle of Four Roses and smoking and talking in the sun. The same as a set of retired guys who get together around the same benches in some same corner of Central Park, maybe, or the way the old Irish guys pass away the afternoons at Angelo's Ebb Tide before the youngsters move in on them. Over on the other side of the rails, up and down, there were groups of women doing the same. And I ached at the ordinariness of this scene, and how it was the parody of life just overhead.

Lionel was greeted by everyone as we moved along the jungle floor, where in this particular neighborhood of what I came to realize was a whole lower world there were narrow footpaths that the people had burned down to bare ground and cleared of

roots and litter and sumac stumps for easy passage. Lionel
returned all the greetings with an open-palmed wave, and in his
Roman collar he looked to me to be the pope himself.

And I looked back up to the world above, where it began at the
parking lot fence. And another memory upturned . . .

. . . in which Patty, as I first knew him before the days of the
gang out back of Blind Mary's and before he was called
Buddy-O, had won yet again the game he loved the best of all.
And the day I found his secret for winning.

I saw Patty run into the little shed back of Blind Mary's, the
shed that later became our hangout, and I and the others
surrounded the shed. But Patty did not come out, and when we
went into the shed he had disappeared. And this was not the first
time he'd done this—always mystifying us with his running into
the shed and disappearing. He would wind up nearly a block
away, almost clear down to Forty-fifth Street, then he would
double back and holler at us from behind, in gleeful triumph,
"All-ee all-ee in free!"

And one day I searched the shed and finally found his secret,
the sliding door he had made of a floor plank. Underneath the
plank was a crawl space, which led into a gap between two of the
big rocks of the ravine wall. And then there was a long tunnel cut
into the gap, along an upper ridge of the ravine bank, some of it
so narrow that I had to slither on my belly to pass.

That was how Patty had done it, how the great Buddy-O had
mystified us; we were all young and dumb enough for a while
back then for him to get away with it.

Now, from way down below on the jungle floor, I strained my
middle-aged eyes to see if I could find the starting point of the
tunnel along the upper ridges of the bank. I thought I spotted the
two big rocks, but I could not be rightly sure. . . .

And now where we walked, underneath the great concrete
bridge that blocked sunlight and trapped the fetid air and
strangled all sound, it had become intensely black and wet.
Lionel moved like a nimble cat, able to see in the dark; but I saw
nearly nothing. I was a blind man, with no experience at

blindness; no experience in making my way by sound and by helpless trust in others, and knowing the uneasy anticipation of a stranger's touch.

I calculated that we had reached Forty-ninth Street when Lionel suddenly turned upward along the east bank of the ravine. He told me to move in close behind him, to feel for the steps and the handholds that would take us upward. And as we climbed, I felt his warm breath and mine, suspended in the dank air as frosted puffs.

The stones and rocks and even the soil underfoot were slimy, and more than once I slipped, barking my knee or shins. The ravine wall, at times only inches from my face, smelled of urine and smoke and rotted paper. And my hands and arms brushed over the pulpy remains of dead rats and squirrels, dragged below the bridge by scavenging dogs who would eat their kill in hiding.

Something screeched and clicked. Then wild flapping sounds. "It's a nest of bats," Lionel explained. He had turned his head toward me, but I could not see his face as he spoke. "We disturbed them somehow. You got to watch out because they're clumsy as all hell and likely to bang into you when they're scared or confused." And as he was telling me this, something in the air thumped against my back, then at my legs. And my throat clogged with a sickly sweet taste.

I think I would have passed out cold if we had not then come onto a narrow ridge partly illuminated by a shaft of light from a crack in the overhead bridge, a crack along the sidewalk bordering a street. The crack was big enough for me to see a woman's feet going by and a child's feet beside her.

And Lionel stopped.

We had come upon a small wood hut, which Lionel said was home sweet home. He put a key into a padlock and opened a door.

The hut was constructed of boards that Lionel had dragged down into the jungle, one by one, over the years. It was wedged firmly into a crevasse in the schist, anchored by stones and mud and stubby tree branches. Inside, there were planks covering slits in the walls so that Lionel could peer out into the dark world below the bridge.

There was only the one room to the place, about ten feet square with a ceiling not much over six feet high. Lionel made light with three kerosene lamps, and he warmed up the place by touching matches to coals in a small hand-built stove that he had vented out through one side of the hut and up to the open air through the crack in the bridge overhead. The piping he had used was the heavy-gauge steel-plate pipes that are always stolen from the subway repair yards uptown in Inwood.

Lionel removed his heavy coat and his hat, and soon the place grew so warm that he also loosened his shirt and took off the Roman collar. And I realized that I had not very often seen him without that collar, or bareheaded; nor had I paid much attention to anything he had to say to me over the years, nothing much beyond what I had found immediately useful to me.

I stared for a moment at his bushy head, sifted with gray. I do not know why this is, but old men living in the streets have the healthiest hair I have ever seen, even if it is greasy or lousy or otherwise unkempt; it's those of us who enjoy the usual indoor comforts whose hair keeps sliding off.

I guessed Lionel to be about seventy years old. There were all the wrinkles to tell me that and the rounded shoulders and the flattened chest. And his face and hands were browned and seamed from the years and from a long and untidy life, though I guessed he was fair-skinned as a boy and young man. His face was sunken from losing teeth. He wore a denture plate, but it did not fit properly; for all I knew, it might have been somebody else's plate once.

There were two pieces of furniture in his place, not including the ledges and shelves he had cut into the walls to hold his belongings, mostly magazines and newspapers and canned food. There was a cot and a pile of tires arranged in the general shape of a couch. Lionel sat down on the edge of his cot, and I took the tires.

Back behind Lionel was a ledge with a little stack of books on it and a fourth kerosene lamp, unlit. This was probably his reading lamp. There was an ashtray on the ledge with a lot of tan-colored butts in it.

He offered me Bull Durham loose tobacco and some tan

rolling papers. I did not want a cigarette, but I made one anyway to be sociable. We smoked. Lionel apologized for not having any coffee or booze to go along with the cigarettes.

As we talked, I realized that Lionel's midwestern nasal twang was the sort of accent that might make a cop think he was a simpleton, if the cop happened to be simple himself. Which I have to say I had been for a while there.

For now I learned that Lionel the Holy Redeemer was also the king of the jungle.

TWENTY-ONE

"**Y**ou ask me how I got to be king of this jungle, hey?"
Lionel pulled on his chin.

"There's the short answer," he said. "Which is, I'm the oldest
and smartest coot around this place. There's the longer version,
too. . . ."

Then he pulled a pair of thick eyeglasses from his shirt pocket,
and when he put them on his blue eyes grew big. He said that
seeing the person he was talking to helped him to be serious
about what he had to say.

"I started out a regular sucker, and worked like everybody
else. I didn't have no schooling or opportunities like that. Christ,
Hock, I honestly forget how come I didn't have opportunities. . . . You get to my age and you're just happy to remember
how to talk, so you don't worry about what ran away out of your
brain.

"Well anyhow, I worked all the usual crappy jobs. I swept up
in different shops out in Michigan where I'm from, worked in the
auto plants a while. I sold stuff door to door all through Michigan
and Ohio, then Pennsylvania and on into Jersey, where I spent
a lot of years in Passaic. And all the way along the line I'd meet

up with guys who would be proud to say how they had twenty
years' experience, say, which I couldn't help thinking was about
one year's experience twenty times.

"I ain't going to apologize for my poor attitude when it comes
to respectable jobs, okay? I found out that jobs is a lot of hard
work and not enough money to live like a human being,
especially if a guy's married and has kids.

"So, what I did was I started helping myself to what I needed
as a decent human being. Which is what they call stealing, for
which they were all the time putting me up in various traps when
they caught me at it.

"Well, all that time I spent in traps I mostly spent reading—
when I wasn't too busy laughing off the queers and their warm
and loving suggestions. This was finally my education.

"I read lots of history the times while I was in the trap. For
some reason, history books are very big with the people who put
together your prison libraries. I don't know, maybe they figure a
dusty old history book isn't going to get the cons too overly
excited. What it did to me was teach me to read between the lies,
but I guess I'm just naturally a cynical bastard, you could say.

"What history is—and you being a cop, you'll appreciate this,
Hock—is a police blotter of the major crimes of the world.
Which include all the different wars that killed off millions of
deluded little guys, and also all the other horrible doings of
various bastards down through the centuries. And also down
through history, I learned how rich people have been spreading
the propaganda that property is sacred and should not be stolen
because they happen to own practically all the property.

"So you might say, my study of history taught me how my
instinct was right and proper: the only thing a sensible man
ought to be is a thief. Of course, there's thieves and then there's
thieves.

"Being an honorable thief, I made it my rule never to steal
nothing from the poor since number one I'd be hurting them and
number two they ain't likely to have nothing worth my time
stealing. This is a completely different approach to being a thief
than what you see with the thieves in business and industry and
the thieves that get voted into high office; these are the ones who

got their snouts so deep in the mash that it don't matter to them
who they steal from, just so long as they steal—which is like
breathing to them.

"What I always did as an honorable thief was steal from people
who had insurance, which is a fine and decent thing and which
does everybody a favor. First, you're doing the owner of
whatever you steal a favor since you give him a little excitement
in his life. And then you do the insurance company a really big
favor since if there's any publicity at all about the theft of that
sacred property you just clipped, then it just delivers up more
policy business and sometimes bigger premiums, too. And it also
does you cops a favor since running after thieves makes a cop feel
important. . . ."

Lionel finished his cigarette. He stubbed it out on the floor
and rolled another one. I declined one for myself.

"But I eventually had to stop being a credit to society," he
continued, "because being a thief is, sad to say, a young man's
game.

"So, my shaky hands and my run of unluck when I started
realizing how old I was getting forced me into retirement. And
retirement—oh boy! That's another horrible injustice of the
world, especially since there's no pension for an honorable thief.
And I don't even dare go ask nothing from the Social Security
neither, since that would only just be inviting a lot of trouble
from the G—and I always make it my very strictest professional
rule not to get funny with Uncle Sam, who is a killer.

"Well, that brings me up to date in an awful big hurry, Hock.
I'm leaving out many thousands of details, some that'd make you
blubber, maybe, and others that'd make you laugh like hell.
Anyhow, here I am an old man, which in my personal book
counts for a lot.

"Of course, I'm a *poor* old guy, as you can see very plain.
That's because I lived a decent life. And I ain't bitter about all the
time I spent in the trap, and the times they put me in the
laughing academy neither just because I developed a habit of
spouting off my theory on property and how it ain't true at all
that it's sacred. . . ."

Lionel raised his hand and chopped the air, and it looked very

much to me as if he were at least somewhat bitter. Or at least a
little crazy on account of the truth as he saw it, which maybe was
true.

"Maybe you're wondering how I myself wound up living in
the jungle?"

I said I had been wondering.

"I had a regular room on Thirty-ninth Street over by the
kosher slaughterhouse on Eleventh Avenue that ain't in operation
no more. I suppose one of these days it's going to be some condo
apartments or like that—Parve Arms, they could call it. Well
anyhow, I'm really bad off for several months, on account of how
they put me in one of their rooms without windows at Bellevue
for a while—which you can see prevents me from stealing
anything for a while, which makes me therefore unable to pay
the landlady.

"One thing leads to another, and there's an awful day when I
find myself at the point where my landlady has nailed down my
trunk and if I go back to my room she will no doubt nail me
down, too.

"So, that was twenty-five going on thirty years ago or
thereabouts, and I been living here since, rent free. And brother,
you think you folks up top have seen some wild changes in the
world?

"Christ Jesus, Hock, what was here when I first come down to
live was not what you'd call a debutante's delight—but at least
we were decent and honorable, even though we might have been
financially without any money. Oh, once in a blue moon
somebody'd maybe go off his nut from eating sterno or swallow-
ing down some hooch with too much lead in it, or something like
that—but it was just nothing like what this rock cocaine stuff has
went and done; that and greed, and how it's sinking us all down
to the level of insane rabid dogs.

"Well—" And Lionel suddenly stopped.

And he sighed, and this was a terrible sigh from deep inside
the soul of an honorable thief; a sigh with the sound of a
thousand years behind it, the sound of a man who knows that
whatever wisdom he has tried to give away is only one quirky
grain of sand on the beach.

"I think what I want to make you understand from what I'm telling you, Hock, is there's not much honor to the world anymore. Not even here in the jungle, it pains me to admit. Even here we are losing sight of how to be decent men and women. And I'm feeling so old and weak after I've went and dedicated my retirement years to being king of this jungle—and always trying to keep at least my little kingdom here free and innocent of this dangerous notion I mentioned before, about how property's supposed to be sacred."

He was through talking for a while. His face went hazy and he looked past me, maybe resting until he could come to the point of helping me find what it was I needed to find in his jungle, in his kingdom below the streets. And he would come to the point, I knew, for the simple reason that if he helped me, he would be doing us both a great favor.

I looked at the top of his bushy old head, at his thick matted brown hair shot full of crooked gray streaks. When a man has never known his father, he looks at men roughly his father's age the way I do—wistfully, measuring their appearance against how they might imagine their unseen father's aging process.

My own father, were he walking the earth, might look something like Lionel. My father, who had written what I had instantly memorized long ago, *The world's gone cockeyed, and a moral truth doesn't have a tinker's chance against the devil without vast armies; and God's very own sweet army doesn't have a chance without spies and betrayals and secret codes and treacheries and propaganda and the very thickest plots and all other manner of deception and cruelty required to preserve a man's civilization. . . .*

And so often, in the dark, the ghost of my father would be sitting on the edge of my bed telling me things. . . .

And it occurred to me that this place where I sat with this beat-up old bushy-headed wise man—Lionel, who had forgotten half his name in the fog shroud of his hard times; Lionel the Holy Redeemer, earning nickels up top from deposit cans and bottles, and sometimes taking a few little dollars from me as a snitch; and Lionel the king of the jungle, too—could well be the start of the money trail.

*   *   *

I touched his shoulder. "Lionel?" He looked at me, but I couldn't say he actually saw me. I touched him again. "Lionel?"

Then he sighed heavily again and said, "Aw, I'm sorry, Hock. I went away there for a while—where, I don't know. I'm a little weak in the head, as you can see plain. This don't hurt nobody else, but it's no comfort to me."

"What you just told me is interesting," I said, "and I wouldn't like it if you told anybody, but there's a lot you say that I go along with. And if this country was a monarchy, I would not kick about your reign."

And then Lionel laughed. Quietly at first, then hard, and then helplessly. He laughed for maybe two full minutes, great and gawping laughter, at the end of which he struggled for breath and his eyes streamed back of his glasses. He laughed in gratitude for sweet laughter itself, which was not abundant in his world anymore. And when he was through at last, Lionel owned the beatific smile of a hot thirsty man who had just been given a glass of cold beer.

"You're a right one, Hock," he said. "Even with all the copper in you, you're still basically the choirboy I hear you was a long time ago. . . . So, why don't you go on and tell me what it is you're wanting from me?"

"I want to tell you what's been happening since the day I moved back home to Hell's Kitchen. I have a very slippery case assigned to me, and I need to tell you about it, and I want to hear whatever you have to say about what I'm going to tell you . . . and who knows but maybe you'll be a big help to me."

"Well, go on," Lionel said.

So I started out by telling Lionel how it was that Buddy-O had steered me to my apartment on Forty-third Street, then how Buddy-O had been murdered and the meeting that we had never had and how Howie Griffiths had found Buddy-O's body—and then how Griffiths wound up dead in my own bathtub.

"Aw, holy Christ, Hock—he croaked out in your own place, hey?"

I also told him about how Buddy-O said there was a stranger in the neighborhood, a black guy running around asking questions about the protocols of hiring a cannon. And I told him about the note ice-picked to Griffiths' chest. And the threats against Father Love on the cards. . . .

And I thought about how well I had summed it all up while I watched Lionel scratch his head in thought.

His only question after all that was, "So, what'd Griffiths say was the reason he come across Buddy-O dead?"

I answered, "He told Detective Aiello, who was the first commander on the scene, and he told me, too, that he'd just heard about Buddy-O blowing off about a score of cash. So Griffiths, being a good little rent collector, said he dropped in cold on Buddy-O to see about his settling up on a lot of back rent."

"You buy that, Hock?"

To myself I had to admit that yes, I had bought just that; I had seen Howie with the sweat pouring off his butter skin and Aiello grilling him and Howie looking so guilty of *something*, I only naturally figured that he could not have had anything to do with Buddy-O's murder. Then I had talked to his widow and had my eyes opened to the fact of Howie being quite the greed-head, not to mention a self-admitted "disciple" of this Daniel Prescott tycoon with the cockamamie book and maybe the itch to add the White House to his real estate holdings. To Lionel I said, "At this point I am open to everything besides what the late Howie Griffiths claimed on the one and only day I saw him alive."

"Yeah, well, I would think it's best to keep an open mind on old Howie," Lionel said, snorting. And this made me remember how Aiello had informed me that Griffiths had been making inquiries about *me* and where I happened to live in the realm of Empire Properties, and how this was very soon after our chat in the late Buddy-O's place.

I asked Lionel, "In the interest of keeping an open mind, it has come to me that just before Griffiths got to be toast, he went and fired the super in my building—and then you and Griffiths are seen having a little chat right outside of my place. So what did you and Griffiths have to talk about?"

"Your super seen me? That crazy spic who went and threw all them bloody pennies all over Griffiths?"

"That's the witness all right. His name's Ricky."

"Yeah, well, Ricky's kind of a nutso. But I like his style."

"Never mind about that, Lionel. Just spill about what you and Griffiths had to talk over."

He sighed. "What I was doing with Griffiths was, I was trying to get this fat pink crud to leave us the hell alone down here in the jungle."

"What's that supposed to mean?"

"Money, Hock! What's anything mean to a crud like Griffiths and a sorry old grifter like Buddy-O Devlin? Ain't you been listening to nothing I've been painfully trying very hard to fill you in on?" Lionel made several sounds of exasperation and then said, "Griffiths and Buddy-O were partners, you could say— partners in making trouble for regular suckers living up top in apartments, and partners in making trouble even for us decent types down here. I'd been talking to them both, trying to at least get them off our backs down here. . . . See, it was Buddy-O who started the trouble we got now, which since the last time you lived in Hell's Kitchen was when you were a choirboy and you just can't know how terrible things—"

"Now, by *trouble*, are you talking how you're losing sight of how to live decently . . . like you've been telling me?"

"That's it exactly, Hock. And hallelujah, I always suspected maybe the light would dawn on some cop if I could find the right one. . . . See, I tried talking with Buddy-O, then with Griffiths, and, well, you seen how far that got me.

"So now since I done all that one tired old poop of a retired honorable thief could of done to keep us in this-here jungle free of that dangerous idea I mentioned, I got to now talk to a cop, and—"

"The dangerous idea—you mean the gag about property being sacred?"

"That horse shit, yeah."

"Okay. But Lionel, I have to tell you that I'm starting to have trouble following the point now."

"Aw, Christ-a-mighty, choirboy! Ain't you got any imagination? Ain't you making the connections here yet? You, a right

guy and everything, and even a detective who's got a regular
wage to prove it?"

"Suppose you just make the connections for me? And maybe
you better leave the 'choirboy' stuff alone from now on."

Lionel shrugged. "Well, I don't mean to get you all snorty and
snarly at me, I only just wonder sometimes if you understand
how the choir ain't singing around here no more."

"I understand."

"Okay then, look—what's the real estate picture look like to
you, up top there living in your no doubt crummy apartment
where you're maybe sweating out the rent every month like
everybody else?"

"Desperate. It looks desperate—"

"*Desperate*. I like that. That's a damn true enough word for it.
Thanks to guys like Griffiths and Buddy-O, who never personally bothered me up until lately, which is why I told you I
mainly like him . . . but old Buddy-O, he really got his nuts
jammed in the ringer now, didn't he? What he done to us, I
figure he brought it on himself, though."

"What, exactly, was Buddy-O doing to anybody down here?"

"He starts coming around the various entrances to the jungle,"
Lionel said. "This was about six months ago when it was warm
out. He hangs around the entrances, noting down on a pad who
lives where and at what end and all. You know from seeing
yourself now how we got our good part of the jungle and our bad
part. And then what Buddy-O does, he starts talking to some of
us next, then hiring certain ones to do things . . ."

Lionel paused and waited for me to ask, "What things?"

"I ain't saying here that *all* of us can be corrupted and hired off
like this, Hock. Okay? Me, for instance, and the rest of us who
got our heads clear on the idea of property, we like to call
ourselves decent. . . ."

"Okay. But what things was Buddy-O hiring some of your
corruptibles for?"

"Well, nothing at first that seemed any great shakes. He'd pick
up some bad bottle gang, for instance, and he'd pay them off in
Thunderbird or Wild Irish to have them just set around all day
outside some particular apartment house where the landlord's

trying to make things as unlovely as possible for the rent payers. See now, I wouldn't care if that's as far as it ever went since I don't carry no torch for nobody who would think it's *icky*—which I myself have actually heard a lot of newcomers around here actually say—if some guys are setting around and looking more or less like . . . well, looking like you, Hock. See, I got no sympathy for that kind of riffraff, and I figure maybe they deserve getting screwed out of their apartments. . . .

"But then I hear how Buddy-O gets himself hooked up with the fat pink creep Griffiths, and then the two of them started taking this little game of undesirable denizens way the hell out of fair bounds."

I asked, "How so?"

"Well, first of all, to appreciate this, you remember how Buddy-O was a guy all the time running his little two-bit scams?"

I nodded yes.

"Maybe he started picking on us because he was getting tired of that small-potatoes stuff he'd been running," Lionel said. "And maybe since he was a guy teetering on the rim of middle age and all the time thinking of his salad days back when the Westies was going strong around here . . .

"And Hock, this's only my hunches, okay? But I'm an old guy who's seen a lot and who has an awful lot of time for thinking and reading between the lies, like I say—so who knows, I might be right on the money. Anyways, what I think is—Buddy-O was trying to broker a new kind of a gang for a new kind of a gangster. Get my drift?"

Maybe I did, but I did not want to acknowledge this yet. So I said, "Why don't you spill it for me nice and slow."

TWENTY-TWO

Lionel put two more coals into the stove and lit them.

"Well, sir, here's my theory," he said. "I figure Buddy-O would go around, like a broker, see, and he'd hire up a string of the very worst elements of our life in the jungle—and then he'd put out the string for your creep Griffiths, who it so happens was in charge of the Flanders Hotel. Get it yet?"

I didn't say anything.

"Griffiths would put up these lowlifes we got in rooms at the Flanders," Lionel said. "And he'd make sure they got plenty of dope and booze and like that, to keep them docile, and this'd be keeping them in storage until the more specific jobs of work would come up. . . ."

"You mean to say—?"

"Ho-ho, so you're maybe seeing the connections at last, Detective Hockaday?"

I had not meant to speak aloud. "Maybe, but don't let me stop you."

"Okay. I was just getting to the out-of-fair-bounds part of this. . . .

"See, the landlord creeps of this city—by which I'm talking

here of your biggest boys, not your little weasels and stupes like Griffiths and Buddy-O was and not your little guys with a walk-up or two who are living right on their own premises, neither—they're all the time at night going to sleep with dreams of really big filthy wads of dough. But when they wake up, they know they can only get that kind of dream dough when they somehow get rid of all them lowball rent payers they still got on leases—in places like your own Hell's Kitchen dump where by law they can only charge them up for a huge profit instead of an obscene one, which with a little twist of the law itself and a lot of help from some string of undesirables they can maybe introduce to the neighborhood. . . ."

I was seeing very clearly by now, of course. And I already knew who I had to go see right after I finished with Lionel, the king of the jungle.

"So, at the very same coincidental time as your new kind of gangster is taking over New York City—these creep landlords, okay?—you naturally see how Buddy-O with his own sugar-plum fantasy dancing around inside of his head is figuring out some way of how he can help make dreams come true for the big fish. And so he starts putting together—"

I finished it for him. "A new kind of a gang."

"Yeah! A new kind of a gang for a new kind of a gangster. Oh, I tell you, Hock, this city never sleeps, hey?"

"Never, I'm afraid."

Lionel said, "So that was the racket, see. Buddy-O, he'd find the rum-dums and the crackheads and the pross and the chickens from somewheres out of our worst elements here in the jungle, then he'd herd them over to the Flanders where Griffiths'd keep them on deck until the day when he'd install them in apartments in some building he wanted to make into a hellhole—so that regular suckers would have to move out and make room for what the gangster landlords are nowadays calling *renovations*, by which the law allows the landlord to hike up the rent to something obscene, which is nowadays called *fair market value*. You follow me?"

I did, I said.

"The way it worked was beautiful, if you want to look at this racket from the creep point of view," Lionel said. "You install some wolf pack of crackheads or pross or your plain ordinary screaming New York psychos into some apartment that's gone vacant in what is mainly a house full of your regular rent payers. Then these suckers who are only trying to raise their kids halfway respectable, or maybe thinking they got the right to go home after working their butts off all day and open a can of beer and sit around in their shorts without having to be scared out of their gourds about gunfire out in the hallway or something . . . well, this type of sucker, he moves on. . . .

"It's what is known in the real estate dodge as *turnaround profit*. You keep turning around the tenants, see, and maybe you add some cheap capital improvement like new plasterboard or some-thing, and the law says you can hike up the rent every time. So naturally, you keep turning them around, and you can naturally see how undesirables could help out the cause of turnaround profit.

"Christ Jesus, Hock—maybe they was even fixing to do just that in your very own building there on Forty-third, you know? They canned your super, which is usually the first sign of what they have in store for the house."

Maybe indeed.

Lionel said, "And maybe now you also finally got the connec-tion about why I am so hardened against this horrible idea of the sanctity of property?"

I said, "Yeah, I read that real clear now. But tell me this, Lionel—what do you make of the black guy running around trying to line up a contract on somebody? And what about the young black kid I told you I chased down here to the jungle—the kid who was the shooter up in Harlem last Sunday, who put Father Love away in the hospital?"

Lionel took off his glasses and rubbed the thick lenses on a relatively clean patch of his shirt. Which did not do the glasses much good. "Well, Hock, I have been thinking hard on that one, and I can't get anywhere near the money with it, not like I'm pretty sure about Buddy-O and Griffiths and how they were running their turnaround profit racket."

He sighed. "Tell you what I think, though," Lionel said. "It's

pretty clear it's one of us down here in the jungle that's mixed up
in the Harlem shooting. Maybe I even seen this guy you're after,
but from the way you describe him to me I can't say. If I knew
him and if I knew where he was down here, Hock, I'd rat him
out right here and now, God help me. That's because number
one I don't hold for that kind of violence, like I said; and number
two, it's not doing the rest of us no favors drawing the interest of
cops to the jungle—and nothing personal, Hock, but that
includes even you. . . .

"Well, when I tell you I don't know where he is here, you just
got to take that on faith. I'd steal from you, but I would never lie.
That's another strict policy of mine. Anyway, I can tell you this
much: the young black guy you're after, he don't live around this
decent end of the jungle, otherwise I'd know him good. So he's
probably holed up at the far end, which you know about from
your little pursuit of the other day.

"Sorry, I know that don't pinpoint too much for you. But hell,
I'm only the king here and I can't know everything. Except
maybe something that might help you understand how it is a
man feels at first when he takes the fall down to here."

I said I could use all the help he wanted to give me in this way.
I have found in the detective trade that understanding why a
man does something is as good as a physical clue.

"Right from the start," Lionel explained, "you're mad as hell
since your mind ain't yet clear about this property idea everybody's ramming into your head since your birthday. And you
ain't got any property, so you're mad.

"And you look around at what you find yourself living in, and
the fact that some of us are working jobs every day up top and
still have to live down here on account of how we can't afford the
landlords—and you start counting all the bodies down here,
which I guess maybe is two thousand or so. Well, you naturally
figure that since there's so many of us pushed or pulled or fallen
or whatever that there's no hope—just like you and everybody
else already knows there ain't any justice.

"So night after night, there you are laying around dreaming
how you want to go hunt down anybody who ever done you a
bad turn and stuff their mouth full of one of these ugly bats

flying around here, and sew their lips shut. Real awful dreams like that, dreams just about as awful and destructive as the ones the landlords are meanwhile dreaming in their beds.

"Well then, that kind of thinking passes by and by. Which is natural since if it don't, then your head would explode on you. Your madness kind of smooths, out, like. . . .

"Except for the fact that it's *still* night after night and you're *still* laying there under the cold stars of Manhattan and you're looking up at black and realizing how you're going to die a zero—and that it don't matter, that nobody gives a rat's fanny, and that you ain't going to be a memory for nobody—"

Lionel leaned over and opened the flue on the stove and poked the coals for a last whiff of heat.

"At which point, maybe you see there's nothing to lose, you know?

"Maybe you gravitate to the mud and the anger up at the other end of the jungle. And you live there with your wine and your dope and your cigarette butts you keep dry behind your ears; you live without a drop of hope in your heart. But you live, that you do—at least so far as a medical doctor would count it as life.

"But all day long, you think the same thing over and over and over . . . and you assume that folks up top living with warmth and regular meals and some laughs, the kind of way you lived once yourself maybe . . . you assume . . . well, you assume they can hear what's howling inside your head down here. In God's name, you'd naturally assume that people could hear what you're silently screaming at them every day in your degradation: Fear us!"

I felt things curling up inside of me and on top of me and under me as Lionel said this. *Nothing to lose.* He coolly observed my discomfort through those bottle-thick glasses of his, through his wildly magnified eyes. *Fear us!* His pale eyes grew brighter now, now that he could see how I was beginning to connect one idea to another.

Property . . . sin . . . lies . . . truth . . . deadly assault . . . murder . . . theft . . . fear . . .
Theft.

TWENTY-THREE

The sky was hazed and the sun was a blotch of yellow white and fading west rather quickly by the time I left Lionel's hut. And the air felt like it so often does in New York on a November afternoon with twilight an hour or so away, like wet wool.

I walked with Lionel along the rusted tracks, toward the spot where I could climb back "up top" to Hell's Kitchen. And to the next set of gummy footprints I could find along the money trail.

Out from under the bridge that protected Lionel's hut and scores more from the snow and rain, the wide commons area of the jungle was thinning out with the coming nightfall. Already the jungle was gray and purple with shadows.

Along both sides of the ravine, small groups of men and women—and here and there what seemed to be families, with children and dogs, too—crouched around cooking fires. The light from the fires softened their faces, and there was as much talk going on as eating—the way it was in people's homes before television silenced everything. And the scents of cabbage and chicken were as thick as I remembered from my own mother's kitchen.

We passed by half a dozen men I had seen earlier, huddled

around a boisterous game of dominoes spread out atop a makeshift picnic table. They were insistent on using up the final minutes of daylight. Nearby, a woman bent over a trickle of water along the tracks and rubbed pieces of clothing between smooth wet stones; I saw that several of her fingers were missing, as if she had rubbed them away. A young man with a hammer worked on a lean-to he had built into a niche of rock, pounding down support stakes. And everywhere we walked, ancient mariners roamed the paths cut through this peaceable end of the jungle, muttering to themselves, or else laughing aloud, or else talking to absent friends of times gone by.

Before I left him, I shook Lionel's hand and said, "Thanks, pal, it's been an education."

"Well, I'm pleased to hear you say that," Lionel said. He looked around him quickly and added, "Good luck."

Every detective in New York should have such an education; maybe Lionel the snitch ought to be on the Police Academy faculty, maybe he should have a tenured professorship at John Jay. Listening to him was an exercise in remembering that when a cop finds a case short on specifics, he should pay very close attention to the evasions and to the motives and to all the sketchy riddles—even to the unsolved riddles of long ago, to a past that might well overlap with the present. And hadn't everything been this murky from the start?

Tommy Neglio himself was so squeamish about specifics that he had hustled out of town, down to the warmth of some island obscurity with no telephones—until the little storm he'd assigned me blew over. And then everywhere I happened to turn to bounce a few random questions, hadn't the result been riddles? Hadn't they all seemed to speak a language of riddles—Samuel Waterman, Jr., *and* Sr.; Lynette Griffiths, Howie's unmournful, Bible-spouting widow; Roy Dumaine; Mona Morgan . . . even Labeija?

"You're in show business, you shouldn't let your face get rearranged too much. If you ever get mad enough to swing on somebody in the business same as you, you're obliged to keep your blows as low as possible. The lower the better.

"It's only the decent thing to do. People who don't understand the

*reasoning that's back of this rule, they call it dirty fighting. But you can
really see how it ain't. . . ."*

This I remembered Labeija saying to me the other night at the
Pigalle, that night when I *wasn't* sapped from behind by somebody hiding in the darkness outside a stripper's dressing
room . . . where Mona Morgan sat inside with her painted toes
and drank herself ugly, for reasons she did not care to disclose.
More riddles!

I remembered this as I worked my way upward along the
shadow-drenched east bunk of the ravine, pulling along the
fingerholds and finding my footing so easily in the intelligently
chiseled steps . . . as if I had lived for years in the secret jungle
down below the streets of Manhattan.

Secret? A gash of sorrow and want in the heart of New York
City is a secret?

Now I had been educated, now the jungle was not a secret
from me. Now I could honestly call myself a detective, for I
knew that a secret is never stronger than when it is laid bare to
those unwilling to see.

As I rose closer to the level of the streets, I began to hear the
dull roar of uptown traffic on Tenth Avenue and the more urgent
pull of time. And I heard a woman's voice calling.

"Yoo-hoo!"

I looked around me and saw nothing but rocks and shadows
and scraggly trees. Another ten feet or thereabouts and I would
be at street level. I looked back down to the floor of the jungle
and saw the neat crisscrossed pathways, and the little fires, and
Lionel walking slowly back toward the bridge and then under it
to his hut.

"Yoo-hoo, Hock!"

And then I saw her.

"Yoo-hoo . . . Merry Christmas, Hock!"

It was Heidi leaning out from a sunlit gap between two small
boulders just below the lip of the parking lot where I had entered
into the jungle. I could see her head and shoulders only, and the
hanky she waved. And I realized that she had found shelter in
the spot where Buddy-O, as a boy, had fashioned himself the

escape tunnel under the trapdoor of the old shed behind Blind Mary's house.

I moved sideways to a spot where I could get a better look at Heidi and to where she could hear me easily. And there I stood on a flat ledge that protruded from the face of the ravine bank, about six feet below the parking lot.

"How are you, darling?" I asked her.

She only smiled at me, then finally she said, "It's been snowing, you know."

"I know that, Heidi."

"Isn't snow lovely?"

"Yes, it is," I said. "Are you warm enough?"

She adjusted something on her head, and I saw it was earphones to a Walkman radio. She turned her face into the last shimmer of a dulling sun, breathed in the darkening light, and then looked back out at me.

"What?"

I said again, "Are you warm enough, Heidi?" If only she could climb up and down the face of the ravine, I thought, clear down to some shelter and under the watch of the king of the jungle. But not with her legs.

Heidi was thinking about her answer, was about to say something, and then there was a shuffling noise somewhere in back of her where I couldn't see. The sound distracted her, she glanced over her shoulder. And when she turned back toward me I saw worry in her mottled, uneven face; then the worry drained away and was replaced by the idiot-serene expression worn by so many homeless women I see.

"Have you got coffee for me?" she said. "Cream and sugar?"

"I could get you some, all you want. Why don't you come with me and we'll get coffee?"

She smiled. "Oh, thank you, Hock, but no. I'm leaving here soon. . . . Never you mind about me, I'm going to be all right. It's been snowing, you know. Isn't that lovely?"

I heard the shuffling behind her again. And Heidi heard it, too, but did not move this time. She only waved her handkerchief and smiled and then slowly leaned back into the cut between the rocks, and I heard her say, "Merry Christmas."

I climbed the rest of the way up, to the opening in the fence around the back end of the parking lot. And then I walked along the fence toward a smaller opening—little more than a space between the fence bottom and a crumbling bit of asphalt paving where Heidi must have slipped through by rolling sideways and then dropping a few feet down into the cleft of rocks.

She sat listening to her radio. She knew I was standing overhead, but she did not care to speak to me anymore, not about coffee or leaving where she was for someplace warm. Not about anything.

And so I walked home.

"I figured you'd be calling again. Damn me, I should have put some money on it. Like maybe I could have won another porterhouse off you, which you could offer me if you want I should help you out again, Hock."

I told Aiello that I now owed him two dinners at The Palm.

"Well, okey-dokey, then," he said. "So just tell me what you need to know this time around."

I heard him light a cigar on his end of the telephone line, and I could taste the cigar he had given me when the two of us stood talking over Buddy-O's body in the building right across from mine, which in fact I was looking at right now while I was standing in my window with a double of Johnnie Walker red rolling around in a nice big glass full of ice.

"This call is unofficial, okay, Aiello?"

"Sure. But the steaks—?"

"That's official. I just have to ask you something about the two homicides you caught."

"Devlin, and then Griffiths in your bathtub."

"Yes. Both of them stark naked."

"Yeah, which is why Sex Crimes gets the word first on account of what I told you's policy nowadays about moving in quick on anything that looks like maybe it's, you know, fag bashing."

"Now, with Buddy-O—Devlin—it looked like he just came out from the shower, which is why he wasn't dressed."

"That's the way it plays, Hock. He's only wearing a towel, we checked out the plumbing and we find how he ain't been corn-holed or nothing. So?"

"So you kicked it to the PDU."

"Correct."

"What about the clothes he might have laid out to wear?"

"That's the funny thing, there weren't no clothes laid out, and there it was right in the afternoon and Devlin looks like he's getting dolled up and smelling good to go meet somebody—"

"Which would be me. He was supposed to be telling me something, and we were supposed to have a drink together."

"Yeah, so I guess that'd be it. Anyhow, there wasn't nothing laid out like he'd wear for a meeting—no jacket, no trousers, no shirt and tie."

"Did you check the closets?"

"As I recall, we done that. But that's part of the report we kicked, so if you want the details, you're going to have to find that out from the PDU, Hock."

"Okay. Now let me talk about Griffiths. The night I find him dead in my bathtub, it was right after you telephoned to say he'd been making inquiries about me since it happens I'm one of his tenants—"

"No kiddin', Hock?"

"Yeah. Anyhow, you said something, too, about how Buddy-O had 'a certain message' for me, and then how Griffiths told you *he* was trying to get hold of me himself?"

"Sure, I remember."

"He didn't say what the certain message was?"

"No, Hock, he sure didn't. And don't be thinking I didn't ask him. Which I did. But Griffiths says to me, 'Well, let me deal with Detective Hockaday direct if you don't freaking mind.'"

"That sounds like him."

"It ought to, it's his exact words." Aiello coughed and then said, "Say, wait a second here—if old Howie went and turned up in your damn *bathtub*, then was he wearing his clothes or what?"

"He wasn't."

"Well, where was the clothes?"

"I don't remember seeing them around in my apartment," I said.

"Well, shoot, Hock, he sure as hell didn't walk up there to your place in his damn birthday suit on a cold night, now, did he?"

"Not very likely."

"I suppose you're pretty sure it ain't some faggoty thing going on in your apartment? Nothing personal, Hock."

"I'm sure."

"So, what the hell—?"

"Good question."

And then I told Aiello it was helpful just to have another cop with good instincts to talk to, and we set up a couple of tentative dates for dinners at The Palm. If I could string out the Father Love assignment long enough, I would put in for the Aiello expenses and Inspector Neglio could not complain and I would stroke Aiello pretty well with no wear and tear on my own wallet.

Then I telephoned the detective unit and spoke to Lieutenant Russ Templeton, who was in charge of the afternoon shift. Templeton was good enough to look up particulars in the PDU "unusuals" file, and he confirmed both my suspicions about both of the precinct's fresh homicides.

"Well, in the case of your Mr. Devlin," Templeton said, "we show that nothing's missing from his place, apparently, except whatever clothes he had in a couple of different closets and some dresser drawers. Well, a couple pair of socks was left, but that's it. Every other stitch was swiped.

"Then with your Mr. Griffiths, we find the only thing that's dressing him is an ice pick. We don't find any clothes that'd fit him anyplace else on the premises—which is your premises, I see here, Hock. You check your own wardrobe there lately?"

I told him I did not have much that would interest anybody out stealing clothes. And I thanked him for the favor.

It was now six o'clock minus a couple of minutes. I thought back over the very long hours of the day, clear back to when it started in the standstill dark of the early morning when I woke up in bed with a bandage covering the crack on my head and Mona Morgan all sobered up and looking swell sitting there by my bed while an old geezer of an off-the-books doctor was poking through my liquor supply; then a long and pleasurable lie-down with Mona, followed by an impossible dream of our spending a good and uncomplicated kind of life that never existed for anybody; then the call to the Flanders Bar to come meet Lionel, then to discover how the Holy Redeemer was the king of the jungle besides and how much he had to teach me about the literal underworld; then another of my run-ins with Heidi the bag lady. . . .

And it was not over yet, this long, long day. As I would discover more darkly into the night, it was not over by a long shot.

I stepped to the sideboard and poured myself another red. Then I telephoned an East Side law office to see if the place was maybe still open for business, and if a certain associate was maybe still at his desk. Which it was, and which he was.

From the doorway to his thirty-fifth-floor corner office in one of those grim granite boxes on Third Avenue with wraparound windows that do not open and are tinted black and look like silos wearing sunglasses, a plump secretary wrung her hands and squawked an apology to her boss for my intrusion.

"Jeez," she said, "I'm awful sorry, sir. But he come in here flashing a badge and all, and I didn't believe he was an actual police officer, though, from the way . . . well, you can see how he's *dressed*. . . . And well, he just wouldn't wait or nothing for me to check with you, he just barged—"

The boss waved her off, and she turned in midsentence and gave me a knife stab of a look. And she bustled on by me in a cloud of rosy-smelling perfume, and I noticed how she looked like a bag full of doorknobs from the back.

When she had left and closed the door, I said to her boss, "You're looking well, Junior."

"The name is Waterman—Mr. Waterman. And when you wish to see me, please call up my office and book an appointment." He spoke in a get-lost kind of tone I have heard before, and he looked at me over a pair of silvery half-frame reading glasses with a get-lost kind of expression I have seen before.

And so I just stood there silently looking at him and waiting for him to crumple, the way I have done it many times before. Good old Tommy Neglio had taught me this particular detective's trick. It never fails.

"You want your ears to work a hundred percent, Hock, then learn to keep your mouth shut. Suppose you want to sweat some perp. . . . Believe me, just stare at him and keep quiet. Just look at him like he was a pair of shoes you might want to buy. No human being in the world can take this. Being human, they'll right away blabber what you need to hear, whether they mean to or not . . ."

So there I stood, looking at Junior like he was an interesting pair of shoes.

He had his long manicured fingers spread out in tents on his desk to support him as he leaned forward slightly at the waist and glared back at me through his half-frames. He wore an English custom shirt with bold blue stripings and a spread collar and French cuffs linked with gold braid. The tie was solid maroon and looked to be cut from raw silk. A navy-blue cashmere blazer lay draped over the back of a side chair.

"I don't much care for your style, Detective Hockaday."

Naturally, I gave him no response. Instead, I began walking around his office like I was looking for something.

I walked along a wall full of the standard red leather legal texts and precedents and ran my fingers along the bindings. And then I walked over to a grouping of oxblood leather club chairs circled around a low table so anybody sitting there could look south on Third Avenue, clear down to the Williamsburg Bridge from Delancey Street to Brooklyn. The table had a few chunky glass ashtrays on it that were empty, some yellow legal pads that were blank and a big square marble vase in the center full of flowers that were dried.

The place was very full of potted date palms, set in little clusters. And in with the palm clusters were specimens of Waterman's collection of two-foot-high leather-bound animals—rhinoceroses, hippopotami, bulldogs, alligators, a few snakes, bears, lions. I have often seen such animals, but in two places only: law offices and expensive Madison Avenue haberdasheries favored by expensive lawyers.

"Do you hear what I'm saying?" I heard Waterman saying.

I didn't say anything. I just looked at him some more, moved a little closer to where he stood behind his desk. I concentrated my eyes on a vein in the middle of Waterman's forehead that started twitching.

And then I decided to give him a break, so I asked, "How's your old man doing, Junior?"

Now Junior was not talking. He turned to the credenza behind the desk and took a cigarette out of a silver box and lit it. There wasn't anything else on the credenza except the newspapers and some neatly stacked correspondence.

When he turned back to me he was blowing blue-gray smoke out of both sides of his mouth, like a dragon. His forehead vein twitched, and he said, "That's what you came *here* to find out?"

Naturally, I did not answer him.

So Junior said, "I was up at the hospital this afternoon . . . there's no change, he's still in the coma."

"Would you mind if I used your telephone?" I asked.

"What for?"

I picked up the receiver from a telephone console unit and said, "Do I dial nine first or what?"

"Who are you calling?"

I started dialing, and about halfway through the number I said, "What do you think would happen if I rang up Harlem Hospital and asked the police uniform guard up there outside Father Love's room if you were up there to see him today?"

"What?"

"Didn't you hear me?"

I stopped dialing when I had only one more number to go. And I looked at him.

"I don't have to sit here and take any—"

I said, "That's correct, you don't. You don't have to answer any question I might want to ask right now, or tomorrow or the next day. And you have the legal right to tell me to go to hell, and you can call out your building security guys if you want, too, and have me forcibly evicted. Is that what you want to do, Counselor?"

"I—"

"But you would really then get my curiosity very aroused, and then I would naturally want to formally interrogate you. Of course, I know I have to advise you about your right to have an attorney present during all questioning. Isn't that right, Counselor?"

"Look here, I'm not trying to hide anything."

"Oh, you're not? Did I suggest you were hiding anything?"

"No, but—"

I hung up the receiver. "I think all that I did was suggest that right here in front of you I should pick up the phone and dial Harlem Hospital to see if you were, in fact, where you told me you were this afternoon."

Waterman sat down in his chair, and the stripings of his shirt seemed a little less bold. "Okay, I wasn't up at the hospital today, so what? I only just said that, without thinking. . . . It seems to me that's what you'd want to hear. Only I *do* know his condition, since I did actually telephone—and there's no change, like I said, and if you want, you can check whether I called or not—"

"What about the other day when you phoned me at my place and said you were calling from the hospital?"

Waterman's smooth brown face went ashy, and he said, "Actually I wasn't calling from the hospital, I was calling from right here at this desk. You want to call that a lie, that's okay. What does it mean, anyhow?"

"I don't know, Junior, what?"

Junior stubbed out his cigarette. "I don't have time for this," "and I don't even know what *this* is. . . . Are you accusing me of something here?"

He got silence from me.

"I suppose you suspected me since I was out watching your apartment that one night and since I followed you that Saturday downtown to Police Plaza?"

I picked up his blazer off the side chair and folded it carefully and set it on the end of his desk and sat down in the chair and asked him, "Tell me, Junior, what kind of law practice do you have here?"

"What?"

"Something wrong with you, Junior?"

"You want a drink?" he asked.

"Thanks, no," I said. "I'm going to ask you once more: What kind of law practice do you have here?"

"The boring kind. Torts, contracts, insurance. That sort of thing."

"You do pretty good, Junior?"

"What do you want, Hockaday?"

"You got some important place you have to go to tonight?"

"As a matter of fact, no. I just want to know what'll get you out of my office."

"Why don't you ask me again about a drink?"

"No, I don't think I will. I think I'll just ask you what the hell you want out of me here and now."

"Well," I said, "what about a client list."

Waterman pressed a button on his telephone console, and his secretary's disembodied voice said, "Sir?"

"Please get Detective Hockaday our standard client list."

And then he took his finger off the intercom button and asked me, "Why not—what could it hurt?"

"I don't know, Junior, what?"

TWENTY-FOUR

There is a certain recognizable pause at one point in the midevening in Hell's Kitchen Park, which is just up Tenth Avenue from my place. This is the time when day turns to night, no matter what the sun will have to say about the shift.

Lights in the handball court are automatically cut off, by means of a computer terminal somewhere in the city parks department, and the players waste little time in taking their leave; neighborhood dog walkers and various other strollers step livelier as they pass; in the warmer months, anybody sitting out on a nearby stoop is well advised to retreat indoors and turn up the radio or television volume in order to drown out the troubling sounds to come; skels awaken from muscatel dreams, rising from the park benches like wooden ghosts, and then they shuffle off into the outer reaches of the darkness—most of them down into the holes and huts and cold spaces between the rocks in the jungle, as I now have come to learn.

And then for a few odd moments out of the day's rhythm, Hell's Kitchen Park stands innocent and empty. As innocent and empty as all the claims by the politicians of New York and Albany and Washington that government and other such forces

240

of goodness are at war with what goes on in this park all through the night and into the dawn.

Dawn in Hell's Kitchen Park very often begins with somebody discovering a corpse that was recently somebody who could not just say no to the young men wearing hooded sweatshirts and unlaced high-tops who stand around chanting. *Set you straight, man? . . . I got splim right here. . . . You want Red? . . . Strawberry? . . . Got some China White, too, man. . . . Ecstasy! . . . Yo, crack it up, crack it up. . . . Yo, pass me by, you don't get high. . . .* Dawn in Hell's Kitchen Park is morning in America.

And every morning in America also brings the politicians' set speeches on the evils of dope and dope fiends, which are as likely to purify Hell's Kitchen Park as a Sunday sermon about fallen women is likely to make a congregation chaste. And while the speechmakers drone on, there are many others who figure on moving in on the pushers in the hooded sweatshirts and organizing them as middlemen in a vast national economy and who see the whole enterprise as an excellent means of capitalizing many more conventional sorts of business ventures. Which is commonly known as banking.

I am not the only cop around who could tell you from what he sees on the job that decadence would not stand a chance if it were not for moralists in high places. And I am certainly not the only cop around who mainly looks the other way since there does not seem to be much percentage otherwise.

But if the day should ever come when maybe the president of the United States—a guy who says he is so tough on the drug thing that he has dribbled his own presidential pee into a paper cup so that an official United States chemist can confirm that he is not, by God, a doper—would ask a regular cop like me how come drugs are as American as apple pie, I would have two things to say to him: if the people who own the government ever want to get serious about crimping the far-and-away biggest business in America, banks from one end of the country to the other will be turned inside out and upside down to track all the money laundering and tax evasion that is going on—which is precisely how the feds finally nailed Capone; and everybody in my neighborhood and in all the Hell's Kitchens everywhere else knows that a pipe full of crack costs less than a hot meal.

So now I mostly avoid the park. Mainly because it pains my middle-aged heart so much to see what is going on there now that I have finally come home to Hell's Kitchen. And also, I cannot stand listening to the language of the blank-faced punks hanging around the park drinking beer and smoking joints and waiting for something—anything—to happen to them. Not because their language is loud and vulgar, but because it is so imbecilic and so numbingly repetitive.

But tonight I felt I had to show up at Hell's Kitchen Park. That was where Mary Rooney and the tenants of my building who had all been so kindly asked to uproot themselves had planned the neighborhood rally to protest all the lousy things that Hell's Kitchen landlords were doing lately to make everything in the neighborhood all the more agonizing for those of us too senseless or too poor or too brave or too ornery and stubborn to go someplace else and live.

By the time I left Waterman's office on the East Side and reached the park, it was nearing eight o'clock and the time of the great recognizable pause in the usual cycle of the place. Only now, a full block away from the park and out of sight in a taxi moving across a side street with the windows rolled up tight and the cabbie's radio blasting salsa, I knew there was to be nothing at all *usual* about tonight in Hell's Kitchen Park.

The air was cold and clear, and from over on Tenth Avenue it was filled with the electronically amplified complaints of neighborhood tenants who one by one stepped up to a microphone rigged up on a makeshift stage to tell the whole city they were mad as hell and were not going to take it anymore. Ordinarily, the park would have been pitch dark because of the fact that the drug dealers keep the surrounding street lamps shot out of service. But tonight the park was blazing with the light of television kliegs set up so the rolling cameras could get everything right for the eleven o'clock newscasts.

There might have been five or six hundred people, which was a very large crowd to pack inside a small neighborhood park.

Which made everything all the more fevered and therefore newsworthy for the cameras.

Right when I turned into the park, there was an old guy up at the microphone with an angry red face and a big jutting chin like Mussolini and also the same kind of slashing right hand. He was winding up the outrageous story of what was going on in the building where he lived, which turned out was right next door to mine and which turned out was also managed by Empire Properties in the person of the late Howie Griffiths.

"So that's how it started with us," the old guy was hollering. "First no water, then no heat, then no lights in the hallways, then he fires the super. . . . Next thing you know, the landlord sends us over a whole bunch of whores to take over the three rooms in the back of the second floor, which brings us the plague of stinking-drunk johns all hours of the day and night. . . ."

The old guy slashed the air and pinched his nose with his thick fingers and went on, "And they're slamming and banging up down, up down the stairs, and then they start pounding on anybody's door at all—they must be crazy, these stinking johns, they must think all the women in the house are whores like the landlord's whores! And maybe you think this is some funny thing we got the whores and the johns screwing up the house— but I tell you, we all are honest people and we ain't so strong no more at our age, and we are so very frightened!"

A lot of the men in the crowd started whistling and shouting at this, and all the women cheered on the angry old Mussolini look-alike. And then strictly out of habit, I looked around the edges of the crowd, and sure enough I spotted a dipper working leather up out of back pockets and out of handbags.

So I started clapping my hands, too, and cheering and moving slowly sideways over to where the dipper was working his trade with a good right hand. Not the fastest I have ever seen, but good. When I was near enough to him, I bumped my shoulder against his right when he had his mitt full of somebody's pocketbook and was pulling currency out of it. Everything spilled down to the ground.

"Watch it, pal," he hissed at me.

I just stared at him and the money he was holding in his hand,

and I said, "Say, brother, can you spare any of that for me? Times are hard, you know."

"Fuck off and get a job, creep."

And then he turned to move away from me. Which was when I clamped a hand on the back of his neck and persuaded him to face me again so that he could see the gold shield on the chain around my neck as I pulled it up over my collar.

Then when I let go of the shield, I reached down when he was not looking and took hold of his good right hand, and specifically his middle finger. Which I bent backward until I heard a light popping sound, which I was able to hear even in the tumult of Mary Rooney's protest rally since I know just what to listen for when I am forced to do this. Also, there was the look of considerable discomfort in the eyes of the uncharitable dipper.

"Oh, holy Jesus, it's police brutality!" he hissed again.

"No, not at all," I said. "Police brutality would be if I was to reveal you to a few of the bigger guys in this angry crowd we have here around us and let them decide what to do about you."

He seemed to shrink as he hissed at me. I kept pressing back his very loose middle finger, yanking it forward and then pressing it back again.

"Oh, holy shit—!"

"So what I am doing here is saving your life. And what I would like you to do for me, since you owe me your life, is to bend down and pick up the pocketbook you just had and give it back."

"What the holy hell—?"

"Don't debate me, or next it's your thumb, pal, which I can tell you is even worse than what you're going through now."

Wheezing, he bent down and retrieved the pocketbook when I let go of his finger. And then he tapped a lady on the back and said, "Did you drop this, ma'am?" And she took her pocketbook and clasped it to her chest gratefully, and smiled at the man with the loose finger sweetly, and shot me a dirty look.

And then the dipper loped away, and I watched him and felt a little guilty about putting a man out of work so close to the holidays.

Meanwhile, there was a young woman with red hair and a red

coat up on the stage, and she was yelling about what her landlord did to her building, which was down Ninth Avenue and up a few blocks from the Ebb Tide and which was a place that not surprisingly was managed by Empire Properties.

"This fat pink guy from the landlord—this Griffiths guy we've been hearing so much about—he sent around a carpenter maybe a couple of months back," the young red-haired woman said.

"Only the carpenter looked funny, not like a carpenter. And I realized that the only tool he had on him was this big hammer. He didn't even have a toolbox, this guy.

"So when I step out from my door because I see him hammering away on the steps out in the hallway, I ask him what he thinks he's doing. He looks up at me and says, 'Lady, the landlord sent me to fix the loose steps.' I tell this character with the hammer that we don't have any loose steps and he starts snarling at me and he gets up and starts coming up the stairs and he says, 'Lady, you wouldn't want a loose goddamn head now, would you, sweet thing?'"

The crowd roared, and it sounded very ugly and very violent, and the young red-haired woman continued, and I saw that Mary Rooney was standing down behind the stage with some note cards in her hand. And Mary Rooney was hopping from one foot to the next, half to keep warm and half out of excitement.

"Well, I ran back into my apartment and rang up the 911 police emergency number and said there was a guy with a weapon coming after me. . . . So, it took about twenty minutes, of course, before the cops came. . . ."

And the crowd made a deep nasty sound at this.

"During which time, the so-called carpenter kept hammering down in the stairwell someplace. And when the cops finally came, one of the officers had a talk with the guy and the other one came up the stairs to my apartment.

"And it turned out, of course, that Griffiths had in fact sent over this guy with the hammer for God knows what reason and the guy lied and said he didn't threaten me at all and the cops said there was really nothing they could do. . . .

"Well, a couple of weeks later the stairwell and the hallways stank so bad we all thought there were all kinds of dead rats in the walls . . . and then finally I made the obvious connection, and I told my neighbor's husband what I thought and he rips up the stairs where the so-called carpenter from the landlord was making his so-called repairs and he finds paper bags full of rotten anchovies.

"So—neighbors and friends—what do you think of *this* fine business practice by Empire Properties and our dear landlord, whoever the hell he might be. And I hope he's watching now!"

And the young red-haired woman held up a rude finger for the TV cameras to see. And the crowd was very loud and very approving of her contempt.

And I noticed a couple of red flashing lights reflecting on a stretch of steel fence. I turned around to see a couple of squad cars from the Midtown-North precinct pull up near to the park entrance and officers inside the cars getting a look at us all. Then it occurred to me that this was our only police presence, so I walked up to one of the units and identified myself to the uniforms inside and asked if there happened to be an active rally permit for the demonstration.

Which there was not. Apparently, Mary Rooney had not troubled herself about this small detail, which might conceivably mean legal trouble for her and anybody else who got up on the stage to incite the crowd. On the other hand, it happened also to be very illegal to peddle drugs in the park, yet it seemed that such a sin was still stalking this end of Gotham. Even so, I thought it a good idea to see about talking Mary Rooney into calling a halt to the proceedings and letting the TV news carry the ball the rest of the way.

I shouldered my way through the crowd, slowly up toward the stage in hopes of catching Mary Rooney before she stepped up to the microphone herself to let fly. But I was too late.

There she stood, the tiny old lady who lived down below me and wrote letters to dead relatives on the other side and who seemed to be fading off to the company of those relatives herself. And now her eyes danced brightly in the kliegs, and she was so alive in this cause that was so much bigger than herself, so full of energy she freely borrowed from the crowd down around her.

She was also mad as hell and brandished a ball bat to illustrate this. And then here and there in the crowd there were others with ball bats I had not seen before. They drummed the bats on the ground as Mary began speaking, drummed their support and their unspoken threat to demonstrate a fool's courage.

"Friends!" Mary Rooney shouted into the microphone. "Neighbors across all New York!"

And the crowd was deafening now.

"Friends, let an old lady tell you what we're up against tonight!" She glanced at note cards in her free hand, the one that did not hold her ball bat. "It's so much more than our little apartments, it's so much more than even our neighborhood here. . . .

"We are all up against the end of the American dream, I tell you true! Yes, the times have changed that much. In America today, you can work hard and live decent and it all gets you where?"

And somebody in the crowd shouted up, "Nowhere!" And then the crowd picked up the response and started chanting, "Nowhere, nowhere, nowhere." And those with ball bats beat the ground in a ferocious tattoo.

"And it's evil times, too, it is! When you can no longer make the American dream work, my friends—they're tellin' you it's *your* fault!"

The ball bats pounded, people chanted, "Nowhere, nowhere, nowhere, nowhere . . ."

And Mary Rooney, her voice cracking in the frigid air, shouted, "Look around you, my friends! It's not just your apartments that're bein' taken away from you . . . it's all of the old neighborhood, too! And not because you good men and women haven't been doin' the decent, responsible job—a day's work for a day's pay—but because of something you and me cannot see; because of some financial decision that's maybe made halfway round the world that maybe'll nudge up the profit margins a point or two, if only you'll just please kindly drop dead or out of the way of this lovely progress, eh?"

The ball bats were sounding increasingly dangerous, and now some of the television cameras were cutting away from Mary in search of a bit of blurring riot weapons. I looked back over my shoulder and saw more squad cars pulling up at the park entrance and felt something sour in my stomach.

"And who profits the very most from all this human wreckage, my friends? Eh? It's the bastard landlords, is who! And I'm sayin' tonight . . ."

Mary Rooney waved her ball bat up over her old gray head, and everybody's mouth in the crowd was hollering different things, all of them angry and mindless and perfectly understandable even so.

"I'm sayin' they ain't lords of the land—"

And of course, I knew what would come next and what would touch off the fuse. And also I knew there was not one damn thing I could do about it.

"They're the scum of the earth!"

The fuse was lit, the crowd began a whole new and much more powerful chant. "*Scum-of-the-earth, scum-of-the-earth, scumof-theearth . . . scum . . . scum . . . scum!*"

"Now then, friends and neighbors," Mary shouted, her voice nearly gone now. She waited for the crowd to quiet some. "If you want to do somethin' about all this for once in your lives—then I'm tellin' you, follow me!"

I was shoved from behind by people shoved from behind themselves, by all the other people suddenly bobbing in a tidal crowd. And then, surging through this crowd from the side entrance of the park was a line of men with ball bats of their own—men who were clearly not a part of the original crowd and surely no partisans of Mary Rooney. And they were shouting something I could not make out and clubbing people as they worked their way toward Mary at the microphone. Women shrieked.

And Mary shouted her last into the microphone: "Follow me, friends, and let's march up to Empire Properties and do what cries out for doin' in the sweet name of God and justice!"

The cops were moving in now from the main entrance, and the goons with ball bats were pressing closer from the side entrance, clubbing down anyone in their way, and Mary Rooney's partisans with *their* ball bats looked to me to be losing heart.

And Mary Rooney herself stood up there on the makeshift stage, merely a wide board stretched out between two steel oil drums, and waved her own club overhead, and her eyes danced in the television lights.

And I heard the sound of a shot, then another one. More shrieking, more people felled by clubs.

And Mary shouting, "Scum of the earth!" into a dead microphone.

Then the crack of one final shot.

And screams. And Mary Rooney falling from the stage. Her frail body fluttered through the television lights and landed soundlessly on the ground.

I bulled my way past half a dozen men, then fifteen to twenty television ghouls. And I knelt over Mary Rooney, who lay on her side. I turned her body so she could see me and slipped a hand beneath her head. Her upper chest was covered in red wetness, and there was a look on her face that made me think—right there and then, in the middle of the violence and panic—of that dusty crowd of photographs in the plastic Woolworth frames on the top of the fireplace mantel in her apartment, pictures of all the fair-haired, light-eyed, solid-legged Rooneys down through the generations.

She blinked when she saw me, and I might have thought she smiled. She groaned, almost pleasantly.

Then before she was no more, Mary Rooney said, "And didn't I promise you I'd pull off a donnybrook, Hock? Oh Crikey, but wasn't it a lovely wee revolution?"

TWENTY-FIVE

But did it mean anything, Mary Rooney's lovely revolution?

I asked myself this question as the crowd circled around me and murmured and I held Mary's head and felt how cold it had become, and she moved her lips into a smirk even as she was dead. And I asked it again when the EMS unit plowed through the crowd and crewmen jumped out the back of the ambulance with a gurney, and one of them covered her face and body with a brown blanket.

The heart had been cut out of the mob then, and the five or six hundred neighborhood tenants began gradually to disperse, some with bruises on their heads and shoulders and hands and blood streaming from ears and noses and split lips. People walked on legs gone wobbly with the fear that quickly replaces cheap courage, and as they moved from the park they looked about for more bodies aground, but there was only Mary's own. Shots had been fired and everyone had heard them, the same as I had; but only Mary was a casualty of her revolution.

And so did it mean anything?

There were no arrests that could be made, not for any specific acts of violence. Ball bats littered the ground, but none were held in anyone's hands; there were no men fleeing, no men who looked in the least out of place. And in Hell's Kitchen Park, where the custom in recent years has been to keep one's eyes to oneself, nobody had seen anything in the way of a club landing across a head or a gun barrel raised in the air.

Hours later, at the precinct station house, patrol cops questioned some of the neighbors of my very own building and some from the nearby houses managed by the Empire Properties Real Estate Company. The way it played was, Mary Rooney had worked feverishly to turn out a crowd of abused tenants; she had made certain that someone on the other end of the telephone at Empire Properties knew of the rally and knew there would television news reporters to cover the event just in case an old lady managed to inspire a mob to trash the real estate office.

And Empire Properties, it would clearly appear, called out a gang of its free-lance goons to go put down Mary Rooney's mob before it had the chance to move from the convenient confines of the park.

Knowing what I did of Howie Griffiths' idea of hired help appropriate for the firm, I had little doubt that Empire Properties had no better professional ethics and that almost anybody in the office could keep the supply of goons and all other manner of objectionable soldiering on for the betterment of the bottom line.

Could any of this be confirmed? And if so, did it matter? And who would ever pay for the tragedy of Mary Rooney's righteous riot besides Mary herself?

Did it mean anything?

Meanwhile, now that the party was over and the park was back to normal, the young men in hooded sweatshirts and high-tops were back on their posts. . . . *Yo, crack it up, crack it up.* . . . *Yo, pass me by, you don't get high.* . . .

I do not remember how it was that I traveled from the station house up to La Club Pigalle. Maybe I hitched a ride with a uniform patrol unit, maybe I flagged a taxi. Maybe I walked since I could not bring myself to go home. Maybe I stopped for a few jars at the Ebb Tide.

All I knew was that it was half-past midnight and I was sitting at a table along the sidelines of the dance floor. And there was a candle in a glass bowl, and I had a double of Johnnie Walker red in front of me, and there were guys moving slowly and clumsily across the floor to the music, and there were "girls" talking baby-doll talk.

The sad little band up near the runway stage was doing a not half-bad job accompanying Labeija, in her blue spot, dressed all in black and silver and singing a good poky rendition of "Easy Living," her voice soft and thick through the smoke.

Girls were settling their partners at the tables around the floor or back along the wall in the banquettes. Drinks flowed. I had another myself. And everybody smiled. And a parade of strippers started up and the room was jolly, and Mona Morgan waited in her dressing room in her painted toes, and I hoped she was not drinking.

And Labeija joined me at my table. She said, "How's the patient?" I rubbed the back of my head. The bandage had come off somewhere along the line, and I felt bare skin where the doctor had clipped me.

I said, "Oh, you mean . . . That's small stuff now."

"How in hell did it happen, though?" Labeija asked.

"I was hoping you'd tell me."

Labeija took a breath and said, "All I know is that Mona was plastered—she sometimes gets plastered, I'm sorry to say—and then anyhow, I hear her yelling down the stairway that you was mugged up by the dressing rooms. . . ."

"Anything like this ever happen here before?"

"Nothing like this, never!"

"Okay. But the fact is, somebody was up there in the shadows and caught me one pretty good. Now the question is, did he come back down the same way I went up? Or is there some other access?"

"There's a door to the fire escape that's up there according to the law. Anybody from inside the club could get through that door, then drop down to the street in back."

"What about coming up from the back street?"

Labeija thought about that for a second. "From the street, I *suppose* somebody could get up to the fire escape platform, if he was a good climber. But somebody would have to open the door for him from the inside. See, the way it works is there's only the inside bar and it's just not possible to get through it from the outside—unless you have dynamite, which I guess we'd have noticed, or unless you have somebody in here who knows to open the door for you."

And of course, I remembered the very same kind of a door up at the Healing Stream Deliverance Temple. The door from the basement, at the top of a stair, leading to the side alleyway and barred only from the inside.

I asked Labeija, "And who gets up the stairway to those dressing rooms where all your girls are?"

"Well, you can see we don't have a guard or anything. But we never really needed one, Hock. We don't have rough types here, and the girls and me and the barmen, we all keep a good eye out on the stairway."

So that was about as far as I would get on the subject. So I changed it and asked, "You say that Mona gets drunk from time to time?"

"Well, yeah . . . it's a worry. I got worries with every girl."

Labeija did not elaborate on this, except to say, "You know, Hock, I don't go trying to figure out anybody else's regrets since I never got a handle on my own. The way I see it here, either Mona tells you what's on her own mind or you never know. Anything from anybody else, that's just useless and sloppy talk."

So I shut my mouth and put back my drink. Labeija did not like the way I did it and said it almost looked to her like I was drinking to hurt myself and asked if I cared to say what was on my own mind.

I told her what had happened in Hell's Kitchen Park and some of what happened when I had the tour of the jungle.

And Labeija said, "This city is being dragged into the gutter by people wearing ermine."

"That one I have to tell to a friend of mine in the jungle," I said, slurring the words.

"You want to lie down, Hock?"

"Yeah, but I'm not too sure about the getting-up part afterward."

"I got a couch in the office and you're welcome to it."

Which is the last thing I heard her say before I staggered across the Pigalle floor, past the bar and up to the front where Labeija kept her cluttered office. I lay down and was out in seconds.

"Hock, you awake?"

I looked up and saw cream-colored silk pleats, then light in a window with heavy drapes drawn aside to let in the morning and walls that were glazed and red, and an oval mirror on the wall at the end of the bed. Not a couch, but a bed.

And there was Mona, in a big terry-cloth robe and her hair wet from showering. She had been at her closet and saw me stirring.

"How—?"

"I don't know that I've ever seen a human being so completely wiped out," Mona said. "What a job of it I had getting you all the way up here. I had to pay the cabbie twenty just to give me a hand walking you upstairs. . . . Do you remember any of that, Hock?"

I shook my head no.

"The driver thought you were dead drunk, but I didn't say anything since I figured he'd never understand what you're up against. . . . Labeija told me what happened last night, and she told me something about your going down into those old railroad tracks or whatever they—"

"What time is it?"

"Noon. Would you like coffee?"

"Oh, please, yes."

Mona left the bedroom. I got up from the bed and looked around for my clothes, which I finally discovered were neatly laid in a big chair in the farthest end of the bedroom back around the side of a dresser so they were out of sight. I could not blame her for that.

I was stepping into my pants when she got back with the coffee, and she said, "What's your big hurry, lover?"

"Hurry? I don't know if I'm in a hurry, I don't know what I'm in. . . ."

"Here's the morning news line, Hock. Maybe that'll give you a clue. Father Love—no change in condition up at Harlem Hospital, still in the coma. Mary Rooney—the TV's got her labeled a crazy lady-slash-tenant activist who was shot to death by some unknown assailant in what they call in TV talk your 'tragic mishap.' The cop PR line is open investigation on Mary Rooney and no new clues in the Father Love thing. So, it looks like you've got a desk day stretched out in front of you where you try thinking inside out on all the little clues you've already got to worry about, but not hurry about."

"Very efficient."

"Well, somebody told me once that a cop wants to know the news the first thing when he wakes up."

"Who told you that?"

"Girlfriend of mine. She used to be a tin wife."

"Oh, so you know the phrase?"

"The subject's been interesting to me lately. So I've been hearing things. You know. Girl-talk things."

"Being a tin wife, it's not a lot of laughs."

And then I realized, since Mona was laughing and pointing at me, that I was standing with one pant leg on and no shirt and no underwear and my hair pasted all over the place.

"Maybe I ought to take a shower."

"And maybe you should get hold of yourself with this coffee." Mona gave it to me.

She looked on the top of the dresser while I sipped the coffee. And then she picked up the paper that Sam Waterman had given me.

"What's this, Hock? It was sticking out from the side of your pocket, and I thought it might be something important."

"Maybe, maybe not. That's the client list of a law firm where Father Love has got a son working as an associate attorney. You know, I told you about Junior."

"Yeah . . . the son," she said. And then she looked out the window for a moment. She still held the paper in her hand, and now she studied it. "These names here—I never heard of these outfits, and you'd never know what kind of business they're talking about.

"I mean, Hock, what is this 'Forty-four Associates, Inc.,' or the 'Fifty-second Street Group' or the 'Greentree Club' or . . . Oh, none of it *means* anything to me."

"What I'm going to do is give it to Legal Division to run down the identities in the assumed-name registrations with the city, except that sometimes you have assumed names maybe up in Albany or even Boston or down in Philly. . . . Maybe in a week, if I'm lucky, I'll get some answers.

"These are speculators who want to be shy," I explained, "and so they think up these innocuous names to paper over some conflict of interest or another, the conflicts being totally immoral but totally legal. Which is very choice meat for many lawyers."

"You're saying that Father Love's kid represents dummy corporations?" Mona asked.

"Dummies, yeah."

"Hock, I know how I can get this information for you real fast—lots faster than your department guys can get it. Really, I mean that." She clasped her hands together, crumpling the client list. And then she smoothed it out and put it back on the dresser.

"I believe you," I said.

"Once, I had this very heavy admirer, a very big financial guy. . . . Oh, don't worry, we're nothing anymore. I can call him up, he'll do anything for me, and the guy really knows his way—"

"Okay, go knock yourself out, kid. You want to save the poor taxpayer a couple of dollars, that's all right by me since I'm one of the people wasting the taxes a lot of the time."

"Hock—don't you realize, we are talking the *money trail* here?"

She said this in a red-faced excited way that told me Mona Morgan might be even savvier than I already knew her to be.

I said to her, "There's all kinds of trails, kid."

Then I showered and dressed and kissed Mona so-long for the day, and she made me promise to remember and give the club a call so I could leave her a message about how it looked for tonight. And I walked down the stairs and out the door and down the avenue toward my place, which was something I dreaded but which is where I had to go for some fresh clothes.

And my step was very ungainly as I went along because I had

this sense of responsibility to a woman all over again; and among other things, this can make a man who has been down that particular trail before shake like hell when he gets to thinking about it.

Once again, there I sat with Father Love's business cards set out in front of me on a table drawn up to my green chair. I had chili heating on the burner, and the radio was playing.

I read each of the cards three or four times, slowly. Then I said each of the biblical verses out loud, slowly:

"There is none righteous, no, not one. . . . The heart is deceitful above all things, and desperately wicked; who can know? . . . The fathers have eaten a sour grape, and the children's teeth are set on edge. . . . As a dog returneth to his vomit, so a fool returneth to his folly. . . . If a son shall ask bread of any of you that is a father, will ye give him a stone?"

And then I picked up the telephone on the stand next to me, and through the fog of the years, I dialed a number from the very heart of my boyhood memory.

A woman's voice answered and confirmed that I had remembered the number: "Holy Cross Church."

I said, "Ma'am, my name is Detective Neil Hockaday, I'm with the New York Police Department. . . . Actually, I was a choirboy there at the church many years ago. . . . Well, I've got to see one of the priests right away. It's a matter of life and death."

"Oh my," the receptionist said, "it's always that one or the other around here. Hold the phone a minute, will you?"

"Yes—"

And she was gone. In a minute or two, a man said, "Father Kelly here, how may I help you?"

"Father—Kelly? Cash-Box . . ."

And the priest began to laugh. "No, there's no relation," he said. "That was a long time ago, so I've heard from the old-timers in the parish. I'm Timothy Kelly, and I'm thirty-two years old. The other Father Kelly—Cash-Box Kelly—died about 1961, I think."

"I guess that would be about right," I said. "Look, Father, I'm very sorry, I—"

"Never mind, then. You're . . ."

"Detective Neil Hockaday. I need only a small piece of your time, right away if you don't mind. I happen to be only a few blocks away."

"Always happy to be of help . . . and to a former choirboy. Come right over, please."

Heidi was sitting on a standpipe outside a pharmacy on Ninth Avenue and West Forty-second. She watched me as I waited to cross the avenue.

"Coffee, dear?" I asked when I'd reached her side.

"Isn't that what I always have when you're around?" she said. "Why should today be any different?"

And so I ducked into the deli a few doors south and bought a cup and returned to her.

She pulled off the lid and sipped.

"Good. Cream and sugar, regular. You never forget."

"You're very welcome, Heidi."

And then a wild idea struck about a vacant apartment below my own and how I might help Heidi squat there for at least the winter, and if the landlord wanted to give me any trouble about it, then I would deal with that, too. The important thing seemed to be to make Mary Rooney's riot mean something.

"How would you like to live where I live, Heidi? It's warm there."

"What are you talking about, Hock?"

"There's an apartment that's open in my building. I could get you in there."

Heidi laughed a phlegmy laugh, and when her face bunched up, it looked as if laughter hurt her.

"Just how am I going to be paying rent on some proper apartment, Hock?"

"You wouldn't have to. You'd be a squatter."

"Oh no, so they could come throw me out into the cold after I'd become used to the warmth. No thank you, sir. I'll stick to what I know, if that's the case." She tugged her balding fur coat more tightly around her shoulders and sipped more coffee.

"Really . . . look, you'd be all right. I'd protect you—"

"I had men tell me that. No thank you, sir."

"Please—"

"I'll do nothing of the kind, and nothing else that leaves me beholden to a man for anything . . . even though I have made the exception in your case of accepting coffee."

Heidi had said none of this angrily. Her words were flat and unemotional, she only stated the facts to me as a sort of bare-bones outline and explanation of maybe some long-ago trauma involving a man. And what woman of any station had not known the same? There was nothing personal to it, except for the apparent fact that she was willing to trust me more than other male strangers.

Then her demeanor changed entirely, exactly when a light dusting of snow began to drop and wet the street. She smiled sweetly and spoke again.

"Hock, it's all academic anyway. As it happens . . . and don't you go telling anyone now, promise?"

"Yes, I promise."

"I've got myself a place!"

"You do—where?"

"Oh, that I cannot say, to no one."

"Will it be warm?"

"Oh yes, warm and lovely again, like I used to know. . . . Look, it's snowing . . ." She turned her face to the sky and let flakes fall on her hard skin. "Isn't it lovely?"

"It is, Heidi, it really is."

"You know, I wish I could tell you, Hock. I really do. But I can't, and I cannot tell you why. But just—don't you be worried about me. I've learned quite a piece here in the streets, and down in my little hole in the wall where you saw me the other day . . . when you ventured down into the jungle, you know."

"Yes, of course. I remember."

"I'll be warm, there's even a fireplace, I'm told . . . and I *do* thank you very much for the thought of helping me squat

someplace in your very own building, but you must understand
that's not for me."

"Okay."

"Just don't worry. I'll be warm. And . . . well, I shouldn't
say this, but I think I'm even going to be able to work again."

"Is that so?"

"Oh yes . . . maybe. We'll see."

"What kind of work do you do?" But of course, I knew she
would stop it there.

"Merry Christmas, Hock."

"Merry Christmas to you."

"I'll be seeing you, I hope."

"All right, then."

And I left her there with the coffee and headed around the
corner on Forty-second to Holy Cross.

Father Timothy Kelly was a slender-built man with blond hair
and a bushy blond mustache and a confident and forgiving face.
Women would call him handsome, men would regard him well,
as something like the ideal good-natured younger brother who
would always come home to family reunions at Thanksgiving
with a fine-looking girlfriend for everyone to meet and size up as
a potential in-law. Yet here he was a priest.

We shook hands and took our respective places on either side
of his modest desk in his narrow office with all four walls bare,
save for a sepia-tone photo of Pope John Paul. Father Kelly's
desk held everything in the office except for what was in the
wastepaper basket. There were all the day's newspapers, a
remarkably small Bible, a couple of spiral-bound notebooks, one
of which was opened to where he had been working in pencil.
And an old telephone of the type I remember from the 1950s.
And a sandwich in waxed paper.

There was no ashtray in sight, nor any decanter and glasses.
Not even sherry. The priesthood had changed.

The chair I sat in was a painted oak library chair, and it had
a sliver in it that was digging into my left thigh.

I reached into my coat pocket and handed Father Kelly the

cards with the death threats. He looked at them without
expression and said, "I've read of this, of course. What would
you like me to do?"

"Well, I thought there might be some connection to the verses,
Father—"

"Tim's fine with me. In fact, I'd much prefer it. Unless you
want to call me Cash-Box for old times' sake?"

"No, I'll call you Tim. They call me Hock."

"Okay, Hock. Now, a connection?"

He took one of the cards and looked at the verse reference and
opened up his Bible and leafed through the chapter until he
found it, in slightly abridged verbiage. And he read the context
verses around it.

He did the same with two more of the cards.

And then he said, "I don't get it. Now, I know from the
newspapers that these were dropped into the offering plates up at
this Harlem church, that they're meant as . . . threats against
the life of the pastor, this Father Love."

"Yes."

"But . . . well, let's try one thing more. Come with me, we'll
have to go to the library."

And when we got there, Tim pulled down a thick red book
and asked me, "Have you ever heard of the Concordia, Hock?"

"No. Should I?"

Tim waved a hand in the air and said, "No, not necessarily. It's
just a common reference that's used by biblical scholars and
school kids, maybe you used it back years ago and you don't even
remember."

He walked to a table and plopped the Concordia down, and
we sat. And Tim took one of the cards again and looked up the
first few words of the verse, then read off the cross-indexed
subject heading to me.

"Here's how it works, Hock. You take the first card, and the
verse begins with, 'There is none righteous . . .' So we look
that up and find it grouped under the biblical subject of
Imperfection.

"So now, hand me another card."

I gave him the one with the verse that began, "The fathers have eaten a sour grape . . ." And this turned up under the heading of Parent/Child. As did the verse that began with, "If a son . . ."

"All right," I said, "how about this beauty?" I gave Tim the card that had the verse beginning, "As a dog returneth to his vomit . . ."

"I can tell you that without even looking, but I'll check myself anyway," Tim said. He leafed some pages and said, "Right—that one's under Sin."

Finally, there was the verse, "There is none righteous . . ."

Tim found the answer. "We're back where we started, at Imperfection. So that's what—?"

I said, "Imperfect twice, Parent/Child twice, and one Sin."

"So now, you want a young priest's theory?"

"Sure," I said.

"I think that whoever selected this stuff went to the library somewhere and picked up a Concordia—it's in any reference department, whatever version of the Bible you care to read. Whoever wanted to threaten this Father Love of yours, he had a message; that's my theory. He wanted Love to know that someone out there knew he was a very serious sinner. About the parent and child thing . . . well, I don't know. Do you?"

"He's got a son," I said.

"Well then?"

"Well what?"

"Go after the son!"

"Do you watch a lot of television, Tim?"

"My share of it, I guess. . . ."

I stood up and thanked him for his time. And told him how he had been a very big help to me. Father Tim beamed.

Then I left him and headed slowly back to Forty-third and Tenth. I considered stopping over at the Ebb Tide, but then I remembered about the chili I left on the burner that I forgot to switch off. And this gave me visions of Mary Rooney's exploding Dinty Moore stew.

So I hurried along. But not so fast not to notice that Heidi had left her standpipe outside the pharmacy; not so fast not to notice how she had dropped something she might later miss. A headphone to a Walkman radio.

I picked it up and put it in my pocket, and trotted home.

TWENTY-SIX

The smell was familiar and strong. Somewhat smokier than usual, I thought. But still, a good and hearty scent and quite in keeping with the historical odors of the hallway outside my apartment.

I slipped the key into the lock, pushed open the door, and stepped unhesitatingly inside.

The sight and smell of my chili spitting and hissing and growling and bubbling up over the rim of the cooking pot, and then coagulating into rusted globs and great heaving crusted pools on the stove top . . . well, it was nearly enough to turn me into a salad eater.

I used paint thinner, a scraper, and Brillo pads to clean up as best I could. But nothing short of a fire was really ever going to make my kitchen right again. . . .

I thought of my mother's kitchen, and the way we were. And Uncle Liam from Dún Laoghaire coming to visit. Uncle Liam and my mother in the kitchen together, whispering things about my father. Uncle Liam with his sleeves rolled up in the kitchen, teaching my mother how to boil down thick pig's blood to make Irish black pudding for breakfast.

I considered the dietary staples of my involuntary bachelorhood: chili, eggs and bacon, takeout Chinese.

I remembered a day years ago, Judy and I at Jones Beach. I with my hard flat belly and Judy with her long slim legs. She came running at me on the beach and she leaped into the air and locked her legs around my waist and we kissed in the sun and the salt air, and we were young; and we made all those watching us envy us for what we had so plentifully that day. . . .

When I was through with the futility of cleaning, I poured myself a generous glass of red, and in order to get myself over and through it all I picked a Sinatra recording from my small collection and played this. Every cut had to do with memories and dreams and tears.

I sat on the couch under the window, where Judy had sat with her feet tucked up under her. Where I had looked at her knees.

The sun went down over the river. Another day closer to Christmas.

The telephone rang.

"Hock, I thought I might catch you in before I went on down. . . . What's it look like for tonight?"

I did not feel good about this, but I had to tell Mona, "Sorry, kid, I'm lousy for anybody tonight."

She did not say anything for a couple of seconds. And I figured she knew for herself how it is sometimes that you should keep the dark side of your personal moon exactly that.

"Sure, Hock. Tomorrow, then."

I had another generous drink. And then after I called for Chinese, I unplugged the telephone. And watched Fred MacMurray and Barbara Stanwyck and Edward G. Robinson in *Double Indemnity* on Channel Thirteen. And fell coldly to sleep.

Late in the morning I dressed in jeans and a Ragg sweater and went down over to Pete Pitsikoulis's All-Night Eats & World's Best Coffee. Wanda the waitress with the Santa Claus button on

her apron string came over and ran a wet cloth over the counter
space in front of me and tilted her head to the far end of the
counter and said, "Your lady friend's settin' over there in case
you didn't notice."

And there was Mona, her back to me. She was drinking cocoa.
And I don't know what it was, but something did not look right
about her.

So I went over and tapped her shoulder. She did not move, as
if she were unable to feel my touch. I tapped again and said her
name, and then, slowly, Mona turned to me. Her face was dry
and drawn. But I could see how she had been crying.

"Hiya, Hock." That was all for a while. Her arm lay resting on
a newspaper. "You get the morning news line?"

I had not, I told her.

Mona stood up and gathered her things and pushed the
newspaper into my hands. "I have to go now, Hock. I'm tired,
real, real tired. Call me sometime, later."

I looked at the cover of the *New York Post* and its big
block-lettered banner over Father Love's photograph: FATHER
LOVE DEAD.

The story inside did not have much to say beyond the fact that
Father Love had slipped over the line into death during the
night, and that the police had no new leads in what was now, of
course, a murder.

There were a couple of lines in the story that were quotes from
Roy Dumaine about how the great work of his mentor would be
carried on faithfully, and there were some other predictable sorts
of quotations from other preachers in town. But not a single
mention of Father Love's real name, nor any mention of survi-
vors.

I put down some money for Wanda, to cover whatever I might
have ordered in the way of a breakfast.

And then I left Pete's and walked east along Forty-second
Street nursing a growing hunch. At Grand Central, I took the
number 6 train down to the City Hall subway station.

For the balance of the day, I sifted through ledgers and card
files in the Vital Statistics Division of the New York City Clerk's
Office because the computers were "down."

* * *

By week's end, during which time I did not once manage to find Samuel Waterman, Jr., at home or on the job, the plans were announced for Father Love's gala funeral.

Also, I never did find what I was looking for at Vital Stats. However, I left a set of reference dates (approximates) and names (subject to aliases) with a young clerk called Buckman, who said he would do what he could, but that he was unable to promise miracles, what with a lot of downtime lately on the computers. I told him there was a day not so long ago when there were no computers to speak of and things seemed to clip right along. As I was telling him this, young Buckman looked at me the way you would look at a man with a large dent in his head trying his best to talk without drooling.

I called up Mona more than once that week, and she kept telling me how she was sick and did not want to be seen sick, and of course I knew what she meant by that. She did tell me, though, that she was on top of the business about running down young Sam Waterman's client list and that she would get to me just as soon as the results came in.

I thought about calling Judy out in Queens and felt lousy for having this instinct, which I could see plainly was nothing but a selfish fear of the unknown. I managed to think better of acting on the urge.

And it occurred to me, too, that during this personal and professional limbo that there was one glaringly strange thing. Something that was not happening.

There I was with one murder officially on my head and three of them by my personal count, and the connections were looking stronger and stronger. And yet at the very same time it still seemed to add up to nothing.

And Neglio never telephoned me.

His staff down at Police Plaza said they did not know when to expect him back from Bimini and that so far as anybody knew, I was still on the delicate assignment of the Father Love case and that I was supposed to conduct my investigation as I saw fit.

*   *   *

The first public viewing of the remains of the Most Reverend Father Love took place on Saturday afternoon in the grand marble lobby of the Holy Stream Deliverance Temple of Harlem. It was plenty big enough to accommodate the tens of thousands of admirers and listeners and all the others who wept and sang, the multitudes who were given a chance to peek inside the gold-and-mahogany coffin containing Father Love—as well as his entire collection of jewelry.

It was a day full of sharp winds and sleet, yet the lines waiting to move through the lobby on a policy of three minutes inside per person stretched four full blocks up Lenox Avenue. Everybody wanted to get one last look at the handsome almond-faced preacher and all the diamond stickpins that were going to be in his tie and all the diamond rings on all ten fingers as they were said to be laid across his chest and the jeweled Rolex on his left wrist.

Everyone wanted to see, for the last time, the last great star of the old Harlem movie palace that had become Father Love's own religious theatre. Now passed on to the glowering Roy S. Dumaine, who had dressed for the day in his own version of the trademark Father Love black mohair suit and who was none too pleased to have me taking up space inside the lobby for way more than the three minutes everybody was allowed.

From up at the top of the stairs leading off to the men's and ladies' lounges, the Holy Stream Deliverance Temple Praise-Sayers sang the choruses of "The Old Rugged Cross" over and over and over as the people streamed by, the women weeping and the poker-faced men stepping away from the coffin to touch Roy Dumaine's hands as a gesture of respect to the new order of church business. And there stood Roy like a Mafia don, a white lily on his black lapel. The place was also lousy with yellow-and-white funeral sprays and bodyguards in dark suits and bow ties and thickly folded arms.

From up near the Praise-Sayers, a deacon would occasionally step forward to intone to the shuffling crowds below as they made their way past the bier, "Here at the Holy Stream

Deliverance Temple, my friends—you come as you are. You got a hat, you wear it; you don't got a hat, don't worry about it. You want to dress up, that's just fine; you don't want to dress up, and that's fine, too. . . . God's here, He's standing right there beside our own Father Love, and He's come to take him up home to glory . . . and God, well, He's not looking at your clothes, He's looking at your heart. Somebody turns around and looks at you funny because of your clothes, well, you just let me know about it. . . ."

And then some other deacon would step to the microphone and say, in a more forceful tone, "If you love the Lord, touch someone and tell them you love the Lord . . . and Lord, send deliverance down to us for what has happened . . . send your deliverance like a two-edged sword! . . ."

I watched all this going on, and all the television news outfits filming the event for viewers in New York and beyond—three European capitals and Tokyo besides. And just when it occurred to me that I should maybe walk over to Dumaine and ask him why it was the one deacon kept talking about clothes, in came a contingent of young and old ladies dressed in fishnet stockings and bright green and yellow and red gowns like the girls wear at the Pigalle, and slit up the sides and wigs and falls piled high on their heads and long false eyelashes and furs tossed around shoulders.

There might have been thirty of them who passed through dressed like this, every one of whom lingered over the coffin and reached in to touch Father Love one more time, to caress his face—or a ring. Several of them leaned full over and into the coffin and kissed Father Love's stony forehead or one of his cold, embalmed cheeks.

I made it to Dumaine's side, and he would not speak to me about this, except to say, "God's looking into their hearts, like the deacon says. . . . That's it, now."

Then after he had told me this, I saw a woman move along behind the fancy ladies dressed as I had never quite seen her before, except for the balding fur coat.

Heidi wore a dress under her coat, something long and purple that looked like a pretty good grade of wool and warm. And she had a broad-brimmed felt hat that she wore tilted over the bad side of her face. She had good shoes on, too, and heavy hosiery that covered her ulcerated legs.

And rouge on her gold grimy cheeks. She looked nearly pretty, and I started moving toward her from behind.

Then when she came right up beside Father Love's coffin, Heidi bent and gave the preacher her final embrace, and the smacking of her lips on his dead skin echoed in the marble lobby. And the voices of the Praise-Sayers swelled in the final verse of "The Old Rugged Cross."

And then another familiar face on the line making its way up toward the coffin. Mona Morgan, moving along with her gloved hands clasped together in front of her like a good Catholic girl walking near the altar. She saw me look at her, blanched and looked down, and then recovered.

She took her look inside the coffin, then broke from the line and came to me. She pushed back a veil that fell over the brim of a black felt hat. I smelled whiskey on her breath when she spoke.

"They told me you'd be here," she said.

"Who?"

"I called you at the precinct."

"I see."

Mona looked around, then back to me. "This isn't the time or place, but give me a call later. Make sure I'm home, then please . . . come over. I've got the report back, from my friend—remember? The names along the money trail—the names behind the dummy corporations. I think you're going to be surprised."

"What about your show?"

"I'm not dancing tonight . . . I don't know if I ever want to work again. I . . . oh, just come see me tonight, Hock."

I knew I would call when I had the chance, but I did not feel all that interested or excited—or even grateful that Mona had come through for me. This was another of Neglio's principles of being a cop, the memory of which popped rather neatly into my head right then: *You never let the public get the impression they're doing you any favors. You just make them feel like they're doing what they have to do.*

So I thought about that some and watched the proceedings for about an hour or so and did not see how there would be any further percentage to my hanging around. I looked around for Mona but could not find her.

And then I left the church and made my way across 125th Street for the A train, with maybe the thought of stopping in for one or two at the Baby Grand, which had a black wreath in the window out of respect for the passing of Father Love that changed my mind for me.

Which left only the sober ride downtown on the A train. After which I was too tired to do anything about being sober, so I just began walking home from the Times Square station.

Just before I turned into the doorway of my building, I saw something through the sleet blowing down Tenth Avenue, something that had eluded me now twice, something that quickened my blood. I did not look directly at it, afraid to scare away the young guy in the old man's clothes hanging around looking at the pinball machines across the way at Runyon's.

I proceeded into the doorway of my building and then from the inside waited until I had the cover of a truck moving up the avenue between me and the killer I was after—the big dopey kid who'd shot down Father Love in front of me, the kid I'd chased down into the bad end of the jungle.

Running with the truck out there in front of me, I reached a doorway directly across from Runyon's that gave me cover from the killer's view. He just stood there at the window with his big dopey face staring at the machines, just the way Runyon had told Aiello he'd looked in the window the day Buddy-O was killed. And of course, the chances were excellent that the guy I was now tracking had done Buddy-O *and* Griffiths *and* Father Love, and I was beginning to get the idea.

He must have seen me reflected in the window.

The kid started running up Tenth Avenue, not even looking back at me. And I had no choice at all but to pull my .38 and give chase and warning shots.

But he kept on moving, never looking back.

He reached the corner of Forty-sixth Street and the parking lot, and I lost sight of him as he ducked down and ran between the cars and otherwise made shooting at him to stop him an impossibility.

But since I knew the entrance to the jungle, I knew which direction he would be moving through the lot and did not waste any time.

I saw him pull back the flap of the fence and I took a shot and missed him. Now he looked back and took a shot himself, and if I had not seen the piece in his hand and dropped in time, I would have taken the bullet somewhere in the stomach, where there are lots of main arteries and you are pretty well guaranteed to die.

It only took me a second or two to reach the flap of the fence and then another second to realize that he'd dropped into the gap between the boulders where I had seen Heidi—and the noise behind her that was made by someone I had not seen, and the same hole I remembered from way back when in the days of Buddy-O's gang.

And so I knew where he would come up next.

All-ee, all-ee in free!

I ran down the block to Forty-fifth and tried to figure where the tunnel that Patty Devlin had used when we were all kids might be today. I guessed at the crumbling edge of exposed foundation beneath an abandoned auto garage, a crack in the wall big enough for a man to squeeze through.

And I guessed right, judging by the wheezing and scratching sounds I began to hear from inside the dark crack. I moved just around the edge of the garage wall out of sight and waited.

I heard him crawl out from the hole in the wall. I peered around the corner, gripped by .38 service revolver in my right hand, and then when he was moving out toward the avenue away from me, with his back to me, I made a shooting tripod and yelled, "Halt!"

But he never turned, and he did not run.

"Halt!" I yelled again.

He didn't *hear* me.

Which made it all the easier. I just stepped out from the wall and ran up behind the killer and rammed my .38 into his spine and watched his own piece fall to the wet ground.

He spun around, and I held the revolver up to his face with

both hands and yelled, "Halt!" again, figuring that maybe he read lips.

The kid looked confused and tried to step to one side and maybe run, so I clouted him against the side of his head with my revolver and he fell down to his knees.

And did not make a sound, because he couldn't.

I stepped around in back of him while keeping my .38 pressed to the top of his head. Then I used a foot to shove him belly down. And I sat on his back and pulled out my bracelets and cuffed him up.

Then I pulled him up to stand and give him a shove in the general direction of the precinct station house. And we walked, in two kinds of silence.

I spent an hour doing the paper on a booking for suspicion of murder, and then I caged the kid.

And I do not know why, but when I looked at him I felt sorry for the poor bastard. But trusting my instinct, unclear even as it was, I kept the news of this very important collar from Mona, who had news of her own.

Just before I left the station house, I received a call from Lieutenant G. L. Keene up at the central Harlem station house.

"You want a good laugh, Hock?" he asked.

"Always."

"Father Love's lying in state, right? And he's going out flashing the rings and the stickpins and all, right? I mean, diamonds right there in the box about to go six feet under with him, right?"

"Right."

"Somebody had other ideas. Most of the jewelry was stripped clean of his dead black ass, Hock. How's that for mourning?"

TWENTY-SEVEN

"**A**ll right, I've got it all in my notes here someplace," Mona said. She moved papers around on top of the *secrétaire* until she found a pad. "Okay, here goes."

I sipped at the glass of Johnnie Walker red she had given me. Also I noticed that she had made space for my brand in her liquor cabinet.

"Now you probably already figured out that all these dummy outfits are fronts for real estate speculation," she said.

I had, I said.

"And that one of the dummies turns out to be the holding company for Empire Properties, which is our very own dead landlord. . . ."

Yes again, I said.

"Which means that—"

"Which means Sam Waterman the living is our landlord's mouthpiece, which means he knows about Howie Griffiths and what he was doing, more than likely—and maybe even the connection to Buddy-O. I figured he'd have to be somehow working for either the landlord, or he was friendly with the landlord from way back the first night when I saw him skulking

274

around outside and spying on *my* place. How'd he know what apartment *I* lived in, or that I'd even moved in—unless he was in some kind of contact with Empire or the rent rolls or something, which meant Griffiths."

"Well, you're a little further ahead than I'd figured."

"It's why they keep paying me."

"All right, then—what would you think if I told you that Daniel Prescott is mixed up in this, the guy who wants to run for president?"

"That I also know, from talking with Griffiths' widow, who'll tell anybody who wants to listen to her that her husband was an idiot because he took this Prescott character's book seriously—"

"Oh God, what book?"

"It's called *Me First*."

"Perfect, it ought to sell a million."

"It did, and more. Anyway, Howie got so worked up about it that he did everything he could to become what he called a *disciple* of Prescott's, which offended his widow's religious sensibilities. . . . Well anyway, that may or may not bear on anything. But the point is, Griffiths winds up getting a job with his god, Prescott. And so that tells me that ultimately Daniel Prescott is my landlord."

"Very good. But now here's the thing that ties it all up for you."

I finished my drink.

Mona said, "One of these dummy outfits is called the 'Fifty-second Street Group.' You want to take a guess who its members are?"

"Prescott and . . . ?"

"You've got fifty percent of it."

There could be only one other name, I thought. "Waterman—Father Love!"

"One hundred percent."

"The two of them were in business together—over what?"

"It's what they owned, and what they maybe dreamed of doing with it. Hock, the two of them owned the jungle."

"Now, that is a surprising thing."

I sat down and asked myself a few questions, and when I could I answered myself.

The jungle was where Empire Properties recruited goons to drive people out of low-rent buildings it owned in the surrounding neighborhood of Hell's Kitchen, meaning that people like Mary Rooney were not crazy in the least about what the landlord was capable of doing when fear was cheap and plentiful in the persons of a few thousand desperate souls of the underworld. Right?

And Buddy-O Devlin saw his own opportunity to get back into the gang rackets by helping out the biggest racket going—real estate. Right? And so that is how he got mixed up in the idea of supplying goons to a character like Griffiths, who after all would do anything since he had read Prescott's greed-head book. Right?

And wasn't Buddy-O simply covering his bets like any good upstanding sleazy American businessman by playing both ends against the middle here? He would play along with Griffiths and that bunch, and meanwhile he would snitch to me; and he would *even* hold court with somebody looking for a contract, presumably on Father Love, and maybe make like he could come through on that *plus* make something on the side by snitching to me on this little item as well. That sounded right.

But who found out and canceled Buddy-O?

The kid I had caged was the button, but who gave the orders? Who controlled this deaf-mute kid, and why?

And weren't Samuel Waterman, Sr., and Daniel Prescott a couple of peas in a pod?

I picked up my coat and started to put it on, and Mona started complaining.

I told her, "Sorry, kid, I've got business."

"Oh yeah?" She asked this like she was accusing me of something, which might have irritated me. But it did not. Truth to tell, I was flattered.

"Really, just business, kid."

Then I left.

And I went home to sleep on the job, the job of letting clues and possibilities roll around in my dreams.

In the morning, right after nine o'clock when the Vital Statistics office opened, I telephoned my young friend Buckman.

"Yeah, Detective Hockaday, I was going to call you up today. I think I maybe found what you're after."

Which he had indeed, judging from what he told me. He said he would send along photocopies to me at Midtown-North by police messenger.

I then took a close shave and looked in my good clothes closet and dressed in dark blues and wound up looking pretty sharp. Before I left my apartment, I called up the station house captain and requested a forty-eight-hour blackout on any news to anyone—cops and media, all the same—about the deaf-mute kid I had collared on suspicion of murder.

Then I caught a taxi down on Forty-second and rode over to Madison Avenue, to a very large and very ugly glass-and-chromed-steel box roughly fifty stories high, on top of which Daniel Prescott himself lived and worked in Xanadu—so I knew from reading the society pages.

The lobby of the Prescott Building was a place I had never beheld personally. It was full of polished ferns and palms and expensive shops, and walls that were enormous marble slabs of a startlingly effeminate shade of pink. I managed to get through it all unmolested.

When I reached the elevators that led beyond the mezzanine, however, I was confronted by an officious little man wearing a Hitler mustache and a cream-colored uniform. He asked, "Where do you wish to go, sir?"

"I want to see the Man upstairs," I said.

"You refer to Mr. Prescott?" he asked dryly.

I said that was my reference exactly.

He said patiently, "You do not simply *arrive* at Mr. Prescott's quarters, dear sir, you achieve a presence."

I showed him the achievement of my gold shield and walked past him to an elevator. I pressed the top button, and when the doors closed I saw him wipe his forehead with a handkerchief and pick up his little telephone to talk to somebody.

When I got to forty-seven, as high as the elevator would take me, I was met by another guy in a funny uniform. This one had braids on his shoulders.

"How you doing, soldier?" I asked him. Then I showed him my shield. "I'm here to see Prescott."

This one looked at my shield and the name on it and the number and made a note of it. Then he said, "I'm afraid I don't see your name on today's appointments calendar, Detective Hockaday. Mr. Prescott is available only by appointment. Of course, you understand? If you've some message, I'll certainly be happy to deliver it for you."

"Soldier," I said, "I'd like you to go in and tell Prescott exactly this: Number one, I'm here to talk about a ditch he owns on the West Side along with a murdered guy uptown; and number two, it so happens that Prescott is *my* landlord, and that my neighbors and I had a little tenants' meeting recently during which there was this other murder."

The guy sputtered and turned to go away. He snapped his fingers at a comrade to keep the watch on me. I said to his back, "Tell the general I'll wait right here for an answer."

When he came back, the soldier said, "Mr. Prescott would like me to advise you that in all questions pertaining to the law, he would naturally prefer that you speak to his lawyer."

"Okay," I said, "now go tell him this: I think it would be a very good idea if there was a lawyer on hand, and so I'm going to personally go to a telephone and ring up one Samuel Waterman, Jr., who is one of Mr. Prescott's many lawyers, I am sure—but who happens also to be the son of one of the murder victims I just mentioned."

He shrank away and was gone for several minutes and then returned with relief on his face and invited me to step into the private elevator that would carry me one floor up to Daniel Prescott's celebrated home office. When I got off this elevator, I was met by a woman who owned a figure that had been starved to a sort of perfection, which is the way a lot of women on the East Side look. She was about forty years old and wore square shoulder pads under a red silk blouse. Her hair was black and very well cut and shaped, but her skin was too white. I wanted to feed her a steak.

She held out a hand full of sleek nails and ropy blue veins and introduced herself. "I'm Janice, I work for the Dan."

"The Dan? . . ."

"Oh, we call him that," she said, laughing dustily. "I mean Mr. Prescott, of course. Well, anyway, welcome."

"You could have fooled me, Janice." Shaking her hand was like holding one of my belts.

"Won't you come sit down, over in the hallway?" she asked.

I followed her across an onyx floor that was lined with brass inset pieces. At the base of a stairway with a bronze banister, there was a couch and a floor lamp and a table full of very glossy magazines arranged so that you did not dare touch them.

"How long will I be waiting?" I asked.

She answered me coolly, "I expect you'll be waiting until Mr. Prescott's counsel arrives."

"I'll wait seven minutes," I said, looking at my wristwatch. "That should give Waterman enough time to walk from his office over here to the Dan's place."

"How very reasonable. Would you like to sit now?"

"Not really."

I stood there and looked at an abstract painting by Léger hanging on a chocolate-brown wall, and then a bronze sculpture of a male torso signed by Roberto Estevez. The rest of the stuff in the hallway did not interest me since it looked like somebody's idea of a nice lobby for the telephone company.

Janice watched me looking around and seemed edgy now. She glanced up the stairway a few times. I asked her, "What else is down on this floor?"

"Offices, mostly," she said. "There's a dining room the family uses sometimes, for big parties. . . . Why do you want to know?"

"Just idly curious," I said. Then I lied, "It's nice, real nice."

Janice brightened. "Yes, well, thank you. . . . I picked out many of the things you see here. I call it 'warm modern.'"

"That's just what I'd like for my own place, warm modern."

"Yes, so. It all reflects the taste of Mrs. Prescott, you know, who of course checks everything with the Dan."

"Of course. Is there a library somewhere?"

"Yes, it's up on the next floor. We've just completed it. We've got to get books now. The Dan has great respect for books."

"Of course. . . ."

I turned when I heard a lot of quick footsteps and sputtering behind me, and then Sam Waterman was right there beside me tearing off his topcoat and raising his blood pressure.

"Hockaday," he snarled, "what's the meaning of all this?"

"Get your boy down here, that's all I'm going to tell you," I said.

Waterman was about to answer me, and the answer was not going to be sociable. But instead of speaking he looked up the stairway past the bronze banister. I followed his gaze, and down came the guy with the bad haircut and the muskrat teeth and the pursed lips, Daniel Prescott. He said, "Hello, Sam," and then stuck out his hand to me and said, "Good morning, Detective—Hockaday, is it?"

His hand was wet and thin, and his fingers were too short for a man of his height. Prescott suggested we step into what he called "the salon," which was right off the hallway. This turned out to be a room with a ceiling about twenty or twenty-five feet high with windows all around that showed off the city down below like it was a string of pearls.

We all sat down on some peach-colored chairs. Janice closed the doors, and that was the last I saw of her.

Prescott stared at me and was silent. And I was pretty sure from this that he shared Neglio's tactical philosophy about keeping your mouth shut; no doubt he and Neglio were fast friends.

So I just went ahead, ignoring Waterman.

"Mr. Prescott," I asked, "do you know a Roy Dumaine of the Holy Stream Deliverance Temple of Harlem?"

Waterman spoke when Prescott did not. "Hockaday, do you intend to arrest Mr. Prescott on some legitimate charge?"

"I hadn't thought of that, Junior. Would you like me to book him on suspicion, though? Would you like it if I booked a presidential candidate on suspicion of being a material witness to murder, which is something that you can imagine would naturally make it into the newspapers?"

Prescott looked at me and laughed through his nose. And he said, "Detective Hockaday, I know of a Roy Dumaine and the church you mentioned."

"Dumaine has been telling me some interesting things about your company called Fifty-second Street Group and another one called Empire Properties—which makes you my landlord."

"I'm a lot of people's landlord."

"Gee, I bet that's swell for you."

Prescott spread his arms and moved his head around and said, "As a matter of fact, you can see it is."

Waterman said, "What *interesting things* has Dumaine been saying?"

Of course I was lying like hell about Dumaine and just playing out my own thread.

"Well, Junior, Dumaine tells me that your father—who would be your partner in the Fifty-second Street Group, Mr. Prescott—was standing in the way of attempts by the company to undertake a very heavy development project right there in what is commonly called the jungle—"

"The *jungle?*"

"Where the old railroad tracks are, down in the ravine."

"Oh, yes."

"I've spent a little time down there, Mr. Prescott. You've got lots and lots of tenants living rent free down there. Well anyway, the late Mr. Waterman—who was the preacher called Father Love, who built up a fortune in the church dodge . . ."

"All perfectly legal," Junior broke in.

"Perfectly," I said. "Anyway, as I was saying, Father Love wanted the jungle to remain fallow, I guess, and you wanted to take over the rest of Hell's Kitchen with your other outfit— Empire—and you were so determined to do that that you were employing, indirectly, a known organized crime figure by the street name of Buddy-O in a scheme to put together goon squads from the jungle into low-rent tenements you wanted to harass the people out of so you could rip them down and slap up the expensive buildings."

Prescott was not saying anything, and I thought for a second or two that maybe my bluff wasn't working.

Then: "You're substantially correct," Prescott said. "But you're missing some salient points: nothing that may have been going on in the way of 'goon squads' was ever personally known to me or approved by me; I do not know to this day why on earth my partner sandbagged the railroad ravine project; and my attorney informs me that all of these are quite beside the point anyway since, to put it delicately—"

"Yes, let's put it delicately," I said.

"—anyone directly connected with what you've been talking about is dead."

"Yes, murdered."

"Well . . . that is not my concern, Detective Hockaday," Prescott said. "I'm an honorable man. I think a development project for the jungle, so-called, would have been a marvelous thing for the city. Did you know I proposed to build housing for the poor there?"

"No, I didn't know that."

"Well, that was the plan. And Father Love sandbagged it. I wanted to show that a landlord has a heart, you see." He smiled with his pointy teeth.

"And it would have looked good for a presidential candidate with a great big heart to be doing such a thing."

"Of course. But Father Love wouldn't hear of it. I even offered him a cabinet post in my administration."

"It's a pity, sir. What can I say?"

Junior said, "Are we through here?"

"Oh, yeah," I said. "Only tell your client here about how he shouldn't leave town. You know the drill, Junior."

I stood up and said, "I'll let myself out."

And when I got back down to the lobby with the pink marble I couldn't help laughing. *The Dan!* I went out to Madison Avenue and treated myself to a taxi ride uptown—to see Roy Dumaine, whether he liked the idea of my visit or not.

"Roy, I have to tell you I think we're closing in on this case," I told him.

"Man, that's neither here nor there to me."

"Well, that's where you're very mistaken, Roy. It's going to be here where you'll answer some questions I've got to have answered—or we come get you and haul your ass in front of a grand jury, and who knows what they'll do to you if you irritate me now."

"Ask me your damn questions, man."

"I don't think you ought to be swearing in the house of the Lord, Roy. Tell me—do you have a Concordia around here someplace?"

"Of course."

"Then you know what it is."

"Yes. . . ."

"Did you use it to write out the verses in pencil on Father Love's business cards, Roy? And then did you slip the cards, one by one, into the collection plates—to scare the boss? That's all, just to scare him?"

"I want a lawyer."

"I'm not saying you killed him, Roy, for God's sake. I'm just asking if you wanted to scare your boss."

"This is, like, I'm cooperating with you?"

"Yes."

And this was the bald-faced lie that I gave to Dumaine. In a court of law, I have to swear to tell the truth and the whole truth and only the truth. But there is nothing that says I cannot lie outside of the court, which I do from time to time.

"Okay, Roy, now we're establishing a rapport. Now, the other thing I want to know is, was it you who went down into my neighborhood—Hell's Kitchen—and started making it pretty obvious that you wanted to hire a contract killer, which you actually did not want to do but which again, when the word got out—which it would, of course, being that a black guy comes down to find some mostly Irish buttons and people talk about things like this—would scare Father Love?"

"Yeah, I did that."

"You talked to a guy down in Hell's Kitchen by the street name of Buddy-O about the price of a contract and things like that? And you talked to some other hoods down there about the same thing?"

"Yeah, but like you say, it was just for some intimidation."

"Because you wanted to take over the church here, by scaring off Father Love?"

"Yeah."

"And that's the extent of it?"

"That's it."

"You knew that Father Love lived on the edges, didn't you, Roy? I mean, we all saw the pross coming in to see him laid out in state and all."

"I knew a lot about him, and I kept my mouth shut and my eyes open."

"I'm sure you did."

"I did."

"So, something happened along the way that went way out of control here, didn't it, Roy?"

"To say the least, man."

"But you were sort of counting on it, weren't you?"

"I think I need to stop answering right now."

"Well, okay. You've been pretty helpful. Just one more thing."

"What?"

"Mona Morgan—what do you know about her?"

"Good-looking white woman. Father Love, he liked the white ladies."

"And somebody else, she's called Heidi on the street. She came here and kissed Father Love in his coffin."

"Oh, she's just an old crazy lady used to come around and do work here. A long, long time ago she was pretty good-looking herself. That'd be back when I was a boy. She worked as a seamstress, at different jobs around town where they needed costumes and things. . . . She did up a few of Father Love's capes and robes and things like that."

"Well, thanks again, Roy."

I went back downtown, to the station house, where my collar was in the cage. And I decided to take an enormous chance with him.

TWENTY-EIGHT

I asked Mona to come by my place at six o'clock for drinks, then we would go out someplace nice for dinner—someplace with a canopy outside. The drinks were on the level, but I doubted whether she would have the appetite for dinner. Not after what I had in store for her.

When she arrived, she took the green chair. I waited until she was settled and had a glass in her hand. I looked at the way her pretty neck flowed up out from her blouse and felt about as lousy as I ever have when I have to break the bad news.

The radio was on. Johnny Hartman sang something smooth and easy. Mona liked it but said it did not much go with the expression on my face.

"I'm troubled about what I have to tell you," I said.

"Tell me quick and get out of trouble."

"It's not so easy, not for me and not for you."

"By now you ought to know, Hock—nothing's easy, and nobody's got a say over the hard life."

"I guess that's right," I allowed. "We don't have any choice sometimes but to build ourselves a pleasant facade and then hope and pray it all works out somehow."

And maybe Mona knew what was coming next, maybe she knew the inevitability of a cop someday having such a conversation with her. She laughed sadly and said, "I'll drink to that."

"I thought you might, Mona. I've got a surprise for you."

She did not look like there was anything that I could do or say that would cause her surprise. And that look in Mona's eyes told me I now had it all about ninety-eight percent all connected.

I walked over to the bedroom door and opened it and motioned for my collar to come out.

And the big deaf-mute kid with Mona's blue eyes and his father's almond skin stood there. I said to Mona, "This is your son, right?"

The kid walked over to his mother and touched her face. The two of them exchanged something in sign language. And then Mona looked at me blankly and asked, "You're going to pose me some questions now, Detective Hockaday?"

"I'm going to question some of your poses, anyway."

Mona closed her eyes for a second. Then she drank up what was in her glass and said, "His name is Jim. . . . Would you mind if I asked you how you found out about us?"

"Little by little," I said. "They pay me for that."

"And so now you want the whole story of Jim and me—and . . ." She laughed again. "And Father Love?"

"Yes, that's what I'd like."

"It all started in the nicest way—"

"He passed you the note backstage?" I asked.

"Yes, and then there were flowers and dinner and the rest. . . . And then along comes Jim. Dreary, isn't it?"

"Except for when it hurts," I said. "Can Jim hear, by the way?"

"No. Even if he could, it wouldn't matter much. He's inside of himself . . . well, not right, you know? But he's gentle in his way, in this peculiar context of his own. . . .

"Look, Hock, the thing is—his father would never acknowledge the boy. I couldn't take care of him myself. So I shopped around for a lawyer to help me with a paternity suit, and one by one the members of the bar of justice were not interested in representing me against a very rich and powerful man. . . .

"I had a lot of trouble with the boy, and I never did right by

him. I sent him to school when I could afford it, I made sure he
learned to sign . . . and so did I. But it wasn't enough. Jim
was . . .

"Oh God, Hock, a kid like that marks you for life, and
whenever I think how unfair it all is, I drink hard. The worst
kind of drinking. You know how that is, Hock?"

I said I did. And then Jim said something to Mona with his
hands, and Mona said something back. Jim sat down on the floor
near her feet and crossed his legs and watched me as his mother
continued talking.

"All through the years I tried doing as right as I could by him,
but he'd just run away," Mona said. "He'd always be hanging out
with the types who spend their days down in the jungle.

"There was a woman down there who started taking care of
him—"

I said, "That would be Heidi."

"You know her . . . I see. Well, the two of them had some
kind of strange affinity, don't ask me why. God! Those people
down there, they've got their own little society.

"Anyhow, Heidi loved my boy Jim like he belonged to her,
and that was that, so far as the two of them were concerned. She
protected him, and he wanted to be with her, more than he cared
about being with me, it seemed; and so, like I said, Hock, *I*
couldn't handle the boy all by myself and no lawyer was going to
take my case . . .

"So I let Heidi sort of take over for the most part. Jim would
come to me from time to time . . . he'd hang around, but then
back down into the jungle he'd go. He'd always sneak up on me,
like he was somebody who knew on instinct that he wasn't
welcome at front doors. . . . I sometimes think he's a lot
smarter than he lets on."

I asked Mona, "Did he drop in on you at the club sometimes?"

She sighed and came clean. "Yes. He'd come up the fire escape
from the alley, and I'd let him through the fire door to the
corridor outside the dressing rooms. So if you want to know—
yes, it was Jim who sucker-punched you in the dark that night.
He was frightened, and probably thought he was protecting me.

And he saw you and hit you, and I couldn't say anything about it. You can see that, can't you, Hock? You can see how—"

But she could not go on just then. She touched her son's head and wept. Jim folded his big hands in his lap and kept staring at me, unaware of his mother's discomfort—or the trouble she was in, or the trouble he was in.

I asked Mona, "What can you tell me about Heidi?"

"Very little. I only know she lost a boy of her own sometime years ago. She told me that. And so I could understand her attachment to Jim, maybe as a reminder of her son. I don't know. And I know she had a trade, too. Sewing costumes and clothing, tailoring and the like. . . . I know she did work for Labeija, a long time ago. . . .

"I tried setting up Heidi in some decent place. So she could work, have a regular home. But she wouldn't hear of it. You can't give her anything because she's convinced somebody will only take it away. That's about as clear as I'm able to understand her."

"I know what you mean," I said. "She'll only take coffee from me, nothing else."

Mona nodded. "Well, I thought about some way of working around this pathology with her. And I figured that maybe at the same time I could do something for Jim—and maybe something *to* his father, it occurred to me when I got into it. . . . I guess you could say that little by little, just like you, I figured out something."

"What?"

"I figured first, I'd find something for Heidi that she could believe from the looks of it that nobody else in the world would ever want—some place she'd feel safe, a place she would believe nobody would take away. Well, I found it all right—and right here in Hell's Kitchen. And when I found it, I also found out that it was owned by none other than Samuel Waterman—or Father Love.

"Well, this was pretty interesting. So I went to town on the research of Waterman and his business dealings. And while I'm putting this all together, I let all my suspicions take over my energy; I mean, I'm not going in any certain direction, but I just know I'm going to find out something on Waterman, see? And when I did, it was a doozy. I mean, here I was—maybe the only person in America who had the documents to show that this scamming Holy Roller up in Harlem is doing real estate deals with Daniel Prescott, who wants to be president.

"Well, so I went to him right up there at his church and laid it on the line: Heidi moves into the property I found for her on Fifty-second Street, which means there cannot be any future development that's going to make her feel insecure—or I go to the press about everything going on in the jungle, which I know all about long before you came on the scene here, Hock. And also, of course, I tell the press how it involves Daniel Prescott. I let the press know everything here—Sam Waterman alias Father Love, the goon squad, the tenant harassment, the whole Waterman-Prescott setup. . . ."

I asked, "What did Waterman say to that?"

"He laughed me off at first. But he could see that I meant it and that I was not afraid and that I didn't have so much to lose. And also I reminded him that I wasn't dumb enough to keep it all to myself, and that if anything should happen to me . . . well, the press would be given its red meat by somebody else."

"Your comrade here," I said, "would have been—Buddy-O, I suppose?"

"Naturally. Anything happened to me, Buddy-O would take action. A girl has to cover herself."

"Of course," I said.

"Anyhow," Mona continued, "Waterman finally agrees with me. But just to make absolutely sure, I cut a deal with Roy Dumaine, who is an ambitious man . . . and we figured out a scheme to scare Father Love into keeping up his part of the bargain. . . ."

I said, "So you figured you would write the Bible stuff on the cards and then have them dropped into the collection plates one by one, and—"

"Yes, all of it. But that's as far as it was meant to go. I just wanted Father Love kept off balance, and scared. . . ."

She was frightened herself, and crying again. Jim looked up at her. Mona said to me, "Some facade I've built up for myself, hey?"

"You want another drink, honey?"

She said, "Yes. No. No—make it no."

"Okay. Let me clear away two more things, Mona. Tell me what you know about jewelry stolen off Father Love's body when it was open to public view—and what you might know about a piano stolen out of the church."

Her face cleared up a little. "Oh, that jewelry! You saw everybody dipping into the coffin to kiss Father Love, didn't you? All his girlfriends took a little something, don't you see? . . .

"And the piano . . . God, Hock, I had the worst time trying to get Heidi up out of the jungle where she was staying with Jim. I hit on the idea of the piano when I learned one day that Heidi is a very big fan of the Father Love radio broadcasts. Well, I persuaded Heidi she'd be safe in this old burned-out house I found for her on Fifty-second Street—if the church piano was inside it. So I got Roy to help steal it, and that's the simple truth of that. . . ."

I telephoned the central Harlem station house and asked the captain to order out the pickup of Roy Dumaine—on suspicion of conspiracy to murder Father Love, Aloysius Patrick Xavier Devlin, and Howie Griffiths.

Dumaine could spend the rest of his life complaining how I had lied to him if he wished; the state of New York would be happy to jail him for the rest of his days in lieu of the death penalty.

Roy had made the fatal mistake of admitting that he had met at least once with Buddy-O. That would be the famous meeting over a lunch of Mooseheads and veal sandwiches at the Ebb Tide, the meeting that Angelo witnessed.

There was nothing to Mona's plan of scaring Father Love that involved looking for a murder contract in Hell's Kitchen. That part of it was purely Roy's idea, and he had had to move outside Harlem where he was too well known. He had heard all about what was going on with an old Westy hood down in Hell's Kitchen, and the Westies were notorious, of course, for contract murders once upon a time. So there was a good solid symmetry that any half-competent DA ought to be able to pin on Roy Dumaine, for starters.

When Roy found out that maybe he was not going to be able to find an old-fashioned contract killer in Hell's Kitchen anymore, contrary to his original belief, he hit on another plan. And that involved the big deaf-mute bastard son of Father Love himself. So Dumaine found a way to control Jim and Heidi, too; and he worked out a plan whereby Jim would first kill Buddy-O, who too many people knew was about to spill the whole Waterman-Prescott scam to me—and then Griffiths, who he figured would eventually crack and go to the cops, too. And of course, he wanted Father Love killed.

Jim was the obvious tool. To get Jim to do the jobs, he needed to control Heidi. That would not be difficult: he had only to convince her that whatever he told her to do by way of guiding Jim would be pleasing Father Love.

Roy could assume that if anything went wrong with his scheme, no one would connect him to a crazed old woman living in a hole in the ground down in Hell's Kitchen—or a brain-damaged deaf-mute she looked after.

But such is the fate of facades.

I made one more telephone call and reached an answering machine. I left an address on West Fifty-second Street and the time I planned to be there—and the message, "Family reunion time."

A wire fence with a padlocked gate, taller than a man, enclosed the little yard. Three dressmaker's dummies occupied the yard, held up like scarecrows by poles run through them and sunk into the ground. One wore a dress with lace around a scooped collar and puffed sleeves that fluttered, armless, in the damp breeze off the piers; another, a man's shirt and tie; the third was pinned full of ribbons and dime-store jewelry, so it looked.

But I looked closer now. The jewelry had not come from any dime store. It had come from Father Love's dead fingers, from his collar, from his necktie. The dress on the one dummy—who knew? But I thought it was a pretty good guess that the men's clothing I saw had come from the dead bodies of Buddy-O and Howie Griffiths.

Midnight was a few minutes away. I stood in the heavy darkness, listening.

The wind gusted. A coffee can blew along the sidewalk. Cars and trucks raced downtown over rain-soaked pavement over on Eleventh Avenue. Foghorns sounded softly on the water.

I stamped chill from my toes. And waited. . . .

From inside the house, a ragged voice: "Up from your defilement!"

And then the sound I'd come to hear. . . .

The piano.

She was playing the piano for him, and Jim was enjoying the throb of the strings as he felt them with his hands, the way Mona had told me he could "hear" his father's piano being played.

I had sent Jim along ahead of me and remained in the shadows as Heidi let him into the house that looked as if it were going to fall down.

Now there was another sound. Footsteps behind me. I turned and saw Sam Waterman, Jr., approaching in his trench coat.

"Let's go," he said. Nothing more.

I led the way up to the door and knocked. When Heidi stopped playing, there was still music from inside—a hymn on the radio. Then the hymn died down, and the previously recorded voice of a dead man said . . .

I say money is the root—

The church organist riffed keys.

Money is the root of all . . . good!

The door opened and Heidi looked up at me and smiled, and I said, "I think it's going to snow soon, Heidi. Merry Christmas to you. . . . I see Jim's inside."

"Yes, Merry Christmas." Her eyes were bright. "Would you like to come in?"

But then a troubled look as she noticed the man with me. "Who's this?"

Sam Waterman stepped into a sliver of light, and all the years of suffering drained from her injured face. And she said to him, "Oh my, oh my God, my *boy!*"

Waterman pulled the withered woman against him and held her very hard against his chest. And his shoulders heaved.

EPILOGUE

The high point of my Thanksgiving Day was having a drink with Sam Waterman at the Ebb Tide. He told me none of it had gone the way he ever imagined, but that nevertheless he knew that someday somebody would call him up like I had; someday he would connect with his mother.

He had a lot of work ahead of him. There was the matter of arranging legal representation for his half-brother, Jim. And for his mother, Heidi.

And I had some work ahead of me as well. I wanted to find out about my father, of whom I knew so very little. And was what I knew a pack of lies? I decided I would do something—someday—about following the lies. I wanted badly to know a day when my shoulders might heave the way Sam Waterman's shoulders had heaved.

Then there was the matter of Mona Morgan. Before I could tell her anything that would give her another scar, she came to tell me she was going home. "Like you came home yourself to Hell's Kitchen, Hock . . . home to where *I* belong."

We would write, we told each other. And maybe I would take

the train up to Rhinecliff someday; Mona said she could not imagine me ever leaving the city.

Judy sold our pretty little house in Ridgewood just before she went off with her Pflam to visit out west somewhere in the turnips. She telephoned to say she wanted to send me half the money from the sale, which according to her lawyer she did not have to do. But she said I should have some money to fix up my place in Hell's Kitchen some.

I am still waiting for Judy's check.

Inspector Neglio appeared back in New York a few days after the indictments were handed down against Roy Dumaine. He asked me to come see all his slides of Bimini one day, which I said I would, in order to tell him that I would like to pass along my sentiments to a friend of his.

"Tell the Dan I expect him to be an exemplary landlord so far as I am concerned, and friends of mine, too. And you could also tell him that I am going to break my rule about voting if I hear he's on the ballot; I'm going to go vote for the other guy, and maybe I'll do something else to express my displeasure, too."

Neglio said he would indeed pass this on to Prescott.

And I felt a sense of victory, but only in the slightest way. I have always heard people say that victory is sweet. But I doubt it; I doubt that big victories are ever sweet, let alone the ones so small they can be won by a cop.

I doubt that we will ever find who killed poor old Mary Rooney, for instance. And I have every confidence that we will still mostly ignore the jungle.